Half Staff 2018

A NOVEL

John Morse

IDLEKNOT PRESS

This is a work of fiction that takes place in the future. Names, characters, places and incidents are the product of the author's imagination or are used fictionally. Any resemblance to actual events, locales or persons, living or dead is coincidental.

Idleknot Press
www.idleknotpress.com

Morse, John

  Half Staff 2018

  ISBN 978-0-9976450-1-9 (paperback)

  ISBN 978-0-9976450-0-2 (eBook)

To my wife, Carole
1 Corinthians 13

Contents

Part I.

Chapter 1

Washington, DC
August 20, 2017

What a perfect day for a ballgame! Past the halfway point in the season, the Washington Nationals were hosting the Milwaukee Brewers and hoping to improve their dismal forty-three wins and eighty losses record. Thousands of loyal fans would brave the stifling heat and drenching humidity to get to the Nationals Stadium for the last of the summer series. Washington would be starting up again after the long hot recess, and the pace would be unbearable by mid-September. People wearing ball caps with the stylish pretzel "W" and red baseball jerseys were swarming towards Southeast, Washington. The combat zone of the District of Columbia had been transformed in the late 1990s from a drug-infested slum to a vibrant neighborhood anchored by the stadium on one end and the re-furbished Navy Yard on the other. The Department of Transportation built an impressive headquarters building right on the water surrounded by loft apartments and several new hotels. Hundreds wedged into the Yellow Line train as it came up from the last underground stop at the Pentagon, banked to the left and emerged into the bright sunlight flooding the cars for the short trip over the Potomac. The rush to the Stadium started early.

The District Department of Transportation added two extra cars to the Yellow Line trains for game day to handle the large family crowds. None of these Yellow Line cars, including the extra ones, would make it to the next stop at L'Enfant Plaza. Just like one of those planned high-rise demolitions shown on TV, three of the Metro's heavy reinforced concrete bridge foundations were instantly pulverized in a perfectly timed series of massive underwater explosions designed to produce shear stresses which would destroy the thick bridge support structure, twist the tracks and tear them like a piece of tablet paper. The conductor had no time to react as the tracks suddenly veered to the right and downward like some amusement park ride.

His hands were still steady on the controls as he saw the muddy Potomac River rushing into view. Eight Yellow Line cars followed each other into the water. The sound of forty tons of steel and aluminum shearing and twisting drowned out the screams of the eager Nats fans, tourists, and weekend workers, as each car slammed into the car ahead, trying to find space for their seventy-five foot lengths in less than thirty feet of water. It was similar to the massive fog-induced collisions on highways in the West involving fifty automobiles or more, but turned on its head, vertically, with forty feet between the bridge and the water and another thirty feet to the bottom. Each of the eight cars carried well over one-hundred riders with several near their maximum capacity of one-hundred and seventy five. The last car landed on its back, speared in its mid-section by car number seven before breaking into two pieces which hesitated on the water's surface for several long seconds before sliding off on opposite sides and disappearing. There would be many no-shows in the Stadium today. Some died of blunt force trauma, others more slowly by drowning as their common metal caskets tumbled to the bottom and filled with muddy water. Many tried to escape by breaking the fixed windows on the way to the bottom. The large fixed picture windows separated the living from the dead by a thin piece of tempered glass about a quarter inch thick. The bodies thrown around inside the trains added to the panicked stampede of fear and caused scores of people to drown just beneath the surface. Ironically, the Nats won anyway.

Chapter 2

Bucharest, Romania
August 21, 2017

A city of stark contrasts, Bucharest's crumbling facades stood between strip malls and still wore the faded trappings of the brutal Communist dictatorship that kept the city at a stand-still for decades. It had been almost twenty years since Nicolae and Elena Ceausescu were given due process in a ninety minute trial and unceremoniously machine-gunned in the square on Christmas Day. Hundreds of the city's gritty survivors gathered to see the fitting end of a cold and ruthless dictator who robbed Romania's spirit and soul. The area around the bodies had been trashed and smelled strongly of urine. Empty bottles and cans littered the ground. A veteran limped up to the body of Elena and unloaded a mouthful of yellow spit onto her bare feet. Someone needing a pair of shoes had torn the cheap Russian loafers from the stiff limbs. They'd taken the socks too, marveling at how the feet were so clean and looked as though they'd been carved from a block of Italian marble. Up the street from the square stood the Athenee Palace Hilton Bucharest, a grand edifice resembling a stately government building from a bygone era. The magnificent structure had been architected by a German and built in 1914. Years of exhaust-borne dirt and grime stained its marble exterior.

Mr. Brown seemed an odd name for the dark, olive-skinned man who carried a United States passport and stayed a single night. The front desk clerk asked him if he needed any help with his luggage. He replied with a painful smile and a shake of his head, holding up a thick black engineer's flight bag. The automaton at the desk ushered him out with a cheery "Have a wonderful day!"

He walked out into the sunlight and turned right. Around the corner of the hotel past the casino were a series of apartments with first floor shops sharing a common roof and dirty, depressing brown stucco walls. The fourth store front housed an adult shop featuring live shows, magazines and videos and a large selection of toys. For months, people living in the squalor here noticed the acrid smell of chemicals. A local doctor observed a disquieting number of his patients complaining of migraine headaches. The authorities had been called several times, but nothing ever changed in Bucharest. The local police had the building under surveillance for several months but not because of the sudden onset of migraine headaches. No, there was another more sinister reason.

Mr. Brown took the ancient lift to the fourth floor and knocked on an unmarked door. A small man's head appeared as the door opened slowly and after recognizing the expected visitor, swung open wide. The man ushered him down the hallway into a large bedroom converted to a makeshift laboratory. Two men worked silently sealed in an inner room isolated by heavy translucent plastic sheeting that billowed the walls before it was evacuated through a connecting room. Inside the plastic cocoon, the open plastic drums emitted visible vapors that looked like a chemistry teacher's worst nightmare, but neither man paid any attention because they wore industrial air masks to complement their protective chemical suits. The familiar transaction was completed mechanically, wordlessly. Mr. Brown opened the flaps on the top of the hard-sided bag and banded bundles of Romanian Lei were replaced by two dozen plastic blocks which looked like oversized computer power supplies. The high grade C-4 explosive had been made without the taggant chemical to identify it. He nodded to the small man and left the bomb boutique. He'd been there for less than five minutes. Now outside, he only needed to deliver the case to a locker at the train station and drop the key in the sharps box in the men's bathroom. A simple and straight-forward task with generous compensation and no W2 form required from an employer he would never meet. A dream job by any standard. Little did he know these power supplies would wreak havoc 5,000 miles away months later. On the other hand, he didn't really care.

Chapter 3

Doha, Qatar
August 22, 2017

It was very early in the morning, but the wires were still full of news about the tragedy in Washington. Some commentators feebly speculated the Yellow Line disaster might be linked to America's crumbling infrastructure. Most questioned whether this could possibly be another terrorist act. The evening editor at <u>Al Jazeera</u> received a claim of responsibility from Al-Qaeda on the Arabian Peninsula within minutes of the event. But this attack was dramatically different than recent Al-Qaeda attacks. The editor picked up the phone and dialed a local number.

"Nadir?"

"Yes, who is calling me in the middle of the night?" The voice on the phone sounded irritated and confused, like someone being roused from a deep sleep.

"It's Khalid from <u>Al Jazeera</u>. I hope I didn't disturb you." The editor smiled knowing that whether Nadir was sleeping or busy with one of his wives or mistresses, he was disturbed. He said, "We got a message via the usual sources about the train attack in Washington. It seems like you are stepping up your campaign, and I wanted to see if you wanted to make any specific comment before we go to print? As always, you would not be identified." There was an uncharacteristically long pause before Nadir responded in a clipped voice.

"I will call you back."

Khalid drummed his pen on the desk and then sat back in his chair. Nadir's response was certainly not what he expected. Usually, he had a well-rehearsed script and talking points at hand, and such calls turned into a one-way press conference. The editor knew full well that <u>Al Jazeera</u> served as Al-Qaeda's bullhorn to the rest of the world. It was reality and he'd gotten over it. Real journalism had disappeared from the landscape and would not be appreciated by the masses anyway. Entertainment was today's stock-in-trade. The state of journalism and reporting aside, Khalid sensed Nadir was not on his game tonight. Nothing concrete could be gleaned from his response, but his long pause seemed strange. He dismissed the possibility of Nadir not being aware of such a large scale attack and filled his cup with American coffee left on the burner for hours. Strong and bitter, it would keep him alert until Nadir called back.

"Khalid?" The question came as the phone was answered.

"Yes."

Now fully engaged, Nadir rambled on for several minutes cursing the United States and exclaiming that the infidels just witnessed the first of many such attacks which would be coming to America's heartland. He ended the statement with one of his classic lines.

"Make no mistake; Al-Qaeda's strength and reach are growing daily. More people are ready to sacrifice everything for our holy cause. We are everywhere. You remember Paris in November last year? The worldwide caliphate is now a reality. My friend, how many more Yellow Lines will it take for America to wake up to the reality that they can never win this fight?"

Nadir delivered the diatribe in the familiar angry voice Khalid expected.

"Do you want to make any specific comments about this specific attack? The wire reports are projecting 300-400 casualties," asked the editor evenly.

There was another pause before the phone went dead.

Chapter 4

Boston, Massachusetts
October 15, 2017

The man enjoying a large black coffee pushed his right hand up under his glasses and pinched the corners of his eyes, leaned back in his chair and smiled confidently to himself. The West neither understood the enemy nor its tactics. Throwing money at problems worked against the Russians to end the Cold War almost thirty years ago. Everyone jumped on the bandwagon without even asking where it was going. Today, the US economy lacked the muscle to win a spending war of attrition.

He shook his head in disbelief and took another drink from the paper cup. Sure, the Anti-Terrorist units formed since 2001 were now tied together by a sophisticated intelligence-sharing network with instantaneous links to allies overseas. Coupled with the continued success of the drone campaign in Pakistan and Yemen, and the Special Operations units operating in Libya and elsewhere in Northern Africa, the mood in the United States had grown more confident but the continued high unemployment rate and a still-skittish stock market dominated the news.

Early candidates for the United States' 2016 Presidential campaign crowed about the Administration's success in breaking Al-Qaeda's back, and the nightly news pundits declared a cautionary victory against terrorists on virtually every front. Dealing with the savagery of ISIL proved problematic but even the horror of mass be-headings or immolations got only fleeting coverage. The liberal idea that things would improve on their own if only we would offer greater understanding and friendship had taken root and those who advocated tighter borders and more government spending were all too often drowned out by the go along, get along press.

The story about a terrorist plot to carry out coordinated bombing attacks around central London appeared as a small sidebar near the back of Section A of the Boston Globe. The combined intelligence resources of the United States and Britain had been successful in uncovering the communications nodes used by Al-Qaeda and the hundreds of groups it had spawned since the 9/11 tragedy. Yet these successes were tested with much greater frequency than was reported in the press. Reflecting the political mood, the press slowed the linking of obvious terrorist events to Al-Qaeda and its affiliates.

ISIL proved to be cleverer with communications, using mosques for written communications which were then encoded and published in a string of newspapers unwittingly carrying orders in their "Help Wanted" or "For Sale" sections. Internet gaming provided a simple and undetectable means of global communications. At times almost complicit, the White House spin doctors all but outlawed the term terrorism, and the term's use in the same sentence with Islam or Muslims had risen to the level of a journalistic capital offense. While the task of preventing attacks remained a 24/7 effort involving thousands on both sides of the Atlantic, a cavalier attitude took hold on the United States' side of the effort. The people being protected seemed to take it for granted, something the government was expected to provide. The Boston Marathon bombing in 2013 brought home the reality that lay just under the surface of the pervasive calm. The terrorists could strike almost at will and nothing could prevent a well-planned attack from within.

The coffee was very good—hot and strong—warming him to face the blustery 35°F temperature of an early-winter afternoon in Boston. Draining the cup, the man stood and headed towards the door, folding the paper and carefully adding it to others in the overflowing recycling bin. He tossed the cup into the trashcan, buttoned up a heavy dark topcoat and pulled on his gloves before pushing the glass against the bite of the wind. The cold numbed the exposed flesh on his face as he began walking up Boylston Street towards Boston Common. His pace was confident and leisurely, knowing a new type of terror had been unleashed that would cover the front page and have the pundits' back-peddling from their sanguine predictions. Day-to-day life would move from predictable to uncertain and fear would spread like wildfire.

He slid into a grimy Yellow cab and said "Logan."

The latest Al-Qaeda statement contained a dire prediction that in years to come, children in the United States would never see the American Flag flying at the top of the flagstaff. The pledge made it very clear. Al-Qaeda's objective was to make certain the Stars and Stripes would hang at half-staff each and every day.

Chapter 5

Washington, DC
October 22, 2017

Having just returned from a very successful G-7 meeting in Vienna where he'd reinforced cooperative efforts with allies on a range of issues including those related to both terrorism and cyber-security, President Samuel Chapman looked back on his first ten months in office with a pained satisfaction. He'd lived up to his campaign pledge to kick-start the economy with permanent tax cuts and ramrodded legislation through both houses which his party controlled. Sure, he had to make some concessions, but the fact remained he'd done what he promised though at a terrible personal cost. Between the morning briefings, endless sidebars and the European penchant for late dinners each evening, he'd given all the energy he could muster to the recent overseas trip, including meeting separately with every journalist wanting to interview him. So it did not surprise his wife, Ann, when her husband started to fall asleep at the table during a quiet lunch on his first day back. After lunch, she suggested he take a nap. He protested feebly, and she walked him to the bedroom and made him promise to stay put. Minutes later, she buzzed his appointments secretary to have his afternoon schedule cleared. President Chapman lay down and fell asleep almost immediately. Sadly, he never woke up, suffering a massive heart attack within the hour.

The Chief Justice swore the Vice President, John Bowles, into office the same afternoon in a hasty ceremony concluded before Samuel Chapman's body lost the last of its internal heat.

Chapter 6

Virginia Beach, Virginia
November 10, 2017

Dan Steele felt a fleeting pang of regret as he walked down the glistening hallway of Seal Team Two Headquarters into the Commanding Officer's office. He knocked on the door as he entered the office.

"Good morning, sir."

Commander Hank Owens looked up from the stack of papers and charged around his desk, starting with a handshake that became a bear hug. The skipper steered Dan over to two brown leather arm chairs salvaged from the Pentagon years before when a newly-appointed Assistant Secretary ordered an immediate change in his office furniture.

"So tomorrow's the big day?"

"Yes sir," Dan said, with a wide grin on his face.

"We're going to miss you."

Dan studied the clean shaven square jaw and bright blue eyes that grabbed your attention and wouldn't let go. The meticulous white uniform was spotted with insignia. Dan's eyes went to the single row of ribbons the skipper wore. A handful of men still living wore the pale blue ribbon with five white stars...the Congressional Medal of Honor. The public citation for the award told a short hand story of how a US Navy Seal platoon had been pinned down on an isolated mountainside in Afghanistan that was deemed too dangerous for close air support or helicopter extraction. The mission ended with 11 of 12 Seals dying.

The skipper leaned back in the chair knowing that nothing he could say would change anything, but he still felt an obligation to try to keep the best Seal he'd ever served with in a Navy uniform.

"I know we've talked about it before. Even now, I can put the toothpaste back in the tube if you want to change your mind and stay."

Dan chuckled and tried to stay serious, but he'd prepared for this "Hail Mary."

"Skipper, I've made up my mind. It's my time to move on. I owe it to Jill and the boys."

Changing course, he asked, "What are your plans?"

"Nothing concrete yet. We'll leave tomorrow after the paperwork is completed and head-up to Jill's folks' house in Newport for a few days and then follow the coast up to Maine. I figure we'll take about 30 days to decompress and then we'll come back here and see what we want to do next. Jim Trainer is trying to expand his dive shop over in Chesapeake and told me I could help him for a few months before I start looking for something permanent."

"Nothing more specific? I've never known you to not have a plan!"

"I know, but I need some time to unwind and think things through."

"Have you got any leads? Hooking up with Trainer doesn't sound like a good option. Hell," the skipper said, shaking his head, "I bet you haven't even put together a resume."

His brow furrowed, Dan said, "You're right. I started a resume last week, but it's a little hard to translate Special Operations Force work into something that can be understood or even done in most workplaces. I don't think Walmart would be interested in my ability to turn anything into a weapon or subdue an irate customer with some gentle physical persuasion." Both men laughed.

"Well, there's no question you'll land on your feet. Look, I know a lot of people here in Tidewater so let me know if you need any help." The skipper knew Dan would do it on his own and would not ask for help. He was just that kind of person. He would do favors and offer assistance to anyone else and follow-through with it but would rarely ask anything for himself.

Hank Owens reached for a small wooden box on the side table and handed it to Dan. The wood's finish was smooth and warm, crafted from a very dark, tropical-looking wood with yellow swirls interlaced with the growth rings. It seemed heavy for its size.

"It's made from quarter-sawn Bocote, a very dense and durable African wood."

Dan opened the box and saw a gleaming, black pocket knife. Dan lifted the knife, startled by its feather weight.

"The case is titanium and the blade is ceramic. I've made two of these. One is in my pocket and this one for you."

It was awkward...both men stood and faced each other. A final strong handshake and Dan left the office wiping tears from his eyes. As he re-traced his steps down the hallway to the Quarterdeck, he thought how could it be this hard? Seal Team Two was a tough crowd. Each of these elite warriors projected a swagger and an edge that they brought to everything. It just didn't end with the ops. They brought it with them every day, wore it like a badge of honor and too often paid dearly with failed marriages, alienated families and addictive behavior. Their only normalcy was the team, where each and every one acted as their brothers' keepers. In their usual environment, nothing else really mattered.

Dan saluted the Duty Officer and walked outside. The hot sun and high Tidewater humidity never felt better.

Chapter 7

Virginia Beach, Virginia
Veterans Day
November 11, 2017

Dan Steele couldn't imagine how anyone could be happier. He glanced at his wife from the driver's seat. Jill's short blonde hair swept over her high cheekbones. She pushed a few strands back into place and continued talking to the towheaded twin boys in the back seat.

"Boys, get ready to go over the bridge and through the tunnel." She always sucked in a mouthful of air through her teeth to make it seem even scarier.

The jeep had just started heading north across the Chesapeake Bay Bridge and Tunnel, a 20 mile span on the "Follow the Gulls" route connecting Virginia's Eastern Shore with Virginia Beach. The Tidewater area was a Navy town with most of the ships in the Atlantic Fleet calling Norfolk home. Dan looked forward to see the flat Virginia coastline in his rear view mirror.

Hampton Boulevard, the main drag into the base used to be lined with locker clubs, tattoo parlors, strip joints and bars. The shore patrol couldn't keep up with the fights, thefts and mayhem. Sailors were poorly paid and treated like second class citizens. What had been built up to provide the care these young men needed mired them down in the mud. The home of the Atlantic Fleet, Norfolk was a town to avoid and was universally regarded as the right place to insert the enema tube if anyone seriously wanted to clean up the Navy. However, Norfolk shed its image of a sailor's town over the last thirty years.

After nearly six years of active duty, Dan and Jill had grown tired of the unpredictability of active duty life, particularly his frequent absence. The two had met in Newport, RI during his time as a trainee at the Officer Candidate School. Running in opposite directions on a narrow sidewalk, they passed each other in front of one of the storied mansions along Bellevue Avenue. Both of them stopped and couldn't really explain why, but it was if they had been searching for each other for years and finally met. The two stared at each other as they closed the thirty feet separating them. Dan first broke the silence.

"Do I know you?"

"No, I don't believe we've ever met, in this life or a previous one."

"This is very strange. Why did you stop?"

"I was going to ask you the same question."

"Where are you on your run?"

"Just finishing, how 'bout you?"

"About halfway through but I am happy to skip the last three miles to find out who you are."

Outwardly a curious match, at 6'3" Dan's frame dwarfed Jill, petite at 5'3". He had dark hair and a strong jaw. With much softer more delicate features, Jill's blonde hair was short and kept in place by an aqua blue headband matching her eyes.

"Do you like coffee?" she asked.

"Sure."

"OK, let's jog down to Thames Street and solve this mystery."

"Pre-determined" is how Jill described it after the first day when they stayed in their shorts and running shoes, drinking coffee and getting to know each other. Inseparable, the two became good friends first and then fell in love. Both believed they were simply meant for each other.

Sixty days later, Dan graduated from OCS and left the following day for San Diego to attend Basic Underwater Demolition School (BUDS), a grueling prerequisite course for Seals with a 75-80% attrition rate. Dan felt a huge void when he and Jill began to separate. He tried unsuccessfully to sugar-coat the situation.

"I'll probably wash out and be sent home after the first week. Then we can get married and live a more conventional military life for the rest of my four year commitment. I'll get my teaching certificate, and we'll grow old together teaching right here in Newport."

Jill knew better. She didn't object too strenuously because his plans always included her.

"Sure. You are a natural leader and will probably be the top graduate in your class. Wash-out? I don't think so!"

A life-long Newporter, she grew up in old clapboard colonial down on the point, a quiet community separated from the downtown area previously frequented by unruly sailors serving on Atlantic Fleet cruisers and destroyers. Her father worked as a diesel mechanic in a local boatyard and just couldn't get enough of the fresh salt air. The family lived simply within spitting distance of Narragansett Bay. Jill studied hard, played soccer and became a star of the cross-country team despite her compact frame and short legs. She graduated with honors and headed to Brown University in Providence on a full scholarship, getting her undergraduate degree in biology with enough education credits to earn a teaching certificate which she leveraged into a job right back in Newport, teaching seventh graders the secrets of life. Jill could not understand her classmates' un-ending quest for romance in high school or college. Full of energy and head-turning attractive, she had a full life and loved living it and did not need to get tangled up with a man to complicate things. Living with her parents in Newport after college seemed practical to her.

Dan learned that Jill had a very good active mind and, more important, possessed lots of common sense. Within weeks of the run that changed both their lives, he realized that Jill's mental capacity exceeded his own, and he should just be happy she was much smarter than he was. Dan grew comfortable with the realization and never needed to verbalize it specifically. He just wanted to spend all his time with her.

While Jill had complete confidence in Dan and his strength was something she welcomed in her life, Jill also had a strong foundation and the self-reliance of a New Englander. She had conviction and a black and white view of right and wrong. A wonderful mother, she lived for the two boys they'd brought into the world together, raising them with love and caring and setting an early knowledge of where their bounds were.

Dan's upbringing was starkly different. An only child whose parents had been killed in a tragic head-on collision with a strung-out trucker trying to stay awake on Route 81 in western Virginia, Dan had become self-reliant at an early age. His parents were spending all their time and energy on keeping a small market going with the prospects of a larger box store coming to nearby Roanoke that would eventually force them to close. They were generous people and could not stand to see anyone go hungry, so the tray beneath the register cash drawer was stuffed with IOUs and cash register receipts which would never be paid. They were eking out a living but the family appreciated what they did have, and it seemed the important things were always there. The trio was tight knit and loving.

He and his father always took a few days off during deer season in the fall and would fish together on one of the fast moving streams in the area in the spring and summer. His simple, uncomplicated life got very complicated in the fall of his senior year when his parents were killed. An exceptional student, his teachers encouraged him to go on college. He knew his only hope of attending college lay in an athletic scholarship. Dan led the football team and gained the attention of the Virginia Tech scouts in his junior year when the team went to the State Championships for the first time in twenty-two years.

The sale of the grocery store barely covered the property taxes. He moved in with his mother's sister and her family for the remainder of his senior year in high school and got recruited by Virginia Tech as a football player. He rode the bench for the first two games and realized the starting quarterback played at a level that would pave the way to the NFL. Dan convinced one of the coaches to have him lead the "special" teams for kick-offs, punts and goal line stands. His work complemented the powerhouse offense, and Virginia Tech reached the conference finals two years straight. There had not been a kick-off return or punt return for a touchdown for two seasons—a school record.

To keep in shape, he swam in the off-season and got invited to join the swim team on a scholarship after an impromptu free-style race when he beat the top swimmer by ten yards in a 100 yard race. He'd always been a strong swimmer and effortlessly adapted to competitive swimming, captaining the team for his junior and senior years. A Navy recruiter convinced him the Seals could use his talents. It turned out to be a very easy decision. And one that led him to Jill.

Dan began to resent the time he had to spend away from his family. He was always either on a mission or preparing for the next one. Special Ops had become the "go to" branch of the military in the nation's undeclared wars and fight against terrorism. He vowed to make up the lost time with Jill and his two laughing boys in the back seat. Smiling to himself, Dan knew in his heart it would never get any better than this. He did not know how wrong he was.

Chapter 8

Philadelphia, Pennsylvania
Veterans Day
November 11, 2017

The Transportation Security Agency's new recruitment center opened its doors in the shadow of City Hall just two weeks prior to Veterans Day and had already met its first month's projections of offers to screened and qualified candidates despite the fact that more than fifty percent of the walk-ins failed to meet the minimum standards and were not moved to the next processing step. Another fifteen percent would wash-out of the training program. Compared to other US Government jobs, TSA standards were set low. Too low for most of the seasoned hands: recruiters joked that all you needed to do was fog a mirror and pass the urinalysis testing on your test day and you were in. Right downtown and with a nearby parking garage accepting TSA validations, the Center attracted a large number of potential applicants from the decaying and corrupt "City of Brotherly Love." There were few real job opportunities in the city, and the applicant traffic was heavy. Four agents rotated from their normal airport duties and staffed the center. This was great duty: no airport hassles, no passenger complaints or investigations, per diem pay which allowed you to pocket some extra cash, and a standard work day with every Holiday and weekends off.

"Dave Gadsden?" asked the young man. A tall, muscular man with a shaved head topping a sparkling white TSA uniform with razor sharp military creases straightened behind the counter.

"Yes, that's me." He stood and extended his hand to the boy and smiled. "What can I do for you?" The big brass buckle was polished to a rich, deep shine that was clearly part of a daily routine.

The son of an itinerant farmer from Monck's Corner, South Carolina, Dave Gadsden starred as a left guard on offense and middle linebacker on defense for the High School making it all the way to the State play-offs. Big Dave went 110% on every play...football would be his ticket out of Monck's Corner. The small town's official description, "where life is a little slower, a little calmer, and a little bit sweeter", attracted many of his teammates and friends who would live out their entire lives struggling and then die, having never ventured outside South Carolina's low country. He hated the smell of the paper plant that permanently scented the air and made the stifling humidity even more unbearable.

His hopes ended violently near mid-field when a pulling guard from Summerville slammed into his right knee on a well-executed trap play. Dreams of continued gridiron glory were dashed in a heartbeat, though he did have the distinction of being the first member of his family to complete high school. Some consolation! He enlisted in the US Air Force soon after graduation.

Dave thrived in the service...he listened closely, appreciated the certainty of the routine, and loved the disciplined and predictable environment where there were rules for everything. He gravitated to flying and became a C-141 loadmaster, leading his team with the same drive that made him a star on the football field. His strength, stamina and focus coupled with his model military bearing supported a strong service reputation as a man people would listen to and follow. He gave the Air Force twenty years, rising to the rank of Master Sergeant. He thought joining the TSA would be more of the same. He was determined to become a standout there as well.

The recruiting center opened its glass doors on Market Street right on time and Big Dave clapped his hands loudly and raised the energy level with his booming voice "Another day to excel, people. Let's make it another great one! Let's go!"

The young man who asked for Dave Gadsden shook his hand enthusiastically.

"Good morning, Mr. Gadsden, I'm Jose Santos. Happy Veterans Day!"

Jose had been carefully selected. His tall athletic frame was a rich brown, a mixture of sperm from Puerto Rico and an egg carried from Guatemala. Manuel and Maria, his common-law wife of twenty-two years, lived with their family in a dilapidated tar-papered shack no bigger than a garden shed. Built long ago to house seasonal workers, the shack had been abandoned when mushroom farming became more profitable. The family accepted their current living conditions...there were no hopes or dreams of anything better in the small eastern

Pennsylvania town they called home. Manuel worked the mushroom farms, spending most of his waking days in a dank humid atmosphere that came from the ground and the fetid mushroom compost which gave him headaches and caused fits of violent coughing that only subsided with cough medicine and clean air. He feared his constant wheezing would shorten his life, but there were no alternatives for someone who didn't have the papers to get another job. Many others found themselves in the same boat. He would continue working and make the best of it.

The Santos family was devastated when Jose was struck by a car just outside Kennett Square, the mushroom capital of the world. The driver didn't stop. Jose nearly died because the splintered bone in his shattered leg severed the femoral artery and only some quick thinking by an EMT saved his life. The doctor showed no emotion when he came out of surgery still wearing a sweat-soaked gown.

"Are you Jose's parents?" he asked. Maria gasped and fell to the tile floor when the doctor explained the clinical facts. There was too much internal damage, and the crushed leg couldn't be saved. He'd done what he could with no heroics. The boy's family was not going to pay, and he knew he'd get called by the medical director to justify why he'd done so much. Only four years out of med school and already numbed by a profession where most physicians remained detached and aloof without any involvement or feeling...not enough time or energy for that.

A few days after his discharge, Manual and Maria thought they'd won the lottery when a man appeared out of nowhere and offered not only to handle Jose's medical bills but also to provide a used Buick station wagon to the family. Six weeks after the accident, Jose's leg was fitted with a high-tech composite prosthesis in a private clinic. Jose couldn't believe his good luck in having some benefactor make all the arrangements and pay for his custom-fitted leg. He quickly learned to walk and felt very positive about his future. From time to time, Brian the benefactor called Jose on a cell phone he'd given him, asking about his leg and how he was doing, and how the station wagon was running. Later, he also asked him to do a couple of things around the city and even paid his cab fare. So Jose looked forward to visiting the TSA recruiting center and presenting David Gadsden with a distinctive wooden pen engraved with the US Air Force logo and words "Top Loadmaster."

Brian surprised Jose with a new cell phone just that morning and tested it with a call as the two of them sat in Brian's car, just before he entered the TSA Recruiting Center. Jose was thrilled. This was going to be a great day. Brian promised he would take him to the city's interactive science museum, the Franklin Institute, later in the morning.

Towering over the boy, Dave smiled broadly as he examined the new pen and excitedly exclaimed "Wow, Jose, this is just great. What a surprise!" He extended his hand again and asked, "By the way, how did you know I was a Loadmaster?"

The two were both smiling and still shaking hands when the composite shell of Jose's prosthetic leg disintegrated into thousands of razor-sharp shards followed closely by an ever expanding circle of steel pellets which surrounded the twelve pounds of C4 explosive that replaced Jose's flesh and bone.

Gadsden's torso fell to the floor, his shaved head landing between his polished black shoes. The white TSA uniform with its sharp military creases was torn from his body in the blast. The polished buckle lay several feet away, its shine covered with a bloody froth. The TSA banner hanging from the ceiling was shredded. The first responders estimated fifteen to twenty people dead, about a half dozen who might die before the day ended and perhaps ten others who would wear their injuries for the rest of their lives.

22

Chapter 9

Newport, Rhode Island
Veterans Day
November 11, 2017

Suzanne Murphy was the Chief Chemist at the Newport Water Department located just off Connell Highway opposite a strip mall. Newport boomed after the US Navy left the town in the 1970s and had become a haven for tourists attracted to the town's mix of traditional New England and yuppie-smart. Sure there was a Starbucks down on cobble-stoned Thames Street, but there was also a marine hardware store where you could buy mooring line and bottom paint as well as the popular white-soled boat shoes. What bothered the locals were the tourists who jammed the narrow streets and started spreading out to the few good restaurants in town. Newport had a reputation for bad restaurants. Most of the waiters were hung-over drunks recruited that morning. But nothing could compete with the town's history and feel. The ocean made it different.

Bill Schmidt sat back in his swivel chair and relaxed. Everything was green on the gauge board in front of him, and he mentally started the list of necessities for tomorrow's trip out on the bay on his buddy's boat. He expected a good day of fishing. It was getting late in the season for striped bass but the blues still chased the bait fish in the Bay and they could always do some bottom-fishing off Fort Adams. The weather was going to be perfect... chilly, 4-6 knots of wind out of the south and waves of less than one foot. He made a note to check the tide tables when he got home. Six more hours to go in his shift, and he'd be heading out the door. Bill pulled a magazine from the middle of the stack which filled the bottom desk drawer...the glossy pictures had nothing to do with game fish but reminded him of the huge collection of raunchy magazines from the Chiefs' Quarters of USS Spruance (DD-963) where he served as Chief Engineman.

The main gate light briefly flickered, but it often did when the wind came off the Bay. Cuts in the maintenance and operations funding led to a number of problems recently, and the team started to cut corners. Suzanne had done a good job holding on to the people assigned to the Water Department. But with everything else being challenged by the budget, Bill knew the people were next to go. A bank of monitors showed an unbroken view of the perimeter fence and main gate. Bill returned to the magazine wondering if what he saw was the work of a plastic surgeon who had gotten a little heavy-handed with the silicone.

Schmidt was startled and nearly fell out of his chair when the control room door opened. He still had a shocked look on his face and a single red hole in his forehead when Dan Lewis came in to take over the next morning.

Sometime that night, a small tank truck backed up to the aeration beds. Two men uncoiled a rigid rubber hose and pulled it over to the first pool. One man opened the valve and let the tank empty quietly with gravity. Even in the darkness, the two men could see the cloudy liquid eagerly spread across the first bay. The bacteria would be carried through the miles of pipes connecting Aquidneck Island's water supply. After discharging their cargo, the two men left by the front gate and drove through Middletown into the night.

24

Chapter 10

Chesapeake Bay Bridge and Tunnel
Veterans Day
November 11, 2017

Traffic was light, and the Jeep was moving along effortlessly. Dan felt a real sense of freedom. The uncertainty of what lay ahead after this unstructured period of decompression shifted to the back of his mind. They were approaching the first of the two tunnels which mated with the bridges and provided a deep water channel for the US Navy and many commercial carriers transiting through Hampton Roads.

Initially opened in 1964, the Chesapeake Bay Bridge and Tunnel replaced the ferry service with a 20 mile combination of elevated roadways resting on thousands of concrete piles and two mile-long tunnels exiting on man-made islands. In 1999, a parallel southbound lane was completed. Water depth along the roadway varied from twenty-five to one hundred feet and the vertical clearance over the tunnels ranged from forty to eighty feet to accommodate the busy port of Hampton Roads that was also the US Navy's homeport of Norfolk, Virginia. Most of the Navy's aircraft carriers were stationed there, and those floating airfields needed more than fifty feet of water between the surface of the water and the bottom to keep their massive underwater hulls afloat.

He looked in the rear-view mirror and instructed the boys to "hold your breath" when they entered the tunnel. Each of the boys always tried to hold their breath longer than the other, but usually it was Dan who ended the game when he burst out laughing at his sons.

He felt relaxed, but his military training also kept him keenly aware of his surroundings. There was a truck in front of them and a minivan behind them as he pressed lightly on the gas pedal and signaled to pass the truck. He glanced over his shoulder as an added precaution. He was just pulling even with the truck when he felt the road tremble under the car. At the same time, he saw a geyser of water shoot from the right side of the tunnel, tumbling the small sedan in front of the truck as if it were a Styrofoam cup. Dan slammed on the brakes at the same time the Jeep was engulfed by a wall of water that swept it around like an out of control water ride at Busch Gardens, scraping its roof on the top of the tunnel before rolling upside down and settling to the bottom as it filled with muddy seawater.

He unbuckled his seatbelt and reached for Jill. He pulled her from the passenger seat into a narrow pocket of air at the floorboard of the overturned car. Limp and unresponsive, she had a thready pulse but no other sign of life. Her open mouth signaled that she'd been knocked unconscious by force of the water slamming the Jeep upward and sideways. The boys remained underwater, their lifeless bodies buckled into their car seats and hanging upside down. The impact of the water and rollover forced the air from their little lungs and replaced it with dirty seawater. He knew of children who survived after minutes of being submerged in water, but there was no hope of that outcome today.

For a moment, Dan thought it would be better to die with his family that day, but then his survival instinct kicked into overdrive. Hundreds of feet of wreckage separated the Steele family from their next breath. What a situation. Out of the Navy, having survived two wars and multiple special operations, took the uniform off yesterday only to lose his family and to die at the bottom of the Chesapeake Bay in a tunnel today?

In the seconds it took the Jeep to fill with water as it was being thrown to the left by the torrent of water, Dan was holding his breath, his mind sorting through the options. He knew the Jeep was upside down on the bottom or atop some other poor souls that would also die today. After forcing a couple of deep breaths into Jill's lungs without any response, he kissed her and let go of her limp body. He took a long final breath before the water pressed the sliver of air out of the Jeep.

"Orient" Dan disciplined himself. How long had it been? What are the facts? OK. Bottom of the bay trapped in a car one hundred feet from the surface. How far were they into the tunnel? What was the lateral distance between the car and the tunnel point of failure? Unable to see and maybe a minute to go before he'd gulp some dirty seawater and drown with his family. At this stage, he thought again about taking the easy way, resigning himself to that fate or resisting the drowning death Seals fear most. Head-pounding, mind focused and in automatic, Dan remembered the emergency "Spare Air" tank in his bag in the back of the car. Awful choice. He climbed over the second seat where he hoped his two young sons' deaths came without the panic that comes with conscious drowning. He touched each of their faces. Could he make it out with Jill and the boys? A simple no. Blind, Dan tore himself from the second seat and desperately pulled himself along the roof line, found his duffel bag and felt along the seams until he found the zipper and opened the bag's mouth. He was conscious of his motions getting slower and at the same time feeling the intense urge to open his mouth and take a fatal breath of water. There had been no time for hyperventilation. Lungs now burning with a familiar feeling he knew all too well and with no visibility, he questioned his decision again as he pawed through the bag looking for the bottle that might save his life.

Known as "Gills" to his fellow Seals, Dan had the ability to ration the air in his lungs like no other Seal could. Mental concentration had more to do with it than lung capacity.

Chapter 11

Fresno, California
Veterans Day
November 11, 2017

The Mayor of Fresno, Laura Sanders, had just finished presiding over the 10:30 a.m. opening ceremony to begin the west coast's largest Veterans Day Parade. Begun in 1919 to honor returning World War I veterans, the city's Armistice Day parade preceded the formal declaration of a National Holiday in 1954. This year, over 10,000 people were expected to participate in the parade that included marching bands from around the country as well as floats and a large number of active duty military personnel. Laura was seated in the center of the VIP bleachers in front of City Hall flanked by the Lieutenant Governor and the Commanding General of the California National Guard. State Senators and Representatives as well as town officials jockeyed for positions closer to the Mayor where they all knew the cameras would be focused. This year, TV and print media commitments had risen dramatically. The forecast called for a sunny 70° with clear skies for the parade start at 11:15 a.m.

In addition to opening the parade, her public affairs team had orchestrated a number of other opportunities for her to take the podium. It would be a momentous day for the city and especially for Laura who was the odds-on favorite to win the next governor's race. She was being groomed for the position. Twice that year she'd been invited to Washington to explore her political future with the Democratic National Committee.

Thirty miles east of Fresno at the edge of the Sierra National Forest, two helicopters had taken off during the Mayor's opening speech and flew west at a low altitude. No flight plan had been filed, and the helicopters were not part of the parade festivities.

Downtown was thronged with thousands of sightseers lining the parade route closed off earlier that morning by the Fresno police department. As they'd done since 9/11, the police department had inspected all the floats and vehicles that would take part in the parade and had screened all the bands and military units. Every year, the police chief complained about the parade's impact on his budget and questioned the rising cost of the additional security, but the Mayor's office insisted that public safety was first and foremost. A first responders' command post was established at the mid-point of the route. The morning briefing by the local FBI agent revealed no unusual activity or particular threat. Everyone felt confident that the only challenges would be the usual lost child or maybe a couple of veterans drinking in public. Fresno was ready!

The longstanding commemoration of the day began as a lone bugler started playing a mournful version of "Taps" at 11:11 a.m. to mark the ending of the 'War to End All Wars' in the 11th Month, 11th Day, and 11th Hour. At the same time the two helicopters were seen flying low up the main street towards the reviewing stand. The two helicopters were identified by the general seated next to Laura.

He leaned towards the mayor pointing with the scrambled eggs that covered the bill of his uniform hat, "Those are special forces helos. I flew one in Iraq." Laura tried not to pay attention to the general, annoyed that he would start a conversation during what was supposed to be the most solemn moment of the day.

The pair seemed harmless enough, soundlessly keeping their distance and hovering short of the reviewing stand. Darkly tinted egg-shaped glass wrapped and protected their cockpits. As if on cue, the bugler's last note seemed to invite the craft forward where they hovered on either side of the reviewing stand as if ready to take their place among the bands and floats getting into final position a few blocks away.

Laura's questioning look to the uniform on her left turned to shock as the fuselage doors of both aircraft opened to reveal ugly black metal snouts. Heavy caliber incendiary rounds began pouring out of twin barrels to the left and right. The bleachers were methodically raked by the cannon fire so that the red, white and blue bunting seemed to outline an area that had been colored in with bright red. The same happened on the other side of the street where the cannons cut down the media stands. After ten seconds, the two helicopters separated, one flying slowly down the main street spitting fire into the crowds that were attempting to flee and the other flying back the parade route and using both a forward cannon as well as the side cannons to savage the marching bands, floats and military units that were all assembled to commemorate the end of a war. This looked like the beginning of another one. It was a bloodbath of the cruelest type. Everyone was a target that day.

With their mission apparently complete, the two helicopters took positions at either end of Main Street and then flew towards each other. Witnesses claimed later that the two helicopters were flying twenty feet above the pavement when they collided in front of the reviewing stand in a brilliant flash of magnesium and unspent fuel, the rotor blades snapping off and becoming scythes that cut everything in their paths. Laura Sanders' political aspirations were unexpectedly thwarted that day because she and everyone else in the reviewing stand were dead.

To the east, a team silently collapsed the portable antennas that provided a radio link to the two helicopters and stowed them in plain white utility vans. Two of the men controlled the event using what appeared to be ordinary gaming consoles. The third had viewed the carnage on a split screen monitor via a live video feed from each of the remotely controlled drones. It had been executed flawlessly, and the casualties were horrific. The trio fanned out over the small area, crisscrossing their temporary operating base to ensure there was nothing left behind.

With the equipment loaded, the leader gave the signal, and the three vehicles sped off in different directions. The operation was perfectly executed, and the team had followed the timeline precisely. What two of the drivers didn't know is that another timer had already been activated that would trigger a powerful blast in thirty minutes in each of their vans. There would be little left when the police arrived at the two separate sites forty miles apart. The third van was abandoned in a nearby town where another car had been parked awaiting its arrival. The driver tapped a brief message into a small pager and looked forward to a few cold beers somewhere down the road.

Chapter 12

Chesapeake Bay Bridge and Tunnel
Depth: Sixty feet
November 11, 2017

Dan found the 'spare air' bottle in his bag. The small cylinder about the size of a water bottle had been presented to him during the Seal Team Two's farewell roast the night before. He insisted on including wives and girlfriends at the event and hoped that this departure from previous formats would keep the night a bit more civilized. He grasped the first model of a self-contained rescue device that contained less than two cubic feet of compressed air, the equivalent of thirty breaths relaxing at your picnic table. Here, blind and trapped under the bay, Dan's breathing rate increased with the panic he felt. He calculated his odds at 10,000 to 1. As he turned the small valve on top of the tank, Dan wondered whether it had been used or had any air in it at all. He put the mouthpiece in his mouth and drew in a full breath of old, metallic-tasting air.

He found a child's 'Sea Hunt' style mask that had been another gift from the evening and pulled it over his head. The mask skirt was brittle and leaked, but it was better than swimming blind with nothing to protect his eyes. He pulled himself over the back seat, crawled along the roof and after saying a silent, painful goodbye to Jill and the boys, exited the jeep through the driver's side door, blindly feeling his way ahead…but to where? Maybe he was just postponing the inevitable or making a difficult problem worse for the recovery effort that would be underway in the next week.

The entire team came to Dan's send-off, and he'd been given the spare air bottle and mask by Tom Bryant as one of the many joke gifts. Dan and Tom had reported to the Seal Team within a couple of weeks of each other. They'd become good friends ever since the stupid challenge that had been spawned after they'd completed a training operation from a wet submersible Seal Delivery System that had been developed to insert six Seals to the objective area from a ship or submarine operating ten to fifteen miles off-shore. On the trip to the beach, the two had argued about the length of USS Wisconsin (BB-64) that was saved from being scrapped by joining Missouri, New Jersey, and Iowa as floating museums. The Iowa class battleship had become a popular attraction on the Norfolk waterfront and was berthed right downtown at Waterside. The argument ended with Tom betting Dan that he could swim the length of the ship underwater. Dan quickly took the bet and thought nothing of it until two months later.

"Hey, Dan," boomed Tom's voice in the conference room after the usual Wednesday meeting. "The ship is 884' long…you still want to swim or do you want to just hand me the win without getting wet?"

Dan's mind flashed back to the long, cold ride to the beach. Without a thought he said, "You're on."

That night Dan told Jill about the bet. She was not happy.

"You've got to be kidding me. You are supposed to be an adult. We've got two boys who want to be just like their dad, and you come up with this stupid manhood challenge. I can't believe it."

When they were first married, Dan would sputter and try to defend his actions but soon learned that Jill would not buy it, and her sweet disposition could turn cold as ice. He found that his only viable strategy was to let her vent long and loudly without trying to explain himself. Over time, he'd worked hard to limit the number of times he'd engaged in what she so correctly called s squared or Seal Stupidity.

Since this kind of wager would never be sanctioned by the Seal Team's leadership or the Norfolk police, it would take place at night. Dan and Tom donned their masks and fins and jumped into the harbor with several team members watching from the deserted pier. After a few minutes of hyperventilating and agreeing that this was their last stupid wager, the two submerged and swam past the massive bronze propellers swimming about six feet apart on either side of the keel. Tom was kicking strongly and pulled ahead a few feet. Dan could barely see the glow of his underwater light through the turbid water. He wondered how close to the bottom they were swimming.

Suddenly Dan pulled even with Tom and swam right by him. Something was wrong. His first thought was shallow water blackout as he swam quickly to Tom's side. Dan grabbed his arm and there was no reaction. He shined his light into his face. His mask was gone and blood gushed from the middle of his forehead. Dan grabbed the back of his wetsuit and started to drag him along the curve of the hull to the surface. Dan cursed to himself: no buoyancy compensator to speed this trip to the surface, no idea of where he was along the hull and no knowledge of what might be alongside the ship's hull on the surface to make this a longer swim. Oh yeah, most important, his lungs were ready to explode, and he was feeling a bit of panic.

Before they reached the surface, Tom regained consciousness and swallowed several gulps of water. When Dan reached the surface, Tom was discovering the new seam in his skull and wondering what happened. Within seconds, the two were surrounded by other team members who got them out of the water and onto a boat pontoon.

The sun was just coming up when Dan, Tom and several of the team left the hospital and headed back to the base. Commander Hank Owens had paid a visit to the two, muttering about the reports and the questions he'd get on this one once it was splashed all over the front page of the <u>Virginian-Pilot</u>. He'd ordered an immediate "Safety Stand-down" for the entire team as a damage control measure. Dan knew that the skipper's "Safety Stand-down" would be far less painful than the one that Jill would impose when he got home.

Chapter 13

Chesapeake Bay Bridge and Tunnel
Depth: Sixty feet
November 11, 2017

Cold and dark. He visualized the explosion and developed a mental picture of the situation. It was grim. "Orient" he commanded himself. He had about three to four minutes to get to the surface, and believed that he was breathing like an asthmatic suffering from an acute attack. There were three exits. One long one continuing through the tunnel; another long one that would head back the way they came or one up though what he thought was a breach in the tunnel wall. Options one and two were non-starters. The only way out was through what had to be a large fracture in the tunnel wall. He moved out of the car along the tunnel wall, feeling for something that might give him some idea of direction. Within thirty seconds he found what he believed was the FEDEX truck that he remembered being ahead of his car in the slower lane when he felt the tremor and just before the car was engulfed. He reasoned that he was heading through the tunnel and that the rupture would be to his right. He kicked slowly on a route that he believed would lead across the tunnel's width and somewhere close to the breach. He reached the tunnel wall and began swimming along it. Was he swimming in the right direction? After what seemed like a minute, he felt a swirl in the water as he touched a series of heavy steel reinforcing bars pointed inwards like punji sticks. What else might block his way to the surface? He figured he had another eighty to ninety feet to go before he could pull in some fresh air. He thought about Jill and wondered whether to spit-out the mouthpiece and join his family in their dirty water graves. Training prevailed. He would try to pick his way through what was likely a rebar jungle.

Trying hard not to panic, he'd tried to feel his way through the twisted re-bar. Every second counted now. He shivered…the water temperature felt colder, and he knew that he was losing body heat. He pulled himself along the twisted re-bar hand-over-hand searching for a way out. Repeatedly, he moved forward only to find a structural box canyon of twisted metal and concrete blocking his escape.

Just as he started probing another pathway to what he thought was the outer shell of the tunnel, the spare air bottle clanked against a protruding metal spur pulling the rubber mouthpiece out of his clenched teeth. Desperate, Dan flailed frantically to catch the bottle as it fell into the muddy darkness. No luck. He was out of options. He pulled himself forward scraping his torso and shins trying to find an escape route. Arms feeling the way ahead, he squeezed his body through the tangled reinforcement rods towards what he hoped was open water. The idea of filling his lungs with seawater and drowning in a rebar cage petrified him. He pushed off a loose piece of concrete and pressed forward. Home free? Just another fifty to sixty feet to go to the surface.

Dan kicked hard towards the muted light that penetrated the turbid water. His lungs were burning, and he instinctively took a sip of seawater that caused him to cough, exhausting the spent air in his lungs. He was drowning. How much further? The light brightened as he neared the surface and finally gulped a life-restoring lungful of warm, salty air that tasted like diesel fuel. He didn't care what it tasted like or how dirty it was…it was air and that's what he needed. With his mind still racing, he forced himself to orient. He quickly focused and panned the horizon around him, spotting the red hull-stripe of a USCG boat bobbing a few hundred yards away. He started a slow breast-stroke towards the boat, keeping his head above water and enjoying the sensation of the oily air filling his lungs. Thinking about what he left on the bottom made him wonder what might be next. Exhaling forcefully, he vowed to find out what happened and why.

Chapter 14

DHS–Domestic Terrorism Annex
Washington, DC
November 12, 2017

Deep inside a large gray building located on 10th Street Northwest, the DHS Domestic Terrorism Annex was surrounded by museums, galleries, association offices, lobbyists and law firms just a few blocks from the Gallery Place/ Chinatown Metro stop. Admiral James Wright sat at the end of a V-shaped conference table and listened to the initial assessment. His mind wandered as he heard the same old conservative, tentative briefing that provided little new information as to what really happened. These were good people that had been drained of their ability to look at things objectively. Classic bureaucrats, they thought they'd seen it all. This was merely another random collection of some isolated events that would see the front pages for maybe another 48 hours and then be forgotten.

He looked down the table and watched the presentation on the screen. It occurred to him that the person who had chosen the conference table had made a good choice. From his seat at the head of the table, he could see the slides and keep an eye on all the other subtle interactions going on at the table.

"Any questions, Admiral?"

"No. Thank you all." The Admiral sat back in his chair and then pushed forward, putting both his elbows on the table.

The dozen people at the table suddenly were all leaning forward and waiting for the Admiral to speak. One of them was a retired Navy Captain who knew what was coming. He looked at the single row of ribbons centered on the Admiral's left breast uniform pocket just below a set of gold Navy wings. A glance captured a career: Defense Superior Service Medal, Navy Cross and Bronze Star with Combat "V." There were many others, but Wright was an uncomplicated man who shunned the spotlight, avoided the Washington party circuit and didn't have a young, trophy wife. That was all part of the package required to be successful in this town. Wright was a rare, clear-thinking warfighter who firmly believed that everything he did had to somehow be tied to the men and woman on the front lines. If it didn't meet that criterion, then it was of little interest to him.

Sure, he'd been selected and promoted to Rear Admiral but not because of his efforts to impress his chain of command. He'd made it on the front lines, leading aircraft to their targets and being a man that people would follow anywhere, anytime. He was an Old Testament kind of guy who could crack the whip and wash the feet of his squadron or wing at the same time. That's why people naturally looked to him when a problem was messy and complicated. But it was painfully clear that he'd go no further. When the stream of dirty jobs that he'd willingly taken on for his service and for the country slowed, if it ever would, he'd be plucked by the Navy for retirement and replaced with one of those hard chargers on the fast track to more stars.

The President himself had picked Wright out of his J3 position on the Joint Staff and asked him to pull back his request for retirement. Wright was assigned to lead the new domestic terror cell at DHS. He had been looking ahead towards retirement when he and Carole could return to Rhode Island. Construction of their retirement house on the Sakonnet River was already started when he was ordered to the job. He had made the Navy his top priority for all of thirty years and was ready to see the next generation take over. It wasn't because he'd lost his motivation or that time had dulled his insight. No, the explanation was simple. He was ready to settle down, to dig a few clams for some chowder or match his wits against the striped bass that populated Narragansett Bay every summer. He longed for the simple pleasure of shuffling along the rocky beach with Carole deeply inhaling that clean, salt-laden air. Again, that would have to wait.

Jim had told Carole, "Heh, I've been serving at the pleasure of the President since commissioning so I can't say no!" She was disappointed but saw his eyes sparkle at taking on one final challenge. She was also worried: chaos seemed to follow him whatever the assignment. She enjoyed Washington and could certainly keep busy while he worked those long days and sometimes nights at DHS. It didn't matter what time he finished, he'd always come home, and she looked forward to that each and every day. At least this job didn't involve leading a battle group halfway around the world for months at a time. He was driving a large desk, not an aircraft carrier with 100 planes and a dozen warships in company.

"Were there any surveillance tapes from Philadelphia?" the Admiral asked.

"No, sir, TSA set up this recruiting office only a few weeks ago and leased the site for six months. A surveillance system was never requested or installed."

The Admiral removed his glasses and rubbed his eyes.

"So, let's recap." he said, "We've got parade in Fresno with hundreds of dead spectators and vets alike, including the Lieutenant Governor of California, the Mayor and the Commanding General of the National Guard. A major highway tunnel flooded and who knows how many dead in Virginia Beach, seventeen people confirmed dead, another dozen wounded in Philly, and the only thing we know is that a teenager was talking to the TSA chief when some sort of explosive went off. And we've got a water supply in Newport that's full of very virulent bacteria that's got the city panicked and people flooding the emergency rooms thinking that they have somehow contracted the plague from their drinking faucets. All on Veterans Day. Just a coincidence? Are there any dots to be connected here?" The Admiral noticed that most of the people at the table began looking down and studying their planners. He did not expect an answer anyway.

"Look, our Secretary sees the President this afternoon and asked me to come along to provide an initial assessment. There's not a lot of detail here and nothing conclusive on any of these incidents. I guess it will be a short meeting." He stood at the table, looked down both sides and concluded, "I sure hope these things are not connected but my gut tells me that that is just wishful thinking."

He walked back to his office and stopped briefly at his administrative assistant's desk.

"Michelle, I need to be over in the Secretary's office at 1:00 p.m."

Michelle would have Wright's driver pick him up at the building's back entrance and drive him up to the Nebraska Avenue site that DHS had taken over from the US Navy. The site was small and not ideally located for a Cabinet Secretary whose time was spent equally between the White House and Capitol Hill, but USG facilities were at a premium with the government's infrastructure continuing to expand like an incoming tide that never receded. Having to squeeze into a consolidated facility to house most of the Department's operations seemed to be the inevitable compromise. Spreading the organization across the expanse of the General Services Administration's DC office complexes would be too complicated, and the Director would lose control of his expanding workforce. Better to slum a few years on Nebraska Avenue until a larger Headquarters could be built, leased or repurposed.

Chapter 15

Double Eagle Headquarters
M Street Georgetown
Washington, DC
November 12, 2017

The dark black car with tinted windows glided into an underground parking lot a block from the lazy Potomac. A former warehouse had been gutted top to bottom and extensively renovated to serve as the secretive Washington-based Headquarters of Double Eagle Industries. The Double Eagle building façade blended well with the traditional boutique offices that lined Georgetown's M Street. Whether old money or new, those building fronts reflected an abundance of it. Behind those doors, deals were brokered by some of the most powerful men in Washington. Though many lobbyists and think tanks still called K street home, Georgetown had become synonymous with influence peddling and Washington politics. Though not readily apparent, what was unique about the Double Eagle building was its size. The façade ended some sixty feet from the sidewalk and the building extended for another 100', ending just short of the old Chesapeake and Ohio canal.

The building renovation ended at the point that would be appropriate for most offices and the latter two-thirds of the building were nondescript, with few windows and none of the stately glitz. Some of the extra space on the M street fronted buildings had been converted to loft apartments or condos that could be accessed from the side or rear of the building and offered a proximity that attracted well-heeled commuters tired of spending hours on the road each day.

The driver stopped, got out of the car and made a sweep of the empty garage. There were three cars present. He then strode around the car and opened the rear door. The butt of a machine pistol was exposed beneath his jacket.

"All clear, Mr. Spence."

The tall beefy man moved quickly from the back seat, walked a dozen steps to the adjacent elevator and pressed his index finger against a biometric pad. The door opened and closed behind him. Though the Double Eagle building extended five floors above street level, this elevator stopped only in the garage and on the top floor.

"Good morning, Mr. Spence." The voice came from behind a massive mahogany desk guarded by a professionally attired woman who served as his Executive Secretary with an annual salary that had grown to $250,000 dollars in the twelve years since she had started working on the top floor.

He nodded and walked through the open door to his office. Even with all the security, Spence was always on guard, vigilant to the smallest variations in patterns, whether physical or emotional. He could detect change of any sort and had developed a very sensitive coup d'oeil.

Born in the sleepy town of Durres on the western coast of Albania, he'd had an unremarkable childhood, an only child produced by a loving mother and a cold and suspicious father who regularly beat her and the child as well. The family eked out a living with his father, Agim, working at a local garage that specialized in providing new identities for the steady stream of stolen luxury cars flowing in from Europe. Anna cleaned the houses of several families that could afford domestic help.

He spent his childhood like all the children, sometimes fishing off the docks with a hand line, running around the Roman amphitheater in the center of town or hiding out in one of the concrete bunkers that still dotted the street corners and countryside. By the late 1990s, Albania had overcome its national paranoia and was trying to re-define itself after years of corruption. But another crisis overwhelmed the country. In the aftermath of Enver Hoxha's dictatorship, a new optimism had swept over the country, and money had poured into the economy with the prospects of incredible returns. Everybody was bought in to what amounted to a national-level Ponzi scheme of staggering proportion. When the bubble burst, the citizens took to the streets and drove out the new government with several thousand deaths attributed to the chaos of massive, country-wide uprisings. Finally, the UN mustered the courage to recognize the problem and restore some semblance of order. Beneath the surface, men talked of the future and how this would never happen to their country again.

Chapter 16

Durres, Albania
June 1960

The army had discharged a young soldier for a series of crimes that included rape, several assaults on non-commissioned officers, and theft. Three years earlier, a local judge had given the soldier's parents the choice of sending their fifteen year old son to jail or having him enlist in the army. They chose the army, hoping that somehow the discipline would straighten out the boy. He lasted just eight months before he was incarcerated for two years and then discharged. After returning to his home town of Durres, Gjon stayed drunk for about a month. Drunks were common in Durres so he made the transition between military prison and town life without any difficulty. He finally sobered up enough to take a part time job as a middle school custodian. That's where he first met Spence whose world changed forever at the age of fourteen.

At first, Gjon just observed the students and teachers. Prison had taught him some important lessons about time, power and fear. He quickly sorted out the organizational pressure points and had his pulse on all the players in a few weeks. Then, he just begged for money and food from the boys and girls. Within a month, after he'd beaten-up all the school bullies and converted them into his enforcers, he expected that and more as a tribute. His threats were real, and the students were cowed into submission. Spence had watched in fear and kept his distance, and Gjon knew that he had no money to give. What he exacted from Spence was far worse. He began to use Spence as his personal whipping boy. Spence had never stood up to his father and thought that there was no alternative to accepting the beatings and keeping his mouth shut.

Spence endured the abuse until the end of the school year when he felt more protected at home. However, the situation had deteriorated there too, and he was a more frequent target of Agim's alcohol-fueled anger. The clock was ticking, and Spence did not want to return to school and be subjected to Gjon's daily torture. He saved whatever money he could by doing odd-jobs around the neighborhood and constantly scouring the streets for odd pieces of jewelry or coins that were carelessly dropped and lost. One day in August that year, he left the house after breakfast and never returned.

This early education in brutality both at home and in school would have far-reaching effects. Years later, the score would be settled. Gjon endured a long and very painful death that took place over a week's time. The entire event was carried out and recorded as Spence stipulated. He viewed the VHS tapes once and then destroyed them. That was the last time he permitted himself to get caught up in taking revenge. In the end, the bully of Durres suffered greatly before his death. However, it taught Spence that the ledger could never be fully balanced. He never had the satisfaction that he expected and still felt a chill when he saw Gjon's face in his frequent nightmares.

The young boy first made his way to Italy and began a street education that would far surpass anything that he could have learned in a Durres classroom. Much of the first year he lived on his own gave him an understanding of the economic system that worked in the shadows. He survived and even thrived in the gritty streets of Naples and then upped his game by traveling to Rome. In October, three short months after leaving Durres, he formulated and committed to a short term plan to accomplish before his sixteenth birthday: fluency in English, German, and Italian, a University level knowledge of mathematics, economics, and history, several identities that would permit him flexibility and access to the world, and economic means that would provide a secure base to achieve his goals.

Coffee houses and public libraries became his haunts. People relaxed over coffee and the small, crowded shops provided ample opportunity to obtain food and drink and take advantage of the careless behavior of the young people that constantly attended to their social habits. Frequently a wallet would find its way to the floor or a purse would be left hanging on a chair. Spence developed the patience of a saint and a well-honed situational awareness of the patrons and staff and others that might be looking for the same opportunities.

Libraries opened up a whole new world that Spence had never known. His mind was more like a computer than a sponge. He would read a textbook in a single day absorbing all the information and forgetting none of it. Everything lay at his fingertips. He still lived on the streets but had shifted the balance, spending more nights in hostels and shelters than in the open air.

His writing and reading skills became known to several regulars at a coffee house closest to the humanities building, and they would ask him to read their papers before submission. His ideas and light editing led to his preparation of short papers and essays for their classes. Spence found this line of work an education in itself, and the results of his efforts at ghost-writing yielded more and more euros. *Traditional education was such a waste of time and energy* he mused. His goals were now clearly attainable.

In the evening, he would frequent the dark watering holes that catered to the university crowd, boys and girls trying to find their way in an uncertain world, bolstering their courage by drinking too much beer or wine. Spence used these venues as a classroom, testing his language skills and listening to the serious students thinking they could apply the theories learned that day to change the world and laughing at the silliness that was often on display. He placed himself in the classrooms and lecture halls with them, studying how he would fit in like everyone else.

He celebrated his sixteenth birthday in Vienna, Austria where he worked as a dishwasher for a wealthy family. His English language skills had developed to the extent that he was tutoring the son of his employer, a well-known Count who divided his time between Vienna and the family's castle in the Alps. His tutoring paid very well and between that and his kitchen wages, he'd been able to send money to his mother with a note saying that he was doing well and hoped that she would forgive his unannounced departure. He enjoyed an abundance of free time. Spence could come and go as he pleased, enabling him to create a secondary identity that served him well.

Chapter 17

Double Eagle Headquarters
M Street Georgetown
Washington, DC
November 12, 2017

It was 09:05 a.m. Spence sat down at a large oak library table and began his daily routine: first, a glass of ice water while he reviewed his daily calendar. Then hot, black, very strong coffee as he scanned Eyes Only reports, many with US Government markings that he often saw before the intended recipient, an industrial intelligence report prepared by one of the other people having access to the garage, then the Washington Post, Wall Street Journal and the Pentagon "Early Bird." By 09:45 a.m., he'd absorbed all the news and had created a list of calls, emails, and meetings that would be added to his calendar. None of the news, not even the recent events that had occurred on Veterans Day, surprised him.

Double Eagle Industries was a privately held firm that operated its vast network from offices in Berlin, Washington, and Tokyo. Branded as a global supply chain provider, Double Eagle Industries had a broad customer base and world-wide shipping agreements that guaranteed delivery at rates that rivaled the better known competitors in the market. Its specialty niche was the shipment of goods that would be bonded or would require expedited customs clearance or avoidance of the customs process altogether. The company's telephone system was entirely automated and every employee, invoice, shipping label and declaration used the same number in Berlin that routed calls in seconds to the right office or specific employee.

Few connected the company's name, Double Eagle Industries, or its logo that featured two eagles joined together with anything historic or geographic. Though the flag of Albania had undergone a number of changes over the years, it always featured two stylized black eagles with their bodies centrally joined watching left and right, on a field of bright red. To those knowing the country's history, the Double Eagles had over-watched countless attempts to gain independence from outside oppressors and occupiers. Many clung to the legend that the flag had been used by the 15th-century Albanian hero Skanderbeg, who led a successful uprising against the Ottomans that resulted in a fleeting independence for parts of the country for a few years. On a grander scale, some Albanians believed the mythology that they had somehow descended from the eagle, referring to themselves as "Shkypetars," or the "sons of the eagle." Only a handful of Double Eagle employees even knew that any tie to Albania existed.

Spence's name did not appear on the company's list of officers nor was his picture on any Double Eagle Industries organization chart. He worked behind the scenes and managed the enterprise through compartments, limiting access to specific projects to a need to know criterion that he himself set. No one had ever heard of a violation of these project boundaries in the company. Spence frequently enjoined his subordinates to "make the market," a broad brush appeal that could involve almost any approach to shift the competitive advantage in favor of the company.

The "Fresno Massacre" as it was labeled by all the networks' news teams dominated the coverage, and there were on-scene live reports from the veteran newscasters before sunset. The talk shows had hastily juggled their guest schedules, and the terrorism experts were in demand everywhere. The President had called a news conference the previous night to inform the nation what they already knew and to pledge that those responsible would be found and brought to justice. The President's anger and commitment visibly showed through. He was determined to find out who and why and was prepared to use whatever resources he had to hunt down those behind this attacks on the homeland.

The Philadelphia Inquirer labeled the Veterans Day events a national "Wake-up call" in the largest front page font anyone had ever seen. Most of the day's reporting of yesterday's explosion at the TSA recruiting center in Philadelphia stuck to the facts and did not speculate as to the cause. TSA investigators had begun the task of sorting through the rubble and removing the red spatter that covered virtually everything in the room. The FBI was called in to assist.

In a clinical monotone, one local newscaster had confirmed what everyone already knew: "There were several eye witnesses that provided information to the police. The FBI and DHS have been all over the site. However, the TSA spokesman had no further comments because of the ongoing investigation. Early indications point to a suicide vest worn by a single individual. There have been no answers to whether the attacks were connected in any way."

The <u>Virginian-Pilot</u> headlines compared the tunnel flooding to the attack on Pearl Harbor. The first four pages contained the front page format covering the events in Fresno and Philadelphia. The Atlantic Fleet enforced a broad perimeter where boats were intercepted and escorted away from the ships that were tied to piers at the naval base. A no-fly zone was imposed with flight corridors for reduced commercial flights out of Norfolk International Airport. The cities of Norfolk and Virginia Beach were locked down.

At 10:00 a.m., Robert "Jack" Lang and Paul McGovern entered Spence's office. He smiled and motioned to the two black leather arm chairs in front of the table.

Spence looked at each man intently, carefully mapping their facial expressions and body positions before asking, "What do you make about yesterday's news? A suicide bomber in Philadelphia and an apparent tunnel failure down in Virginia Beach? And the parade disaster in California? What's going on?" Spence rarely engaged them in a current events discussion but seemed interested in the near simultaneous timing of these events and curious about their thoughts.

McGovern spun in his chair towards Jack and then replied, "All on Veterans Day. Seems like they might be connected, but I haven't heard anyone make that call, and no one knows what caused the tunnel flooding. God, I can't even imagine being trapped underwater in a tunnel. I'm not aware of any survivors. I talked to some people over at DHS earlier this morning, and there are already calls for the Director's head." A studious man with a round face and a balding head, Paul McGovern's closely clipped blonde mustache seemed to flatten his voice into an emotionless monotone. His unremarkable personality was offset by other skills that Spence valued.

Full of energy and with insight beyond his years, Jack Lang added, "It's too early to know what happened down on the Chesapeake, but some reporter claimed that an aircraft carrier was underway in the middle of the channel when it happened. I haven't heard any other plausible theories, but you can bet that the conspiracy truth seekers will be out in force tonight hitting all the evening talk shows. Philadelphia sounds like someone going postal using a bomb instead of a gun. At the other extreme, Fresno seems to me to be a well-planned technology demonstration carried out by a well-organized and well-financed group that wanted to maximize the media impact. This is distinctly different than be-heading a small group of Christians along the Mediterranean or throwing women and children off a mountain cliff. It has the look and feel of a military operation. My bet is that Al-Qaeda or ISIL is involved."

"Well," Spence summarized, "It's a dangerous and unpredictable world out there. Let's be careful." Spence detected no sign from either man which is what he expected. When the trio was together, the temperature in the room dropped. What the three had in common was the absence of any emotional attachment to anything. They were cold as ice. Spence nodded in Paul's direction and sat back in his chair with his hands woven behind his balding pate.

McGovern began with a geo-political summary of the hot spots around the globe, the overnight market reports and then briefly recapped Double Eagle's international activities. He provided an Executive-level overview of the current status of programs for US Government agencies and ended by announcing a new opportunity coming out of the Department of Homeland Security called HS2.

McGovern concluded, "So it looks as if they will wrap multiple efforts into this large, winner takes all contract for everything from border security to cyber protection."

"What's the estimated contract value?"

"It's not clear how all the smaller efforts will be swept up into this, but during the question and answer session at the program's Industry Day, the Contracting Officer called this the biggest contract since DOD awarded the Joint Strike Fighter. HS2 will have a ten year period of performance and three five year options. Total value will have a T instead of a B. I think that Team Double Eagle is well-positioned on this one. We'll have some stiff competition for sure but no one can touch our past performance."

"What's the timeline from here, Paul?"

"The government plans to get a draft request for proposal out early next year and anticipates releasing the final in the spring. The award is projected before the end of 2018. Of course, the Contracting Officer made the usual speech about the plan being dependent on the out years' funding profile and the uncertainty of the budget given the current emphasis on balancing it and slowing the increase to the national debt. In any case, we need to start planning now. I don't see another opportunity like this one for years to come. By the way, the government refers to the HS2 program as Fortify."

"Team Double Eagle" was used frequently to describe the network of companies that had been acquired and were managed as wholly owned subsidiaries, retaining not only their own corporate identities and business structure but keeping secret their affiliation with the parent. Double Eagle and its subsidiaries had grown a very large and impressive portfolio of multi-year contracts with all the US Government agencies that looked after internal security for the country and had loyal people in positions of great trust within those organizations. Because of the compartmentation, no one knew who might be working for Double Eagle. With this extensive network, Spence gained both access to the United States' most sensitive security secrets and could also influence approaches, methods and techniques. Put another way, he had an invisible hand in every major security decision made and understood its impact better than anyone. He had more insight into the US Government's Homeland Security posture than anyone in the government at any level.

"OK, good. Do any of our companies have any exposure as a result of these recent incidents?"

"None reported so far," replied McGovern evenly.

Spence leaned forward, "Thank you, Paul. We clearly need to go after HS2 and add it to our portfolio. Please start working that with the team. Can you please give Jack and me a couple of minutes?" The big man shook McGovern's hand and walked him across the marble floor to the entry door.

"Son," said the beefy man. Spence always called him son when they were here alone. He began pacing the floor. The leather heels of his capped-toe dress shoes broke the silence of the room and measured his pace for several minutes before he began talking.

"You recall that we lost that Strategic Border Initiative re-compete a year ago. Since then, the program is really foundering. The prime contractor, ABACUS, is losing boatloads of money. The supply chain is broken and many of the small businesses have not been paid for months. Director Lewis is being routinely raked over the coals by the subcommittees in both chambers. It's a mess. I'm told the program office will likely find a way to terminate the contract for the convenience of the government and then re-compete it. The incumbent had the inside track, and the government didn't have the courage to pick the devil that they didn't know."

Lang interrupted, "I thought that we'd had a hand in their current success."

Spence enjoyed Jack's less than subtle sarcasm. He smiled and continued, "Yes, that's true. We had some of our team sell them some defective coax, planted some very ugly viruses in their computer code and sabotaged the workforce. We are in the final phase of turning that loss into a win."

"So, what's up now?"

"OK, let me fill in the squares for you." The big man paced across the floor twice before starting the explanation. "First, I want to compromise ABACUS' standing with DHS and then undo the Congressional support that they are able to muster. I'm still working on the details, but I'm thinking that one way to get the ball rolling is to have the Programs Vice President from ABACUS suffer a personal and potentially damaging security lapse."

"Doug Smith? Forget about it. The guy has a sterling reputation...decorated war hero and a god over at DHS. The agency still loves ABACUS, and Doug is one of the reasons why. He's a choir boy. It seems a little far-fetched to me. "

"Your analysis is right on target. But that's precisely why this initiative will work," Spence replied gently. Spence often spoke of initiatives to refer to those efforts aimed at undercutting a competitor. Jack didn't know much about the special operators that Spence employed but had watched him topple giants before with no Double Eagle fingerprints left on the causes.

Chapter 18

The White House Situation Room
Washington, DC
November 12, 2017

The President leaned forward, putting his elbows on the polished table and pausing before addressing Jim Wright with a mixture of shock and disbelief on his face.

"Jim, I spent most of yesterday in the bunker, and Air Force One is still on a fifteen minute alert. You are telling me that twenty four hours after this series of attacks we're still clueless? We have a mass casualty disaster in Fresno, a TSA center gets blown up, a tunnel collapse, and a water supply full of bugs, and we don't have a clue where these attacks originated? There's no pattern? Has anyone claimed responsibility? Random acts all on the same day? I don't want to jump to conclusions, but this looks like a well-planned, coordinated disaster day for the United States to me. It's got to be Al-Qaeda. Anything from the CIA? Did NSA pick up any chatter over the airways? We need to explain this quickly and believably. The press won't give us very long before they'll expect a full story with all the details. When the Secretary and I met yesterday, I understood that we were early in the process, but by now I expected more answers. What is the problem?"

Known for his ability to navigate out of impossibly bad situations, the White House Chief of Staff looked at the President and then at Wright and offered, "Why don't we start with a DHS press conference to buy some more time?"

As if on cue, the Vice President quickly declared his agreement with the idea of a scheduled press conference, "Yes, let's see if we can start putting something concrete on this story as soon as possible. If DHS called a press conference, it would certainly give us some more time and maneuvering room to get the facts. Mr. President, your statement yesterday afternoon was needed but that was yesterday. People are expecting some explanations today, and we are apparently short on the facts. I can't believe this. What a disaster!"

Growing weary of the spin doctors sitting around the table trying to delay any announcements until all the facts were in, Admiral Wright's mind found an oft-used quote of one of his previous Commanding Officers: *you can put lipstick on a pig but it's still a pig.* And what occurred on this Veterans Day couldn't be covered up, politicized, or made better.

With the Director to his left still apparently shell-shocked by the President's diatribe, Wright took a chance as soon as he could get an opening in the fast flowing, politically correct brainstorming. "Mr. President, I'd like to get back to DHS so that we can start assembling all the pieces of these events and feed something factual to the Secretary by mid-afternoon so that he can prepare for a late afternoon conference." Wright glanced to his left and asked, "Mr. Secretary, do you agree? There was a sound muttered by the Secretary that Wright took for an approval. He continued, "We'll stand-up an interagency task force and get some answers to your questions ASAP."

"Good idea, Jim." The President realized that the staff was merely trying to outdo one another by cranking out ideas and that there was work to be done. He quickly got the team focused. "Look, we've sustained a real shock to this country, and it's going to cause a firestorm if we don't address it quickly. I do not want to be answering questions for the next three weeks on these events. Let's put the facts together and work on an action plan to find out who the hell is responsible and what kind of options if any we have to respond. Roy, please take charge of this. Art, keep me posted. Jim, Good Luck! Thank you, gentlemen."

A savvy politician that had come from multiple terms in the Senate, President Bowles knew what had to be done and made sure that his team was tracking towards a solution. He glanced at his afternoon schedule and asked his appointments secretary to postpone whatever she could. He reached for the untouched cup of coffee that had been poured as the meeting started, knowing that he had a long day and night ahead. The coffee was cloudy and stone cold, but he didn't care. What he needed most were caffeine and time.

Chapter 19

Double Eagle Headquarters
M Street Georgetown
Washington, DC
November 12, 2017

Spence and Jack walked down the carpeted hallway to a private dining room. Seated at a small round table set for two, Spence lifted the crystal goblet of red wine and swirled the contents on the way to his nose before looking at Jack.

Spence broke the silence, "I think you'll like this. It's a Cabernet from Romania." The conversation picked up the thread from the previous meeting.

Jack Lang looked at Spence and shook his head at what had sounded like a crazy scheme that didn't pass the common sense test. But Lang knew Spence better than that. He always was playing the game multiple moves ahead. His brain could assess options faster than a server performing complicated Monte Carlo simulations. But this scheme had Jack wondering…was Spence slipping gears or had he really thought this one through?

"ABACUS is the likely leading contender for this HS2 program, and I intend to make them non-competitive. Some china will likely be broken in the process, but we need to take them out of the running now."

"Hey, Doug and I play racquetball every Wednesday in the Pentagon City Sports Club, and I can tell you that he's in this game for the long haul. He figures that winning Fortify will put him on track to head up ABACUS' Sterling business unit in Colorado Springs. ABACUS is all in on this program."

Spence looked at Jack with cold eyes and said evenly, "Looks like you've got a blind spot when it comes to Doug Smith."

"Blind spot, hell no," replied Lang angrily, "I like beating him on the court and especially seeing his wife when he's out of town."

Spence smiled, his eyes showing their more characteristic warmth. He replied, "Yes, we've got time to position Double Eagle for winning Fortify. You will help us with that win."

Spence glanced at his 'son'. Jack's sinewy body supported broad shoulders and dark curly hair framed a rugged face. Women were drawn to him like moths to summer porch light. Perfectly straight white teeth flashed behind a confident and engaging smile. Jack filled every room with his presence. Spence looked into his deep blue eyes that captured the color and serenity of the Aegean Sea.

The two ate a light lunch, talking about plans for the next few weeks and the rumors about the Washington scene, who was in and who was out, assignments of senior civil servants and military flag officers and the overall attitude of the Congress. Spence prided himself on knowing these details before they were released to the organizational insiders and long before official announcements were made to the general public.

"Jack," he said as he embraced him in a familiar hug, "Leave the details to me. Have a safe trip and I'll see you when you get back from Los Angeles."

The younger man smiled broadly and walked towards the door, closing it softly behind him without looking back. The comments about Doug Smith made him wonder exactly what Spence had in mind when he suggested that a security lapse might be attributed to Doug and what china might be broken. He dismissed any misgivings as he thought about a site visit to one of the Double Eagle affiliates out in LA that dovetailed nicely with the layover that a certain Qantas flight attendant had offered to him weeks ago.

Chapter 20

DHS–Domestic Terrorism Annex
Washington, DC
November 12, 2017

Admiral Jim Wright felt drained as he walked into his office suite. He walked past his assistant's desk and said, "Michelle, we're going to need to bring Sandy in on this one. See if you can find him and have him call me ASAP."

"Yes, sir," Michelle replied with a knowing smile. She lived for the crises and did her very best work when the heat was turned up. When the normal connections to Sandy failed, she felt her pulse quicken as she unlocked the small black box at her desk and punched in a six-digit code that she'd only used once before.

Chapter 21

Appalachian Trail
New Hampshire
November 12, 2017

"What a memorable day" exclaimed Sandy Matthews to himself. He'd been on the trail for five days and felt an unusual energy growing inside him. Because of the early winter, most of the leaves had fallen, and the wind had swept the bright yellows and reds into piles that filled the hollows along the trail. In another month or so, the trees would stand naked, ready to take on another long New Hampshire winter. A fellow hiker told him earlier in the day that there was a chance of a cold front bringing some rain, maybe some snow and some temperatures below freezing that night. Sandy planned to press on for another hour or so before sunset. As soon as the small electronic puck in his front pocket began its incessant vibration, he knew that he would be leaving the trail soon. He silenced the device and pulled out the trail map to find the quickest way to return to the real world. What would it be this time?

Pushing the button on the small pedometer-sized puck had triggered an electronic signal to a communications satellite operating 42,000 kilometers above the earth's surface that relayed his acknowledgement straight to Michelle's desk with a discrete three digit readout that identified him.

"Admiral, Sandy has the message. Do you want me to wait for his call-in?"

"No, thank you, Michelle. He'll contact me directly. Have a good night and try to get some rest. I have the feeling that things are going to get hectic around here."

"OK. See you tomorrow!" Michelle walked to the private elevator, passed her badge over the sensor and hit "B". She would walk two blocks underground and exit the parking garage under her apartment building.

Chapter 22

Somewhere in New Hampshire
November 12, 2017

"Where the hell have you been?" demanded the Admiral through the telephone speaker.

"Good evening to you too," responded Matthews evenly. "Remember the Appalachian Trail is on my bucket list? Well, this morning I began day five of that adventure and was really enjoying the solitude when it was rudely interrupted by a top priority page from you. It's taken me the last two hours to leave the trail and find a place where I've got cell coverage. I'm standing here in the freezing rain wondering what my good friend needs this time. I know that you just didn't call to chat."

"When can you get here?"

"I should be in your office first thing tomorrow morning."

"Good...see you then." Admiral Jim Wright placed the handset on the cradle and said "Thank God" aloud. No one heard him.

Chapter 23

Brussels, Belgium
November 13, 2017

Paul Stevens, the name under which he was traveling this time, strolled through the town square just after 1:00 p.m. The sun transformed the narrow multi-colored facades into something magical. The square was crowded with office workers on their lunch breaks, tourists, and tradesmen going to afternoon calls. Belgian beer was being quaffed in every restaurant that ringed the large, open area. People were returning to their offices for the afternoon, and there was an air of earnestness in their strides. Paul exited the square and walked towards an American hotel several blocks to the east. He passed a number of sex shops with one of particular interest to him. He visited the shop several times a year according to no particular schedule. He preferred to work from the United States and rented a Brussels P.O. box from the shop's owner for clients to contact him with assignments.

Paul Stevens had no memorable physical attributes and a face that couldn't be remembered because it was so plain and ordinary. These features were particularly valuable in his line of work and had served him well for a dozen years. He'd been a middle of the pack naval officer years before and, though he enjoyed the time at sea, it was clear that he would never be a careerist and couldn't compete with the shining stars that were destined for greatness. He left the US Navy after four years, experimenting with a number of career choices before settling on corporate intelligence. That rather broad job description covered a wide range of skills that he had developed over time.

Resourcefulness seemed to be his strong suit. Coupled with no fear of anything or anybody, Paul exuded confidence and delivered on any promise that he made. He had a handful of simple rules: he selected his work, worked to his own timetable and methods. Everything came through his drop box in Brussels, and, when his work was completed, payment was sent via wire transfer to a numbered account in Zurich. People with intractable problems found Paul's approach refreshing, and it put more distance between them and the work he carried out. The terms were simple: 60% on acceptance and the balance upon successful completion. He decided both the when and the how. He'd only been crossed once in twelve years. The 40% balance hadn't been paid for a job completed two years earlier. Paul sent the client just one reminder via his six year old son a year later. The man was discovered by the same son months later hanging from a beam in the barn of the family's country estate. Fear over time is a strong motivator. Despite the long delay, the final payment had been wired several weeks before he collared himself with a piece of nylon line rated at 700 pounds and launched himself from the second floor haymow through the hatch above the ground floor where old cow stanchions lined either side of the walkway. An inexplicable yet at the same time, a neat and tidy end. Once set in motion, an assignment would be carried out as agreed. There was no opportunity to change course.

Paul entered the "Sweet Stop" and went over to a locked viewing booth marked "closed". He entered and ignored the viewing window filled with the gyrations of a sad-faced girl with gigantic breasts and opened the same coin box that was being fed with Euro coins at the other booths for every sixty seconds of the show. He retrieved four envelopes from the coin box, opened the booth door and walked back into the sunlight. Paul liked to have a backlog. It permitted him the luxury of planning his trips and pacing his work. He did not like to rush. He stopped at a nearby park and read all four proposals. Two he rejected outright, one he needed to study and the other he'd already started to plan.

Chapter 24

DHS–Domestic Terrorism Annex
Washington, DC
November 13, 2017

"Sandy, how the hell are you," exclaimed Admiral Wright as he jumped up from his desk and embraced the stocky, somewhat disheveled man wearing a rumpled tweed jacket and khaki pants that had never been subjected to an iron.

"Just great," smiling broadly and showing a remarkable set of large teeth marred only by a friendly gap between the two central incisors just behind his upper lip. The smile pushed his cheeks up so that his dark eyes were barely noticeable behind the slits that covered them. The two men hugged like old friends do, in public or private.

The Admiral motioned to the chair next to his desk.

"You know, I can't believe that we're still solving the intractable problems of our young democracy. Is there anyone else working these problems?"

"Don't know of any off the top of my head, but you'll be the first to know when I find them. Coffee?"

Answering with a nod, the Admiral barked into the intercom as Sandy Matthews rested the well-worn leather elbow patches of his jacket on the edge of the expansive mahogany desk. "I read everything I could about the Veterans Day events. It's hard to fathom. Anyway, you called me. What's up, Jim?"

The Admiral waited while two steaming mugs of black coffee were delivered. "Thanks, Michelle, please hold my calls."

"As you surmised, we have a mess on our hands. It's got lots of moving parts, and I just don't have the talent or experience on this team to sort through it all and understand what's going on. I need a big thinker, my friend."

He slid a thick folder across the desk towards Sandy who ignored it. His friend and colleague had a reputation of keeping a cool head in any crisis, but the stress clearly showed through to people that knew him well.

"So Jim, how is Carole?"

The question had an immediate calming effect. Admiral Wright responded, "Damn it. I'm getting so wound up in this mess that I can't even remember my manners. Carole's fine. She knew you'd be here today and asked that we try to get together for dinner this week. She misses you!"

"That would be great. I'm free every night for the short term, and we'll see if the two of us can double team you out of the office. Remember Jim, you only go around once, and we're not getting any younger. You need a day off to clear your head. You look terrible. How much sleep have you had in the last few days? I expected that things were bad when you called, but I've never seen you shaken up like this. And it's obviously too important to zig when you should zag."

The Admiral ignored Sandy's analysis. He pointed at the folder and said, "That's a chronology of the last few days that captures the pieces we know about, but I'd be lying if I told you we had a grip on things." He looked up at Sandy through a set of tired, bloodshot eyes and desperately concluded, "I'm scared to death about what I might be adding to that folder in the next seventy-two hours. Hell, I don't even know whether these events are connected or not."

Shifting gears, Sandy continued, "so you've got what looks like a stepped up terrorist campaign here at home with events that may or may not be connected, and all your friends at the White House, over on Capitol Hill and in the press are asking you when you'll reveal the complete story, right?"

The Admiral laughed and said, "You've got it."

"Anything from the intelligence side or three letter agencies?" Sandy continued, "And I'm assuming that the political appointee acting as your boss is still completely ineffective and just wants you to clean up the mess?" The Admiral nodded.

"Who have you got in front of this?"

"Martin."

"OK. How do you want me plugged in? Martin is a very capable guy, too bureaucratic and process-oriented in my mind, but we can get along." He took a big gulp of coffee and answered his question, "Look, Jim. Just put me in an office somewhere close and tell Martin to copy me on everything coming in and out. I'll attend the morning brief and whatever else he's got underway. Let me study this for the next couple of days and see if I come up with anything."

"Perfect. It's great to have you here and don't hesitate to call me direct anytime." The Admiral came around the desk, put his hands on Sandy's shoulders and stared into his eyes. "This one scares the bejesus out of me, Sandy."

"I'm on it. Say hello to your sweetheart for me! I will call her tomorrow and hatch a plan to get you out of here for some rest this week."

Chapter 25

Kennett Square, Pennsylvania
November 14, 2017

Fire crews had responded to a fire in an outbuilding on a mushroom farm the previous night, thinking that the farmer might have lost a few tools and maybe some soil additives. Mushrooms were simple fungi that didn't need much to thrive. Once the fire was out, the team spotted a man's arm under the smoldering rubble. There wasn't much in the shed to burn and no gasoline to fuel the fire so it had been quickly extinguished. The blistered arm surprised them. Why couldn't he have gotten out? The farm's foreman admitted that he had allowed one of his best workers and the rest of the Santos family to stay in the building but had assumed that he needed the place temporarily and that they'd moved out long ago.

The police demarcated the scene with bright yellow tape. It didn't take the fire investigators long to discover the three bodies under the tin roof that had collapsed with the walls. It looked like two adults and one young child had died in the fire. The Medical Examiner, Dr. James, arrived at the scene an hour later and within five minutes, told the lead police investigator to call the homicide division. The people couldn't escape from the small outbuilding because they were obviously dead before the fire started. The M.E. left the scene and wondered if he had a clean shirt for the press conference. This would be a big news event for the sleepy community of Kennett Square. Should he wear his black suit?

Chapter 26

Doha, Qatar
November 14, 2017

Nadir was livid. Responsible for coordinating Al-Qaeda operations worldwide, he had simmered for two days waiting for reports from the field about the Veterans Day events in the United States. Al-Qaeda affiliates had spread like wildfire over the past four years, and the rigid control had broken down. ISIL's grip had loosened with the Arab coalition that had restored a fragile order in Syria, but Assad remained in power, and there were still strong pockets of resistance within the city. But to have attacks of this magnitude carried out without his prior knowledge and final approval was simply not acceptable. To Nadir, the operation was out of control, and he vowed to bring discipline and centralized planning back into the organization. Attacks had a simple purpose of advancing the agenda and recruiting disciples that could act independently to make the caliphate a reality. Nadir could not stomach the rogues that were crossing thresholds that would bring more attention to their operations. A delicate balance had to be preserved to avoid the massive attention that the West could dedicate to Al-Qaeda. If the situation in the Middle East stabilized politically, he knew that resources would be re-directed to eradicate the leadership of Al-Qaeda. He had transmitted a dozen queries around the globe and wondered how the operatives would respond. Had they lost control of their regional cells?

Nadir stubbed out his cigarette in the overflowing ashtray and called for another cup of tea. Of the four attacks on Veterans Day, only the contamination of the water supply in Newport had been reviewed and approved for execution. What other players were out there and who was controlling them?

In the United States, the public outcry was deafening. Congressional leaders called for significant increases in funding the continuing war on terror and fueled the notion that all the problems facing the US emanated from beyond its borders. They wanted to fund the activities that kept the ramparts far from the US shores and focus on the countries from which the terror had been metastasized.

Chapter 27

Town Square
Brussels, Belgium
November 14, 2017

Brussels' Grote Markt or Grand Place located in the city's heart is one of the most beautiful medieval squares in all of Europe, where well-preserved 17th century buildings surround an expansive cobble-stoned common. The vibrant bright colors of flags, awning and doorways offset the centuries old stonework. Paul Stevens laughed as he approached the famous resident statue just off the square, a small bronze of a boy urinating into the basin of a fountain aptly named Manekin pis. Dating to the early 1600s, the town dressed the little boy in various suits throughout the year. This day, he was naked.

Paul walked leisurely along a narrow street one block off the square looking for a plate of local mussels steamed with garlic. He was famished. Taking a sidewalk table, he ignored the long list of local beers that were flavored with coriander and other spices and ordered an Amstel draft. He panned his gaze around the small restaurant carefully. All locals except for a young couple more interested in each other than anyone else. The mussels arrived in a metal container that looked like a lidded champagne bucket…exactly what the doctor ordered. His mind concentrated on his next assignment in the United States.

Chapter 28

Virginia Beach, Virginia
November 14, 2017

Dan had been put through the wringer. He'd spent several days giving repetitive statements to DHS, FBI, the USCG, the USN and the local law enforcement teams that were trying and failing to have any influence on how the multi-pronged investigation was proceeding. At least all this investigative churn kept his mind distracted from the constant anguish of losing his family. Known for his even, steady temper and the type of perspective that permitted an almost clinical detachment from any situation headed for a disastrous end, Dan needed to be in control and recognized that he could not get fixated on events beyond his ability to influence.

He lay in bed awake at night reliving the day his family was taken, knowing that no one should have survived. He felt a terrible guilt. When he did try to sleep, Jill was always there, her smile bright and confident. Dan started focusing on how to begin putting his life back in some kind of order. He felt like the sole survivor of a shipwreck all alone on some deserted island. He'd called Jill's parents and promised that he'd come see them as soon as he could. It would likely be weeks before crews would be able to caisson the ruptured tunnel and recover the bodies of Jill and the boys. It seemed to make sense to wait until then or at least what was left could be recovered and put to rest properly. He'd spent a great deal of time in the ocean and knew how its inhabitants could change a body into something that barely resembled its original form in a matter of a few weeks. It was certain that there would be no open casket funerals for the victims.

He tried to keep his personal survival story out of the papers but somehow some sketchy details leaked out forcing him to barricade himself in their modest Virginia Beach house where Jill's scent and her presence filled the empty rooms. The boys' twin beds were empty and painfully quiet. Other than Jill's parents, the only other call that he'd made was to the skipper just to check in with someone who cared that he was alive. Hank Owens told him to call anytime, night or day and promised him any support he needed. He even offered to arrange a meeting with a grief counselor if Dan thought it would help.

"Thanks, skipper. I don't need that today, but I'll let you know when all of this sinks in." Dan felt very alone and a little fearful. He wondered if getting drunk might take away the immobility that had him spending hours on the couch. So far, he'd successfully avoided the press that camped on the street in front of his house by hiking through the woods to a nearby development close to a twenty-four hour grocery store where one of his old shipmates had parked a pickup for him to use.

Another telephone call interrupted him. The Caller-ID showed a DC number so he answered in his customary way, "Lieutenant Steele…I mean Dan Steele." He heard a friendly chuckle in the background.

"Good morning, Dan, this is Sandy Matthews. We don't know each other. I'm assisting Admiral Jim Wright, the Domestic Terrorism Chief for DHS. I know you've answered a thousand questions asked in ten thousand ways since you surfaced, but I'd like to ask you some different questions about what happened last week."

"OK, fire away," Dan replied in a tired voice.

"It would be helpful if we could do this face to face. I can drive down tomorrow from DC, and we can meet anywhere you feel comfortable in Norfolk or Virginia Beach. If you'd like to meet someplace in between that's OK too. And if you feel the need to do any checking on me, you can ask Hank Owens. He and I worked on a project together a few years ago and he can vouch for me."

Dan was immediately taken off-guard by the calm voice and willingness to make the trip to Norfolk. Not a standard practice for anyone working inside the beltway. Leave for a day and your office might be occupied by one of your colleagues before you got back into town. Throwing in Hank's name certainly made his answer much easier.

"Well, the truth is that I've been cooped up here in the house trying to duck reporters for a couple of days now. Let's meet down at Waterside near Battleship Wisconsin. Do you know where it is?"

"Yep."

"When can you be there?" Dan asked.

"I'll get an early start in the morning. Should be there by 10:30 or 11:00 a.m. depending on traffic. Will you have enough warning time if I call you from Hampton?"

Dan replied, "Sure, that'll be fine. I'll see you tomorrow."

Chapter 29

Double Eagle Headquarters
M Street Georgetown
Washington, DC
November 15, 2017

Spence often sat at the library table he used for a desk staring intently at a distant object light years away. He had the ability to align his brain cells and, like a computer, focus all his computational power on the problem at hand. Unlike a computer, he could parallel process all the quantitative and non-quantitative material simultaneously, fusing the data into a feasibility model with a range of outcomes each with a calculated probability of success. Spence was thinking about the DHS contract known as Fortify and had mentally developed a Capture Plan and run it against multiple scenarios. He leaned back in the chair, pleased with his work.

Spence finished his reverie seconds before his secretary appeared with his afternoon coffee.

"Thank you…I just worked through a very difficult problem, and this is just what I need to finish the day."

"You're welcome, Spence." She turned and left him.

Spence sipped the coffee and began thinking about how winning the Fortify program would accelerate his grander goals for Double Eagle. He stared at the painting on the wall as he often did. George Kastrioti Skanderbeg, Albania's 15th Century hero, successfully fought a guerilla war against the Ottoman Empire. Best known as simply Skanderbeg, he was a warrior who fought and won against larger, better trained and equipped forces because he led his men into battle and took advantage of the rote tactics employed by his adversaries. Skanderbeg read the political landscape well and would change alliances when it suited his purpose. He fought for Albania's independence, and his name became synonymous with Albanian nationalism that would irregularly reach a fever pitch and then retreat in defeat time after time. Spence looked forward to the day when the Double Eagle would fly proudly, and Albania would finally get some respect on the world stage. He had been planning for that day for a long, long time.

Spence did not see any glory in facing off with an enemy and fighting a costly war. He was also a student of Sun Tzu, the warrior-philosopher, who taught a pragmatic approach to warfare by devising a better strategy, instead of relying on brute force. His vision for Albania rested on a critical element: to infiltrate every element of the United States' security apparatus so they would be paralyzed by both an external enemy that they could see but also by the enemy within, a group of high level operatives placed in leadership and command positions within the US military industrial complex that could hold the most powerful nation on the planet hostage. The enemy within would always be there and how could the United States or any nation respond? Who could you trust, who would save you? How much was it worth to live in security but pay a ransom to the enemy that lived with you, as your colleague, neighbor and friend?

Part II.

Chapter 30

Waterside
Norfolk, Virginia
November 15, 2017

Dan tried to go out for early morning run but found himself paralyzed with the grim reality of the situation: he'd never see Jill and the boys again, never hear their laughs, and never see the sparkle and delight in Jill's eyes. She was so much more than his better half. Unshaven and mesmerized by the drone of the local news, still dominated by the tunnel collapse, he listened to the newscasters discuss the thousand theories about its cause. Any politician with a tie to Virginia was either in Tidewater or making plans to visit. No shower or shave this morning. Dan gargled some mouthwash and looked at his image in the mirror. His eyes looked like lifeless red hollows, his features sharp covered by pasty ill-fitting skin. Dan pulled on a pair of jeans and a long-sleeved polo shirt he'd worn for days. He slipped into some worn boat shoes and dashed out through the woods. He would stick to the backroads for the trip into downtown Norfolk.

He'd had another restless night, feeling numb and disoriented like the time he was over-medicated for nasal surgery in college. The surgeon let him stay awake during the procedure, and he felt the pressure and heard the crushing of the bones inside his nose. Even with the local anesthesia, it seemed that he observed the entire operation from the doctor's side of the table. He felt groggy for days while the drugs slowly worked out of his system. He forced himself to focus on the meeting ahead.

A fresh cool breeze flapped the vendors' tents along the pier where the USS Wisconsin (BB-64) was berthed. Now a popular museum, the last of the IOWA Class battleships looked better than when it was in active service. Between the legions of ex-US Navy volunteers and some wealthy donors, the ship sparkled with fresh haze gray paint and bright work that glistened in the sunlight. It seemed like a lifetime ago that he and Tom Bryant tried to swim her length underwater.

"Dan?" a voice from behind him asked. Dan found himself facing a short man in a blue windbreaker that covered an open neck plaid shirt and wrinkled khakis. The face was friendly, and Dan immediately extended his hand as if the man he'd never met was an old friend.

"Good morning. Sandy?"

"Yes, it's me."

"How did you pick me out?" Dan asked.

"The Bureau was kind enough to send me your jacket, and there's a striking resemblance between you and the guy that was commissioned six years ago. Truth is, I can almost tell the warfare tribe a Navy guy is from by the way they walk. You walk like a Seal."

As the two walked along the pier past the line of visitors waiting to tour the ship, Sandy continued, "Thanks for coming down to meet me. How are you holding up?"

Dan replied hotly, "About as well as can be expected for a guy who just lost his wife and sons and can't figure out what he might do next." Dan regretted the words as they were leaving his mouth. He'd contacted Hank Owens after Sandy's call. Owens told him to trust Sandy as if he were your buddy on a night mission with a ten percent chance of success. Dan reacted with emotional anger. He was still off-balance.

"Dan, look," Sandy replied directly, "I've got a sense of how you feel but know I'm not standing in your shoes. I just want to turn over all the rocks and find out how this happened and why as quickly as I can, so it doesn't happen to anybody else, ever. If you need more time, I'll come back when you're ready."

Dan motioned to an empty park bench near the end of the pier and said, "OK, let's sit down. I'm still having a tough time dealing with this."

The two had been talking for two hours when Sandy asked, "You know, I had an apple and some black coffee this morning on the way down. I'm starved! You have time for a bite?"

"Sure. I can't remember what I had this morning if anything, but I'm sure getting tired of eating out of a box or can. There's a good sandwich shop up on Colley Avenue that Jill and I used to go to."

"The sandwich shop sounds good," replied Sandy, "I'll buy if you drive."

It was after 3:00 p.m. when Dan dropped Sandy back at Waterside.

Sandy said, "Thanks. This has been really helpful. Here's my card with all my connection details. Call me anytime and let me know if there's anything I can do for you, OK?"

The two shook hands like old friends. Dan had this odd feeling that he and Sandy would be talking again very soon.

Chapter 31

Alexandria, Virginia
November 16, 2017

Paul Stevens arrived at Dulles late in the afternoon after a mid-day departure from Brussels. He checked into a hotel in Alexandria that provided easy access to the Washington Metro system. It had a constantly changing population of transients, tourists, and people who faced the Washington grind every day and were oblivious to anything around them. The glass and steel structures of Crystal City were a stone's throw away and that was the location of his next engagement. He had two full weeks before the annual DHS expo, a three day affair where government officials, contractors, and vendors would make deals in a collegial party atmosphere lubricated by free booze and the prospect of easy money.

Paul smiled to himself as he strolled along the Alexandria waterfront looking for a place to eat. He had started his career in Crystal City after joining a small firm desperate for work and being squeezed out by the big defense contractors that always seemed to attract the best and brightest talent and greased the skids politically to make their competitive selection easy. His company had worked for months trying to get on one of the prime contractor teams for a US Navy procurement but were just not making any headway. They were just too small and lacked the past performance credentials that the government looked for to justify their awards. They needed to change the game, but how? Paul had met with the confident lead of the large defense contractor in the acknowledged pole position. Despite the fact that his company had a great product, he was politely dusted off and not even given the chance to demonstrate the capability. It was frustrating, and Paul realized that his company did not have the financial staying power to survive unless they got a piece of the action. Angry at the way the big company had dismissed him, he quickly decided to take an unconventional approach to level the playing field. Teams had been formed and were completing proposals, and his company looked like it would be left at the station when the competitive train moved down the tracks.

While everyone attended an evening reception with the Assistant Secretary of the Navy at the last conference before submission of proposals, Paul Stevens easily broke into the Business Capture Manager's suite and photographed selected pages of the draft Technical and Cost volumes that were to be submitted to the government two weeks later. His colleagues were shocked when they were unexpectedly invited to demo their product a few days later to the well-known prime expected to win. A formal Teaming Agreement binding the two companies together quickly followed the first meeting. People were stunned when the government's announcement months later named the winner as the company they'd joined just before the proposals were delivered. Paul Stevens displayed the same excitement as the rest of the team when the government contract award was announced. But he was not surprised.

He walked through the old Torpedo Factory on the waterfront that had been re-furbished and now housed a vibrant artists' colony. As he looked past a massive old torpedo, one of many that were cradled throughout the building, at a striking watercolor of Chesapeake Bay, he felt relaxed, and invisible. This should be an easy putt.

Chapter 32

DHS–Domestic Terrorism Annex
Washington, DC
November 17, 2017

"Excuse me, Admiral. Sandy Matthews is here to see you."

"OK, thanks, Michelle," the Admiral said without looking up, "Just give me two minutes and then bring him in."

Five minutes later, the door opened and Sandy walked over to the desk littered with open reports and several yellow legal pads with scribbled notes and reminders.

"Morning, Jim. Did you ever get home last night? You look like you were rode hard and put away wet."

The tired man in the not-so-crisp white uniform shirt laughed easily and asked, "Coffee?"

"No, thanks. I've had my coffee for the day. What's up?"

"The NTSB was called into the tunnel collapse, and they have scheduled a press conference later this afternoon. It's pretty clear at this stage that we are dealing with a well-planned act of terror that took a lot of planning and preparation. They have a temporary caisson in place, and this morning, they started winching the first cars out of both ends. It's real slow work because of the mud and silt that has encased all those cars in the tunnel. They've got temporary morgues set up on both sides to process the bodies. As you can imagine, it's pretty grim."

"Do we know how it was done?"

"Not 100%. The divers that surveyed the outside think that the equivalent of 1,000 pounds of high explosives was detonated on the tunnel shell on the eastern side. Someone suggested that it might be one of those bunker busters that was built to blast bin Laden out of the mountains, but that type of bomb needs a delivery vehicle and we haven't seen anything to suggest an air drop. To do the job from the surface seems like a long shot to me. How something like this can be done with all the Navy ships and commercial traffic coming in and out of port is a mystery, and I can't imagine what kind of equipment would be needed to do it. The White House is reviewing NTSB's prepared statement now, but if they open it up to questions, there is going to be a very nasty reaction inside the Beltway."

The admiral smiled weakly, pressed the intercom and asked Michelle to bring in some coffee then shaking his head, remembering that Sandy had already had his coffee. He needed sleep.

"My god, Sandy, what day is it?" Continuing without a pause, he asked, "By the way, how was your trip to Norfolk?"

"Glad you asked," Sandy replied edging to the front of his chair and leaning on the Admiral's desk. "The guy that made it out from the flooded tunnel is a Navy Seal that just left the service the day before. He lost his wife and twin boys. He's still trying to get on an even keel. Majored in Economics at Virginia Tech, was an All-American swimmer who captained the team, got selected for OCS where he was a Company commander and graduated at the top of his BUDS class. Led a number of special operations in some pretty tough spots all over the world. His operational jacket is classified. He's an operator, a warrior, not a paper pusher. Quick on his feet and has the right instincts. I want to get him on my team."

"Really? You know you can pick anybody you want, and there's lots of talent around. Are you asking from your heart or your head?"

Sandy took a folded paper with scalloped edges out of his jacket pocket and slid it forward in front of the Admiral. "He and I had lunch two days ago. Like I said the kid's still a wreck, but I asked him what he thought about the tunnel breach. He said he didn't know what happened. Then I tried a different tack, challenging him to plan a clandestine operation that involved the placement of a charge against the exterior shell. He drew that diagram on the back of the restaurant placemat in fifteen minutes and identified all the logistics of getting the equipment and communications gear on site with no-one ever knowing. He planned the mission real time, and his plan answers all your questions about how this was done in one of the busiest ports on the East Coast. I need your help to restore his clearance and bring him on the team as a civil servant."

"This is impressive work. You know it will take me weeks to get a preliminary concept out of Martin's team." The Admiral removed his glasses and asked, "OK, he's smart and has a solid record. A good guy, I get it. But is he ready for this, emotionally?"

"That's a fair question. He's having a tough time of it, but I think he needs to do this as part of the healing process. Besides, he's agreed to start tomorrow. I just wanted to give you a heads-up that the approval paperwork will be on your desk today."

Admiral Jim Wright leaned back in his chair, shaking his head and smiling broadly, "OK. Sorry for the second degree. Thanks for the heads-up…I'll make it happen."

Chapter 33

Double Eagle Headquarters
M Street Georgetown
Washington, DC
November 17, 2017

Yesterday's <u>Virginian-Pilot</u> lay on top of Spence's reading stack. He quickly found the article marked on the left side of page three. The picture showed the mayors of both Virginia Beach and Hampton shaking hands and flanked by Paul McGovern and Jack Lang. Spence was delighted. He'd asked Jack to set up some modest press coverage of Double Eagle's pledge of $5,000,000.00 to assist the families of the tunnel disaster that had deeply affected both communities.

The story described Double Eagle Industries as a European-based company specializing in worldwide supply chain management and security solutions. The two Mayors had presented keys to their respective cities and thanked the company for their generosity. Both were surprised by the pair's lack of interest in holding a prime time press conference. That was generally the quid pro quo for donations a fraction of this amount. However, Paul and Jack stipulated that the occasion be marked only by a small office ceremony but were finally persuaded and agreed to the release of a photograph and story to the press as a means of stimulating other donations. A local Virginia bank with branches on both sides of Hampton Roads would administer the funds, and their website and telephone number were provided for others wishing to contribute to the fund. Jack handled the assignment perfectly.

Chapter 34

Norfolk, Virginia
November 17, 2017

Jennie Perkins rose from her desk chair by pushing herself up on its arms and surveying the open room where she and ten other writers occupied tiny cubes separated by fabric-covered gray dividers for privacy. She dreamed for years that her journalism degree would have guaranteed a single office and a flurry of invitations to speak at writers' conferences and attend literary parties. Instead, she'd labored in the trenches for six long years at the <u>Virginian-Pilot</u>. Today's assignment was a filler, a follow-up story on the company that had created a tunnel victims' fund that was reported on two days before. After thirty minutes of unproductive internet searches, she gave up and called her classmate, Pam, the Virginia Beach Mayor's protocol and communications coordinator.

"Heh, Pam, have you got a minute?"

"For you, anytime."

"I'm doing a follow-up to the story we carried on that company that donated five million dollars for the tunnel families and can't seem to get a fix on it. I wondered if they'd left you any contact info."

"Funny you should ask, Jen. Those guys didn't even want the company's name released to the press and insisted that everything be low key. Our friend on the other side of the Bay was furious because he saw this as an event to get more visibility at the State level." Pam added, "Everything was done by phone and neither of the guys from the company had business cards. I was bummed out because one of the guys, Lang, was really hot."

Jennie responded, "Well, at least you get the chance to meet somebody like that. The guys in this office are old, fat and married. Anyway, thanks for the info. See you soon."

"That's strange," Perkins remarked to the computer monitor in front of her. "Let's see if we can tackle this another way." She began typing and then looked up to see her boss peering into her cube making the football "time-out" sign with his hands. Everyone in the office knew that the sign was his way of communicating "drop everything and pay attention."

He followed the gray fabric to the open side and started talking in a brisk staccato, "Jen, Meehan is out sick and Schultz is on his way to DC. I want you to cover the National Transportation Safety Board press conference that begins at the Naval Base auditorium in forty minutes. Here's your chance to get your by-line on tomorrow's front page."

Jennie stared at him, first ready to pounce but retracting her claws seconds later. She knew that her boss had three important traits: a good nose for a story, quick decisions about who should pick it up, and the one that he'd just applied so effectively, the knowledge of the hot buttons that would cause even a seasoned reporter to react like one of Pavlov's dogs.

"I'm on it." Jen knew that the press conference would go long, that the traffic back would be horrendous and that a completed product was needed before 9 p.m.—a small price to pay for the opportunity to have a front page by-line. Her notes on Double Eagle Industries would soon be lost in the slush pile.

Chapter 35

Alexandria, Virginia
November 17, 2017

By 10:00 a.m., Paul Stevens had watched the news and weather on the local Virginia channel, consumed the <u>Washington Post</u> and gotten fueled with two large cups of cappuccino. The hotel was comfortable, generally clean with a good coffee shop within a block and the Metro stop a short walk away. His dark trousers, muted plaid shirt and navy windbreaker blended nicely with the mix filling the streets on this bright, sunny afternoon. A good long walk would finish his local immersion. It was time to get to work. Paul Stevens needed a simple, uncomplicated plan.

Chapter 36

Naval Base
Norfolk, Virginia
November 17, 2017

Jen Perkins got through Security and entered the auditorium just as the Base Public Affairs Officer was finishing introductions of the team.

The National Transportation Safety Board spokesperson took the podium. "I will read a prepared joint Navy-NTSB statement and then answer questions." The lead investigator was conspicuously absent. She picked up a copy of the release from an adjacent folding chair and was thumbing through it while listening to the monotone from the stage.

"The failure of the tunnel's pressure shell was caused by the detonation of a high explosive charge that led to a catastrophic failure of the reinforced wall surrounding the dry side of the structure. We have examined a number of scenarios involving the possibility of accidental explosions and ruled them out. While we have not established the timeline or the exact materials that were used, we have concluded that the failure of the Chesapeake Bay Bridge and Tunnel on November 11th was most likely the result of a deliberate act by person or persons unknown. As such, we cannot rule out that this was caused by any number of terrorist organizations, including Al-Qaeda or one of its affiliates. We have collected a great deal of evidence and will be analyzing that over the next several weeks and months. NTSB along with other USG agencies, including DOD, is now overseeing the recovery effort of the people lost in this tragedy and removing the vehicles trapped in the tunnel so the structural assessment can begin. Are there any questions?"

Jen sat patiently through all the questions, most of which were answered with the predictable comments about an ongoing investigation or that further responses would be speculative at this time. There just wasn't much new on the story. She caught up with one of the recovery team after the press conference, and he told her that more than thirty cars and trucks had been winched out of both ends of the tunnel and that the occupants as well as dogs and cats were covered with crustaceans finding an easy meal. A number of sharks had also been encountered in the tunnel, trapped in the mud. Jen had a new angle and would work-out her story line on the way back to the office. She would be very pleased to see her by-line on the front page in the morning.

Chapter 37

Alexandria, Virginia
November 18, 2017

Sandy Matthews lived in the northern part of Alexandria in an old shingled colonial home on the Potomac River. Developers had been eyeing the site for years, visioning high end condos that would feature unobstructed water views and the convenience of a boat slip in their front yard. Sandy bought the house from a Georgetown Political Science professor that he'd gotten to know early in his Navy career. The two had become good friends when Sandy attended the National Defense University where he'd earned a Masters' Degree in Strategic Studies and National Security Affairs, a largely Political Science curriculum designed for military officers with a career that would be helped along by an advanced degree. They'd kept in touch and saw each other from time to time after Sandy left the Navy.

During one long evening at the house years ago, the two talked over a bottle of small batch Kentucky bourbon. For decades, the professor had applied himself vigorously to the study of bourbon and considered himself a self-taught connoisseur. He smacked his lips loudly and declared emphatically that this single barrel was the best the distillery had produced in the last fifty years.

"Sandy, I'm hanging it up at the end of this academic year and moving out near Gettysburg. You know that I've been working on my last book about the Civil War for twenty years and figure I've got maybe five years to finish it. I could stretch that to ten years if I could stop drinking bourbon and smoking these Cuban cigars, but bad habits are hard to break, and I'm too old to change."

"Come, on," Sandy teased, "You've got more energy than most of your grad students and are stronger than a draft horse. I'll bet you'll live to 100."

The old man laughed and shook his head. "No, my days are numbered, and I'd like to finish this project before heading to the happy hunting ground. Anyway, I wanted to see if you'd be interested in buying my little house?"

Sandy looked around the familiar living room at the bookcases and filing cabinets and replied, "It's certainly more appealing than my condo but I can't afford this place. It's way out of my league."

"I've got no one to will it to, and the idea of having this place go on the market and being razed to make room for some high rise is not what I want to do. Money's not the issue. I'd be willing to sell you the house in exchange for the price of a small place in Gettysburg. And I can tell you that the real estate out in Pennsylvania farm country is a bargain compared to Alexandria. What do you think?" He continued, "This house is full of history that will vanish if someone like you doesn't take it. Before you answer, let me show you the lower level."

"What lower level?" asked Sandy, "I've been here in the living room and in the kitchen and used the bathroom a few times. I assume that you've got a small bedroom or two on the second floor, but you're too close to the water for a basement."

The professor moved to one of the bookcases and unlatched a side panel. The bookcase opened smoothly to reveal a black hole.

"Put down your glass and let's go."

The professor switched on a light and Sandy watched his head move lower and disappear. He crossed the living room and followed a staircase down to join the professor on a thick-planked platform that overlooked a huge stone-walled bay that extended the ground-level foundation by twenty feet. The two continued down an adjoining set of stairs until they reached a catwalk made of heavy granite blocks that surrounded the floor of what appeared to be the bay of an old dry-dock. In the middle of the bay, a miniature submarine made of cast iron rested on a short keel block in a heavy wooden cradle that extended up the sides of the hull. Black like a seasoned frying pan, the shell of the submarine had been sealed with a protective coating that kept the exterior free from rust. It looked like something that belonged in a museum.

"Is this what I think it is?" asked Sandy.

"Yes," exclaimed the professor, "If you believe that it is a vintage submarine. But that is only the obvious part of the story. Actually, two miniature submarines were secretly commissioned by the Department of the Navy soon after Lincoln's inauguration and were put into service near the middle of the Civil War. What you are looking at is the vehicle designed to carry the President to safety if Washington were ever overrun by the Confederate Army. The bay would be flooded and the sub would clear the cradle and head out into the Potomac. I'm told that there used to be a covered boat house at the Navy Yard where the primary sub was berthed if the President had to be extracted. This was the back-up. Actually, the stonework started in the 1820s as a commercial dry dock. The project went belly-up after several floods scared off the investors. The man that built this house took advantage of all the foundation work and lived here until the War Department took over the house as a secret armory. With the looming prospect of a southern assault on the city itself, the bay was re-purposed as an escape route for the President. The Navy Yard boat house is long since gone, and no one seems to know what happened to the other submarine. As you can imagine, the controls are very primitive, and it's designed to be propelled by three people turning a chain driven direct gear train. One revolution of the hand crank equates to a single turn of the propeller."

"Why isn't this in the Smithsonian? I would have never guessed that civil war contingency planning developed to this extent. And no one knows about it. What's in the crate?" asked Sandy, pointing his hand in the direction of a large, modern-looking packing crate positioned on one side of the submarine.

The professor slapped the outside of the ten foot by twenty foot packing crate and replied, "Believe it or not, this place is still on the Presidential contingency plan—it's got to be near the bottom of the list, but this was delivered about five years ago in the dead of night. The Secret Service told me that it holds a modern submersible that was designed to evacuate the President and two others in the event of some attack on Washington if he couldn't get airborne. It's incredible that a plan like this is still on the books. And every year, they come down and service it. Our hard earned tax dollars at work!"

The professor walked to the Potomac side of the bay and pointed out the large, riveted iron door that kept the water out. Along either side were heavy machined metal rails that guided the door to flood the bay from the Potomac. In the background, Sandy could hear the low hum of some motor-driven pumps that were taking care of any seepage of water past the mating surfaces of the door and the rails. The sea wall itself showed no evidence of leaks.

As they climbed back up the stairs to the main floor, the professor pointed out the workshops, offices and sleeping quarters that ringed the bay, built to accommodate President Lincoln if he needed to stay for any length of time.

He said, "Every year I have to get briefed into this plan by the Secret Service and must promise not the reveal this location or its contents. Other than them, you are the first person who's seen this, and I guess you have no choice other than buying the place now, for National Security reasons."

"Well," said Sandy, "I'd be lying if I told you that I wasn't intrigued by the house before you showed me the catacombs. Now, I'm hooked. As long as we can work out something financially that I can afford and leaves you whole, I'll buy it. Do we have to get the Secret Service's permission?"

Chapter 38

DHS–Domestic Terrorism Headquarters
Washington DC
November 20, 2017

"Morning Dan, welcome to the organization!"

"Yeah, good morning, Sandy. I'm glad to be on the team and anxious to get started."

"Well, you got through orientation and have your access badge and an armload of disclosures to read and complete. That's the toughest part of the job here. I've managed to grab an office for you right down the corridor. I'll walk you down there and show you the kitchen and coffee service on the way."

"OK, great," he replied as the two left Sandy's office. "How'd your session go with Admiral Wright?"

"Very well," replied Sandy stopping in the hallway, "First, before I forget, I got a call from NTSB this morning, and they've concluded their investigation on the 14th street Metro bridge collapse last summer. All the cars have been recovered and bodies removed, and they've collected all the evidence they need. The contractor hired to repair the bridge is ready to start work, but there's a final government dive planned down there tomorrow morning if you're interested. We've got a couple of FBI divers, three from DHS, one from DDOT, and you've got a slot if you want it. I made no commitment, Dan. Don't know whether or not you are ready to dive again? "

"I'm absolutely ready," replied Dan without hesitation, "I've just got to get some gear."

"That's what I thought you'd say. The Explosive Ordnance Disposal team down at the Navy Yard will get you outfitted after lunch, and the dive boat will leave from East Potomac Park just south of the DC side of the bridge tomorrow at 08:30 a.m. There's a temporary pier there that the recovery crews used."

They walked further and Sandy pointed out the kitchen and copier rooms until he stopped at doorway marked with Dan's name in a brass frame.

"Here's your executive office, Dan. I had the IT people get a classified system installed for you, and one of your packages will guide you through the log-in process."

He slid a red-covered report marked SECRET across the desk. The classified report had been "sanitized" by the CIA before being released to DHS. It consisted of a single paragraph summary based on an interview of a known Al-Qaeda operative that had been picked up in a sweep in Yemen.

"Subject stated repeatedly that the summer's Yellow line incident in Washington, DC was not an Al-Qaeda operation."

Dan closed the folder and looked at Sandy.

"How much stock do you put into these reports?"

"It depends," Sandy replied, "They run the gamut, and I think of them as just another data point that's out there for potential correlation with something else or discounted altogether."

"I think we should talk to the FBI about it," Dan offered, "They are right down the road in Quantico. Seems to me that it might be worth a follow-up. What do you think?"

"Yeah, I agree. We need to follow every lead we can to see where it takes us." He glanced at his watch and exclaimed, "I'm headed to another meeting…good luck tomorrow! My extension is 3451 if you need anything."

As he returned to his office, Sandy thought about Dan's family still entombed in a Jeep at the bottom of the Chesapeake Bay Bridge and Tunnel.

Chapter 39

14th Street Bridge
Washington, DC
November 20, 2017

Seven divers stood in a semi-circle at the stern of the work boat deck listening to a US Navy Master Chief Diver outline the dive plan.

"The tidal effect will be minimal this morning, and we expect a slight southerly current during the dive this morning. No precipitation of any kind in the forecast. You'll be diving in teams, and each team will be assigned to survey one of the damaged concrete support piers. Visibility is about four to six feet at the bottom. Depth varies from twenty-five to thirty-five feet. This will be a forty-five minute dive, and no decompression will be required. The Metro cars have all been brought up and transported to a NTSB-controlled yard just south of here. The site has already been carefully surveyed, but if you find any personal effects in the rubble, please mark them with your GPS recorders for collection. There is a large barge with dual cranes anchored to the south. It's got a four point mooring and should not interfere with our dive."

The Master Chief looked down the line of divers and concluded, "We'd like to come back with the same number of divers as we left with so let's do this safely. We'll be over the site in ten minutes so get with your buddy, check out each other's gear and let's get ready to dive. Any questions?"

Dan was buddied up with two other divers, one from the District Department of Transportation and the other from the FBI. He had made it a practice not to dive with two other people because it took too much effort to keep track of each other and tended to distract people from the mission. However, Dan silently swallowed his protest and reminded himself that he'd gotten a last minute invitation to this dive, and he was certainly not the guy in charge. Second thoughts rushed through his mind that he pushed away but couldn't get rid of the nervous despair that he felt before going into the water. He shook hands with both the other divers and noticed that the DDOT diver had a small pneumatic spear gun strapped to his leg.

"Do you think there's anything edible down there to spear?" Dan asked.

The diver just grunted and ignored the question. The three stepped off the diving platform and stayed together until they reached the bottom. The FBI diver took the lead with Dan and the DDOT diver in trail. They reached the base of what used to be the trestle foundation, and the FBI diver signaled that they could circle the jumble of reinforced concrete that had once supported the Metro tracks and meet back at the same point in ten minutes. Despite the fact that the depth of water would be no greater than thirty-five feet, the plan to dive independently and then re-group raised a red flag. Again, he reminded himself that he was not the dive master and pushed his uneasiness aside.

He and the other diver responded with an "A-OK" sign and would try to stay as a pair. Dan swam to the edge of the scattered structure and then retraced his path trying to make sense of the jagged concrete shards of various sizes that lay strewn across the bottom. The DDOT diver matched Dan's speed and stayed about six feet to his right. The foundation had been violently ripped apart by a powerful explosive force and the sight of the twisted reinforcement rods reminded him of the cage at the bottom of Hampton Roads that he'd escaped from days before. It caused him to shudder. The rods had been bared and twisted by the explosion or bent at sharp angles connecting adjacent pieces of concrete that looked like dumbbells. Similarities between this explosion and the one in Virginia Beach would likely be found. After several minutes of trying to relate what he was seeing here on the bottom to the sketches of the foundations that had been made by NTSB based on divers' reports and side-scanning sonar, Dan wondered why he'd been so quick to come on this expedition.

Startled by a rough tap on his shoulder, he turned to his left and saw the muzzle of the spear gun pointed at his chest. There was no time to react. Dan felt the spear hit the left side of his chest and then saw the business end of a large serrated knife that looked like it belonged in a commercial meat-packing house pointed at his abdomen for the coup de grace. He grabbed the extended wrist guiding the knife and pushed it away. He and the DDOT diver were face to face. Dan went into full combat mode. He began to notice things that previously he would never have missed. This was not a typical diver: his regulator mouthpiece was strapped behind his head and his low profile mask was built for close encounters. With dark determined eyes visible behind the tempered glass, he was compact, agile and strong, clearly on a mission to kill his new diving partner. Dan cursed himself for not continuing his daily PT since escaping the tunnel. He felt slow and thick. What a way to begin diving again!

With their arms hugging each other and the knife still extended, Dan quickly realized that he would lose this fight unless he gained some sort of advantage. His breathing became quick and labored. His arms spasmed with tension, and both legs were beginning to cramp. Suddenly, the other diver reached over Dan's right arm and grabbed for his regulator and mask. He countered with a weak uppercut to the man's chin at the same time protecting his regulator and mask. The combatant deftly maneuvered behind him and wrested his arm from Dan's weakening grip. He managed to parry a knife thrust to his side and grabbed the outstretched arm with both of his hands, twisting the wrist and forcing his attacker to drop the knife. A small victory to be sure, but there was a price to be paid. The attacker had reacted quickly to losing his knife by snaking his arm securely around Dan's neck where his strength was clearly an advantage. Dan pulled on the diver's arm with both of his hands to break the hold. The grip against his neck tightened as he strained to pull in another breath from the regulator. The other diver's arm felt like a twisted steel cable being used as an oversized garrote. Desperate and with no leverage, his mind began to drift, and he knew he would lose consciousness in seconds.

His fin touched something solid on the bottom. It must be a large chunk of the foundation. His long legs kicked hard as he arched his back to break the death grip on his neck. The grip remained tight and steady. Dan was starting to black out. He put all his remaining strength into a series of kicks and tried to twist out of the grip. Suddenly, the garrote loosened, and Dan twisted to find himself face to face with his foe. But there was something different. A dark liquid was seeping out from the edges of the regulator still strapped into his mouth. Dan grabbed the collar of the man's buoyancy compensator and kicked towards the surface as best he could with both legs still cramping. The dive boat was anchored fifty feet away, but Dan's wild thrashing on the surface quickly got the crew's attention. A safety swimmer dived into the water and reached Dan seconds later. Too winded to talk and with the muscles of both legs in spasm, Dan wordlessly turned over the limp cargo and started to slowly pull himself towards the boat with his arms while extending his legs. Making slow progress, he started to replay the bizarre events that had unfolded moments before.

Dan could barely hoist himself onto the diving platform before dropping his tank and climbing up the short ladder to the after deck. He looked over at the Dive Master and the safety swimmer working in unison trying to revive the other diver. A narrow stream of fresh blood streamed down to the deck edge and overboard. That's when Dan noticed what appeared to be a thin piece of ridged steel poking through the diver's wetsuit just under his chin.

"What the hell happened down there?" the Dive Master demanded through his CPR rhythm.

"I don't know who this guy is, but shortly after we got down below he tried to kill me with his spear gun and then a knife. This guy had a mission, and he came damn close to achieving it."

The coxswain came out on deck and gagged when he saw the blood pumping from the diver's neck.

"Master Chief, I just got a radio call from DDOT. The diver supposed to be onboard for this morning's dive was found dead in the park's maintenance shed about thirty minutes ago." The coxswain gagged again before heading back to the wheelhouse.

The other divers returned to the boat in pairs, and the first FBI diver to step onto the bloody deck took charge of the scene. He cordoned off the deck area and secured the dive bag of the imposter. He used the ship-to-shore radio to ask that some investigators meet the boat when it landed. A light tarp covered the body with a channel of blood flowing across the deck and finding its way to an overboard deck drain.

With all the divers accounted for and gear secure, the Master Diver ordered the boat underway. They tied up to the temporary dock minutes later. Dan knew that he'd have to provide an account of what happened and wondered why he had been targeted. The steel spear point was still hanging from the left pocket of his buoyancy compensator. He opened the pocket and extracted it. It was very light, probably titanium and tipped with a point of razor sharp steel blades that reminded him of a hunting arrow, a killing tip. Dan also found the case knife that he'd been given by the skipper that he'd tucked into the outside breast pocket of the buoyancy compensator. The impact of the spear had deformed the titanium case into a shallow U, saving his life. Dan felt a real rush of anxiety wash over his body as the last ten days flashed by instantaneously through his brain. He just wanted it all to go away.

Sandy Matthews threaded his way through the growing number of unmarked cars arriving at the park, flashed his ID and maneuvered quickly to meet Dan as he stepped off the boat, still wearing his wet suit.

"Are you OK? What happened?"

Before he could respond, the lead FBI investigator held up his badge and whisked him away for questioning. It was clear that he had no intention of having his crime scene or any evidentiary statements contaminated by external sources. Dan shrugged a *what can I do* signal to Sandy. He followed the other divers and crew to a trailer that NTSB and the FBI had occupied during the recovery. After spending nearly two hours with several agents relating the story in as much detail as he could remember, he was dismissed.

It was noontime. Dan was famished and felt like he needed a shot of something to put the morning behind him. He found his rental car with a sheet of paper under the windshield wiper. The paper demanded "CALL" in block letters with an "S" underneath. He peeled off the wetsuit and pulled on a pair of sweatpants and a long sleeved jersey. The agents had kept his buoyancy compensator, what was left of the knife and the spear point.

Dan started the car and auto-dialed Sandy's secure line. He answered immediately.

"Are they finished yet?"

"Yes," replied Dan, "For now. I gave them all I could but I'm sure there will be a follow-up. Guess it's better than writing some of the after-action reports that I've had to put together. "

"What are your plans?"

"I'm accustomed to working more than two days a week, but this DC pace almost killed me this morning."

"Glad you haven't lost your sense of humor."

"After today, I know that I need to get back into some sort of training routine. Even in my best form, I couldn't be sure of surviving an attack like that. I just got lucky."

"Understood," replied Sandy, "It's clear that someone had you in the crosshairs this morning. Take the day to clear your head. I'm not sure why but it's certain that you are on someone's target list. They came too darn close. Look, if you want some extra security, just let me know. We'll be shut down for Thanksgiving and Friday. I'm going to visit my parents so I'll see you next week. Take care."

Chapter 40

Washington, DC
Thanksgiving Day
November 23, 2017

Jill's favorite Holiday was Thanksgiving. She'd spent three Thanksgiving Days alone with Dan deployed on operations to places that were never revealed. She would invite other wives and families from the team to join her, preparing enough food for a small army. Now she was gone, and this holiday would never be the same. Dan even missed his small contribution to Thanksgiving, insisting that Jill vacate the kitchen after dessert and leave the clean-up to him. He'd been asked to carve the turkey one year and made such a mess that Jill took over, and he never attempted that traditionally manly task again. There would be no more turkey dinners together. He resisted the self-pity by staying determined to find out who caused this tragedy. However, the future just didn't look that bright. What he'd give to have Jill and the boys back again.

Dan took advantage of the office shutdown to get in his doubles, hard, twice-a-day workouts that would force him to get back into shape. But he still had trouble sleeping and felt that he had fallen into dangerous pit of emotional quicksand that kept sucking his body down deeper. "When would that change, if ever?" he wondered. He changed his running route and paid more attention to everything around him.

Chapter 41

DHS–Domestic Terrorism Annex
Washington, DC
November 27, 2017

Dan started the day with a tough run around Capitol Hill shrugging off the brisk fall weather. He'd gone into work early Friday after Thanksgiving and began to catch-up on reading the intelligence reports that had filled his desk tray.

The FBI investigators called to follow up on last week's dive.

"Dan, do you recall if the diver had any accent or used any unusual words when you talked to him."

"He didn't say anything to me. The only communication that I recall were the standard hand signals that every diver uses. But he never spoke a word. Why?"

The agent responded, "Well, we found no ID, no car and can't match his prints. The Medical Examiner put him in his late twenties, very muscular and hard. He's got a few interesting scars that look like they were stab wounds, an old burn on his upper thigh, several broken bones in his hands and feet and a crude eagle tattoo on his upper arm. We've initiated a facial recognition search of the INTERPOL database and sent a photo of the tattoo over to forensics to see if they can cross it with anything. You were not dealing with a run-of-the-mill hit man. And you were right about the spear point. It's custom-made of titanium and sharp as a razor. No manufacturer's marks or numbers on the spear or the gun. Clean as a whistle."

"Heh, I'll sleep better tonight because he's not out on the street. I re-played the incident and the interview over the weekend and don't think I missed anything. Thanks for the update. One more thing, I'd like to get my knife back. I know it's ruined but my last Commanding Officer made it for me, and it stopped that spear."

Chapter 42

Alexandria, Virginia
December 04, 2017

The DHS Expo officially opened on December 5th but everybody arrived the night before for the welcome reception that featured the best food of the week and free drinks. This was the time to size up the competitive landscape and to arrange sidebar meetings where the work really got done. Doug Smith was easy to spot. Tall, lean and handsome by anyone's standards, he looked like he'd just walked off a Hollywood set as a leading man. Standing in a circle of admiring ABACUS colleagues, his animated face and radiant smile exuded confidence. Paul Stevens was also in the room, and his plan for the evening was far different than Doug's.

Minutes after drinking a glass of red wine, Doug felt strangely nauseous, excused himself and promised to return shortly. He never did.

Paul Stevens intercepted Doug as he left the elevator on the ninth floor and escorted him to a room just down the hall where a small cast was ready to perform. The short one act play that Paul orchestrated involved two women, a young blonde boy whose features made him look much younger than his twenty-five years and a photographer whose credits included some of the best known adult magazines that catered to the sexual fringe. Like all morality plays, this one had a straightforward purpose: to isolate a man from the comfort of a loyal employer, an admiring customer and shatter the stability of his family. The cast was paid handsomely including two weeks that they would spend hundreds of miles from Washington. From opening until curtain call, the play had lasted less than fifteen minutes.

Paul Stevens pocketed the thin memory card containing the photos and led a dazed Doug Smith back to his room, propping him up in a side chair. He laughed as he hung the "Do Not Disturb" sign on the door. He exchanged his waiter's uniform for a dark wool coat, driving cap and glasses and walked through the lobby head down, exiting the hotel into the night.

He departed Washington by train later that evening and printed selected photos the following day at a convenient drug store with a photo kiosk. The photographer had been very skillful with Doug as the star. His acting was nothing short of brilliant. The entire cast seemed to be enjoying themselves whether singly or as a group. He addressed four large manila envelopes: the first to Sue, Doug Smith's wife. The second to Dale King, ABACUS' CEO and Doug's mentor at ABACUS; the third to the Chairman of ABACUS Board of Directors and a fourth containing the memory card to a post office box in Dallas where it would be secured in a safety deposit box if Paul needed to make another copy or, if he were killed or compromised, released to the local police department. He would not go down alone. He mailed the packages from a curbside mailbox at the airport and flew under a different name, vanishing to his next assignment.

Chapter 43

Double Eagle Headquarters
M Street Georgetown
Washington, DC
December 07, 2017

Spence arrived at the office as usual. He completed his daily routine and typed out a quick coded text to Jack Lang who he hadn't seen for several days. There was a report in the business section of the <u>Washington Post</u> that caught Spence's eye, announcing that Doug Smith from ABACUS had left the company unexpectedly for personal reasons and that he was pursuing other unspecified interests. None of the photos had been published, and there was no scandal surrounding his abrupt departure. But, he was gone, and Spence knew that ABACUS would be hard-pressed to replace him with anyone that could lead their team to recover the momentum and build the customer trust to win Fortify.

Chapter 44

Newport, Rhode Island
December 10, 2017

Surreal. Dan wanted to think he was still sleeping and in the middle of a nightmare but knew that the sharp, cold wind off the bay cut as real as the minister's words. He tried hard to be strong, at first choking back the tears but now letting them flow down his checks.

"Ashes to ashes, dust to dust. We commit Jill and her two sons, Alex and Andrew, to a beautiful, blessed place where life is eternal, and there is no pain and suffering. We express our sorrow and hope to Jill's parents, Tom and Susan, and to Dan, her loving husband and the father of these two fine boys whose lives have been cut short for reasons that only God knows. Let us pray."

His mother's sister planned to come but had been laid low with the flu. She and Jill were two different people who'd quickly became good friends. They shared a love for reading. She enjoyed the two book clubs she led in Roanoke while Jill tended to be a solitary reader. He always wondered how Jill could be reading five to seven books simultaneously, but she did and there were books spine-up on many horizontal surfaces throughout the house. When she had five minutes to spare, she would retrieve one of the books and pick-up the story as if she'd never put the book down.

Dan held Jill's parents' hands as the somber ceremony ended. They were staunch New Englanders, very private people who rarely showed emotion and understood the cycle of life and death when it happened in a natural way. But Jill and the boys did not die that way. They were left at the bottom of a watery grave for weeks while the fish and bottom creatures found their bodies a new source of easy food. He had left them there and saved himself. As they left the grave site, Jill's father pulled at Dan's topcoat. His bare hands were strong and sinewy, reddened by the cold. The blue veins stood out from the skin that had thinned with age.

"Dan," he said in a cold and uncharacteristic harsh tone, "I want you to find those responsible for Jill and the boys' deaths. Find them and teach them the eye for an eye covenant. Do you understand me?" The tone of the command from the kind and gentle man that he'd known since he'd first met Jill shocked him.

He gripped both the man's forearms and looked him in the eye, "I promise that I will do everything in my power to make that happen." He looked at Jill's mother and gathered Tom and Susan into a long hug, held them closely and pledged, "I promise both of you."

He stayed with the family for the rest of Sunday and most of Monday. They talked over the many childhood pictures of Jill and the several photo albums that had captured the boys' growing up. He was surprised at how completely Jill had documented those happy years. Many of these photos he saw for the first time. Laughing and crying seemed to be the only emotional expressions left for the three of them. Numbed by the events that brought that fateful day back as if it were yesterday, he finally said his goodbyes late Monday afternoon and started the trip back to Washington. A new fire began to burn deep inside his chest. *An eye for an eye.*

Chapter 45

Quantico, Virginia
December 12, 2017

Dan fought his way through the morning city traffic and turned south towards the Marine Corps base at Quantico. Sandy had scheduled a meeting with the FBI investigator assigned to assemble the evidence from the Veterans Day incidents and to determine if there was anything to connect them.

Meg Andrews opened the door to the crime lab and stepped into the hallway. He had expected the typical FBI agent that you see on TV: dark-haired, tough and business-like. Meg didn't fit the mold at all. She stood about five feet tall with a well-proportioned but diminutive frame topped with shiny copper hair cut just above her shoulders. Her eyes were light green and had a striking transparency. Her flawless light skin had a constellation of freckles under her eyes and across her long straight nose. The bright red lipstick seemed out of place on a mouth with pert lips. She exuded an air of efficiency and matter-of-factness, someone very dedicated who followed the book. Meg checked Dan's identification card and had him sign into the nearly empty log book placed on a podium outside the evidence lab door. The "lab" was actually a cafeteria that had been slated for demolition. Divided into sectors, the evidence had been color-coded with shipping tags and segregated into four discrete areas representing each of the Veterans Day incidents.

After a quick orientation around the floor's perimeter, Dan asked, "It looks like you're working a 100,000 piece jigsaw puzzle here and don't know how many pieces you have or even whether they all belong to the same puzzle?"

"That's a good analogy," Meg said brightly, "And I don't want to sugarcoat the situation, but we've made some progress here in the common area that you might be interested in." The two walked over to another part of the floor that had been cordoned off with bright pink surveyor's tape and contained tagged material from each of the areas.

Both Meg and Dan put on latex gloves and paper booties before lifting the pink tape.

"I'll tell you upfront that the links are still a bit tenuous at this stage, but I've got some preliminary ideas. No conclusions yet," said Meg, flashing a smile that revealed an even set of white teeth.

Meg seemed to be cautious and methodical, traits that were aligned with this type of work. Dan wondered whether she might get so far down in the weeds with the myriad details that she would not see the big picture.

"Good morning," boomed a strong, energetic voice behind them. Both turned, and Meg introduced the man approaching the tape as her boss, David. He obviously kept track of what outside visitors were visiting his facility and made sure that he met all of them. Tall with wire-rimmed glasses and a professionally styled shock of brown hair, he looked more like a college engineering professor than an FBI agent. He ran the FBI Training Academy in Quantico and had been quick to offer the cafeteria for the forensic work after the Veterans Day attacks.

"Welcome to Quantico, Dan. Glad to hear that you are part of the DHS team. Meg has been doing some great forensic work for us here. She's a very focused and dedicated scientist. If there's anyone that can find the correlations between these incidents if they are out there, it's Meg. Is there anything new?" he asked Meg from behind the pink tape.

"Not this morning. I was just telling Dan that any physical evidence links between these events are still speculative, and we are letting the evidence and science lead us to findings, not the other way around."

"Good. Let me know if you come up with anything new. The Director is keenly interested in this project. Dan, it was a pleasure to meet you and again, welcome. I'm sure that'll we'll get to the bottom of this. Please give Sandy Matthews my regards."

"Yes, I'll do that," Dan replied, wondering how he and Sandy might have been connected in the past and thinking that his glib welcome seemed too practiced. David nodded, did an about face and headed out the cafeteria doors.

The two turned back to the evidence, and Meg surprised Dan by immediately complaining about her boss's constant interest in her work, saying, "He might as well take over the effort for all the time he spends down here. I guess there's a great deal of pressure from above to come up with some answers. I know it sounds petty to complain and I really enjoy my job and all, but there's just something about him that rubs me the wrong way."

Dan replied, "Look, I'm new to all of this and don't consider myself an insider by any means, but I do know Secretary Lewis and my boss's boss, Admiral Wright, are under the gun to find any linkage that exists or rule it out altogether. Based on what I've seen here so far, that's a tall order."

"Well," replied Meg, a frown pinching her face, "What I've been able to put together scares me a little. And it's more a case of what we expected that didn't show up. Let me explain. Ever since 9/11, we've been working on a database that has tried to fingerprint every terrorist incident by looking at the sources for materials, assembly methods and packaging. This is extremely sensitive data, and I really can't tell you anything more except that our research is very sophisticated, and we are generally able to profile the attack. It's all been after the fact but we are getting closer to triangulating the key overseas sources."

"Makes sense. Is there anything new or different in these Veterans Day events?"

"That's just the problem with this material. We are looking for correlations against our database and frankly haven't found any. There have been a few things that would point to Al-Qaeda but they seem too contrived. A shard of metal with some Arabic characters stamped on it…that sort of thing. My conclusion is that these attacks were put together by a new team or organization that has left no fingerprints."

"A new Al-Qaeda affiliate?"

"Maybe. But what I'm really thinking is that there is an independent cell that's working right here in the US."

"What points to that?"

"That's the problem. It's more my gut than the science, but I can tell you that we've picked up much more US-related content in the material that we've collected from these sites."

"Could they be trying to throw us off the scent?"

"That's possible. They are obviously a very clever bunch and are testing us each and every day. It scares me." She shivered involuntarily. Meg's confident exterior belied the personal vulnerability she felt.

"If you're right, that is different and frightening. I've always been hopeful that Al-Qaeda would not be successful in recruiting people from here in the States." He felt a sudden wave of emotion as he said the words and turned his head away from Meg and the evidence scattered all over the floor. Recovering, he cleared his throat and asked, "By the way, did you get anything from the Norfolk tunnel failure last summer?" Dan didn't know whether Meg even knew about his personal connection to that tragedy.

"Not much. A lot of the evidence was either destroyed by the explosion or silted over by the tides. The reconstruction effort began shortly after they'd removed the cars and people in them, and everything in the tunnel ended up being pumped back into the bay so we may have lost some evidence there. We did get a fix on a high-tech boring machine that may have been used to excavate the silt and sediment that covered the tunnel to place the explosive. We traced it to a small company in Switzerland that manufactures mining equipment, and our investigative team is following up with them. The company only manufactures a few units each year so our team is tracking down all the units sold in the last few years."

The two spent several hours examining the evidence floor, failing to find anything that Meg overlooked. She got additional pieces in several times a week but the stream had slowed to a mere trickle and some of the stuff sent in had no connection at all.

After removing their gloves and booties, they walked out to the lobby. She promised to keep him in the loop if her investigation produced anything new.

"Thanks, Meg. I appreciate your taking the time to show me where you are on connecting the dots. I'm sure we'll be talking soon." He saw the start of a faint smile on Meg's face before he left. He wasn't sure what it meant but he certainly liked her professional approach to the investigation. Plus, she seemed like someone who could be trusted.

He left the base with a growing worry. Home grown and directed terrorism was a whole new ball of wax that no one was ready to deal with. Already after 2:00 p.m. the beltway traffic would be starting in an hour so Dan headed east from Springfield and went into downtown Alexandria for some crab cakes and coleslaw before heading home. He decided that a good run would give him a chance to think about what he'd learned in Quantico and see if he could make any other connections to Meg's work.

Chapter 46

DHS–Domestic Terrorism Annex
Washington, DC
December 12, 2017

Dan found a well-used manila inter-office mail envelope in his basket when he got to the office the next morning. It had been routed to DHS from an unrecognizable office code at the Naval Sea Systems Command at the Washington Navy Yard. He unwound the red string figure-eighted around the two plastic buttons on the back. Inside the outer envelope was a plain business envelope with his name and DHS typed on the front. He examined the envelope and held it up to the light just to make sure that it didn't contain an unexpected gift of anthrax. Satisfied, he carefully opened the envelope with a craft knife that he had inherited with the desk and unfolded a single typed page:

If you are interested in some information about the Veterans Day events, come to Dubai. Next Sunday at 7:00 p.m. in front of the aquarium.

Not dated or signed, the letter invited him to a busy public place. Dan and Sandy got on Admiral Wright's calendar later that morning.

"Good morning Admiral," Dan began. "Here's the letter that was routed in a guard mail envelope from NAVSEA. I don't want to read too much into the contents, but it was addressed and routed by someone with knowledge of what I'm doing here. It could be a set-up, but the aquarium is inside the Dubai Mall which is a very open place. In my previous job, I operated out of the United Arab Emirates a number of times so I know the lay of the land. Sir, we are getting very little traction on this investigation, so I think it's worth a shot to see if there's anything there."

The Admiral turned to Sandy for his input.

"Jim, I agree. Sure, it looks like a long shot to me, but we just don't have any better leads today. The only thing I worry about is his safety."

"Look, this is obviously a 'come alone' invitation, and if I show up with a team, the meeting probably won't happen," said Dan, "I'd rather take the risk and see if we can learn something."

The Admiral found Dan to be level-headed and resolute. He also knew that he had assessed the situation and quickly determined the actions required. Admiral Wright looked hard into Dan's brown eyes. They were clear and confident, not the eyes of a reckless man not caring about his own safety.

"The only thing that I insist on is that we fly you over there on one of our aircraft, just to make sure that someone isn't setting you up along the way. I'll get Michelle to make all the arrangements for a departure from Andrews Air Force Base Saturday morning."

The Admiral got up and came around the desk, shook Dan's hand and clapped him on the shoulder. "I'm glad you're on the team. Good luck and watch your back."

Chapter 47

Dubai, United Arab Emirates
December 16, 2017

Thanks to some very strong tailwinds, the unmarked Gulfstream touched down in Dubai after twelve hours in the air. During the first part of the flight, Dan relaxed in the reclined seat and sorted through the events of the last month. Frequent images of Jill danced through his mind as he entered a self-induced trance that he often used to visualize missions and mentally prepare for the "what-ifs". He woke up halfway through the flight and managed a few push-ups and some stretches in the generous aisle between the seats. The sole passenger, he kept hydrated and helped himself to a sandwich from the fully stocked pantry. After landing, the plane taxied to a private terminal where he was met by the security officer from the United States Embassy and hustled through the Diplomats line at customs and immigration. The two exited the terminal where a large black SUV stood waiting at the curb.

Dan opened the door behind the driver and immediately noticed that its weight signaled bullet-proof glass and exterior armoring. Both the security officer and Dan got in the back seat as the driver moved into the heavy traffic. Previously a modest seaside city with walking paths and water taxis to ferry people across Dubai Creek, a narrow inlet that separates Deira and Bur Dubai, the city had grown at an exponential rate. Zoning guidelines were initially non-existent and with the rapid expansion came painful limitations of the highway system, sewage and water as well as the penchant to build more elaborate structures.

The security officer offered some color commentary on Dubai while the car inched through the traffic. Dan listened politely before telling him that he'd spent considerable time in the United Arab Emirates, mostly in Dubai while in the Navy. The Embassy had arranged a five star beachfront hotel. Just before they arrived, the security officer offered Dan a local cell phone and a high tech wire with a range of three miles.

"While I appreciate the offer, I expect that I'll have better luck in getting information without them. I've got your number at the Embassy, so I'll keep you posted and will definitely connect before the return flight. And don't worry; I'll fill you in on all I learn." Dan had dealt with these security experts many times in his short career and knew that they expected official visitors to rely on them for the latest intelligence. Too often, they also acted as the self-appointed Political Correctness squad, thinking that they needed to protect the good name of the United States and keep the Embassy staff on the straight and narrow.

Not used to that kind of rebuff, the security officer sniffed, "Have it your way tough guy. But just be aware that you're still a stranger in a strange land, and no one will have your back."

He ignored the comment, laughed and said, "Hey, what's new? Thanks for your help getting me here."

After checking-in to the hotel, he enjoyed a light room service mezze with fresh pita bread, hummus, stuffed grape leaves and assorted olives washed down with a few ice cold beers from the minibar. He idly flipped through the TV channels before crawling into bed, hoping that he'd see the morning light without any unexpected visitors.

After a surprisingly good night's rest, he woke before dawn, pulled on his shorts and running shoes and took a long run on the white sandy beach before its daily manicure. He knew that a long run would help offset the jet lag and help prepare him mentally for that evening's meeting. Though he'd been there just two years ago, the city's incredible pace of change surprised him as he jogged along the beach street that would soon be attracting locals and tourists alike. Though the mild winter weather in Dubai would limit the number of beach-goers, people that grew up on the ocean seemed drawn to it year round, and many families would brave the seventy degree temperatures to have a picnic on the sand. He stopped multiple times along the route trying to catch anyone following him but never saw anything or anyone suspicious. *Yes, they are a clever outfit.*

After a breakfast of fresh squeezed juice, toast and strong black coffee at the terrace restaurant, he read The National and returned to his room to see the red message light blinking on the desk phone. A man's voice simply said: "Seven o'clock, alone, aquarium." The message removed any doubt that his arrival was expected and that the network of watchers could cover all the city's hotels. With his location known and the ample opportunities to cause him harm, Dan felt at ease and confident that the meeting would provide some information but not his assassination.

He found a tourist's history book on the United Arab Emirates in the lobby and read about its startling transformation since the seven tribal emirates had joined together in 1971. The history book had obviously been approved by the internal government censors and omitted some of the details about the royal family and tribal power struggles that had attended the consolidation. The CIA Fact book that Dan had read on the flight gave a more accurate account. The United Arab Emirates had remained a close ally of the United States for years, sending troops to Afghanistan and later leading combat missions over ISIS positions in Syria, Iraq and Yemen.

Well-educated and progressive, the ruling family acted as benevolent dictators and had set a course for the country that would move it away from reliance on oil and gas revenue in the future. The country set the bar very high with expansive internal development plans, free education and health care and support of women's rights. Here, women were able to drive and were not subjected to any hard line mullahs insisting that they replace their western garb with the traditional black flowing abaya.

With so few signs of its past, Dubai had become a western city at heart and offered a glimpse into how progressive the Middle East could really be. However, even Dubai had not been spared from the reach of the Muslim extremists. Recent plots had been thwarted by the wide-spread intelligence and special police units. The few that had been carried out had been contained, with the results usually blamed on a third country national that would be deported post-haste. In reality, there were few such deportations. Sometimes, there was little left to deport after the perpetrators were interrogated by the local authorities.

Following a late lunch and a brief combat nap, Dan swam a mile in the Olympic-sized pool. After a brisk shower, he dressed in a blue polo shirt, khaki pants and brown loafers. The winter air felt tropical as he asked the doorman to hail a cab. Twenty minutes later, Dan entered the sprawling Dubai Mall that combined 5th Avenue and Rodeo Drive into an air-conditioned sanctuary of shopping and restaurants. He had an hour before the meeting and used the time to get acclimated. Navigating the mall was straightforward as English, Arabic and International signs and symbols were used to guide shoppers and sightseers alike. He wandered at a determined pace, ducking into shops and making excursions between the mall's multiple floors to see if he were being followed. Unconsciously, he looked for little gifts to surprise the boys and more useful things for Jill. He snaked his way through the crowd that had gathered at the elaborate water park at the base of the world's tallest building to see the lighted water show set to popular music and featuring fountains shooting 200' into the air.

He followed the signs to one of the world's largest indoor aquariums. The tank was filled with large regional specimens, including sharks up to eight feet in length. A single sheet of Plexiglas–the largest in the world—separated viewers from the millions of gallons of seawater and the thousands of creatures that lived in it. It reminded him of the aquarium located near Cannery row in Monterrey, California where a seventy foot slice of the Bay had been transported to a multi-level aquarium complete with living kelp and an accurate tidal movement.

Dan glanced at his watch at the same time he heard a woman's voice from behind him.

"It's really a magnificent sight, don't you agree Mr. Steele?" Dan guessed that German was the speaker's first language.

"Yes, it is quite a sight, particularly in a mall." Dan turned around and took a gamble, saying, "With all the restaurants here, I bet that there must be some good schnitzel close by?"

"You are right, Mr. Steele," she said smiling, "Please follow me."

While on guard and with his mind's 'fight or flight' mechanism turned up to its highest sensitivity, Dan stayed several feet behind the woman leading him through the mall. Tall, blond and perfectly proportioned, most men would follow her anywhere. After a brisk fifteen minute walk, the woman stopped and pushed open an invisible unmarked panel that blended perfectly with the wood grain on either side of it. Surmising that sensors had been placed in the corridor's ceiling to monitor their progress towards the hidden entry, Dan followed and heard the door close with a soft metallic click. She led him to another door and delivered instructions in a no-nonsense manner.

"Please get completely undressed and put on a set of green scrubs that you will find in the locker. You will be going through a very sensitive metal detector so do not try to bring anything along. Clear?"

After passing through the metal detector, he was shown into a small, darkened room with two chairs. The shadowy figure of a man dressed in the traditional white thobe that covered him from his neck to just above his leather sandals sat in one of the chairs and motioned for Dan to take the other. The lighting in the room had been set to keep the man's face in the shadows.

"I am pleased that all the advanced information we received on you is accurate. We knew what to expect, and it's helpful not to complicate this meeting with any sort of electronic devices. Your colleagues from the Embassy were intercepted so they will not be joining our conversation."

He nodded without comment, wondering if he would have the time or energy to visit the security officer before leaving Dubai. Calm and confident, he showed no surprise, while waiting for the man to speak again.

"What I want to convey to you is that our Al-Qaeda organization takes responsibility for adding some bacteria to the water supply in your city of Newport, RI. We killed one of the workers at the facility in the process. I think that you call it collateral damage in the States. An insignificant loss when thousands of our people have been killed while your government targeted our leaders with their little remotely-controlled planes carrying missiles. Innocent women and children are not our leaders, do you understand?"

Dan fought to keep his anger from showing physically or in his voice, replying in a measured way, "Neither were the 3000 Americans...men, women, and children... that your organization slaughtered in 2001. I do not know how many more innocents were killed in Fresno, Philadelphia, or in the Chesapeake tunnel."

The man sat back and took stock of his guest, pausing the conversation for what seemed to be minutes.

"I understand your reaction. Allow me to get to the main point: no Al-Qaeda organization was involved in the massacre in Fresno with the helicopters or caused the tunnel flooding in the Chesapeake Bay. We don't like the city of Philadelphia and did not have one of our young men go to paradise by blowing up your TSA recruiting station. I'm telling you this because our organization needs to continue expanding and recruiting soldiers that believe in our movement. If the United States thinks that we are responsible for these events in America, they will declare war on our wide-spread affiliates and never find those responsible. There will be too many deaths. Many innocents from both sides will be killed in the process. Do you understand Al-Qaeda is a political organization more like a state than a centrally controlled terrorist organization? We've moved beyond the goals of Hamas or Hezbollah or even ISIS. We are beginning a kind of new cold war with the world, similar to the standoff that the United States began again with the Russians in 2015. Do you follow me?"

"Yes, I do," said Dan in an even monotone, "So if I am to believe your story that neither Al-Qaeda nor any of its radical off-shoots is responsible for these attacks, who is?"

The man leaned forward in his chair. Dan could faintly see the end of his long beard framed on each side by the traditional head-covering for men.

"I do not know. We have many agents in our network asking questions and listening. We will find out, but it may take some time. And as you know, we are a patient people. I know that you and I will never see eye to eye on this struggle. As a former US military soldier, you can never understand our motives. But we believe in them just like you believe in yours. We are on opposite sides of an issue for which there is no bridge. We are both men fighting for different causes. I know some things about you and admire your courage. For that reason, I give you this information."

The man stood and turned and walked to an unseen door leaving him alone. The woman with the German accent opened the other door and asked softly: "Are you ready to return to your world?"

The two walked back to the aquarium without a word. She left Dan standing in front of the clear acrylic panel, seemingly mesmerized by the wide range of sea life and wondering what to make of the brief meeting. Who was the man? He left the mall and walked the bustling streets back to the hotel. Dan called the Embassy security officer from the hotel and related that the meeting had been cancelled at the last minute when the other side discovered that a team from the Embassy had accompanied him.

"What do you mean?" the security officer asked feebly.

"I think we both know what I mean," Dan replied angrily. "Call the pilots and tell them I'll be there in thirty minutes."

"I have a car lined up to take you from the hotel to the terminal," the security officer sputtered.

"No need," said Dan angrily hanging up the phone. He packed his overnight bag and left the hotel in a cab. The Gulfstream took off thirty minutes later, and he immediately fell into a deep sleep that lasted for the first seven hours of the flight back to Washington.

Chapter 48

DHS–Domestic Terrorism Annex
Washington, DC
December 18, 2017

Without Jill and the boys, Dan had little to look forward to during the Holidays. He'd gotten a number of calls and email invitations for parties from some of his old shipmates and a few colleagues at DHS but found his only solace in working, turning over every stone that came across his desk and constantly pinging people for additional details, more thorough analysis, and faster responses. His internal priority was to find those responsible for his family's death. The national security aspects presented a more complex problem that became a lesser-included investigative case.

For months, Dan had been sifting through all the evidence he could find on the Veterans Day attacks trying to discern a pattern or new clue. None of the leads had led anywhere. He worked like a madman, fueled by endless cups of black coffee and sustained by two hard work-outs every day, laughing at the irony of being in the best physical condition in his life while holding a desk job in DC. His life had taken on a different direction and a single-minded purpose: to follow every lead, work through all the bureaucratic roadblocks, and break down the institutional barriers that separated him from the truth in order to find his family's killers and to hold them accountable. He read all the reports he could find, visited all of the sites and soon became the un-official point man for the investigative effort. He gutted an adjacent office and set up a war room, thinking that it might help piece the puzzle together. Sandy continued to help him navigate through the Washington maze and mended fences when he pushed too hard. But mostly, Sandy let him follow his instincts. He had no interest in putting a bit in Dan's mouth.

"It's Meg from Quantico. Can you talk?"

The two talked at least three times a week. She proved to be a meticulous investigator, and he trusted her thorough, scientific approach. Uncomfortable with preliminary findings or working theories, Meg preferred to reach the end of her effort before offering anything as a fact. Dan agreed with her approach as long as she shared all the raw data points with him.

"Sure, Meg, what do you have?" Dan asked expectantly.

"If you're hoping that I found the Holy Grail or finally had a scientific breakthrough on the case, I'm going to disappoint you. If, on the other hand, you believe that small steps even in the wrong direction are better than no steps at all, then you'll feel better."

"I'm all ears."

"Well, as I mentioned before, we traced that boring machine to a small Swiss company. We nailed down five of the six units they produced in the last two years, and one of their engineers verified a Quality Assurance etching inside the drill head we recovered from the Chesapeake, so we've now found the sixth unit. It completed quality inspections and was shipped in June of 2015."

"And?" anticipated Dan.

"You have a very bad habit of trying to jump to the bottom line before hearing the background. Don't worry; it will only take another three minutes." Meg continued, "This drilling machine was purchased by a company in Oman and shipped by sea via Genoa. The ship was registered in Moldova for an operator in Singapore. I hope that you appreciate how complicated these Flags of Convenience shipments are to follow."

"No, but I'd like to learn more next time I visit." Dan hoped that his sarcastic tone didn't come through as clearly as he spoke it.

"So the ship first docked in the Black Sea port of Constanta, Romania to pick up a load of lumber. There, it was entangled in a tug boat accident where the local dock master drowned. The Romanian courts would not permit the ship to leave port. That started months of haggling between the owners, the crew and the Romanian officials. Bottom line is that the ship was stranded for over four months before being sold to a new owner in Albania. Before leaving port, the drilling machine was removed from the cargo hold and the shipping documents were modified to list the drilling machine as a metal lathe. It subsequently cleared customs in Constanta and was shipped by a local freight forwarder to a mining operation here in the States in West Virginia. The shipment arrived there in February of this year." She paused, "Are you still with me?"

"Good work, Meg." Dan's mind was working at full speed to link the synapses that led to the underwater bombing of the Chesapeake Bay Bridge and Tunnel.

"I've got more!"

"OK, I'm ready."

"We also got a lead on the helicopters that were used in Fresno. Turns out that there are a number of manufacturers of this type of helicopter and its many variants. Those particular units were assembled in an aircraft chop shop outside of Tucson, Arizona where the cannons and ammunition trays were mounted at the same time. The refit was completed in September, and the buyer brought his own test pilots to fly the aircraft prior to final payment. The people we interviewed claim that the test pilots didn't say a word but were obviously ex-military. The buyer specified a very simple dashboard and gauge sets and paid cash. His pilots flew them away into the sunset."

"Good!" exclaimed Dan, "You are making great progress. Keep going!"

"I saved the best for last. The chop shop guys posed for a photo with the pilots. No name tags or patches but get this: one of the guys had a small tattoo on his wrist that we enlarged and got a computer-aided rendering. Guess what it was?" Meg's voice questioned.

"I don't' know," said Dan, "Was it a heart with a dagger through it with the words Death before Dishonor?"

"No" said Meg, exasperated, "It was a double eagle that looked just like the one your diving buddy had. Like I said, it's not a breakthrough, but we're finding new pieces to the puzzle."

"As I recall, we didn't get any much data on that tattoo. I know that the FBI sent a query off to INTERPOL. Where do we go next with that?"

"Dan, you're not going to believe this, but I just looked up Albania on my computer, and the country's flag features a two headed eagle just like the tattoos. I need to get someone on this. By the way, do you know where Albania is?"

"No," Dan lied. Meg needed to get to work, and he needed time to think. The jigsaw puzzle suddenly seemed less complicated.

Chapter 49

DHS–Domestic Terrorism Cell
Washington, DC
December 21, 2107

Dan and Sandy met the Admiral in his office for a brief update. Dan reviewed the progress since the last meeting and told them both about yesterday's conversation with the FBI.

"I think we've got a strong link between some group working from or being coordinated from Albania. The presence of these tattoos on at least two people involved in these attacks is not coincidental. I've got the CIA looking into any organized nationalistic groups in the country that could plan and finance such an operation. Albania is a very poor country which has been the red-headed stepchild of Europe for centuries, and they've never been known for anything other than an occasional short-lived spurt of nationalism. Admiral, I know this still sounds very tentative and sketchy, but that's where we stand today."

"Thanks, Dan. I sense that we are on to something."

As the meeting ended, Sandy Matthews invited the Admiral and Carole and Dan to his house in Alexandria for a drink the following evening.

"I'm in," said the Admiral.

Dan affirmed, "Me too."

Chapter 50

The US Congress
Washington, DC
December 21, 2017

    It had been a very different year for the Congress. Their year-end recess had been delayed to complete work on the Fiscal Year 2018 budget. It was late, and it still had some shreds of pork left. However, it represented the first real bi-partisan effort in years to include specific language and a significant increase in funding for the war on terrorism. The final appropriations bills quickly passed by a wide margin in both chambers by members anxious to get out of town before the Holidays.

Chapter 51

Sandy Matthews' home
Alexandria, Virginia
December 22, 2017

"Well, this has been one hell of a week." Sandy raised his glass towards the Admiral and Dan. The three were unwinding in his house in Alexandria. The winter sun had already set, and the crackling fire in the stone hearth made the room very comfortable. Winter on the Potomac seemed to always find its way into the old house, and keeping the chill at bay was a chore that Sandy willingly accepted. His former professor loved living in Gettysburg and had given up cigars to guarantee that he'd finish his seminal work on the Civil War.

"Thanks. And Dan again, welcome to the team," the Admiral exclaimed extending his glass in his direction. "You've had a rough transition, and I really appreciate your help. Like I said in the office, I'm feeling very positive about the direction you're steering this effort."

The daily grind at the Annex had become very frustrating: a series of repetitive dead-ends on the investigative side, bureaucratic food fights, and incessant pressure from all quarters for definitive answers. Admiral Wright continued to get dragged through the knothole, and the people between him and President Bowles were happy to see him take the spears. It reflected the classic Washington Fifth Law of Thermodynamics: "If the heat's on you, then it's not on me." Sandy thought that a few hours' break from the action would probably give the trio some additional energy and perhaps a different perspective. They'd been slogging together for what seemed like months without a break, and Admiral Wright hadn't had the time to get to know Dan at all.

"I was hoping that your better half would be able to join us tonight, Jim," said Sandy as he added another oak log to the fire, "but then again, if Carole were here, Dan wouldn't be able to tell us about the nice German girl he met in Dubai."

All three added a series of rapid fire comments to the visual image that Sandy raised. It reminded Dan of some of the Seal team's pre-mission sessions that ended with tension-easing laughter all around. In the end, the three men hooted like frat brothers until they cried. Dan realized that he hadn't let go in almost six weeks since leaving his family at the bottom of the bay. The Admiral regained his composure first.

"Truth is that Carole figured that this was more an after work boys night out so she's off to a movie with some friends. I hope to beat her home tonight. That will be a first!"

Sandy had offered a rare, small batch bourbon recommended by his old professor, and the level of honey brown liquid in the bottle fell rapidly. From his chair, he glanced out the street-front window surprised to see two large yellow bulldozers being offloaded from low flatbed trucks onto the adjacent street. They looked like large earth-moving dozers with engines capable of pushing tons of stones and gravel with their twenty foot blades that stood taller than most basketball players. Dan and the Admiral joined him at the window.

"Is this Alexandria's approach to urban re-development?" asked the Admiral. "Those things are going to tear up the street with their weight."

The unloading process had also drawn the interest of residents astonished at the size of these behemoths invading their quiet neighborhood. Once unloaded, the machines shut down until two large panel vans marked Commonwealth of Virginia SWAT Team arrived on the scene simultaneously, discharging armed black-clad fire teams in full combat gear on either side of Sandy's house.

Any questions ended abruptly when the bulldozers were fired up and maneuvered abreast of each other as if starting a drag race. On signal, both started moving directly towards Sandy's house. The SWAT teams took well-rehearsed flanking positions that effectively surrounded the house. Sandy moved towards the door when the first well-placed shots thudded into the siding followed quickly by three tear gas canisters shattering the living room windows. Sandy reached for the phone…it was dead. Small red laser points began to dance over the living room walls.

All three men hit the living room floor where Admiral Wright calmly observed that they were hemmed in, and the Potomac seemed like the only alternative. That avenue closed moments later with the sound of two helicopters, hovering just over the water a hundred yards away, with their spotlights bathing the house with a broad swath of intense light that illuminated the living room like a summer sunrise.

The Admiral spoke first: "Gentlemen, I am feeling a little like General Custer at Little Big Horn. Any ideas?"

Sandy quipped, "Remember that old song, 'Nowhere to run, Nowhere to hide'?"

Dan slowly raised his head for a better view and several rounds went whizzing by. The vise was closing quickly on three sides on the ground with the helicopters guarding any escape route by water. The side-by-side bulldozers were steadily moving forward clearly positioned to scrape the house into the water with one deliberate, deadly push.

The Admiral and Dan watched Sandy belly crawl across the room. He rose high enough to reach the side of the bookcase, activating the switch and opening the door to the lower level. His hand was picked up by the sharpshooters on one side of the house and shots splintered the woodwork. Sandy motioned for the two to follow, and they crawled over to the threshold and followed Sandy into the brightly lit bay below.

"Hide in the basement?" thought Dan. "You've got to be kidding me! I'd rather take my chances in the water than to wait until the sharpshooters would have a chance to shoot all of them like fish in a barrel." The low, throbbing sound of the big diesel-powered dozers was louder.

Sandy explained the bay in a few clipped words on the way down the staircase. "Dan, figure out quickly which one of these vehicles you want to use, and I'll open the watertight door at the other end of the bay."

He quickly surveyed the old iron clad and pulled the cover off the crated submersible that looked like something he had seen before. There was no time for an in-depth familiarization. This was on-the-job training with a very specific purpose: to save their lives.

There was no hesitation. Dan took charge and called out, "We'll take this one. You and the Admiral get in as quickly as you can. How do you open the door?"

Sandy pointed to two yellow levers on the forward bulkhead on the river side as he climbed the ladder and disappeared into the small dank green craft. Moving forward, Dan hoped that the water came in the bottom rather than the top because he still had to cross the bay, climb up the submersible and close the hatch so they wouldn't drown like rats in a flooded pipe.

Dan pulled on each of the levers, and they didn't budge. Despite the now deafening sound of the bulldozers, he could hear heavy boots above in the living room and knew that it would be seconds before the SWAT team found the door or the bulldozers opened up the bay as the house was pushed off its stone foundations. Chunks of flooring, concrete and stones started to fall into the open bay from the street side. Laser aim points swept the granite blocks of the catwalk.

Dan knocked a safety pin out with the palm of his hand and pulled both handles down hard. The lights dimmed as electric motors started to move the door downwards and an arc of muddy water poured over its top. The door was moving much faster than he expected. Dan ran along the granite catwalk that surrounded the floor of the bay and jumped for the hook of an overhead crane, catching it with a single hand. The hook had been preserved with a thin coat of grease, and he nearly lost his grip as he swung through the air and made a very hard and painful landing atop the crated submersible. He glanced up and saw the edge of one of the bulldozer's blades appear between the frame of the house and its foundations. The pushing had begun. Dan dived through the top hatch of the submersible head first, quickly spun around and closed the watertight scuttle. He then crawled over Sandy and the Admiral to reach the control console. A barrage of bullets was ricocheting off the pressure hull as Dan completed a ten second orientation. He hit the "power" button on the console and nothing happened. Already waterborne, the crated submersible was being pushed hard against the rear granite wall by the water rapidly filling the bay. He needed to get moving to avoid having the propeller jammed against the wall or be trapped under the foundations' overhang.

He found a red override toggle switch and flipped it on. He pressed the power button again and the control console lit up. He threw the throttle ahead, hoping for some movement. The craft shuddered as Dan coaxed it forward, talking aloud, "Come on, come on, let's move."

Dan turned to his passengers and exclaimed loudly, "Hold-on, this could be a rough ride."

Throttles full ahead. Turbid water partially covered the viewing ports as Dan urged the craft forward to escape yet another watery grave. The buoyant sub snapped the crate's top timbers and the sides fell back from cradle supporting the submarine's hull. Two seconds later, the three were violently jolted as the craft rammed into one of the side walls. He checked the position of the rudder and spotted a digital compass on the console. Now completely waterborne, he swung the rudder around to head east and gingerly eased the throttles ahead again. Another hard metallic scrape on the port side and suddenly silence enveloped the craft. It had cleared the sill and was out into the Potomac at full throttle plowing a furrow through the soft silt bottom. He adjusted the dive planes, raising the bow slightly and clearing the bottom.

Admiral Wright craned his neck and looked at the back of Dan's head: "That underway wasn't pretty, but I'll give you a 4.0 on getting the job done. Sandy, are you OK?"

"Yeah, just fine. I suspect that my little house will need some minor renovation after this evening. And I'm getting nervous that hanging around you two means that I don't need to look for any enemies on my own. Nice job, Dan. What about the helos? Where are we headed?"

He had gotten a feel for the submersible's controls and gauges. He'd backed off on the throttles and set the course due east at just about two knots. An electronic chart system showed their location in the middle of the Potomac about 200 yards from Sandy's house.

"Unless either of you have another suggestion, I'm going to head northeast for the Anacostia River and Washington Navy Yard where we should find some friendlies and maybe a place to berth Sandy's folly." Sandy responded with a groan and mumbled something about saving everyone's hide.

Dan continued, "I hope the helos have been recalled. But I don't think they can do much to us as long as we stay submerged. Of course, I really didn't take the time to see what they might be carrying. "

"Sounds like a plan," the Admiral chuckled. "What kind of comms gear do you have up there?"

"Looks like a UHF radio with a handheld mike and a black box with a keyboard and message monitor…probably a SATCOMM terminal of some sort. I didn't stop to see if there were any external antennae on the hull or whether there's a trailing wire on the surface. I'll see if I can raise someone on Harbor common. I doubt that any of our guests will try to take on this submersible along the way but just hope that we don't run into any other traffic enroute. We are traveling blind."

"Sandy, before I forget, maybe you can tell us why you had two submersibles in your basement?" asked the Admiral.

Sandy told the strange story about his former professor at NDU and the night that he learned about the floodable bay under the house. Because this site would likely be eliminated from the Presidential escape plans, Sandy told them about the contingency plans and the yearly visits from the Secret Service concluding that he'd never actually use either vessel. There seemed to be no reason to protect the information any further. He also admitted that he'd never been curious enough to know what the inside of the vessels looked like and had certainly never taken the time to learn how to operate them.

Twenty minutes later, two US Navy Rigid Hulled Inflatable Boats arrived and escorted the surfaced submersible to the Navy yard. Two F-16s from Andrews Air Force Base had also been scrambled to ensure that the transit remained uneventful.

Chapter 52

Double Eagle Headquarters
M Street Georgetown
Washington, DC
December 22, 2017

Except for the throng of last minute shoppers and usual crowd of people walking to the boutique restaurants that dotted Georgetown's streets, it was a quiet evening. Spence sat in the darkness of his office enjoying the solitude while he waited patiently for a report on the evening's events a few miles south in Alexandria. The operation had been meticulously planned, and he had reviewed every detail carefully. He trusted the leaders and had great confidence that the manner of execution and the clues left behind would lead authorities to Al-Qaeda. Cutting off the head of the snake had always been an effective tactic, and Spence had no doubt that this event would really stir the pot with the public and with the Congress. The outcome would include cries for more funding in a futile effort to stop these violent terrorists' attacks. In reality, additional money would prove counter-productive, as it would permit Spence to further infiltrate the nation's security network. Fear would widen the funding streams to combat the external threats, and the focus of the special anti-terrorism teams from multiple organizations would be right where Spence wanted it: on Al-Qaeda and its affiliates.

A small screen lit up on a pager in the middle of Spence's desk. The signal had been routed through multiple nodes around the world but reached his device seconds after transmission. Spence looked at the screen which showed just the number "2". Spence pounded the table in anger causing the little device to jump up from the desk's surface and land face down. "2" signaled mission failure.

Chapter 53

Washington Navy Yard
Washington, DC
December 22, 2017

A chilly wind coming off the Anacostia River greeted the three passengers, as Dan skillfully landed the submersible alongside a finger pier at the Washington Navy Yard. It had been born in the new nation's infancy, first opening in 1799. It became famous for the construction and design of warships and later specialized in ordnance technology that included the battleships' sixteen inch guns. Still a very busy place, the yard hosted the Naval Sea Systems Command as its primary tenant, continuing its historic role as the ship engineering and technology center for the US Navy.

Dan recalled visiting the yard with Commander Hank Owens to look at some outfitting for a dry Seal Delivery Vehicle prototype that had been built as a Research and Development project supervised by the Office of Naval Research. The two were called up to Tingey House, the original quarters of the first Commandant, to have supper with the Naval District Commander, an old classmate of Owens. The two had a lot of catching up to do and drained a bottle of scotch in the process. As the designated driver, Dan just had a beer before dinner. The evening ended when the Admiral showed the two to a guest room where Owens immediately fell asleep in his summer white uniform. It was a short night. After a carafe of hot coffee with the Admiral and neither accepting his invitation to put the hair on the dog, Dan and the Skipper piled into the sedan and headed back to Norfolk. The Skipper fell asleep before they'd cleared the beltway. Dan never knew what real snoring was until that trip south.

Those awaiting the arrival included a number of Navy divers that quickly embarked on the submersible. The trio was met by the Navy District Washington Commander, a Rear Admiral, and whisked away to a conference room in the Headquarters Building where a larger group had already assembled. The DHS Intelligence Chief began the impromptu briefing.

"Admiral, the attack in Alexandria appears to have been well-planned and well-executed. You and your team were the targets, and the tactics indicate that the objective of the operation was to kill all of you. We are still trying to get our arms around all the elements of the attack. Here's what we know now. Several Alexandria police cars were used to re-route traffic from the waterfront area and the vicinity of Mr. Matthews' home. We are not sure how those cars were obtained by the perpetrators. The 911 emergency communications infrastructure was compromised and routed to a third party node we are still looking for. The call center staff thought it was an unusually quiet night. No one was notified. The telephone company logs show multiple calls from the waterfront area and nearby side streets so it appears that the neighborhood watch program is working well."

The Intelligence chief recognized that his attempt at humor had backfired, and he pressed on, "The bulldozers were abandoned. One of them is completely submerged in the flooded basement of your home, Mr. Matthews. The choice of bulldozers is odd, and we assess that the planners believed that your house was built on a slab foundation. The tactical vehicles used in the operation disappeared. We found large temporary, peel-off decals used to make these vehicles look official in a dumpster near the Huntington Metro Station. It's not known how the vans were marked underneath those decals, but we've requested the videotapes from the station. The entire operation took less than fifteen minutes. The Alexandria police force had been successfully diverted to a major fire that erupted at the Federal complex off Eisenhower Avenue in the southern part of the city. As you might have guessed, that report turned out to be erroneous. This was planned with the precision of a military operation that had been rehearsed multiple times beforehand."

The intelligence chief nervously took a drink from his water bottle and continued, "We did not capture any of those involved and what we have left at the scene is a small battlefield. There's no surveillance coverage in the area. Maybe some of the eye-witnesses can provide some more detail, but frankly I'm not hopeful. The helicopters flew from the Maryland side and followed the Wilson Bridge before hugging the shoreline until they took positions to the east of the objective area. No flight plans had been filed, and the spotty radar tracks did not conform to any threat profile that would have triggered an aircraft scramble in the National Capitol Region. Emergency vehicles, EMTs and private ambulance services were dispatched all over the city as a further diversion. A folder containing a timeline and a schematic of the area with Arabic notations, a set of Russian night vision goggles, and a commando knife of unknown origin have been recovered. Once daylight breaks, I'm sure other artifacts will be found. In my judgment, the scale of the attack and the planning that went into it point directly to an Al-Qaeda operation. That's all I have for the moment. We'll have a more comprehensive update for you tomorrow Admiral. Any questions?"

"Thank you," Wright looked left and right to see if there were other questions. Dressed in charcoal grey slacks with a long-sleeved dark green plaid shirt, Wright exuded the command presence of a combat aviator addressing his squadron in the ready room before a combat mission. Getting up from his chair and turning to face the hastily assembled group, he made a sobering net assessment: "I'm sure that we were targeted, and this attack was obviously designed to kill us. It makes me wonder who else might be on the target list. I think we should bring in some of our military special ops guys to analyze this operation and give us any insights they can on what we are up against. I expect that the Secretary and I will brief the President tomorrow afternoon, and we need to get ready for the press. They will be all over this. Again, thanks for the update, and I hope that we'll have something more definitive tomorrow. This pattern of attack, carried out by professionals with little or no conclusive evidence left behind, is getting very old. People are getting impatient and fearful and expect answers. We are targets right here inside our country. Our ramparts are no longer an ocean away." The Admiral paused and smiled, looking directly at Sandy and said, "Thanks for a memorable evening," laughing as he left the room.

Chapter 54

DHS–Domestic Terrorism Annex
Washington, DC
December 23, 2017

Alone in the office, Dan fought the despair alone. He thought that he could be headed for a clinical depression or worse. He anticipated that the first Christmas without his family would be tough but had underestimated its paralyzing effect. He'd seen this happen to some of his fellow Seals particularly after a high risk overseas operation where no contact with the home front was permitted. Losing anyone was a gut-wrenching experience, but he'd never had to deal with the emptiness that he felt these days. Sometimes he caught himself staring blankly at the walls, thinking about Jill and their boys and wondering whether what happened in the tunnel was just a nightmare that he would suddenly wake up from. He stopped himself a number of times from walking down the hallway of his apartment to tuck in the boys.

Everyone around him seemed to be in the Holiday spirit. There were a string of parties that he'd been invited to, some with friends that really meant something and others where his name showed up on the guest list because it was organizationally correct or people felt sorry for him. As people rushed out of the office every afternoon, complaining about the traffic and time it would take to get home, he stayed in the office with nothing to look forward to other than his next workout. The office would be lightly staffed over the Holidays, and he desperately needed a change. He wrote a quick email to the Admiral and Sandy and headed out the door, not sure where he'd end up but now committed to getting there.

Chapter 55

Washington Post
Washington, DC
December 24, 2017

Sunday's edition of the Washington Post carried the Alexandria incident on the front page describing it as a major DEA raid aimed at shutting down a cocaine transshipment point that was using miniature submarines to bring the white powder into the United States from Colombia, right under the DEA's nose. The raid occurred after months of surveillance and cooperation with Colombian authorities. The DEA Administrator apologized to the city of Alexandria that was subjected to the raid with no prior warning but stressed that secrecy and timing were crucial to minimize potential casualties. An internal investigation had been ordered to pre-empt the inevitable calls from Congress for the Administration to identify a scapegoat for the lapse in good judgement.

The storyline had been penned by Sandy Matthews to stop the spreading fear that continued to grip the country after the Veterans Day attacks. For the real investigators, there were muddy boot-prints, hundreds of spent cartridge cases and a couple of large bulldozers that had been stolen from a mine in West Virginia. Beyond that, there was nothing. After a thorough daylight search using metal detectors and dogs, no other evidence turned up. The story confirmed that a submersible used to transport drugs had been seized and towed to the Washington Navy Yard for inspection and evidence gathering. Another miniature submarine had been found in an underwater cavern that had been fitted with workshops and support equipment to re-package and distribute. Authorities estimated that more than five tons of cocaine could be transported into the United States on every run. The President had invited the team of DEA agents and their Colombian counterparts to the White House for a private recognition. There would be no press coverage of the event to protect the identities of the officials from both countries.

Part III.

Chapter 56

Virginia Beach, Virginia
December 26, 2017

Dan drove home on Christmas Eve and spent Christmas day drinking a bottle of bourbon that he consumed in the darkness of his quiet living room. Bright strings of light were strung everywhere in the neighborhood but he couldn't pull himself out of the bleak funk that pulled him down. Waves of emotion seemed to crash down on him like those in a powerful surf zone. The next day, he drank cup after cup of coffee, feeling more miserable as the day went on. He couldn't sleep or sit still. He had tortured his body with alcohol but that hadn't touched the grief and anger and loneliness that he felt. His pounding head constantly reminded him of his bitter solitude. No tree, no decorations, not the gift he always hid on the tree for Jill. Just a deafening silence.

Dan suddenly woke and stared at the little light through puffy eyes and finally recognized his phone blinking. He'd missed a call. Still groggy, he felt his muscles involuntarily twitch when he saw the Washington, DC area code and hit the redial button. His mouth felt like it was stuffed with cotton, and he wasn't sure that he could even speak.

"Sandy Matthews," crackled the familiar voice over the line.

"Hi. What's up?"

"President Bowles called the Admiral and asked that the three of us come over for breakfast tomorrow morning to give him an update on where we stand on the investigation. No slides. No staff. Just a small breakfast roundtable with the Commander-in-Chief."

"OK. I'll drive up later tonight and see you in the morning."

"How are you doing? You don't sound like your usual energetic self."

"I gave myself a real bad hangover for Christmas and feel like I've been run over by a truck."

"I know it must be especially tough for you during this time of year. We'll meet the Admiral in his office tomorrow at 07:00 a.m. and go over to the White House in his car. That way we can compare notes before we sit down. Breakfast at 08:30 a.m. Are you going to be able to make it?"

"I'll be there."

Despite the sudden rush of adrenaline flowing through his body, Dan wondered if he could recover enough from the alcohol poisoning and emotional whiplash to make it back to DC and be prepared for the meeting with the President the following morning. He headed to the health club in a nearby mall that offered both a steam bath and a sauna, determined to sober up and to never again repeat this approach for treating his depressed mental state. It hadn't done anything to get him closer to finding his family's killers.

Chapter 57

The White House
Washington, DC
December 27, 2017

"Good morning, gents. Thanks for joining me." President Bowles sat down at the table set for four. "So, I hope you've had some time off and are enjoying the Holiday season." The President looked at each of the men in turn and then turned his attention to Dan.

"I know this is hard for you. Thank you for continuing the fight. I am personally very pleased that you've joined this team. The country needs our very best talent on this effort."

"Thank you Mr. President. Working on this investigation is all that matters to me at this point." Puffy and bloodshot, Dan's eyes told a different story.

"Well, it's important to me to get an unvarnished update about the investigation and see what's next. Sometimes things get filtered on their way to my desk, and I appreciate knowing what's really going on. I'm sure you understand that there is an army of politicos always trying to package and re-package what gets briefed to me and what I read. It sometimes scares me."

The Admiral nodded towards Dan.

"Mr. President, let me give you the last slide first. I'm convinced that three of the four Veterans Day attacks were carried out by one or more well-organized, well-financed terror cells operating within the United States that are not directly affiliated or linked with Al-Qaeda in any way."

Unexpectedly, the President dropped his fork and grabbed for his napkin. His hands shook like a man with an uncontrollable palsy as he stared in horror at Dan.

Clearly upset, he challenged Dan's assertion: "Are you saying that there's a terrorist group here in the States? Anarchists or Neo-Nazis? Where's the FBI on this? Jim, are you on the same page?"

Admiral Wright had never seen such a baffled look on President Bowles' face. There was also fear. The President wiped his mouth roughly on the starched white linen napkin, cutting his lip in the process.

The Admiral paused and then responded calmly, "I'm afraid so, Mr. President. With the facts we've been able to put together, that's the most plausible conclusion. I would caution that our case is largely based on circumstantial evidence, and we'd all be very pleased to be proved wrong, but I think what we are up against here is a home-grown threat that we have not even seriously considered. We certainly have concentrated on what terrorists could do here in the States but have always assumed that the plans and the people would be infiltrated from outside CONUS. That's simply not the case. You just can't sugar-coat what we've learned."

The President looked like he was about to throw up his breakfast. All the color had drained from his ruddy face, replaced with a dry parchment color common in long term anemia. He took a gulp of water, sat back in his chair and stared at each of the three men at the table, dumbfounded. He unbuttoned his collar and loosened his tie to get more air into his lungs, partially regaining his composure before responding.

"This is shocking. It could drive the entire nation into chaos. I just can't believe that we are facing an enemy trying to overrun our nation whether here or overseas, and at the same time we've got people inside the walls working with them or for their own objectives." He paused and wiped his mouth again. "I blame myself for looking at all these attacks through the 'it couldn't happen here' lens. I really took my eye off the ball, and didn't even think about other less obvious solutions. Hell, I didn't even ask the right questions. On one hand, I think I owe the nation an explanation but on the other, I'm reluctant to make this widely known because it could very well have dangerous consequences. People will be paralyzed with fear. There will be a run on every gun shop in the country. I've seen what happens when paranoia takes over, and it's not pretty. We just can't afford that. Jim, we are in a tough spot. What do you recommend?"

The Admiral responded, "Mr. President, I'm concerned that we'll waste a lot of valuable time and put the bad guys on alert if we have a press conference and announce that a new terrorist cell is at work inside the country. We will also give those organizations an opportunity to join forces and to complicate our efforts to keep them out. You remember what happened a few years ago when people found out that Americans were coming home from Syria without any special screening. My recommendation is to bring in some talent from each of the key agencies to form a special task force at a classified level and see if we can get a fix on what we are up against. I'd like to ask Dan and Sandy to hand-pick that team. We'll keep it small, and we'll need your backing to get the best athletes and keep them."

"And we'll still maintain our 24/7 watch on the international front?"

"Yes, Mr. President. I don't know any other way to tackle this, but in my judgment, we've got to move fast and stay very nimble. Essentially, we're starting from scratch."

"OK. That makes sense to me."

"One final thought. What really scares me is that I suspect there may be some people on the inside, within our government, that are working for or supporting this group. That's why we need to keep it small and vet every member of the team. We'll get you an 'Eyes Only' plan by the end of the day and identify the draft picks that we'll need from the agencies."

"Fine. What about our big DHS contractors…can they help?"

"Yes, we'll look into that as long as we can screen them like the others," replied the Admiral.

The President rose from the table and shook hands with the three men. Some color had returned to his face but he was still clearly shaken by the revelations.

"Good luck, Jim. Call me directly anytime you need my help."

"Thank you, Mr. President."

Chapter 58

DHS–Domestic Terrorism Annex
Washington, DC
December 27, 2017

The three walked through empty corridors, and the Admiral sat at his desk motioning to the two chairs in front.

"So, the President agrees with our recommendation. Can you pull together a plan to discuss this afternoon? As far as I know, I don't have anything on the calendar except that Carole expects me to be home for dinner with the grandchildren tonight."

Sandy responded, "Sure, we've already got the plan outlined and identified the "A" players we want on the team. How about 2:00 p.m.?"

"Fine, see you then. And thanks for joining me this morning. Personally, I feel that I let the Director and the President down. I'm the guy who's been asleep at the switch." The Admiral shook his head, and then turned his attention to the monitor on the right side of his desk. The meeting was over.

Sandy and Dan stopped in the hallway outside the Admiral's office.

"I don't know many of the inter-agency players or any of the DHS Industry reps. How do we bring them in?"

"There are just a handful of them with the right tickets so the pool is pretty small. Let me take a crack at that. Let's get together at noon in the war room."

"Right, see you then."

Dan felt like Mr. Phelps in the original "Mission Impossible". The President had given them a free hand to define the team to widen the dragnet. He reviewed the bidding: they will have picks from all the three letter agencies. He thought about Meg from the FBI. He could probably have someone with more experience and horsepower, but he'd rely on Sandy to choose the heavy hitters. He could trust Meg.

The Admiral opened the folder, read the package deliberately with his hands pressed on either side of his face. He grunted and handed it back to Sandy, "Terrific effort. Both of you know how important this is and you certainly got the boss's attention this morning. Dan, I'm 100% confident about having you lead it. Let's get this over to the White House ASAP. I feel like the clock is already ticking."

Chapter 59

DHS–Domestic Terrorism Annex
Washington, DC
January 03, 2018

Dan had contacted most of the team via secure means in the days since they'd sent the plan over to the White House and had it approved within hours. The Holidays made it tough to get anything started, and he reasoned that it would be best to start after the kids had returned to school and most people were back at work. Having the right people was critical to the effort's success, and a logical start would improve the chances of attracting the principals they needed.

Dan stood at the head of a polished rectangular table in a small, windowless conference room in the building's basement that had been equipped with secure laptops, data terminals, and encrypted landlines. No personal cell phones or other electronics of any kind were permitted in the room.

"Good morning and welcome to DHS and the Domestic Terrorism Annex. I'm Dan Steele. This effort is classified SECRET for now, and I'm certain there will be compartments applied as we pick up speed. You have been selected to serve as part of a team for an effort code-named "Stormy Weather." The scope has been briefed to the President and will be executed under the authority of an Executive Order that has been placed in the folder in front of you. On top of that folder is an in-briefing and non-disclosure form that I'll ask you to sign. Meg Andrews from the FBI will witness your signatures and collect the forms. One other administrative item: you were nominated for this assignment by your Agency, so if you believe you have a conflict or higher priority work, please raise any issues with your organization. To begin, I'd like to go around the room and would ask everyone introduce themselves: name, parent organization and any specific expertise you'd like others to know about. We've got a lot of ground to cover, so let's get started."

After introductions, Dan briefly introduced himself as the team lead. He saw a number of glances from some of the old hands, and the looks questioned whether he was up to this type of challenge. He walked to the screen and began reviewing the recent attacks one by one and offering the correlating evidence that several of the attacks had not been orchestrated by Al-Qaeda or any of their known affiliates.

He talked non-stop for two hours except for answering an occasional question from the team. No one could doubt that he knew the subject cold, and his grasp of details impressed many of the people around the table. He summarized with the team's charter: "We have strong evidence confirming that recent terrorist attacks originated within the United States and have been carried out by organizations not affiliated with Al-Qaeda. Stormy Weather has a straight-forward objective: to examine the evidence and to develop an intelligence network that will identify the source and sponsorship of these attacks and create some actionable leads for our intelligence and law enforcement agencies. This threat is real, and this is as urgent a task as any we are facing today."

After the presentation, several team-members suggested other ways the team's premise could be validated and volunteered to follow-up using resources within their parent organizations. By the time the team had hammered out the plan forward and agreed to a meeting rhythm, it was mid-afternoon. Several people approached Dan after the meeting with a range of comments, most of which were positive and helpful. There were the expected complaints and also some dire predictions, but overall he was pleased with the participants and their initial level of interest.

When the others had left, Dan came over and sat down in a chair next to Meg. "Any thoughts on our team or the kick-off? Seems like we've got a mixed bag of some real professionals and some other folks that see Stormy Weather as another bureaucratic drill that will result in nothing other than adding another accomplishment to their resumes. Frankly, I don't know most of the folks that came today, but I was surprised that your boss was the rep from the Bureau."

"Yeah, it doesn't surprise me," responded Meg glumly, "I'm sure he raised his hand for this assignment. He's all about what's next in his career. If the President or Director for that matter is interested in something then you can bet David will be fascinated with it."

Dan grinned, "I get it. I'm glad that you were available. The first thing that I'd like to do is get a real fix on our team. Call me paranoid, but I want to make sure that we are dealing with known quantities with clear track records. If I need to change someone out, I'd rather do it sooner rather than later. Can you take that on?"

"Sure, already started. I'm nervous too. Let me see what I can pull together on each of them so you can see exactly who's been assigned to your Impossible Mission force."

"Good analogy. The big difference is that Mr. Phelps started selecting a team from people that he knew. Based on what we've put together so far, the groups involved in these attacks are experts at planning, executing and covering their tracks and may have some people in critical slots inside the government. Maybe both. I just want to make sure that this Task Force does not provide another conduit of information going back to the bad guys. Who's to say that one of the people we read into the program this morning won't feed it back to the people we are trying to get a fix on?"

Meg shook her head, "I can't believe that we have to worry about a mole on Stormy Weather but you're right. Someone could undermine this effort and we'd never know it."

Meg continued, "By the way what are the expectations for reports up the chain?"

"None have been levied so far, but I told Sandy and the Admiral that I'd give them a weekly update. I'm not 100% confident that this group can generate anything valuable week after week, but I'll stick with that schedule until someone has a better idea." Dan leaned forward on the table and looked intently at Meg. "I just want you to know that I'm really glad that you're on this team, Meg. I can count on one hand the people I trust in this town, and you're one of them. Thanks."

Meg blushed, "OK, let's hold the compliments until you see if I can produce anything useful."

"Deal." Dan sensed that she was not comfortable with a comment that could be interpreted as something more than it was. He smiled, shook Meg's hand and left the conference room.

Chapter 60

Double Eagle Headquarters
M Street Georgetown
Washington, DC
January 08, 2018

"It's good to see you!" Spence continued around his desk, extending his hand and then wrapping Jack into a familiar fatherly hug. "I've missed you. What's going on with the Task Force?" Spence licked his lips in anticipation of the inside news that Jack would deliver.

"DHS has put together quite an impressive group from all the agencies. There's an ex-US Navy Seal by the name of Steele who's in charge. He's still a little wet behind the ears as far as the Beltway goes but seems to be a quick study and a clear thinker. One of the guys from the CIA told me that he was at the bottom of the Chesapeake Bay in the tunnel when it ruptured, and he managed to survive but he lost his wife and two kids, so he's personally motivated to see this through. Anyway, they've read us all into a special access program that they are calling Stormy Weather. They've gathered some pretty compelling evidence that some of the terrorist activities of the last six months have been the work of independent cells operating here in the States that may not be aligned with Al-Qaeda. The parade out in Fresno has produced a number of leads, but it's still fragmented and mostly circumstantial. Whoever's been behind these attacks has left little behind. Anyway, the team's charter is to assess the evidence across the board and to see what else can be uncovered to support or refute it. Right now this theory is based on a small amount of shaky data so it could go either way. Like all things with DHS, we are operating on a short fuse. This effort was initiated at the President's direction so it's got some high level interest and support."

Spence scowled, "Sounds like another bureaucratic effort to justify more funding at DHS." Spence's face softened and he smiled, "As you know, Double Eagle and our subsidiaries take the lion's share of the

DHS budget so we will no doubt benefit from more funding. We are protected either way."

Jack countered, "No, I really do believe that this is a serious effort. Whether it's Al-Qaeda working here in the States or another group is still the question. I was surprised that they traced those bulldozers that were used to tear-up the Alexandria waterfront to a mine in West Virginia. You remember that happened just before Christmas. The paper claimed that the DEA had uncovered a cocaine trafficking node supplied by some submersible. I was told last week what really happened. Evidently the group has very good intelligence and orchestrated an attack on the leadership of the Domestic Terrorism Cell at DHS, including Admiral Wright. It turned out to be a very close call and clearly had been well-planned."

"Yes, I agree. It does sound serious to me."

"Didn't Double Eagle have a mine out there in West Virginia?"

"Yes, we did at one time, but I recall that we sold it several years ago," Spence replied in a monotone.

"Well, there was also a story about a Swiss drilling machine that had been recovered from the tunnel disaster that was traced to the same mine. Anyway, they are finding things and trying to triangulate the evidence, but it's very flimsy at this point. I'll have to say that I'm a bit skeptical of the whole proposition."

"Jack, it's important that you stay engaged here. As I've said before, it's always good to have someone on the inside, and we can use all the information generated by this group in our effort to position for the Fortify opportunity. What's the name of the guy running the show over there?"

"Steele, Dan Steele."

"OK. We'll get some additional data on him and the others on the Task Force."

The two discussed the team for nearly an hour. Spence seemed very interested in all the details, and Jack chalked that up to Spence's commitment to 'making the market'. Jack knew that Spence would do almost anything to influence and shape a situation to his own advantage. Though sworn to secrecy, Jack only felt a passing pang of conscience when providing all the internal details to Spence. After all, Double Eagle served DHS as a major contractor, and Jack knew that Spence was committed to keeping his business base and expanding it into other areas. What Jack didn't know was how ruthless, cold, and deadly Spence could be in creating that market.

After Jack left, Spence buzzed his Secretary and asked her to set up a "Business Circle" meeting with Paul McGovern.

Chapter 61

Double Eagle Headquarters
M Street Georgetown
Washington, DC
January 09, 2018

Spence walked down the hallway into a conference room that looked like a situation room in the Pentagon. Each of the six seats at the table was fitted with a personal monitor and key board as well as a communications suite offering secure landline, satellite, and a voice scrambler. Three sixty inch large screen displays covered the front wall. The "Business Circle" graphic filled the center screen.

While most companies portrayed the power structure in a top level organization chart depicting the key leaders and their span of control of people, revenue, market placement and key customers, the business circle plotted the relative position of all the Double Eagle subsidiaries to the inner circle or corporate core operations. Organized simply, both the business elements and their leaders were characterized by their location within a series of ten concentric circles that identified the proximity to the core and the level of sensitive information that each individual leader had been cleared to receive. There were hundreds of locations all over the world that were tied to the company. However, most of those companies were in the outer rings separated from any connection to innermost circles by a web of ownership and compartments that allowed Spence to control what everyone knew about the centralized control that he imposed. Only the inner circle had full knowledge of the Double Eagle organization and a vote on organizational changes.

Spence took his seat at the head of the table and studied Paul McGovern's face to his right. The two had known one another since their childhood years, played together in the amphitheater in Durres, and both had been the targets of Gjon's abuse. Paul had taken a different path out of Durres but the two had remained in contact via a primitive coding system that they'd developed as children growing up in the era of Ian Fleming's James Bond. As children, they played a team of secret agents stopping the plots of evil doers. For the last twenty years, the game had turned more serious, with real people and less distinction between the good guys and the bad. In a sense, their childhood world had been transformed into what was displayed on the large screen at the end of the table. McGovern was one of the six people in circle one, the innermost circle, and someone that Spence trusted more than anyone in the world.

"I just spoke with Jack this morning, and he filled me in on the progress of the Special Task Force that convened a week ago under a classified Presidential Directive. Seems like they've been poking around the evidence from Veterans Day, the Virginia Beach tunnel, and even our recent failure in Alexandria and concluded that the attacks might have been organized from inside the country. This is very troubling. It turns out that the Task Force lead is that US Navy Seal that somehow survived the tunnel collapse. You'll recall that we tried to take care of him during that dive on the Metro Bridge. Now he's turned up again and that group is digging deep and uncovering some sloppy efforts that could expose the company and undermine our strategy. It makes me nervous."

"I agree. We've had a couple of operations that left some loose ends but do you really think there's any real risk of exposure?"

"Yes, I do. Look at our West Virginia mining operation. The investigators have already traced the bulldozers and connected that boring machine from Switzerland to the same mine."

The front screen responded to the keystrokes and mouse that Paul deftly navigated on the table. The center screen showed the Starwood Mine Company logo and a picture of its manager. Flanking the center screen were financials on the left and a traditional organizational chart on the right.

"The mine is a circle eight company so we are well-insulated from anything that the Special Task Force might turn up." Paul brought up another view that provided the mine's ownership chain that included a Canadian mining conglomerate and a South African Gold Exploration company.

He continued, "They would have to get through the books of multiple companies before they reached our Double Eagle group of companies."

"What level is the mine's manager?" asked Spence.

Paul brought up the manager on the right screen. His resume was displayed with a watermarked "Eight" in the background. Paul quickly summarized: "He's been at the mine for six years and never been exposed to anything other than that level of information. Performance has been solid, and his reports are always on time. We have an "in-depth" on him completed in the last two years. I'll take a close look at that but just don't see how he could hurt us. I'm confident that we are protected on this one."

"Fresno. Paul, one of the pilots posed for a picture at the place that fitted out the planes and exposed his tattoo. We need to make sure that doesn't happen again. I don't want to overreact to these oversights, but we've had more than our share of problems the past few months, and we do not need the Feds getting any closer."

Spence reached out and put his hand on top of his friend's arm.

"We are making progress in leaps and bounds. I just don't want any more setbacks, my friend. We've come too far for that."

Both men sat back in their chairs, talking and laughing in their native tongue as if neither had a care in the world, back in Durres playing the good guys in the Amphitheatre.

Chapter 62

DHS–Domestic Terrorism Annex
Washington, DC
January 12, 2018

After the morning meeting, Meg knocked on Dan's open office door. "Have you got a few minutes, Dan? I've got some initial findings on the Task Force that I think we need to talk about."

"Sure, Meg, come on in," motioning to her to close the door. Dan walked around his desk and the two sat down at the small round conference table. Meg pushed the team roster in front of Dan so he could see where she'd highlighted several names.

"Based on my review and database searches so far, we've got the agencies' "A" players. Most are long time government employees, so there are few questions about their loyalty or allegiance. Some of these people have access to information that only a handful of people are cleared to see, mostly having to do with nuclear readiness and release authority. Those I've highlighted in green. I looked at the team from two angles: their history in government and their professional reputation. I realize that the reputation piece is much more subjective, but we don't want to find out downstream that our reliance just on the official personnel files blinded us to something we should have known. That said, I do have some questions on two individuals that I've highlighted in yellow. Specifically: my boss, David Kline and Robert Lang, from Double Eagle."

"Wait a second. I knew you didn't like your boss after my first trip down to Quantico, but the guy's been nominated by the Director, and it's helpful to have this level of horsepower on the Task Force. He mentioned Sandy Matthews too."

"Look, there's nothing personal driving my concern. Just hear me out, OK?" Dan nodded in agreement.

"David joined the FBI five years ago from a Silicon Valley software firm that developed a biometric package for DHS. He managed a group responsible for getting the package accredited by the government. The systems were supposedly fool-proof. However, there were a number of critical breaches into sensitive databases during the initial six-month start-up."

Dan interrupted, "But don't we generally find software glitches in most all systems during roll-out?"

"Yes, that's fairly common across programs. And, according to my sources, the government usually short-changes the testing regimen or runs out of funding, and the contractors replan the effort, cutting corners and kicking the can down the road. In this case, all the breaches were investigated but a true root cause was never determined. David's role made him a party to the investigation, but no evidence of wrong-doing or negligence ever got documented. I found one snippet that was scanned on a cover page that noted:

"D.K. seemed evasive when responding to the breeches, never admitting that the cause could have been tied to his company's biometric product."

Meg paused to collect her thoughts and then picked up the thread. "What makes me suspicious is that many of the investigative interviews were somehow expunged from the record. His clearance was suspended during the investigation which is the standard protocol. But then there's an unexplained excursion from the process: somehow his clearance was re-instated through an administrative action, rather than the usual process of re-applying and going through a new background investigation. That takes time and I understand that delays may impact a program. There's one other thing. Between the time he left the software company and joined the Bureau, there's a period of eight months where he claimed that he was caring for a sick family member. The problem is that he was adopted, never married and had no family. The personal history chronology that he submitted as part of his background investigation revealed no family at all."

Meg paused to see if Dan was following the story.

"So he pulled some strings and got someone to waive the process," replied Dan. "That happens too often in my view, but there must have been some rationale for fast-tracking the reinstatement. The stuff about his family is troubling but that's something for HR to look at. I think that the files you've collected may not include the documents you'd need to confirm any personal wrongdoing. Maybe he's got a significant other that he wants to keep in the closet? Plus you don't like him, right?"

"That's true but these are just the facts that you asked me to pull together," replied Meg defensively. Dan could see that he'd hit a raw nerve by making a crude reference to Kline's sexual orientation and most important, calling her objectivity into question.

Dan tried to recover and get back on track, "Is there anything in his FBI jacket that raises questions about his loyalty or motivation?"

"No," said Meg, "He's clean. But I still don't trust him. He's always asking questions and wanting to know about the evidence that I've been collecting. There's something about him that just doesn't seem genuine."

"So what can we do? It's a weak argument, and I don't think there's enough here to ask for him to be removed from the Task Force. But let me talk to Sandy. He may have other insights into David or ideas on how to move him. I trust your instincts and promise to run this to ground. Just be prepared to continue to work with him. Now, what about the other guy, Robert Lang? My first impression is positive...seems like a good guy to me, at least for a contractor."

"In Lang's case, there's just not much there. And by the way, he goes by Jack. Foster child that bounced around a lot. He's been working for Double Eagle since he graduated from Columbia with a degree in Economics. Nothing out of the ordinary at Columbia. Bs and Cs and no academic awards. Kind of a loner with no affiliations or extra-curricular activities. Lived in an apartment off-campus. At the company, it appears that he's more a business development guy and "front" man for the company. His track record is pretty thin. He's never been a program manager and just has a "meeting" friendship with the DHS Staff. Double Eagle has trotted him out a number of times for Award Fee presentations, and he's always got an amazing grasp of the facts. He's very steady and likeable. I'm told that one of the government managers changed his award fee evaluation during a presentation because of Jack's explanation of a late delivery. He is particularly even-handed in discussing the company's performance and presents objective evidence to support their self-assessments. There's less public data out there on them than I expected. It's a large, privately held firm that specializes in supply chain and security services. Most of the folks here at DHS speak very highly of them...professional, responsive, know the rules and follow them and perform at a level above the competition. "

"So what's wrong with him?" asked Dan.

"Well, the only thing that bothers me is that he lives in the fast lane. Lots of foreign travel, frequent vacations and multiple female contacts. He seems to live well above his W2 and that's the red flag. Bank records are in synch with his wages, and there are no known investments or other income to support his lifestyle."

"Maybe the women are paying the freight," Dan offered, knowing that Meg would quickly find a hole in his response.

"No, I've checked them out too. None of them has the means to support someone else living the high life. They may look and act the part but can't afford it."

"OK, Meg. I've got it. Seems like we've got a squeaky clean group with the exception of the two that you've found. But I just don't see anything here that rises to the level that I'd need to make the case for removal. Maybe Sandy can get David quietly re-assigned based on some higher FBI priority and the fact that you are so ably representing the Bureau. I think we'll have to keep Lang. He's one of the only cleared contractors, and Double Eagle is already so deeply embedded in the Department that that in itself could prove problematic. Just because the guy has a way with the ladies does not disqualify him. We'll just have to see if anything else turns up. I can tell you that this former Navy Lieutenant did not have the means to even think about the high life let alone live it."

The next day, Dan thanked David for his contributions and announced to the team that he would be leaving the Task Force for a higher priority "Special" assignment within the Bureau. Ten minutes later, Spence learned that one of his insiders was now on the outside.

Chapter 63

Boston, Massachusetts
January 17, 2018

Beverly Inshore, Inc. had been working in Boston for years, building breakwaters, constructing and repairing seawalls for coastal towns on both the south and north shores, the Army Corps of Engineers and investors trying to develop some of the limited Boston waterfront. Its owner, Dave Rowe, had seen all the ups and downs in the waterfront business. Of late, it seemed all down. There had been no technology breakthroughs that made the jobs any different than they'd always been. It was hard, dangerous work that required barges and cranes to support tough, strong men that would move huge granite blocks into place or drive piles through the mud and sediment down to the bedrock to keep the storms from the city's foundations and to prevent sinkholes from swallowing pieces of choice real estate. Beverly Inshore had a spotty business record and a particularly bad reputation for fighting over contract terms, scope changes and acceptance criteria which most people believed was a direct reflection of its owner's prickly personality.

For forty years, Rowe had worked the waterfront, thriving on the tough manual labor, the miserable winter weather and killing the aches and pains by maintaining a constant level of intoxication. His leg had been crushed by a ten ton block of granite that had unexpectedly opened the lifting eye on a wire sling as he was wedging the stone into position on the top of a breakwater. The doctors argued for amputation, but Rowe insisted that they close the wounds and splint the leg. The result was a knee that couldn't bend. It was fused into position and had to be swung around like a stick. It's didn't matter to Rowe. He kept his leg and found ways to compensate for his lack of mobility.

The long winters forced him to lay off most of his crew in December but they were happy to collect unemployment checks and knew that he'd call them back come spring. In addition to the pain, Rowe's other constant companion was a crooked black cheroot that rarely left his mouth. He removed the cheroot after Paul McGovern unexpectedly made him a cash offer to buy the company. He looked deep into McGovern's eyes trying to see a flinch or a glance away from the fixed stare that could penetrate a man's inner soul. Seasoned by many years in a rough and unforgiving trade with vicious competitors and high levels of payoffs and corruption, no one could pull the wool over Rowe's eyes. The few that had been successful over the years were long gone from the area.

"I think I've got a good fix on all your company's assets and their condition."

"Now how exactly did you do that? Who are you, anyway?" said the man, who was both intrigued and angry that someone could access his private company details.

"We specialize in companies that might be niche players in a market where the business base could be easily expanded or whose location offers other business advantages. As you might expect, this requires detailed background research. So, I am aware that your principal asset is the floating spud crane built in 1958 with a limited lifting capacity and a thinning hull. You also have a work boat and a single barge that needs to be constantly pumped. And then there's this grand office complex that would make an ideal spot for a convenience store."

Rowe sat at his desk, seething at the recitation of the condition of his company but also knowing that the assessment was startlingly accurate.

Noting Rowe shifting uneasily in his chair, Paul McGovern pressed his attack, confident that he could hammer the cigar smoking owner with facts until he called "uncle". He continued, "By my calculations, Beverly Inshore's balance sheet would confirm that you are losing about $4,000 dollars a month, have zero contracts in your backlog and virtually no chance of getting further city contracts until the discrepancies from last year's OSHA inspection get resolved. In short, Mr. Rowe, I am prepared to make you a reasonable offer to expedite the sale of your company to an interested party. You will not be a rich man after the sale, but you'll be on a solid financial footing which will no doubt open many opportunities. Do you have any questions regarding my valuation process or its accuracy?"

Rowe's silence answered the question.

"So, the party that I represent is prepared to offer you $500,000 for the sale of the company's assets and assumption of its known liabilities providing there are no liabilities that we've not yet uncovered."

Rowe withdrew the cheroot and talked through the cloud of smoke as he exhaled. "First, I don't like you mister. Second, what's the catch? You are offering to buy Beverly for a half million dollars when I haven't brought in that kind of cash in eight years. I've got one contract that I've pulled in this year worth about $400,000 to replace some core stones and re-set the armor stones on a breakwater over in Nahant. You haven't eyeballed my books, but you've got some good inside information on our operations. You are right, I don't have a backlog. You don't look like a guy who's spent a lot of time on the water, and your hands look like some Boston politician who gets a weekly manicure. We don't see that out on the spud barge, I can tell you that."

"You are right. I'm an indoor cat. I don't pick the companies to acquire, and we use different processes to make our valuations and projections. My buyer frankly believes that this is a business with growth potential that can be realized with new ownership and a modest cash infusion. They've got a great record in turning-around businesses and are convinced that Beverly is a good candidate. I was sent here to see if we can come to terms and to close the deal, simple as that. No tricks, no catches. Just a straightforward business deal. What do you say?"

His anger subsided; Rowe looked at the man with disbelief. "Well, I don't know who's doing your prospecting for you, but I'm certainly interested in your offer. What's your timeline?"

"I'd like to close as soon as you can."

"In case you weren't aware, and looking at your suit and shoes you aren't, it's winter here in Boston and the slowest time of the year for us. My crew is usually laid off for several months of unemployment, and I get them back in the spring. With the harbor freezing over, I thought you'd be trying to make me a lowball offer. But, $500,000 dollars in cash is an offer that I can't refuse. There's obviously something here that your company sees that I don't but that's not my problem. I'll tell you what. Draw up the papers, give me a $250,000 down payment, and I'll be ready to close the deal tomorrow," thinking that he'd call the man's bluff.

McGovern reached into his briefcase and pulled out a legal folder. "Here's our proposed settlement. Let me know if it's acceptable to you, and I'll wire the down payment to your bank this afternoon. We can close the deal any time after that."

The folder lay unopened on Rowe's desk. The cheroot left his lips briefly followed by an acrid balloon of smoke that hung in the air. Rowe's leg felt better than it had in years. He pulled himself up from the chair, shaking McGovern's hand and said, "Wire the cash today, and you can take over by the end of the week."

After the man left, Rowe shook his head in disbelief and sat back at the desk. He reached into the bottom desk drawer and pulled out a bottle of scotch. It was a large bottle of what he could afford. He filled the dirty coffee cup on his desk and spoke aloud, "this might be the last time I ever drink this rotgut." Suspicious yet hopeful, he still couldn't believe that this was happening. He'd wait until the money showed up in his account before really celebrating. He would have sold the whole kit and caboodle for the down payment alone. He took a good long pull from the cup and felt it burn all the way down his throat. He smiled and said to himself, "Florida here I come."

Chapter 64

West Virginia
January 30, 2018

Alive with activity choreographed over the years into a mindless process involving massive trucks waiting to be loaded with tons of ore-laden earth taken in huge fifty ton mouthfuls by electric rope shovels, the Starwood Mine's on-site grading and processing cycle ran like a finely tuned machine.

A joint FBI and IRS team arrived at the rendezvous point just two miles from the strip mine at 09:00 a.m. Loaded into two large, black SUVs with tinted windows fitted with bullet-proof glass, the team drove at a steady pace, past countless pick-up trucks that looked like they'd been spared from the junkyard only because they would have required heavy washing first to remove the thick layer of dirt and accumulated grime. Most of the trucks' windows were left open and exposed to the constant dust storms that the excavation produced.

Reaching their destination, the agents, bulky and slow in their tactical vests, fanned out around the double-wide trailer that served as the operations center. The door to the trailer opened before the lead Agent had a chance to knock and announce himself. He held up an official-looking document at the hard-faced man who looked like he'd come right out of Appalachia. The sight of the Agents and the official license being waved at him seemed to have no effect at all.

The man led them into the trailer and made himself comfortable. "What can I do for you fellas?" he asked, leaning back in his desk chair and showing the well-worn bottom of his work boots to the agents.

The lead agent responded, "I'm Special Agent Sands from the FBI. This is Examiner Stubbs from the IRS. We have a search warrant signed by Judge Wilmot that we are executing today and just wanted to let you know that we expect your full cooperation, Mr."

"My name's Curtis, son. Melvin Curtis. We're not used to having any visitors here at the mine. If I'd known you was coming, I'd have dressed up in my Sunday best. Now, just what kind of cooperation are you asking for?"

"Well, Mr. Curtis, there was a drilling machine manufactured in Switzerland that was sent here that we are trying to track down. We recovered parts of that machine at the bottom of the Chesapeake Bay and believe it may have been used in that tunnel catastrophe last summer. We also understand that a couple of your heavy bulldozers were taken just before Christmas last year."

"Yep, I couldn't believe that someone would actually steal those dozers. They took them over the weekend and must have brought their own transports to haul them out of here. Where'd those dozers end up? Will we get them back?" He continued without waiting for a response. "I don't know about the drilling machine. We don't keep much paperwork here on the site, but we can certainly show you what we do have if it will help."

"Thanks. We'd like to look at whatever records you have here and will follow-up if required."

Curtis addressed a man whose desk was covered in paper. "Henry, see if you can find those equipment logs and show them to the gentlemen here."

A young man with thick glasses responded to the request. Henry seemed confused as he began excavating the piles of paper on his desk. He had that unmistakable look of someone who'd been bred from a couple whose family trees had very few branches that had frequently grown together over the generations.

Special Agent Sands glanced back at Curtis who hadn't moved an inch since their arrival. He said, "We brought a number of people with us. If you don't have any objections, we'd like to take a look around the site while Henry is gathering the records."

"Sure, that's OK, as long as none of you boys is from OSHA." Curtis laughed and showed a partial mouthful of teeth stained black from chewing tobacco. Examiner Stubbs wondered to himself if that mouth had ever been subjected to a toothbrush.

Sands left the IRS examiner with Henry and gathered his team outside. "Ok men, we've served the warrant, and I'd like to see what's here. Looks like any documentation or records will be hard to find so split up into pairs and see if you can turn anything up. I think we have enough hand-held radios for every pair so keep in touch, and let's reassemble back here in 90 minutes. Any questions?"

The team covered the open pit, the vehicles, the safety shed and the repair shop, and turned up nothing new. The miners all listened to the same country music station while they were talking about their families and how the hunting season was going. The visit lasted just two hours. Once all the agents were accounted for, Special Agent Sands thanked Curtis for his cooperation and said that they would follow-up with the central office in Morgantown the next day. He noticed that Melvin Curtis seemed fixed in the same position that he'd been in an hour before. Twin dust trails from the SUVs were still hanging in the air when he quickly changed positions and pulled a shiny satellite phone from his desk and dialed a number in Morgantown. The next day's search would turn up nothing.

Chapter 65

DHS–Domestic Terrorism Annex
Washington, DC
February 02, 2018

The weekend finally arrived. Dan felt frustrated. The Task Force continued to correlate data, but the initial enthusiasm had waned, and the team had settled into a bureaucratic grind that bred lethargy. People got tired of the long days with not much to show for their efforts. There had been no big breakthrough, and the team's attitude deteriorated with the monotonous routine. Dan mentally replayed the week's events and concluded that he'd allowed the team to start drifting. Picking up a clean legal pad, he jotted some notes on how he'd get the team re-energized the following week.

Tonight he'd been invited to join a former Navy friend for the Wizards game and took a deep breath on his way out of the office. He'd like to see his old friend but couldn't resolve the internal debate raging in his mind. The mission had become a constant focus, and he didn't have the ability to turn off the work week that easily. It stayed with him. He had no other distractions in his life, except frequent feelings of guilt as he revisited his family's Veterans Day trip over and over. As he exited the building, a sharp, cold wind hit his face. He pulled up his overcoat and quickened his pace, as he walked towards the Verizon Center in Northeast Washington, right at the Gallery Place/ Chinatown Metro stop. Stopping just short of the crowds hustling to the game, he turned around and headed back to the solace of his empty office. He just wasn't ready to add any unnecessary complications to his shattered life.

Chapter 66

Occoquan, Virginia
February 11, 2018

Located south of the Metro area just off the I-95 corridor, Occoquan remained a small town. Developers by-passed the site along the river by the same name. They wanted more open, uncomplicated acreage to build hundreds of tract homes to offer the growing army of commuters heading north to the beltway every morning. The town fiercely protected the small river and resisted any further development. Occoquan's small shops did not attract people with children and lacked all the conveniences that suburbia offered: twenty-four hour-a-day grocery stores, mega home centers, drop-off day care, drive through coffee shops and wide-ranging sports and academic programs to satisfy the yuppies. But Occoquan did appeal to Meg. She avoided the things that attracted so many of her colleagues and found the quiet, laid back town to her liking.

A thick winter fog had settled into the Capital region overnight and hung over the still river. It enveloped Meg as she opened the front door of her small townhouse to take her dog on his morning walk. Meg really liked living out here. The commute to Quantico was far better than the hike to DHS as she'd found out since driving to the Domestic Terrorism Annex the past five weeks. However, working on the Special Task Force stimulated her, and she particularly enjoyed working for Dan. Clear-headed and focused, he listened to Meg and seemed to value her input. What she liked best was that he frequently used her as a sounding board for his ideas prior to engaging the rest of the team. She felt like part of something important and worthwhile.

As her little Boston bull terrier, Corky, stretched his legs along the damp sidewalk, Meg spotted a man headed towards her. Strange, she knew all her neighbors in this small neighborhood, and few were up at 5:00 a.m. Involuntarily, her muscles became taut. She moved off the sidewalk and into the road, giving the other person a wide berth. Dressed for winter, the man wore a long dark wool overcoat and a brimmed hat pulled low on his brow. He looked like he was deep in thought and did not even acknowledge her.

Just before getting to her house, she spied the man again and stayed on the sidewalk, quickening her pace so that she would be up the walkway and on her porch before the two met again. He also quickened his pace. As they approached each other, the man opened his coat like a flasher, and Meg spotted a shiny pistol. At the same time, she felt a sharp sting in her side and fell into the man's arms as she lost consciousness.

Hours later, Meg's neighbor spotted Corky scratching the front door with the leash still attached to his collar. Meg didn't answer when he rang her bell and knocked loudly. He returned home and called the local police. Meg's car was parked in the driveway, and the house security system was armed. With no response to another round of knocking, the uniformed police officer returned to the office and called the FBI.

Chapter 67

Double Eagle Headquarters
M Street Georgetown
Washington, DC
February 11, 2018

The small window in Spence's paging device lit up. Spence lifted the small machine and smiled. He spoke several words aloud to himself in his native tongue that conveyed something positive, some good news. The fact that Spence had an inside man at DHS on the Special Task Force was important. Jack had kept Spence apprised of the team's efforts and had pin-pointed some specific areas that Spence had the opportunity to "clean" in advance, thwarting any collection of data and avoiding any connection with Double Eagle. But that really wasn't enough. Spence wanted to know what Steele and his close-mouthed assistant were planning next and how he might outflank their efforts.

Spence expected that the loss of Meg Andrews would have a negative impact, but the objective was to learn enough to take down the Task Force as well. Momentary set-backs could be overcome. Spence was annoyed with his team's recent failures and couldn't understand why these "easy" domestic operations were proving so difficult. He made a mental note to talk to Paul and ask him to formally look into the lapses. Meantime, he needed to follow-through on an important VIP event. The Double Eagle organization needed to begin planning. This had to be a zero defect operation.

Chapter 68

DHS–Domestic Terrorism Annex
Washington, DC
February 13, 2018

Meg had been out for two days. Dan found it very odd that she hadn't even called. There were lots of people out with the flu that was going around, but it just wasn't like Meg to not call in or leave him a message. There had been no email from her. That was unusual too. Meg usually spent a few hours on the weekend catching up on the team's progress and frequently sent out follow-ups and reminders. She copied him on all the key items that they were tracking. Dan relied on her to keep the routine progress reports flowing and make sure that all the moving parts of the Task Force were integrated.

Where could she be? He wondered aloud. Nearly 11:00 a.m. and not a peep. His desk phone rang angrily. Maybe this call would answer his question.

"Good morning, Dan Steele," he answered.

"Mr. Steele, this is Doris at reception down on the first floor. There are a couple of FBI agents here to see you."

"OK, thanks, Doris," he replied, "I'll be right down." This happened frequently on the Special Task Force. He routinely met with reps from multiple agencies and never dismissed a data point, even if it initially seemed inconsequential. Yet the timing of this call alarmed him. He worried that Meg might be in trouble. Seal Platoon missions had taught him valuable lessons in developing situational awareness from all available sources even if the dots later proved to be outliers. He passed through the security turnstile and approached the two agents in the lobby. Both looked like they came from central casting, a Laurel and Hardy pair.

"You Dan Steele?" asked the beefy one with the high and tight military haircut and traces of a donut's confectioner's sugar creating snowflakes on his suit.

"Yes, that's me," said Dan evenly. He didn't understand why but he immediately felt defensive and his autonomic flight or fight adrenaline kicked in.

Everything quickly became a blur as he was handcuffed and unceremoniously led out of the building and into a waiting black sedan with tinted windows. The two agents remained incommunicado during the trip over to the FBI Headquarters building that was just two blocks from the DHS Annex. They drove into an underground garage that opened with a key card that Hardy waved past a sensor at the entrance.

Dan endured a brief "in-processing" where he surrendered his wallet, cell phone, car keys and DHS badge before being escorted into an interrogation room. It reminded him of the US Navy's SERE (Survival, Evasion, Resistance and Escape) school that he'd attended in the mountains of Maine. Only there the instructors were decked out in Eastern European uniforms, and the students knew that the course restricted physical abuse to provocation and verbal attacks. That had been a cake walk compared to his BUDS training. He wondered who might be observing from the other side of the large window covering the wall opposite his chair.

One of the agents slid a photo across the table and asked Dan if he recognized the woman.

"Sure, that's Meg Andrews. She's on a team I'm leading in DHS."

"When was the last time you saw her?"

"Last Friday afternoon. She left the DHS office about 6:00 p.m. to go home. I had a couple of follow-up emails from her on Saturday morning and expected her back here in DC bright and early Monday morning."

"You married Mr. Steele?"

"Yes…well no." Dan stammered, "I lost my wife in the Chesapeake Bay Bridge and Tunnel collapse last summer, so I'm not married any longer."

"What is your relationship with Ms. Andrews?"

"She was the Bureau rep assigned to my team at DHS looking at domestic terrorism. I first met her down in Quantico last fall. What's this all about anyway?"

"Were you involved with Ms. Andrews?" the beefy agent leered.

"No." Dan felt anger coursing through his body and decided that he needed to take a different tack. "Again, I'd like to know what this is about," he said, challenging the pair for an answer.

The beefy agent annoyed him again by responding, "We'll ask the questions. You are here to answer them."

Dan stood up, now in full anger as one of the agents drew a Taser and pointed it at his chest.

"Ever been incapacitated by one of these before? I don't think you'd like it much. Now, sit down."

He took his seat as the other agent sat across from him and started the standard good cop, bad cop routine.

"Listen, Mr. Steele, you are in some deep kimchi. Meg Andrews' body was delivered to our office in Quantico this morning in a large black trash bag. She'd been tortured by someone who knew how to get answers, raped and suffocated. We found her green eyeballs in a jar in your apartment this morning along with a bloody T-shirt that's been sent to the lab. Looks to me as if you are one sick puppy. And we here at the Bureau don't like to lose one of our own. Now, you can make this easy or you can make it hard, but one thing's for sure. You are going to tell us what happened."

Dumbfounded after hearing about Meg, he looked up with a mask of fury, stared at the pair and declared angrily, "Look, I didn't have anything to do with this. I've been set up."

"Where were you over the past four days?"

"Friday night I stayed at the office until about 9:00 p.m. Saturday, I got up and took a long run in the city, down to the Navy Yard and back. Saturday afternoon, I drove to Virginia Beach to check on our house and had dinner with my previous Commanding Officer at a restaurant downtown. I ended up spending the night there and drove back here Sunday afternoon. Went into the office late in the afternoon, ran through my email and got ready for the week. In the office by 07:00 a.m. Monday morning and left about twelve hours later. Played racquetball at the Athletic Club over in the Pentagon until 9:30 p.m. and was in bed an hour later. Got to the office this morning at 06:30 a.m. and pushed paper until my unexpected visit from the two of you. Again, you guys should be spending your time talking to someone else."

The heavy agent with the dusting of confectioner's sugar on his ill-fitting suit put both fists on the table and leaned over so that Dan could smell last night's beer on his breath.

"As I said before, we ask the questions, you give us the answers, and we're not interested in any additional commentary, got it?"

"OK, I'm tired of this exchange," said Dan, "I think that I want to make a telephone call, now."

He stood and Laurel reached for his hardware. Still handcuffed, Dan quickly outmaneuvered him and locked his wrist behind his back. He ordered Hardy to place the Taser on the table. The other agent looked stunned, a deer in the headlights.

He leaned over the man's shoulder and calmly said, "I would appreciate your permitting me to make a call. Otherwise, I might get difficult to deal with. You understand?"

Dan released his hold and then faced both agents, his eyes wide and smoldering with anger. "As I said, I had nothing to do with this. I can make a call and you guys can probably hold me on suspicion but that's not going to help us find out who did this and why. So, how do you want to proceed, the hard way or the easy way?"

Before either Agent had a chance to respond, a speaker crackled from the ceiling, "Sorry for the confusion, Mr. Steele. You are free to go. Agent Conrad will drive you back to your office."

Back at headquarters, Dan headed for Sandy Matthews' office and barged through the door. Sandy listened to the story and became apoplectic by the end. "I can't believe this. What the hell were those guys thinking?"

"I don't know. But what I'm really concerned about is that the bad guys know that we are on to something, and they will stop at nothing to disrupt it, including killing those on the Task Force. They've raised the bidding, and we need to meet them head-on. I'm not ready to tell you how, but I know that we need to change the game. We can't win a war of attrition against an enemy we don't know. Can you ask our physical security team to review the tapes from the last month to see if they've got anything that looks like surveillance on the building?"

Chapter 69

DHS–Domestic Terrorism Annex
Washington, DC
February 14, 2018

The Stormy Weather Task Force had assembled for the mid-week meeting, and it got off to a sluggish start. Prepared to deliver a much-needed wake-up call, the news about Meg's abduction and murder immediately got everyone's attention.

"I don't have many details to give you today. The FBI has launched an investigation, and I'm sure that many of you will be interviewed about your knowledge of Meg and anybody she might have known that could be responsible. The sick brutality of her death makes me believe that she may have been targeted because of Stormy Weather. So, I'd ask each of you to be alert and suspicious. The classification of the program and the team roster has been raised to a Sensitive Compartmented Information level, so that your assignment should not be discussed with anyone at your parent organization without the clearance and need to know. I regret that those of you not cleared to that level will have to leave the room. There will be a security specialist in the main floor conference room in ten minutes to process your de-briefing forms. Thank you for your professional efforts in support of the program."

A third of the team left the room.

After a brief pause, Dan took an entirely different tack. His words came like steady thunder from a heavy caliber machine gun. He saw the people at the conference table as Seals just about to shove off on a difficult and dangerous mission that would almost certainly be accompanied by casualties.

"Our team's task tracker looks like we are stalled without the motivation or momentum to make progress. Stormy Weather is too important to permit missed deadlines or extension after extension on our dates. I'll make this easy. For everything to date, I take full responsibility. We will re-set our schedule, and I expect it to be aggressive. We'll take today as a new point of departure and work through the tasks and dates. I will tell you that I will hold you accountable for work assigned. There will be no changes without my approval before the fact. And for those of you who believe that this is nothing more than an unpleasant wire-brushing that will be forgotten tomorrow, think again. I have asked for and received authority to provide a formal input on your performance ratings via the Director. Your objectives will be what we jointly assign, and I expect stressing goals from each of you. Are there any questions?"

No one had a question. Everyone understood that the team's pace had been shifted into high gear and the driver was Dan Steele.

"OK, team. Let's roll up our sleeves and get to work. We need a detailed plan with clear accountability before the end of the day."

He used a tactic that would have shocked most Washington bureaucrats accustomed to the no fault approach elevated by management professionals and consultants that offered vague touchy feely recommendations on how to positively motivate the workforce or be recognized as an Employer of Choice. He had let his emotion and his conviction show through to energize the team. Heavy-handed? Yes. Effective? Time would tell. One certain outcome: people would either step up to the plate and give it their best effort or be forced to quit. A simple fork in the road.

Chapter 70

CIA Headquarters
Langley, Virginia
February 16, 2018

The Admiral, Sandy and Dan were ushered to a conference room where an emaciated briefer with a shrill voice sounding like chalk screeching against a black board began the brief with the usual classification warnings and disclosures.

"This morning, an international team disrupted a terrorist plot involving a near simultaneous release of nerve gas in train and subway stations of several European capitals. That's the good news. The bad news is that while we watched the plan develop over the last sixty days, we missed the fact that Al-Qaeda initiated a parallel effort using an entirely different communications network. As a result, successful attacks were carried out in three cities—Athens, Barcelona, and Brussels. The trigger on a fourth device failed in Istanbul. Casualty estimates are not yet in."

Chapter 71

February 18, 2018

Virtually all the Sunday papers carried the European terrorist attacks on page one. The ISIS attacks in Paris and Brussels in 2015 and Nice in 2016 changed the way the European governments responded to the growing Muslim population and dealt with the thousands of immigrants from North Africa and refugees from the Middle East. The crackdowns were unpopular but, faced with a choice between order and chaos, most law-abiding people preferred to give up some of their freedoms for internal security. The news reporting varied along predictable lines, but most of the papers hinted similar attacks were headed towards the United States and raised rhetorical questions about the government's readiness to thwart such attacks. US military bases and Westerners continued to be targeted and attacked overseas, but so far the incredible investment in surveillance, intelligence sharing and border security prevented large scale attacks such as 9/11 within the United States.

The ISIS march to Bagdad in the summer of 2014 renewed fears about the implosion of the Middle East, and the United States was fiercely divided when it came to putting boots on the ground. Ground that was already saturated with American blood for what now appeared to be a senseless cause. The United States stubbornly clung to the proposition that what the people of Iraq needed most was democracy, the type born in the US which worked imperfectly to begin with. To think people actually believed our brand of democracy could be exported and made to work in a country that had only known a strong man and remained divided by longstanding tribal loyalties remained a pipe dream.

Until the summer of 2017 and the recent Veterans Day attacks, most of the incidents in the United States were limited to homemade bombs like those used in the Boston Marathon or a lone shooter in Orlando with scores of people killed and injured by a single shooter. Anger jumped off a number of papers' editorial pages where the US Government, particularly DHS, was skewered for its delay in solving the Veterans Day attacks. There were no real conclusions about what group was responsible. The level of fear gripping the country rose measurably every day.

Chapter 72

DHS–Domestic Terrorism Annex
Washington, DC
February 20, 2018

Dan received the autopsy report on Meg. The information extraction process just started when Meg, tied to a wooden chair, jerked her head forward causing a scalpel to sever her carotid artery. Her inquisitor lost the opportunity to use his vast creativity and roll of surgical instruments to compel her to tell what she knew about Stormy Weather. She died with her eyes stoically fixed on the man she defeated. The sick post-mortem activity focused solely on preserving his reputation. The profession set high standards of accountability. His failure to extract the desired information served to eliminate him from one list and to be added to another.

Chapter 73

DHS–Domestic Terrorism Annex
Washington, DC
February 21, 2018

Dan liked to begin the day's work early and could be found at his desk between 06:30 and 07:00 a.m. He got his best work done first thing in the morning and found it was the only time when he could back away from the trees and try to see the forest, often remarking that his best thinking occurred during his early morning shower. He just entered the office with a steaming cup of coffee when the annoying electronic ringer on his desk phone sounded. The phone's window identified the call only by its country code of 971- the United Arab Emirates.

"Good morning, Dan Steele," he answered, anticipating the silky German accent from months ago.

"I thought you might be an early riser. We met some time ago in Dubai. You no doubt are aware of our successes in Europe last week. Al-Qaeda takes responsibility for those operations. It's also to remind you our organization is not responsible for the Veterans Day incidents in the United States except for the one in Newport, RI."

His blood boiled over. "To label the operations in Europe as successful is perverted. I acknowledge your killing of so many innocent people but hoped you would make good on your pledge to identify the groups carrying out the attacks in Norfolk, Fresno and Philadelphia," Dan angrily spat the words into the receiver, knowing his tone was offensive to Middle Easterners. He wanted to provoke his acquaintance into providing more information.

"I grew up here in the Emirates where my father fished the Gulf and tried pearling for a while. His tribe got lost in one of the power struggles, and he never got a chance to enjoy the benefits of our booming economy driven by Petro wealth. But he would often remind me 'Patience is a virtue.' I think this is a phase you should adopt when you talk with people wanting to help you with your dilemma. Don't you agree?"

"Interesting. My father used to tell me the same thing. The only difference is that people, many innocent people are dying every day because of terrorism ordered by your group. We value life and want to stop this madness as soon as possible. So, I will be patient until your group and all the other terror cells are found and burned out of existence."

"I understand your view, but what's underway cannot be stopped. Al-Qaeda or any of our growing number of worldwide offspring did not ruin your Veterans Day. I can tell you that with certainty."

The call ended abruptly.

Mid-afternoon, the inter-office mail cart stopped outside Dan's office, and Alvin carried a thick envelope to Dan's desk and handed it to him.

"Thanks Alvin," said Dan, looking up at the smiling mailman. Alvin silently saluted Dan and headed out of the office. Alvin left the Navy during his first tour because of a heart murmur not detected during his entry physical exam at the recruiting center. He landed on his feet and worked for a defense contractor for several years before moving over to the Homeland Security. There he found an interested and more diverse workforce than the contractors working for DOD. He found most ex-military people appreciated an occasional salute rather than a conversation about the mail he'd just delivered. Dan always engaged Alvin and enjoyed the back and forth that military men seem to share.

He opened the envelope and found a classified assessment prepared for Meg with a handwritten note from David forwarding the report and expressing hope it might be useful to the investigation. Dan took his eyes off the paper, stared to a distant place and thought again about Meg. She'd been his right hand during all of this, and he never even asked if she had parents or a significant other who was dealing with the grief of losing her. Was he developing that cold and uncaring attitude so pervasive inside the beltway?

Turning back to the document, he found it originated at the CIA. It contained a number of country assessments from the field regarding terrorist profiles and known links to Al-Qaeda. Several of the pages were marked Sensitive Compartmented Information and contained nothing more than an uncorrelated chronology of events. Meg provided a narrative starting point related to Stormy Weather and the scope of the Task Force's effort as well as key words to trigger a connection, such as the Double Eagle tattoo, the drilling tool made in Switzerland, Dan's bizarre meeting in Dubai, Fresno, the Yellow Line, TSA Philadelphia, and the Chesapeake Bay Bridge and Tunnel. Much of the material was "off the shelf" meaning intelligence assessments completed for other reasons and just forwarded as a harried station chief's answer to specific tasking. What was the famous Pentagon line? An action passed is an action completed. Dan did not mind spending the time going through the stack of paper thrown together in response to Meg.

After plowing through half of the thick compendium, Dan came across a surprising entry. The report involved a shipping clerk picked up for petty theft in Tirana, Albania.

Arrested before for public drunkenness, the man had a spotty history of skimming cargo and selling it on the thriving black market where the people of Tirana shop similar to westerners going to the mall. Everything imaginable is available for the picky shopper seeking brand-name merchandise. The clerk helped himself to the contents of tri-walls damaged by the stevedores or the trucks transporting cargo between the docks and the warehouses. Sometimes, a container would be pilfered with the custom's seals still intact. Nothing was considered off-limits, and high volume commodities could add 200-300% to the meager wages paid to the supply chain expeditors to whom these goods were entrusted. Most shippers expected perhaps ten percent of the total volume of goods would be lost while in transit.

The police officer ridiculed the shipping clerk for stealing paint and said he didn't have an interest in writing up the report.

"You know Anat, I am tired of filling out all the paperwork on you for every time you steal from these containers. The ports fees, the thefts, the cargo handling and forged bills of lading have given the city a bad reputation. You are supposed to be a responsible employee. How do you expect things will get better when every importer and exporter has to deal with people like you? Why are you stealing paint when you can buy it so cheaply in the market?"

Still drunk and worried the policeman might be annoyed enough to send him away to prison for a number of months that would cost him his job, Anat desperately tried a new course to deflect the focus from him to something else.

"I'll tell you about something I did last year that didn't end up being sold in the underground economy. I was asked by my boss to change a shipping manifest for a piece of cargo forwarded from a ship stranded for months. The cargo came from Italy. The equipment was an expensive Swiss drilling machine. I changed the manifest to list the item as a lathe so there would be no questions about it coming into the USA. My boss told me it would be used in some "tunnel work."

The interview ended when Anat vomited on the floor. The officer's billy club put Anat temporarily out of his misery and his face thudded to the floor, splattering the vomit on the officer's polished boots. The notes were incomplete and made Dan immediately queasy as he read the report and realized this drunk in Albania may have had a hand in his family's loss. He would ask for the previous reports on Anat to see if anything else bubbled up. This could be a breakthrough in the case if it could lead them to the organization which acquired the drilling machine. But, that would be handled as a routine matter taking weeks, and he knew the problem he faced was much more urgent.

Dan jotted some additional notes for follow-up as he continued to study the report and tried to see if there were other dots that could be connected with the vast storehouse of information generated by Stormy Weather.

Chapter 74

Boston, Massachusetts
February 22, 2018

Just a week after the contract between the City of Boston and Beverly Inshore was signed, permits were drawn and initial site preparation work on the Charles River Esplanade began. Sure, they were just getting started, but the city engineer was pleased the company mobilized quickly and seemed so well-organized. Beverly Inshore's site manager briefed the city's engineering team on the detailed timeline and set-up a collaborative website so anyone could access the integrated master schedule, status against the plan, subcontracts, meeting notes and contacts. It would be a first if the company could deliver on the plan they'd offered to the city in response to the competitive solicitation. Not only did Beverly Inshore beat all the other bidders by a wide margin, but they also provided an unusual and persuasive level of engineering detail, even though the company's track record was mixed. The new ownership seemed committed to making the company successful, and this was a solid step in the right direction. The city's sub-contracts team was unanimous in selecting Beverly Inshore for the project and spoke as if this job would begin a new era in city work.

The independent engineering report that led to the contract described the problems with settling of the Esplanade's crown jewel, the Edward A. Hatch Memorial Shell. Completed in 1940, the Hatch Shell was extensively overhauled in the early 1990s. However, the work centered on acoustics and restoring the shell's decorative interior, not on the structure itself. The report recommended excavation of the Charles River side of the structure's foundation, inspecting the piles for deterioration and re-setting the strength members by driving large steel-encased concrete piles down to the bedrock. The work scope also included installing a drainage system to carry away the water that sometimes pooled for days after a heavy rain. The system would route the water down to the Charles via a large drain pipe discharging under the normal water level in order to preserve the ambience of the venue.

Beverly Inshore provided extensive engineering calculations to support the drainage plan and alleviate any concern with the underwater discharge point. None of the city contract managers nor its engineers were aware of the fact that Double Eagle paid a highly respected out-of-state structural engineer handsomely to exaggerate the conditions and necessary scope of repair.

Early planning for the annual July 4th Concert was already underway, and the concert committee developed a slate of potential hosts who signaled interest in the event through their agents, pointing to other similar events they'd fronted. Beverly Inshore's detailed construction schedule contained at least thirty days of float which won the committee over. The structural work on the Hatch Shell would be completed by mid-May. If first impressions proved correct, Beverly Inshore was the right team to select for the project.

A week later, the construction supervisor, Jim Ward, walked through the snow to the job site and couldn't believe his eyes. As he approached, it was clear the job site was professionally organized and surprisingly clean. Excavation work began with properly sized equipment to dig down past the frost layer of the frozen ground. The site was a beehive of activity, humming like a well-lubricated machine. Piles of stone and pallets of plastic drainage pipe were staged with military precision. Site access was controlled and security evident. Jim Ward thought to himself that bringing this job in on budget and more important, on time, might give him an edge to replace the city's retiring senior engineer.

Ward opened the door of the Beverly Inshore trailer and the site manager introduced himself and offered coffee. The two sat at a small table talking about the schedule posted on the trailer wall and adjacent to an easel displaying all the permits necessary to begin work. Jim found the site manager relaxed and friendly. He exuded confidence, saying all the right things and answering a number of questions that revealed his total grasp of the construction field and the intricacies of the project. A native Bostonian, he promised transparency on the cost and schedule with the familiar local accent spoken between brothers. Trust built easily.

"And Jim, one thing I want to tell you right up front is that I view you as my customer. You will be the first to know of any schedule delays, material issues, or worksite problems. Or anything else. I promise you."

"I appreciate it," Jim replied. "I'd rather be focused on the work at hand than answering queries from my boss at city hall or some Globe reporter trying to win a prize for investigative reporting."

"You know we've already had a number of visits down here from the water department and the local OSHA office. No issues at all, but, as you know, it requires keeping a steady strain on all the moving parts. I've got our daily progress meeting over in the production trailer in five minutes so I need to head over that way. Please feel free to stay here or join me if you'd like. If you need anything, just call Joyce and she'll run it down for you. I'll be back in thirty minutes. Just make yourself at home...this is your office too."

The site manager stood, pulled on his work coat and shook Ward's hand with a warm, firm grip. Jim sat there sipping his coffee, relaxed and smiling. He was feeling good about this job.

Chapter 75

DHS–Domestic Terrorism Annex
Washington, DC
February 23, 2018

The courier was obviously new. He had two large sealed cartons about twenty-four inches square that he said were to be personally delivered to the fourth floor, and he needed to have the recipients sign for them. Exasperated with his insistence and unfamiliarity with delivery processes, the receptionist finally told the man she would call the mail clerk to assist him. Minutes later, Alvin appeared in the lobby and spotted the courier. He waved to the receptionist and approached the man.

"Hey, good morning. I'm Alvin from the mailroom. How can I help you?"

"I have some packages here for floor four and need signatures." The broken English caught Alvin off guard.

"Where's Dave? He's usually the one who delivers to this building."

The man shrugged his shoulders.

Alvin replied, "I can sign for the boxes and will deliver them this morning."

The man shook his head and repeated that he had to deliver them in person and get signatures.

Alvin replied, "OK, who are the addressees? I'll see if they are here to accept them."

The man extended his electronic tablet and showed Alvin the names of Admiral James Wright and Dan Steele.

"Fine," said Alvin, "Please wait here, and I'll be back in a few minutes."

Thirty seconds later, Alvin appeared at Dan's door, winded. He took a couple of deep breaths and then spoke.

"Dan, there's a guy downstairs trying to deliver a couple of large boxes to the Admiral and you and claims you have to sign for them. This is no delivery man. He looks like a cage fighter. Tough as nails, broken English and an accent I can't recognize as anything I've ever heard. And the uniform he's wearing doesn't fit. The guy is stuffed into it. I interviewed with the same company years ago, and they always make sure that their employees' uniforms fit."

"How big are the packages?"

Alvin replied, extending his arms: "About this big. Square and all taped up."

Dan didn't hesitate, "OK, Alvin, I want you to take charge and evacuate the building. Get the folks out of here. Exit through the rear doors only and tell them to move a block away. I'll call the bomb squad and will head down and meet the guy in five minutes. Maybe I can buy some time but get moving now."

"Good morning 911, how may I direct your call?"

"Bomb squad." Dan quickly relayed the information. He left the building with other employees and circled back to the coffee shop on the opposite side of the street from the main entrance. He ordered a large black coffee and walked up the building's front steps. He approached the man in the ill-fitting uniform and could immediately see the signs Alvin picked up along with a few others. The man's neck was corded with muscle visible under the shirt. His ears were badly cauliflowered and several white scars were visible on his scalp.

"Excuse me," said Dan as he watched the man turn and assume a combat stance. "Alvin said you have some packages for the fourth floor." Dan continued over to the collapsible hand truck to see if there was an address or office code on the cartons. There was none.

"Who's the sender?" Dan asked.

The man shrugged and then asked Dan to sign the electronic tablet in his hand. "Does the tracking number indicate where these came from?"

Dan maneuvered next to the man and tried to look at the tablet. The screen was blank. What did catch Dan's eye was the tattoo on the man's thick wrist—the double eagle.

Dan went back to the boxes. How long had it been five minutes? Eight minutes?

He looked back at the man and said, "If you don't mind, I think I'll open these up and make sure this material is for us." He noted the involuntary widening of the man's eyes. This was no suicide bomber. This was a survivor. Dan reasoned that opening the packages would cause the detonation or a touch on the tablet's screen would trigger a timer set to allow the delivery man to leave the building prior to a detonation.

Dan faced the giant and asked for his identification, triggering an instantaneous reaction. He reached inside his pocket and pulled out a telescoping ceramic rod that could cause instant incapacitation when wielded in the right hands. And these hands were obviously well-practiced. He backed up as the giant charged.

Dan threw the hot coffee into the assailant's face hoping it might slow down the assault, but the man apparently never felt it. The baton whizzed past his head as he side-stepped the first slash. A lunge followed jabbing him sharply in the sternum as he backed away from the attacker.

Wheeling to his left, Dan ducked through the metal detector portal and hurdled the turnstile, frantically searching for anything that could help him defend himself. He pulled a fire extinguisher off the wall, pulled the pin and aimed the hose at the enraged fighter. A small puff of CO_2 like the pressure from a house plant mister exited the discharge hose. Dan held the empty bottle to parry the next vicious slice of the baton then threw the metal cylinder at the killing machine. He brushed it away like a bothersome fly. Why hadn't he thought about grabbing something other than coffee before this confrontation? The administrative station he entered now appeared like a semi-circular cage, and Dan was no cage fighter.

The giant stalked his prey into the reception area with a crooked smile on his face. He had the advantage and swept in for the kill. Now face to face once again, Dan dodged the baton making a short arc and shattering the Formica desk top in a violent explosion. There was nowhere to run. One solid blow from the baton would likely leave him unconscious. Then, the man would simply activate the timers and leave the building. Cornered, and with no maneuvering room, Dan started a nervous bob and weave as the man approached, baton held high over his right shoulder ready to deliver a crushing blow. Dan crouched and pushed off the bottom of the counter as a last ditch effort to hit the man with a low tackle and get him on the ground. The man adjusted and avoided the impact of a direct tackle. Now on the floor, Dan had run out of any offensive moves. He was an easy target. The large man towering above him staggered with the first shot, but the baton continued downward to split Dan's head. A second shot filled the room and caused a rose to suddenly blossom on the scarred face as he fell heavily on top of Dan's outstretched body as he crumpled to the floor.

Dan pushed the giant off his body and slowly got up from the floor. He craned his neck over the desk and saw a compact uniformed police woman in the distance with a 9 mm pistol extending from her outstretched arms. Calmly, she spoke into her shoulder microphone, "all clear."

He stared at the expanding pool of blood and the ceramic wand still tightly gripped in the man's hand. Lucky again, he thought.

The police officer came through the portal and exclaimed, "Talk about meeting old shipmates in strange places. Dan, I can't believe it's you!" It took him a minute to recover.

The two had seen each other last when Dan's Seal Platoon embarked in a Navy destroyer operating in the Mediterranean Sea. Assigned as the ship's Operations Officer, Lieutenant Cass Thomas coordinated a clandestine surveillance mission into Libya. Conditions on the ground were far different than the intelligence reports described. The team found a well-armed and alert cadre of fighters with an effective perimeter patrol. Her quick thinking during the messy extraction prevented the team being overtaken by several light trucks fitted with fifty caliber machine guns that could have disabled their Rigid Hull Inflatable Boats (RHIB) and left them high and dry on an open beach. The ship was patrolling slowly off-shore about five miles from the beach. Acting as the ship's Tactical Action Officer, she ordered an unplanned Naval Gunfire Support Mission that first turned the dark beach into daylight with a pair of illumination rounds and then directed a lay down of some rapid fire high explosive five inch rounds between the Seals and the pursuing trucks. This effective cover fire enabled the team to beat a hasty and safe retreat. Short and simple, she'd saved the Team.

Unfortunately, her reward was a formal reprimand from a mean-spirited Commanding Officer effectively ending her career. She took the initiative to engage the enemy on her own, and the CO didn't arrive in the ship's Combat Direction Center until the five inch rounds were slamming into the beach. Dan tried to intervene with the skipper on Cass's behalf without success. An odd duck, he took a special delight in setting little "traps" for his junior officers to make sure he had something on all of them. After listening to his request for leniency, the Captain enjoyed reminding him that no one had the right to question his authority or decisions. He summarily dismissed Dan. Cass stayed in her stateroom for a few days and then quietly left the ship at the next scheduled port call. Bitter and confused, she broke off contact with her former shipmates altogether.

"You saved my skin for a second time! I had visions of my head being mounted on that guy's trophy wall."

"Well I didn't have any problem recognizing the bad guy this time," she laughed.

Within seconds, the bomb squad waddled into the foyer, their bodies thickened with heavy blast-proof protective clothing and faces covered with clear shields. Cass intercepted the team and pointed to the cartons on the hand truck while Dan told them on how they might be detonated. They were both shooed from the foyer. Cass decided she needed to reassure the hundreds of shocked employees still shivering in the cold, wondering why they'd been evacuated.

She shook her head, "This is going to be a mess. By the way, I'm ready to collect the steak dinner you promised me years ago and never delivered. I'll call you, OK?"

Cass pushed through the glass entryway doors and headed towards the crowd. By this time the usual collection of police cars, ambulances, EMT trucks and SWAT teams had descended on the area and condoned off a perimeter two full blocks from the building.

Dan needed a drink but resisted the temptation. He grabbed a fresh coffee across the street and walked towards the Metro Center, oblivious to the cold.

Chapter 76

Hatch Shell Construction Site
Boston, Massachusetts
February 28, 2018

With the steady progress Beverly Inshore made during the first weeks of the project, Jim Ward decided he could afford to take a long weekend and go skiing in New Hampshire with his son. Just after the morning meeting, he reviewed the plans for the remainder of the week and took the site manager aside, telling him he planned to take a trip to New Hampshire for some skiing.

"The forecast looks good, Jim. The weatherman is calling for a couple of inches of fresh snow tonight up in White Mountains if that's where you're headed."

Jim replied, "That's what I'm thinking. It's close enough so I can get back here in a few hours if I have to."

"Well, I don't see any problems for the next phase of the project. It's pretty straight-forward. We'll be trenching for the primary drainage system and backfilling it with crushed stone. Early next week we'll have all the secondary drains tied in. That's a witnessed inspection point and payment milestone, so we'll need you on site for the walk-through and sign off. I'll be thinking of you tackling those Black-Diamond trails while I'm here trying to wrestle the main drain pipe into place. I hate working with CPVC in the winter."

"You've got the wrong guy. Green circles are more my style."

The two men laughed as they shook hands, and the site manager returned to his desk in the trailer. He retrieved a new site plan from a cabinet that at first glance looked like all the other city-approved plans but included some additional excavation that no one else knew anything about. He had patiently waited for this opportunity. Smiling to himself, he picked up his brick radio and called the foreman.

Chapter 77

The White House Situation Room
Washington, DC
March 01, 2018

Everyone at the long conference room table stood as the President entered the room. More a military custom, it had gradually become a tradition in the White House because ninety-nine percent of the meetings held in that room in anyone's memory were related to military operations, mostly overseas in Syria, Iraq, Afghanistan and Yemen. Dan knew many of the Seal Team's covert operations were monitored from the same room.

He introduced himself from the podium and began a presentation marked with an alphabet soup of security classifications. The presentation went smoothly, and he responded to a number of questions. At the end, one of the Intelligence Community interns mustered the courage to ask the question on everyone's mind:

"Assuming your assessment is correct, do you have any idea what group is directing these attacks or from where? Do we have any idea of what could happen next?"

"No, I do not. We've tried to define a pattern of these attacks, and we've been through every attack linked to Al-Qaeda, ISIS, Boko Haram, Neo-Nazis, here, Europe, South America, and Africa and cannot find any links between the Veterans Day attacks and others, except what I've described. Without knowing the Indications and Warnings that might signal an attack or penetrating the planning process, it's impossible to predict when and where the next attack might occur."

The intern's likely boss replied, "Thanks, Dan. This is frustrating for all of us. I know you've been coordinating across the agencies, and I've been briefed in detail on the scope of this investigation." He turned towards the President and exclaimed, "Mr. President, we've been following every investigative lead and have gotten good cooperation from our allies. But, we keep running into blind alleys, and frankly I'm not optimistic about finding out who's responsible before the next attack."

The President turned a laser stare at Jim Wright and demanded, "Jim, is there anything you need that you're not getting from any part of my team?"

"Mr. President, at this stage, what we need is some good luck. In other words, to find some evidence that can be tracked, and correlated and followed to the source. Whoever they are, this is a capable group that does not leave any fingerprints on their operations...we don't know if it's a single group or a half-dozen. They've stumbled a couple of times, but otherwise they plan and execute as well as our special operators. We are studying the calendar and wondering when and what could possibly be their next target. We've got surveillance and uniformed as well as undercover teams almost everywhere, but they've not turned up anything yet. I think we are doing the right things, and, as the Secretary mentioned, we've gotten great cooperation from our allies and friends abroad."

"OK, thanks, Jim. Does anyone else have any ideas on something else we could do at this stage?" The table was silent. The President stood and looked towards the far end of the table: "Dan, keep going. We'll get them." He ended the meeting, "Thanks everyone."

As his car left the White House, the Admiral looked at Dan with dark and troubled eyes.

"Great job," he said, "You've really tackled this investigation head-on. Don't get discouraged. We'll get a break in this case. I can feel it."

Dan nodded his head as his mind zoomed to the sites of the Veterans Day attacks, trying yet again to find something that they'd not seen or understood. He was still deep in concentration when the car stopped in the underground garage at the Annex. He found himself back at his desk not even remembering if he talked to the Admiral during the car ride back or after. His brain was focused on something just beyond the right synapses required to grasp and to understand it.

Chapter 78

Hatch Shell Construction Site
Boston, Massachusetts
March 06, 2018

Jim Ward took an extra day off after skiing with his son and returned to the work site hoping the trust he'd put in Beverly Inshore had not been misplaced. It wasn't. He walked along the edge of the trench and inspected the drainage manifold that lay neatly on a bed of crushed stone just waiting for his inspection. Inside the site trailer, he viewed a video taken underwater of the steel sleeve protecting the last twenty-four inches of the large drainage pipe to prevent collapse after the backfill. Everything was in order. Even the grate was welded into place at pipe's termination in the Charles River located about a foot from the embankment to avoid silting. The work simply could not have been done any better. Elated, he tried hard to mask his enthusiasm. He did not want to appear too enamored with the contractor team. After all, he represented the City of Boston.

"Well, everything looks in order. I'll sign off on the inspection milestone, and you can start backfilling whenever you're ready. Good work!"

Chapter 79

DHS–Domestic Terrorism Annex
Washington, DC
March 07, 2018

Cass met Dan in the Annex lobby and while walking to the cafeteria, they recalled the day two weeks before when Cass stopped the giant killing machine from crushing his skull before detonating two cartons of explosives later disarmed by the bomb squad.

"Those cartons were filled with high grade C4 explosive with no chemical taggant which means they were smuggled into the US. I'm not laying the blame on my Customs and Border patrol colleagues, but there was enough material in those boxes to level this building and produce a devastating effect on the surrounding neighborhood."

"Like I said, you saved my skin a second time."

The pair chose a quiet end of the seating area to have lunch and catch up.

"So I left the ship and took forty-five days of leave before getting back here to DC where I grew up. The Navy assigned me to an Admin job over at the Washington Navy Yard where I spent six months partially fulfilling my service obligation before they offered an early out which I took in a heartbeat. I ended up applying for a Defense Security Services job and have been with them ever since. It pays the bills and keeps me busy, but I can't see staying there forever. Plus, the skipper made sure my service record contains an indelible DFC, Detachment for Cause, so my future opportunities working for the government are somewhat limited. How did you end up here in DHS?"

He recapped the highlights of the last few months and told her a little about what he was doing at the Annex. She shook her head in disbelief at the rapid and traumatic changes he lived through. Not wanting to dwell on the pain of the recent past, he shifted the conversation to the present.

"As the Ops Officer, you had a Top Secret clearance, right?"

"Yes, I was also read into a couple of special access surveillance programs we had going on behind the scenes. Why?"

"I'm struggling with this investigation and need some help I can trust. Just wondered if you might be interested in doing something different."

"Working with you here in DC?"

"Yep."

"Where do I sign?"

They both moved to lighter subjects about the previous deployment and some of the characters in the ship's company and the Seal Platoon. He walked with Cass back to the lobby and promised to be in touch.

Chapter 80

DHS–Domestic Terrorism Annex
Washington, DC
March 08, 2018

Dan received a routine INTERPOL report in response to a query Meg sent nearly two months before. The report confirmed there were many Albanians proud enough of their origins to have the Double Eagle needled onto their bodies. At least six tattoo shops in the capital city of Tirana alone offered a variety of artistic interpretations, and the investigators thumbed through photo albums displaying the work that the artists completed over the years. The report concluded that the double eagle tattoos were common and did not seem to be connected with any particular group. Bottom line: inconclusive.

While the report itself did not represent any investigative breakthrough, it convinced him that the answer to the domestic terrorism question somehow involved Albania. He googled the State Department and clicked on the link for the CIA World Fact book. There on the first page was the country's geographic location and its flag: a jet black double-headed eagle on a field of red. He didn't expect to find anything earthshattering in the public domain country background paper, but it did provide some historical context on the country and its tortuous history. He jotted some quick notes for his next meeting with the Admiral.

After the morning meeting with the team, Dan was walking back to his office when he met Jack Lang in the hallway.

"Hey," he said, "Sorry I missed the meeting this morning. I got a late start and just couldn't get through the traffic. A tractor trailer is burning out there on the beltway, and it's just like a massive parking lot."

"No problem, Jack. Nothing new this morning."

"I'm late, and there's nothing new so let's grab some lunch today down at the Indian place I've told you about. It's right around the corner, about a three minute walk. I'm headed into the tank. Let's meet in the lobby at noon."

Dan refused any social invitations from his team but thought recently he should do something more to motivate the group.

"Sure. I'll see you then."

The two were seated at the bay window in the front of a busy restaurant right at noontime, moving past a line of about a dozen people waiting for tables.

"You must be a regular to get this kind of attention," Dan remarked as he glanced at the menu.

"Since this project began in January, I usually make it here once a week."

The Maitre D' brought a basket of hot naan and bottle of imported sparkling water to the table and greeted Jack.

"Welcome my friend. I'm a bit surprised you are dining with another gentleman today. Welcome, sir. I have some delicious spiced lamb today accompanied with basmati rice and fresh dal. Would you like to try it?"

"Sounds good to me, Kamal. Dan, what will you have?"

"I'd like the same thing."

Kamal bowed slightly and headed towards the kitchen.

Dan tore off a piece of the hot naan and asked, "Where do you work when you're not here with the team?"

"When I'm not on the road, I work out of our M street office. Double Eagle is an international conglomerate and business takes me all over the place, mostly involved with the care and feeding of our major customers."

"I know that Double Eagle is one of DHS' major contractors and has a good reputation for program performance. Are any of your customers grousing about the change in your ability to see them because of this lengthy temporary assignment?"

"No. It's really the program team's responsibility day-to-day anyway. I represent the company's leadership when I meet with them. Right now, I don't own any specific program but work on top level customer relations and new business capture."

"What exactly is that?"

"Yeah, I forgot you are new to the acquisition side of things. What I try to do is look for government opportunities early in the planning phases, long before they are known to the masses or posted on the Fed Biz Ops website. We try to match up customer needs with some solution or product we have in the portfolio that is aligned. If we have a solid match then we engage the customer and try to convince them to award a contract to us directly without competition. If we don't have a solution in hand, then we make sure we understand the requirements, shape them as best we can and then decide to submit a proposal or not. Usually all the work done in the pre-solicitation phase is led by what we in industry refer to as the Capture Manager."

"Got it. So is someone managing your Capture now during this period? "

"Actually, I am between assignments so this works out perfectly. I'm not exactly sure what Spence will give me next."

"Spence?"

"My boss."

Dan never tasted any better Indian food. He and Jack got special attention, and he felt a little conspicuous by the meal's end. He checked his watch and told Jack he had to get back to a meeting in ten minutes. Jack grabbed the check, and Dan insisted on paying for his half of the bill.

"I'm a new civil servant and need this job. I can't be breaking any of the rules," Dan insisted.

"Don't worry, no one will even know."

"I will, so what's my half?"

"Twenty dollars."

Dan slid twenty-five dollars over to Jack. "Great lunch, Jack. Here's a few dollars for Kamal for the service. I enjoyed it. Thanks. See you back in the office."

After Dan left, Jack laid a crisp $100.00 bill on the table and left the restaurant.

Chapter 81

DHS–Domestic Terrorism Annex
Washington, DC
March 08, 2018

Dan felt energized after the lunch with Jack. He sent a quick email to a DHS IT lead and an NSA contact. The email had no content, just a subject line: "Execute Internal Watch". He then prepared the equivalent of a high priority international all-points bulletin query on an individual named "Spence" and any connection to Double Eagle and Albania. The query would be widely distributed within INTERPOL and friendly intelligence agencies as well as NATO. Dan smiled to himself as he hit the send button on his computer, the equivalent of putting a nice piece of cheddar cheese on the spring-loaded catch of a mousetrap.

Chapter 82

FBI Headquarters
Washington, DC
March 09, 2018

"Good morning," welcomed the tall, lanky man at the podium as he looked out over a crowd of thirty people representing all the agencies involved in preparations for the President's visit to Boston.

"For those of you I've not met, I'm agent Bill Streeter assigned to coordinate POTUS' visit to Boston. I just have some details to go over with you before we break into the planning cells and run down the action items. We also have a guest speaker, Dan Steele, from the DHS Domestic Terrorism group who will give you an overview of an ongoing investigation of importance to all of us."

The lights dimmed and a large screen filled with an overhead view of the city.

"OK, folks, we are now about 120 days out, and I wanted to bring everyone up to speed on our takeover of the city. In terms of logistics, the Advance Team will depart Andrews at 11:00 a.m. 09 May. We will accept your cargo until 1600 hours on May 7th. Otherwise, you'll be on your own to haul it north. We've booked a hotel overlooking the Esplanade that now occupies the site of the former Charles Street jail."

A few laughs rippled through the room as he continued: "I know what you're thinking, but the jail was converted years ago and is now a very upscale place that greatly exceeds our per diem rate. But don't worry, we are covered by the 300% rule for lodging." The agent continued the briefing for another 15 minutes, reminding everyone that all the information could be found on the secure website before introducing Dan.

"Thanks, Bill," said Dan as he got behind the podium. "What you're about to hear this morning is a summary of a classified effort undertaken by the DHS Domestic Terrorism Unit earlier this year. Our Director, Admiral Jim Wright, asked that you be briefed on another threat we've been tracking which could target Boston. We believe today the Veterans Day attacks in Philadelphia, Fresno, and the

Tidewater area were caused by a cell or cells of terrorists operating from here in the United States. They may or may not be linked to Al-Qaeda or one of its offshoots. We just don't know. What we do know is the group is disciplined, well-financed with worldwide connections, and they don't leave much behind. I can tell you we've got lots of activity going on both here and overseas, but we've not been able to break into their communications nets or get inside their organizations. I know it's not much to go on. I'll keep Bill posted and will share all the leads I can with this team. Are there any questions?"

Most of the people were stunned with the news, some disappointed with the scant level of detail and the remainder so numbed by their years of government service that it didn't even get their attention. There were no questions.

Chapter 83

DHS–Domestic Terrorism Annex
Washington, DC
March 15, 2018

Reports flowed in from all over the world regarding Dan's query on Spence, mostly isolated data points that were arranged on a large magnetic board inside the war room. The Baroness of the Austrian family that had adopted Spence told investigators she remembered Spence as a bright boy and hard worker who was her bedmate on occasion. A University professor also recalled that he was a gifted student with little interest in complying with the school rules or academic standards.

Several minor scrapes with the law turned up too, suggesting Spence deftly managed a network of thieves and fenced stolen goods. Somehow, he managed to keep himself separated from the work itself and was never formally charged. His adoptive family carefully protected the Baron's name, and the police were happy to overlook these minor childhood infractions. Still missing were the details of his emigration to the United States. Also of interest was the lack of any public information connecting Spence with Double Eagle. While no data is helpful in some cases, in this case it was not. Dan wondered whether Jack purposely gave him false information or whether he unintentionally slipped during their conversation.

Of primary importance were the two emails he received in response to his "Execute Internal Watch" order of the previous week. Both emails simply had a + in the subject line. A classified meeting with the two respondents was arranged for the next morning at a Sensitive Compartmented Information Facility or SCIF located at DHS Headquarters.

Chapter 84

DHS Headquarters–Nebraska Avenue Complex
Washington, DC
March 16, 2018

Hundreds of employees already moved to the new DHS complex located in Anacostia on the site of Saint Elizabeth's hospital, a former psychiatric facility with long views of the Capital skyline. However, the secure facility on Nebraska Avenue still had responsibility for answering non-mainstream tasks such as Dan's. The three men met in the bowels of the facility behind a heavy steel door that protected a small room resembling an anechoic chamber. The walls were covered with triangular, pointed foam horns that allowed no sound of any sort to escape. There were no exposed conduits and no communications equipment permitted.

A month before, Dan realized that data from the Stormy Weather special task team might be leaking out. He and Sandy presented Admiral Wright with a simple plan designed to ferret out any insiders who might be serving as information sources for people outside the program. The query on Spence set the approved plan in motion. Both NSA and the DHS IT Security officers created a limited internal and external surveillance capability of phone and computer connections made by Annex employees and select transatlantic organizations. NSA discovered an international call was placed to Double Eagle's central office number in Europe, and DHS IT team intercepted a paging message sent shortly after the query hit the wires from the Annex to an unknown external addressee. The call had originated from an INTERPOL office in Brussels. The page was transmitted by the Admiral's point man for Domestic Terrorism. Dan had what he needed. He mentally prepared a short action list on his way back to the Annex.

Chapter 85

DHS–Domestic Terrorism Annex
Washington, DC
March 16, 2018

Dan grabbed Sandy and the two barged past Michelle and into the Admiral's office. The Admiral looked up and knew immediately the unplanned visit was urgent.

"Good morning men, please take a chair. You've got my undivided attention."

"Thanks Admiral. You recall we set-up the internal surveillance contingency some time ago to detect any Stormy Weather leaks?"

"Yes."

"The query I sent out last week on Spence prompted a call from the Annex placed within a minute of the individual accessing the program database files. The mole is Martin."

"Martin?"

"Yes sir. He has provided information to Double Eagle from our restricted file server that has not been made available to anyone outside the Stormy Weather team."

"God, it's hard to believe. I've known Martin for ten years. I thought he was a loyal plodder more interested in preserving the bureaucracy and following the rules than digging in, but I never thought he would be responsible for this kind of breach. What information did he pass?"

"We are not entirely certain because we haven't broken the encrypted message, but we know it was sent via a data pager and also via telephone."

Dan passed a typewritten page across the desk to the Admiral.

"Here is the transcript of the call picked up by NSA. There are some holes but it doesn't take much reading between the lines to see the information that was passed. Another message originated from INTERPOL shortly after the first so it's clear at least one of these organizations has penetrated both DHS and INTERPOL."

"This is what I call a sucking chest wound, gentlemen. Do either of you have a clue what steps we need to take now?"

"Let's see what Martin knows and then offer him a deal if he's willing to help us pinpoint the nerve center here in the States. One of the counter-intelligence teams from the CIA should be able to extract what he knows by explaining the alternatives he faces," Sandy offered.

"OK, I agree. What else? Dan?"

"Well Admiral, Stormy Weather has reached a point of diminishing returns. As a team, it feels like we are just shoveling sand against the tide. Everyone is exhausted. I have good solid contacts within the other agencies and can reach out if I need something specific. It's time to shift the work to an internal team. One request, though. I'd like to see if you can pull Cass Thomas from DSS to DHS. During the bomb threat, she saved lots of the people who work here, not to mention the building and me. I led a Seal platoon embarked in a destroyer over in the Med where she was the Ops officer, and she single-handedly saved the team during an extraction operation from Libya. Doing so got her cross-threaded with the CO and that ended her career. She's a smart lady, I trust her and I could use a fresh set of eyes. She's got a Top Secret clearance but would need to get read-in to the compartmented stuff. I gave Michelle all the details."

"Done. Anything more, gentlemen? Let's isolate Martin ASAP. I need to make some calls on this right away."

Chapter 86

M Street South East
Washington, DC
March 20, 2018

Admiral Wright invited the Stormy Weather team for lunch at one of the restaurants built to serve the hordes of US Government employees that moved to southeast Washington with the relocation of the Naval Sea Systems Command to the Navy Yard and the nearby construction of a lavish office building for the Department of Transportation. He knew the team struggled with the urgency of the assignment. Special assignments of this sort rarely lasted for more than forty-five days and, with the actions on Martin underway, it was an opportune time to end the Task Force. Standing at the head of the table, the Admiral addressed the group.

"Thanks to your efforts, we are closer to discovering the organization and reach of the group or groups behind the Veterans Day attacks on our country. I salute your individual contributions to this program, and I appreciate the willingness of your organizations to make you available. Our Commander-in-Chief feels the same way and has sent a letter of thanks to each of you via the head of your respective agency."

The Admiral's words would usually signal the end of the event but a large woman in a rumpled suit stood and addressed the group.

"Admiral, this has been the best inter-agency team that I've worked on in my twenty-seven years with the government. Our progress would not have happened without Dan's leadership. I for one would follow him anywhere."

Other similar remarks followed before the group split up and went their separate ways. Dan and the Admiral headed back to the Annex in the Admiral's car.

"Admiral, thanks for getting those letters for everyone. I know they will treasure them."

"You've led some people on this program that will be your friends and will watch your back. As I'm sure you are discovering, that's important here in Washington. You have also made a very good impression at the top. The President wrote you a letter, rejecting my proposed draft and writing it longhand. Here's the copy he sent me."

Dan read the letter. The President unexpectedly invited him to fly to Boston on Air Force One to attend an Independence Day summit with other foreign leaders and dignitaries.

Chapter 87

Double Eagle Headquarters
M Street NW
Washington, DC
March 21, 2018

Jack took a seat in front of Spence's desk.

"I'm surprised the Admiral decided to pull the plug on Stormy Weather. Some of the others were too. Maybe they have concluded that it's Al-Qaeda after all. I'd like to see that group and all their sick offshoots rolled back, but I think we were onto something. Budget issues don't seem to be a likely reason to shut it down."

Spence looked hard at Jack and shook his head. "You are naive. The government is just not that decisive or nimble. Shutting down the Task Force is just too abrupt. The President doesn't commission one of these groups and then stop it mid-stream. And it would be his call, not Wright's. Something in this story just does not ring true."

"I see your point, but the fact that the President signed out letters to the team confirms he knew what's going on. On the other hand, maybe they found something that they couldn't stomach and are keeping it under wraps?"

"I doubt the President even saw those letters. They use an iron hand to sign most of the routine stuff requiring his signature anyway." Spence paused. "Tell me more about Dan. I'd like to understand him better."

"He's a straight arrow. Follows the book, at least in his current capacity. He's managed the team well and has been out front on all the problems we've faced. Dogged determination and an incredible work ethic. All the praise he received at the lunch yesterday seemed a little over the top. He turned red when the woman from the CIA said she'd follow him anywhere."

"How much do you think is going on behind closed doors that the team is not aware of?"

"Hard to tell. Far as I can see, everyone is one the same page at the meetings, and Dan is always accessible. He spends a lot of time every day in the team room so I cannot imagine that he's got a separate or parallel effort on this. Maybe someone else, but not him. Maybe he's now out of a job, I don't know."

"Is there anyone on the team who seems to be a confidante or meets with him separately?"

"No, as a matter of fact, he went to lunch with me the other day, and that's the first meal I've seen him take outside the office."

"How about on the personal front? You know, bad habits, addictions, any chinks in his armor?"

"Nope."

"OK, I just want to be prepared to deal with him if he causes us any problems. I'd like you to keep a pulse on him. I sense he's much sharper than you estimate."

Chapter 88

Vlore, Albania
March 28, 2018

It was a particularly boring night in the police station in the seacoast town of Vlore. The usual drunks were sleeping and a chilly breeze was pushing in from the Adriatic Sea. Only a howling dog disrupted the peace. The last ferry from the Italian port of Brindisi would be arriving in ten minutes, and there were only two more hours in his shift. The desk telephone broke the silence, and he ignored its first two rings. He picked up on the third and heard an excited voice competing with a loud background hum. The call was patched from the ferryboat's VHF radio to a landline.

The Lieutenant grabbed the keys and his uniform hat and gave instructions to the sergeant as he passed the empty cells and left the building. The streets were quiet so he did not use his emergency lights or siren. He had plenty of time to reach the port. Piecing together the Captain's garbled transmission, he knew there was a fight with injuries so he also contacted the local hospital to send an ambulance. Fights were frequent aboard the ferries transporting passengers between the two countries, especially the ones operating overnight.

The clunky looking boat eased alongside its customary berth where two large tractor tires were chained against the pilings to protect the decrepit pier. Two deck hands stepped across to the thick timbers facing the pier and covering its concrete surface, looping tattered eyes of fraying manila line from the bow and stern over large rusty steel bollards. Each stepped back aboard and secured the lines to cleats on the boat deck and then together shoved the gangway forward bridging the gap between the ferry's deck and the pier with a piercing metal to metal screech.

The Lieutenant boarded first and told one of the deckhands to keep all the passengers onboard. He met the Captain at the end of the gangway and disappeared through a door into the interior. Ignoring the hapless deckhand, the passengers went down the gangway or stepped across to the pier and vanished in the night. No one would wait for the

Lieutenant to question them. If it were important, he could find most of them in the city the next day.

Off the main deck's central passageway, the Captain opened a door to what appeared to be an abattoir. Spattered blood covered the deck and walls of the small day cabin. Crumpled on the deck against the single bunk was a man savagely attacked and left for dead. The man's heart was still beating and pumping out blood through a dozen leaks in his body.

From statements taken by the first mate, the man was traveling alone and spent most of his time at the bar since boarding at about 10:00 p.m. for the overnight trip to Vlore. The bartender claimed an argument began about 4:00 a.m. between the nearly dead drunk and an unidentified passenger thought to be an Albanian national. The Albanian challenged the man after he made a series of comments about how stupid his countrymen had been and mocked the national Ponzi scheme that led to yet another economic collapse. A shoving match ensued ending with a spilled drink and threats from the drunk who disappeared several minutes later. The bartender believed he'd probably passed out somewhere. He was discovered thirty minutes before docking by one of the day cabin attendants.

The Lieutenant asked the bartender to describe the man, and he offered a non-descript profile fitting most middle aged men. The bartender did add that the man arguing with the drunk had a long straight scar on his cheek which ended at his chin and a large tattoo of a double-eagle on the palm of his hand.

A small town of less than 100,000 people, Vlore's locals all knew each other and lived in a close-knit almost communal environment. Generations were born and raised there and had little interest in venturing beyond the town. The lieutenant knew the man suspected of the crime. As he left the now deserted ferry, his simple plans for the day, to finish his shift, drive home and join his wife in bed had been dashed. The long night would be followed by an even longer day.

Viorel Stoica did nothing to cover-up his crime. The police found his blood-covered shirt balled up and thrown in the corner of the room. Blood coagulated in the sink where he'd washed his hands and traces of blood were still in the fingerprints he'd left on the bottle of cheap Rakia on the bedside table. Snoring loudly in a tangle of stained and dirty bedsheets, the tattoo could be seen from the doorway on his extended hand. The man cooperated sullenly as he traded the squalor of his apartment for a jail cell smelling strongly of disinfectant. Later the same day, he appeared before a magistrate.

"How do you plead, Mr. Stoica? Are you guilty of this murder or not guilty?" the judge asked from behind the simple table that served as his bench.

"The man had no reason to speak of our country that way. I couldn't take his talk anymore. I followed him from the bar. He called my family animals and said the whole country of Albania was nothing more than Europe's pigsty. There was a pistol in his belt, and he reached for it. I had no choice to save my life. I wrestled him to the deck and then dragged him into an unlocked cabin along the passageway. He was quiet for a short time but then he called my mother and sisters whores. I kicked him. He kept talking so I took out my knife to quiet his tongue. Wouldn't you do the same?"

Without a response, the judge advised the man of his right to court-appointed representation. He signed the order to keep the man incarcerated until a trial could be set.

"Well, is there anything else you'd like to offer the court today?" the judge queried wearily.

"You will see. Our country will rise again to greatness, led by the Sons!"

"By whom?"

The man stood upright, proudly facing the bench and exclaimed, "By the Sons of Skanderbeg."

With a quizzical smile, the judge dismissed his statement and nodded to the deputies. The man was roughly pushed from the courtroom. Fearful of the treatment he would receive from the guards well known for their viciousness, the man successfully hung himself the first night in jail. Everyone seemed pleased with the outcome: no distraught family, no mourning, and no extra paperwork.

Later the same afternoon, the Lieutenant added Mr. Stoica's thin case file to the archives. The "Sons of Skanderbeg" comment raised the judge's curiosity, but he dismissed it without a second thought.

Chapter 89

DHS–Domestic Terrorism Annex
Washington, DC
March 30, 2018

After the first week of questioning, Martin started talking. A skilled team from the CIA and FBI were assigned to the case, and the pair had experience getting government employees to spill their guts without the use of any enhanced interrogation techniques. Both agents were surprised that he folded so quickly, but neither was convinced they'd gotten everything. He told them he'd been recruited as an inside source four years ago, and his task was limited to reporting information in a one way stream to people he never met, in exchange for deposits into an account opened in his wife's name. As a loyal public servant, he claimed that the only information he passed would eventually be released to the public anyway. The endless questions followed a contrived pattern Martin navigated easily. He'd worked in government long enough to know all the games.

"You know, information related to upcoming RFPs and that sort of thing."

"What about on-going investigations?"

"Sure if it looked like something that they were interested in."

"How did you know what they were interested in?"

"Well, it was easy," he answered, "I could track the payments based on what I passed along, and there was no payment for information they already knew."

"How often did you pass information and by what means?"

The information was passed via a numeric pager or international call to a drop box if urgent or to a General Delivery post office box in a Chicago box-pack-ship store if routine. He fell into Dan's trap by using his pager. Martin tried to explain his behavior and justify it to his inquisitors. Unexpected medical bills for his wife drained his savings, and he was just replacing the money he "lost". He'd done this for her and his family. Martin ignored the instructions to destroy any documents related to the deposits into his account. He gave up the bank information he conveniently kept on his computer, and investigators from the Treasury department were tracing the payment streams. The last fifteen to twenty percent of the information Martin knew would be difficult to extract.

"Martin, how would you like to be able to turn this situation around and make a fresh start? We are willing to consider a deal with you but need to understand whether or not you'd be able to work on the right side of the law."

Martin smiled to himself, knowing that the negotiating power shifted, and his position had become much stronger. They want me to continue working here and feed their own information through the same conduit.

"Well, sure. I mean if there's a way out of this mess, I'm listening."

What the investigators did not know is when Martin demonstrated the encrypted pager, he used a password to activate the device signaling that he'd been compromised, so any information he did send would be considered suspect by his handlers. He would tell them anything they wanted to hear to save his skin. He had plenty of money socked away which none of the investigators would ever find.

Chapter 90

DHS–Domestic Terrorism Annex
Washington, DC
April 02, 2018

Cass knocked and then opened Dan's door.

"Lieutenant Cass Thomas reporting for duty, sir."

Dan laughed and jumped up from his desk and shouted, "Hey Cass. Am I glad to see you! Sit down. Welcome to the DHS Domestic Terrorism Annex! You don't have a clue just how happy I am you are here."

"I'm glad someone's happy. My boss over at DSS was not pleased when the "by name" request hit his desk, but he'll get over it. I'm here for six months and that can be extended if the job is still required and you and I are not strangling each other."

"Good. I know your SCI clearance is being processed on the fast track, but I do have permission to read you in to some of the stuff we are working on in advance. Let's go to the War Room and start getting you up to speed."

Using a combination of his badge and a numeric keypad to open the door, he and Cass entered the War Room Dan created from a small unused conference room with a water leak in the ceiling that became an informal repository filled with project files, broken desk chairs, cork boards and posters. Dan emptied the room, had the leak fixed and navigated the bureaucracy to get it repainted, carpeted and fitted on three sides with parallel rows of roller clips where notes, presentations and maps could be hung up and easily rearranged. Well-lighted, the room still had a narrow conference table with six chairs and a light box for projecting. The fourth wall served as a makeshift screen.

"OK, let's start over here. This wall represents what the Task Force put together and the leads that have been generated and are still active. If you thought the Bureau of Naval Personnel moved at glacial speed, you should take a look at some of the other agencies. I'm sure a lot of this stuff got a full chain of command review before being released to Stormy Weather. I've learned first-hand that information is the coin of the realm here in DC."

Dan walked around the table and opened his arms. "On this wall are the international queries that we've made starting last fall when Meg Andrews and I were working together. She died because of this work so I know we are being watched from beyond these walls. Remind me to fill you in on the insider we recently flushed out who kept tabs on the department and Stormy Weather and reported regularly. The FBI and CIA are still working to get more details out of him, but it's slow going. They may try to turn him and get him to work for us."

"There's a lot of detail here, and it's spilled over onto the third wall but we're still nowhere close to connecting all the dots. One thing that would be helpful would be for you to look at all the stuff related to Albania and see what you can make of it. Sandy and I are planning a trip over there next week, but our objectives are fuzzy at this stage, so your input would be helpful." She acknowledged with a simple nod of her head.

He continued the whirlwind tour. "The third wall represents HUMINT reports from Al-Qaeda, ISIS, the Arabian Peninsula crowd and others captured in the last few years. You'll see my reports from a strange meeting over in Dubai with a man trying to convince me that Al-Qaeda was not responsible for the Veterans Day attacks, except for polluting the water supply up in Newport. Truth is, I believe him. The binders on the floor in front of each wall are my filing system and, as you can see, we're on our second course of files."

"OK, Dan, I've got it. This looks like mission impossible. By the way, in the US Navy, we call walls bulkheads, remember? Where's the coffee?

"We can get a cup down in the Admiral's office if you like black oil or let me take you across the street to a coffee shop that opens early and closes late. They have great coffee and you don't have to fight all the yuppies frequenting the better known shop on the other corner. Your call."

"Let's go across the street."

Chapter 91

Woodley Park
Washington, DC
April 04, 2018

Woodley Park reminded people of the early days of Haight-Ashbury in San Francisco. The area attracted an eclectic group of people and cultures living in a bustling tribute to diversity. Perhaps the proximity to the National Zoo drew them in. The Department of Homeland Security announced a second HS2 Industry Day being held in a large hotel with conference facilities rarely used since the National Harbor complex in Maryland opened. DHS had been strongly encouraged by a vocal DC politician to hold the conference within the District. The program revealed the Department had about two hours of presentation material packed into a six hour agenda that allocated plenty of time for networking and glad-handing with the military-industrial complex. After all, it did take one hand to wash the other.

The Contracting Officer presented the usual disclaimers, and the Program Manager provided additional details on work scope, the approved budget and the rough timeline for the Draft RFP. He encouraged feedback from contractors on any hard spots they saw in the draft solicitation, projecting proposals would be required in September and stating that the government intended to make an award before the end of the calendar year. Nothing changed. Once again the government offered an ambitious schedule for the award that was clearly not executable. In today's contracting environment, no one would make an award if they didn't think it was protest proof and the stakes were too high to follow the sanguine timeline outlined by the PM.

Chapter 92

Dulles International Airport
April 08, 2018

No direct flights connected the United States with Albania, so Sandy and Dan flew via Frankfurt, Germany. Though the Admiral offered his own plane, they decided to maintain a low profile to blend in with the 300 new friends electing to make the trip that evening. Sandy was able to finagle an aisle seat forward and Dan found himself wedged between two Germans determined to drink their way over the Atlantic. The layover in Frankfurt provided ample time to stretch. He persuaded the Lufthansa gate agent to give him an exit row seat on the next leg of the flight so his legs wouldn't cramp. Despite the fact that it was only 05:30 a.m. local time, the travelers enjoyed a cold beer. Compared with the transatlantic crossing, the flight to Tirana surprised both of them. The plane departed on time, the flight attendants were polite and responsive, the sandwiches they served were edible and the landing hard but otherwise uneventful.

Chapter 93

Tirana, Albania
April 09, 2018

After a perfunctory passport inspection, they entered the waiting area and spotted the hotel's shuttle driver holding a sign board with their last names scrawled on it. The Mother Teresa airport in Tirana was built on the outskirts of the sprawling city, and the van made its way on a road paved at one time but now rutted with potholes surrounded by broken pieces of asphalt. With only one stop enroute to allow a herder and his small flock to cross the road, the van passed through the countryside dotted with large round-top reinforced concrete bunkers built in the 1970s, following the country's formal withdrawal from the Warsaw Pact. Enver Hoxha, Albania's hardline communist leader, began the public works project that produced over a million of these structures. Several intersections boasted a bunker on every corner, begging the question of whether the military tacticians and the construction crews were ever on the same page. Today, most were abandoned, too deep to excavate and too heavy to remove.

The van snaked through the industrial part of town by way of crowded, narrow and unmarked streets to the city center where a modern structure on a modest rise greeted them. The Embassy made their reservations at the best hotel in the city that offered all the necessary amenities including a well-stocked bar, with both potables and attractive companions available to sooth the weary traveler.

Westerners filled the hotel. What a great target Dan lamented. He asked for a room on the second floor, and the desk clerk told him the Embassy confirmed rooms on the seventh floor already carefully prepared with a welcoming fruit basket and a bottle of local wine courtesy of the hotel GM. To the consternation of the day manager, Dan insisted and eventually got a room on the third floor. The room's last occupant was a heavy smoker. Dan opened the windows to change the air and to assess his surroundings. He used a small electronic device the size of a shaver to see if the room had been fitted with any listening devices and found none. He unpacked and took a quick shower and combat nap before meeting Sandy in the lobby at 6:00 p.m.

They walked downtown across the cobble-stoned plaza in front of the Parliament building for an early supper at a Greek restaurant. The agenda for the next day started with a meeting with the Embassy's Military Attaché at the hotel and lunch with the CIA Station Chief at noontime. Back in the hotel, Dan mindlessly surfed the channels on the small television for an hour before falling into a deep sleep. His expectations for the visit remained understandably low.

Chapter 94

Tirana, Albania
April 10, 2018

After a thirty minute run through the city to shake-off the jet lag and familiarize himself with the surroundings, Dan circumnavigated the hotel to cool off. He found a note from the front desk under his door to call Cass.

"Good morning, what's up?"

"I got another INTERPOL lead in this morning from Austria. This is a record nearly forty years old. A student named Spence Bektashi briefly attended the University in Vienna and provided a local Austrian address. He disclosed his birthplace as Durres, Albania."

"Sounds like a connection. I think Durres is west of here on the Adriatic. At least the Admiral will be satisfied that we are not on a wild goose chase. Anything else?"

"No, you are confusing me with a miracle worker. I've gotten through about one tenth of the material you've collected on this case and will see if I can plow through the rest of it while you're off on this boondoggle."

The meetings with the Attaché and lunch with CIA Station chief yielded nothing new.

After lunch, Dan and Sandy booked a car through the hotel and traveled to Durres. The driver had worked in Durres for several years and offered a non-stop commentary during their windshield tour of the seaside town. He pointed to the Durres Children's Hospital as the newest building in the town. It was constructed seven years earlier. On a hunch, Dan asked the driver to pull over and went up to the front door. There was a dedication plaque at the entryway telling the story in neat bronze letters.

Dedicated to all the Children of this town and
Anywhere in Albania in honor of
Valdete Bektashi
Donated by Double Eagle Industries
July 18, 2011

Dan ran back to the car.

"Sandy, this hospital was donated by Double Eagle Industries in honor of Spence's mother. She is still living just south of here on the coast."

"I know the house," said the driver.

A smiling woman answered the door and invited the trio into her spotless house with a stuccoed exterior, a red tile roof and all modern imported European appliances. Though bent over with a prominent dowager's hump on her back, the woman was pleased to have company and looked like she dressed up for the occasion. Crisply starched, her white blouse fit her petite frame as if it were custom tailored. Her gray hair was drawn back into a tight bun, and her face was full of expression. She offered them tea. She spoke halting English, and the driver helped translate when he could.

"We saw the children's hospital in town. It must be an honor to have a building donated to the town in your name."

"Yes, my son has been very generous. This house he built for me also."

"What is his name?"

"His father and I named him Bekim when he was born. He left Durres and went off to Europe as a teenager and changed his name to Spence. I guess it made things easier for him."

Dan tried to remain calm and patient, but the halting pace of the translated conversation made it difficult. He also wondered about the accuracy of the driver's conversion into English.

"This tea is excellent. Is it local?" asked Dan.

"No. My son sent it from London."

"Thoughtful of him," Dan replied, smiling at the woman. "Do you have a photograph of your son?"

"Oh, yes. He asked me not display it on the wall because he's a private man."

The woman pushed herself up and walked to a hand-carved keepsake chest in the corner of the room, opening the lid and coming back with a thick stack of papers kept together with a faded red ribbon. The first photo she passed was taken seven years ago at the dedication ceremony. There were newspaper clippings from the start of construction as well as pictures, letters and postcards from various

European capitals that any mother might keep. The dots were now connected. After the men left, the woman sat alone in a rocking chair and waited for her son's weekly call. She was excited when the phone rang, and she told him about the nice visitors she'd had earlier in the day.

Chapter 95

Tirana, Albania
April 10, 2018

Dan and Sandy watched the setting sun as they ate local fish at a beach side restaurant and recapped the next steps before returning to Tirana. Neither man could believe what a stroke of luck they'd had with the visit.

Hours later, Dan's hotel phone rang loudly. He heard Sandy's hushed voice on the line: "Get out."

Without hesitation, he grabbed his phone and wallet, opened the window and vaulted the iron railing, landing in a small, empty raised bed on the sloping landscape. He could hear loud voices from the window of his room. Moving in the shadow of the building, he ran up the hill and into a stand of spindly pines ringing the parking lot.

Lights winked on throughout the upper floors of the hotel. Minutes later, an ambulance screamed its arrival at the hotel, and the medics ran a single gurney into the building. He moved to get a better view of the hotel's front entrance and saw the loaded gurney emerge from the bright entry lights. He could see no IV bag or resuscitation efforts going on. Dan had a sinking feeling that the lifeless form pushed into the ambulance was Sandy.

He punched the Admiral's desk phone code into his cell phone and left a message: "Admiral, Sandy and I were ambushed at the hotel in Tirana tonight. I made it out OK, but I'm not sure about Sandy. More to follow."

Dan spent the night inside the United States Embassy and left mid-morning the following day on a plane the Admiral commandeered from the Flag Officer in charge of the US Naval forces in Europe. Sandy's condition remained critical, and he stayed in the local hospital, guarded by US Marines from the Embassy. Important intelligence dots were connected and triggered a quick, violent response that must have been directed from someone inside Double Eagle Industries. Now the enemy had exposed itself and the ongoing multiple front operations could be focused on a single entity. This group, masquerading as Al

Qaeda, had incredible reach and a clear command and control system to react so quickly. Facing a potent enemy and devising the right tactics to beat them was one thing. Fighting against a seemingly omniscient enemy that remained in the shadows was another.

Chapter 96

Istanbul, Turkey
April 11, 2018

Easy to spot, Mikhail Zubov's gray face looked like deeply fissured stone and his large, callused hands were missing both the ring and small fingers. An undercover officer patrolling Taksim Square saw the man enter a small restaurant and called the Lieutenant.

"You won't believe who I'm watching right here in Taksim."

"Bridgett Bardot with a see-through blouse."

"No. And because you will never guess in the next ten years, I will tell you. Mikhail Zubov is sitting in the small place right next to the sweet house where you buy your Turkish Viagra. It's him, I'm certain of it."

"How many are with him? Are they armed?"

"He and one other Russian. The third guy I cannot recognize but he looks local. They just walked up the square and right into the restaurant. I don't see any watchdogs anywhere."

"I'll see the inspector right away and call you back."

Twenty minutes later, a dark blue van parked on one of the square's side streets. The undercover officer watched eight heavily armed ninja-like special warriors emerge and take positions in the front and the rear of the restaurant. Another man wearing a fedora and a thick black mustache left the passenger side of the van and walked straight into the restaurant. It was the inspector himself. All three men were arrested quietly after the Inspector drew his revolver and asked the men to come with him quietly, reassuring them that a detail of special police surrounded the building and escape was impossible.

The word spread around Istanbul and over the government and international networks. Mikhail Zubov, a man who appeared on every terror watch list in every country, had been captured. He was the man responsible for supplying terrorists' special needs around the world, in particular for fissionable material sourced from Ukraine and chemical weapons supposedly destroyed under the watchful eyes of international observers.

After processing and a brief press conference where he was paraded like a red carpet model in front of hundreds of cameras, Zubov found himself in a US-funded rendition center located well under the city in a tiled water cistern with vaulted ceilings built by the Romans centuries before. After the rendition practices had been halted by a prior Administration responding to the pleas from the left, the Istanbul police took over the space for their own interrogations. The first night, Zubov found the lack of any sound in his cell comforting. He smiled, knowing the Turkish government would treat him well. There would be none of the harsher interrogation techniques such as the ones that took his fingers and other body parts not visible when he was clothed. In a sense, he was like a movie star. With so much attention, he would remain the darling of the international law organizations for years to come. With the solace of his rock star status, he fell into a deep sleep.

Chapter 97

DHS–Domestic Terrorism Annex
Washington, DC
April 11, 2018

During the flight back to the States, Dan crafted an action plan and called Cass to start the wheels turning. He's called the office several times and finally connected at 07:00 a.m. Eastern Standard Time.

"Hi, Cass. I'll be landing in a few hours but wanted you to get started on a couple of things, OK?"

"I've been worried sick. Are you all right?"

"Yes, and I just got an update on Sandy. He's still listed as critical, but his condition is stable. What I believe is the gunmen got a tip from inside the Embassy about what rooms we were assigned. I changed my room at the desk and they were acting on old information. I have this feeling they wanted me alive."

"There's no doubt you touched some sensitive pressure points."

"Right. Things are accelerating now, and I know we are getting closer."

"Glad you are safe and Sandy is out of the woods. What's on your action list?"

Dan dictated a series of actions that included all the agencies involved in Stormy Weather as well as Treasury, State, and the IRS. Electronic eavesdropping and plainclothes surveillance of the DC-based Double Eagle Industries building started within hours. Audits by the Treasury Department and IRS were notified the same day. Much to Dan's chagrin, there was insufficient evidence for a front door search warrant of the building but the surveillance actions set in motion would likely generate the basis for a probable cause finding by the judge.

"Anything else?" asked Cass. "I've got six legal pages of tasks here and need time to make this all happen."

"No, that's it for now. By the way, I forgot to thank you for the tip on Spence. With some good luck we are moving in the right quadrant. Great work!"

"My pleasure. Will you be in this afternoon or are you taking the rest of the day off?"

"See you soon."

Chapter 98

Double Eagle Headquarters
M Street Georgetown
Washington, DC
April 13, 2018

Spence stood over his Executive Assistant's desk speaking in an uncharacteristically loud voice and wagging his finger when the elevator opened. He shifted gears fluidly.

"Good morning. Nice to see you Jack. Come into the office so we can talk." He turned back to the desk and delivered his parting shot, "When you locate Mr. Phillips, tell him to come up to the office immediately. I expect him within the hour."

"What's wrong, Spence? You are really wound up about something."

"DHS is playing games with us. They've put us under surveillance. Cameras and plainclothes cops are all over the block. I'm going to have Phillips make some gentle inquiries with the Justice Department and get some answers. We've got lots of friends over there, and I'd like to know if they were in the loop on this or whether it's the work of some loose cannon like your friend Steele."

Jack paused momentarily before responding. "On another topic, did you see the announcement about Mikhail Zubov getting arrested in Turkey a couple of days ago? I'm told he was a real sweetheart within the terrorist community."

"What did your friends tell you about Mikhail?"

"Only that he offers terror weapons to the highest bidder. People beat a path to his door. He's a shrewd businessman adept at lining up sellers and buyers all over the world. A real matchmaker."

"That's what they want you to think. The truth is he is one of the last true freedom fighters. He has helped the people of Georgia and most recently Ukraine fight the Russians. Yes, he brokers arms deals but nothing more exotic than AK-47s or M-16s. I heard a few years ago he diverted some Stinger ground to air missiles from Saudi Arabia, but that was unusual."

"Do you know him?"

"Of course, I've known him for the last thirty years, and he's taken care of a number of things for us."

"Really? I guess I had a somewhat narrow view of your concept of making the market. And your assessment is not what DHS claims. The CIA has been trying to nab him for years."

"Don't be so trusting of all these people you met during the DHS group grope, Jack. They are putting out a lot of nonsense and controlling the press." The words came like short lashes accompanied by a malevolent look which Jack had never seen on Spence. "By the way, what have you heard from Steele?"

"Nothing at all."

Spence's face flushed with red. "I thought I told you to keep track of him. Why haven't you followed my order? Do you think my direction to you is optional? What are you thinking? "

Jack flashed with anger, "I didn't come here to get chewed out. This conversation is over."

Jack pushed the chair back so hard that it toppled over. He walked to the elevator and mashed the button for the parking garage. Two cameras recorded his exit: one was part of the building's perimeter security and the other trained at the garage entrance had been installed the previous day as part of the surveillance effort. Both recorded a clear close-up of his exasperated expression as he left the building.

Chapter 99

Double Eagle Headquarters
M Street Georgetown
Washington, DC
April 13, 2018

Paul McGovern answered Spence's call on the first ring.

"Paul, please activate the device in Jack's phone. I sense he may be developing some views and personal attachments that will not be helpful to meeting our objectives."

Chapter 100

DHS–Domestic Terrorism Annex
Washington, DC
April 13, 2018

"Thanks for seeing me on short notice."

"Sure, Jack. What's up?"

"I had a blow-up with Spence this morning. He's hacked off about the surveillance on our Georgetown building and engaged someone to go directly to Justice about it. Can you fill me in on what's going on?"

"I can tell you this. As you know, Double Eagle is an important prime contractor for DHS. We've gotten some information tying the company to activities and people that raise questions about the company's methods. I don't know all the details and, because you are not publicly held, getting the information we'd like has been difficult. There is no question that the company's performance has made those questions moot in the past. Now they are not. I can't predict where this will end up, Jack, but my personal advice is to start looking at other employment options."

Part IV.

Chapter 101

The White House
Washington, DC
April 18, 2018

The Social Secretary finally got the invitation list chopped through the President's Chief of Staff. She couldn't believe all the effort required for this formality. She'd been in touch with all the embassies for months and rarely issued an invitation without knowing it would be accepted in advance. Standard policy. By later that day, everyone would have the President's invitation to visit Boston for a July 3rd summit on combatting terrorism and to join him and the rest of the United States in celebrating Independence Day. She sent a note to the White House Communications Team just in time for the daily press conference.

"A couple of announcements this morning. The President will host a meeting with a number of world leaders in Boston in early July, and will also attend a number of Independence Day events in the city including the Boston Pops concert and fireworks."

"Can you confirm the leaders attending the meeting?"

"No, I can tell you invitations have been sent, and we are waiting for responses. There will be more on the agenda as it's developed."

Spence was well aware of the President's plans long before the White House spokesman's announcement. There were other plans afoot to make this July 4th celebration a memorable one for the entire world.

Chapter 102

General Aviation Terminal
Dulles International Airport
April 22, 2018

At 06:00 a.m., Spence and Paul departed in a large company jet for the trip to Albania. They arrived in Tirana later that afternoon and were driven directly to Durres. Both men visited Spence's mother and brought her a large basket of gifts from the States. She loved everything about flowers, and the gardens around her small house were planted by a professional gardener and looked like a painting, vivid with colors and bursting with fresh scents. There were several silk blouses and skirts made for her by a Georgetown dress shop. The crisp cuffs and embroidered flowers always touched her. The woman beamed with pride and happiness. The conversation avoided his father. Both Spence and his mother chose to remain in denial that life was once hard and miserable for both of them. They were content to look back only to the time when he was able to care for his mother in this special way. He embraced his mother tenderly before leaving the bright cheery house. In high spirits, she waved from the window as the car pulled away from the curb and proceeded inland.

Chapter 103

Kruje, Albania
April 24, 2018

Kruje reflected the ancient heart and soul of Albania. A fortress city less than twenty miles from Tirana, it was the birthplace of Albanian hero and liberator Skanderbeg. His ancient castle was reserved for this special meeting of the Double Eagle leadership. They served in key positions within the company and also the "Sons of Skanderbeg." Spence scheduled this gathering months before and always looked forward to seeing all these men that he thought of as his other family.

Torches flickered brightly on the rough stone walls of the castle's grand hall as the medieval banquet began. Time had been rolled back to 1450 AD and to an outside observer, this would appear to be a faithful period reenactment. The twenty or so participants dressed like soldiers in Skanderbeg's populist Christian army, and the servers and attendants were also attired in the garb of the time. They feasted on spit-turned wild boar and simple root vegetables eaten with their hands, washed down with a strong fermented mead made for the event. A joyous occasion, there were loud peals of laughter from everywhere in the large hall, and the mead relaxed the mood of the participants.

After a grand entrance of Hollywood proportion, Spence was seated at the head of the long rough-hewn table. An imposing sight, he dressed as Skanderbeg himself, minus the full beard the hero wore. He carried a massive two-handled broad sword Skanderbeg used to kill as many as 3,000 men in the battles he fought. To the side, he placed a helmet crafted from an animal's skull. This gathering of the Double Eagle top leadership included levels one through three, the top two dozen planning and execution leads world-wide. The men behaved like brothers from a large, loyal family. All were tied somehow to Albania's past and certainly its future.

Though shrouded in secrecy, the gathering was known to the people of the town. Most were smart enough to not ask questions. The thought of attending such a gathering uninvited would never cross their minds. Not so for the American CIA chief from Tirana who never cared much about Albanian history or the people who made it. After all, he was a fully trained operative living in an unsophisticated society made up of people abandoned by the rest of the civilized world. He thought himself cleverer than anyone in the group assembled for the meeting. However, when he failed to deliver the meeting password at a checkpoint outside the castle, his fate was sealed. Weeks later, the smell of his decaying body would lead a team of local hikers to his final resting place on a steep mountainside far from Kruje. His body was dismembered and scattered over the hillside with an Albanian flag hanging limply from a sharp metal post anchored deep inside his torso.

After a final late night toast, the men returned to their quarters to sleep. The following day's meeting began after breakfast and followed a more traditional format complete with business suits and a specific agenda. After a series of reports and approval of specific business initiatives briefed by their sponsors, Spence offered a long-awaited update on the grand strategy for the next year.

"My fellow countrymen, my comrades in arms and the loyal Sons of Skanderbeg, I salute you as we begin another year of work to shape the destiny of our country and its people. This has been an eventful year on every front. Our business base around the globe is well-entrenched and secure with the highest profit levels we've ever recorded. Our organization relies on you, and the other Sons, to carry out our plans and to seize opportunities. You have remained alert and moved aggressively to capture those opportunities. Of particular importance, we have furthered our penetration of the United States' internal and external security apparatus and have added even more of the key government employees who make the policy and then execute it to our membership rolls."

He stood and began walking slowly around the conference table fitted in a modern setting sited within the long shadows of the castle walls but not detracting from its historic strength. "Last November's attacks have fueled and reinforced the idea that America is being attacked by Al-Qaeda or one of its many offshoots which are too numerous and unimportant to be mentioned here today. Of course, that was our intent. Suffice it to say that our stranglehold on the government of the world's largest democracy is gaining strength every day, and no one suspects we are behind it. We have successfully

236

evaded any real scrutiny by the US Government and continue to make progress on the domestic front."

Pausing at the head of the table, he looked at each of the men and continued, "I fully expect Double Eagle will be the largest Department of Homeland Security and perhaps the largest US Government contractor at this time next year after our win of a major new security project called Fortify. We will also accelerate the United States' need for increased domestic security after an event planned for Boston this summer. Our 2020 Vision is on track. I look forward to all of you joining me and being part of the new government here in our beloved country."

The formal meeting concluded with a luncheon where each of the men received their financial bonuses for the year, many of which totaled tens of millions of dollars. Extremely generous, Spence understood these bonuses tied each of the leaders to the vision emotionally, physically, and financially. It was a good year for Double Eagle and also the "Sons". After lunch, he led the group in a prayer passed down by Skanderbeg after he renounced the Muslim faith imposed on him by the Ottoman Empire and renewed and strengthened his ties with Rome and the Catholic Church. The well-known prayer invoked the holy trinity for the country's cause and was recited in unison with his war council before each battle. The 'Sons" followed the same practice, and they were certainly about to engage the enemy yet again.

Chapter 104

Tirana, Albania
April 25, 2018

After the guests departed, Spence and Paul relaxed in their rooms at the castle before the night flight back to Washington. Some additional un-manifested cargo had been loaded into the aircraft earlier that evening and a false bulkhead added to the main cabin. The plane took off into a black starless night enroute to Washington. There was no record of the brief stop the plane made in Manchester, NH at 03:00 a.m. to offload cargo and re-fuel before continuing on to Dulles.

Spence's plane landed at Dulles and taxied to the General Aviation terminal where it was met by a group of Customs and Border Protection Agents. The aircraft stairs were lowered onto the tarmac and a uniformed agent stepped into the plane.

"Good afternoon gentlemen, my name's Greely, and I'm from Customs and Border Protection. Your flight plan indicates you've come from Tirana, Albania, and we would like to search your aircraft as part of our random process to ensure compliance with US law."

Ready to deplane, Greely stopped Spence and Paul holding up his hand and continued, "Our search includes interviews with the plane's crew and all its passengers. We will inspect your customs declarations and any baggage and cargo. Don't worry, it shouldn't take too long, and I do appreciate your cooperation." Greely's broad smile and deliberate southern drawl said it all. This was no random search, and Spence knew there would be an unnecessarily long interview required.

He was fuming when he was released two hours later. The inspector said that the thorough search of the plane would take the rest of the day. All the paperwork was in order and the baggage check revealed nothing unusual. External cowlings and interior panels would be removed and inspected with nothing found.

"Well, Mr. Greely, I hope you and your colleagues are satisfied. I will follow-up with the Director of Customs and Border Protection personally to discuss this unnecessary and annoying process that's held me up from an important meeting. My company is a major sub-contractor supporting your organization and its operations, and this trumped-up inspection is anything but random. Paul, please take note of Mr. Greely's badge number so I can discuss his conduct during this waste of time."

Greely responded with a wide smile and looked directly at Spence, "Have a good day, gentlemen, and thanks so much for your cooperation. Bye bye!"

A photographer with the CBP team got excellent photos of Spence and Paul McGovern that would help unravel the mystery surrounding Double Eagle. The photos were sent to Dan as the search proceeded and now he could add the faces to the case he was building. Greely himself had been wired and now had a voice print that could also be used to identify the two in any future conversation the agencies were able to intercept and record.

Within minutes of the photos being released to law enforcement agencies worldwide, Spence knew the search of his plane was planned and confirmed that DHS had stepped up the game. Feeling well-insulated from the investigative effort, he already began thinking about his next move. Two could play this game of cat and mouse, and Spence remained confident Double Eagle would prove to be the most nimble.

Chapter 105

DHS–Domestic Terrorism Annex
Washington, DC
April 27, 2018

Sandy returned to the office in a limited capacity. He'd been medevac'd from Tirana to Frankfurt a few days after the shooting when his condition stabilized enough for air travel. He'd taken two bullets in the abdomen and one in his upper left arm and had lost a large amount of blood. After two operations to reconnect arteries and clean the wounds of metal fragments, he showed no signs of infection and was flown back to Washington. He faced a long road ahead with physical therapy three times a week. As he explained it, the one positive result of the shooting was the loss of nearly fifteen pounds which he tried to shed for years without success.

With Sandy's help, Dan and Cass completed a formal threat assessment of the unknown terrorist group they were still trying to identify and prepared to courier it over to the White House national security team. Dan briefed the Admiral on the contents and explained that the facts as presented would not change or modify any plans or behavior.

"There's no spin in this assessment at all. We present the facts and anything speculative is identified as such. There's just nothing else we can do. Based on what we know now, there is no greater threat in Boston than there is here in DC. Sandy fully agrees with the findings."

"To present the facts is our obligation. The reality? The President's schedule is driven more by politics and perception than by threats. You've done your job, so shoot the report over there and then get back to finding out who's behind this group or groups. By the way, we still haven't gotten anything new on Double Eagle to satisfy the judge have we?"

"No, the surveillance continues. We fended off a query by Justice which would have shut it down but haven't gotten any breakthroughs. CBP did intercept Spence's jet returning from Albania, and we got some good photos of him and his deputy as well as voice prints. Here's what they look like." Dan slid the photos across the desk, and the Admiral studied them intently.

"As you might expect, the aircraft was squeaky clean. Progress is slow."

"Are the audit teams turning anything up?"

"No sir, and they've gone through the books in great detail. The company's Headquarters is in Berlin, but I sense that all the strings are pulled from right here in DC."

The Admiral removed his glasses and looked up at his thinner old friend still in obvious pain, "Sandy, it's great to have you back. How do you feel?"

"I've learned I don't heal as quickly as I used to. I'm getting too old to be flying to distant places and being welcomed with a few bullets. This time I need to pace myself and follow the doctor's orders."

Chapter 106

Portsmouth, New Hampshire
May 04, 2018

An old sport fisherman with a faded signboard "Idle-Knot" across the stern crept out of the harbor with a pair of custom outriggers and a bank of short trolling rods lined up on the afterdeck. The steady throb of the inboard engines signaled to a trained ear that the diesels were properly tuned-up and would deliver all the power needed by a crew headed into the Atlantic Ocean. The new owner obviously put the money where it counted and would save the cosmetics until the end of his first season. Some other operators wondered whether there would be more competition for the summer market when similar boats would go out for full or half-day fishing excursions or whale watching. Though new to Portsmouth, the man at the wheel had the weathered look of a seasoned skipper. His underway plans involved neither fishing nor whales. He glanced at the chart and set the autopilot on a heading to a point due east of Boston. A simple coastal transit of exactly 100 nautical miles, he'd be anchored in Boston Harbor just after sunset.

Chapter 107

DHS–Domestic Terrorism Annex
Washington, DC
May 08, 2018

Despite the photos that were distributed widely through the international security community, new leads on Spence and Double Eagle slowed to a trickle, and the cost of round-the-clock surveillance became a budget issue at every staff meeting. When it came to resource discussions, Dan's operation provided an easy target for those trying to protect their own funds and people. It was a battle he would eventually lose because the green eyeshades would reduce or suspend continued funding, known in Beltway circles as death by a thousand cuts. He needed a game changer to start getting some traction.

Chapter 108

Boston Harbor
Boston, Massachusetts
May 08, 2018

Just after daybreak, "Idle-Knot" lay peacefully at anchor just west of the Charles River Yacht Club, a protected series of slips commanding fees of more than $20,000 a year. Judging by the boats moored there, the owners didn't much care. Located just inside the basin and a stone's throw from the drawbridge which would open for the tall-masted sport fisherman seeking access to the salt water, the club hosted a variety of power boats resting between the finger piers. A sophisticated entry system permitted those with privileges to access the property from the street entrance.

A gentle tidal current caused little eddies to form on the edges of the round mooring buoys that resembled giant bobbers. An ordinary-looking man rowed a small dingy out to the boat and came aboard over the transom. He huddled with the two men making the transit from Portsmouth who waited for his signal before transiting the protected entryway that started under the Charlestown Bridge and led to the narrow fifty foot cut through the old dam now supporting the Museum of Science. The passage funneled all the boat traffic leaving or returning to their moorings at clubs that dotted the inside of the Charles River basin. Amphibious "ducks' catered to city visitors and departed on wheels from the front of the Museum of Science before getting waterborne.

Thirty minutes later, "Idle-Knot" headed south towards the esplanade lagoons, formed by man-made slivers of land that protected the riverbanks like breakwaters and connected to the mainland by arched pedestrian footbridges. The boat anchored again a short distance from the Edward A. Hatch Memorial Shell. Busy with tourist tours, kayakers and other runabouts, no one paid any attention to the two men casting spinners near a known hole in the basin about sixty feet deep where large-mouth bass congregated in the summer. It was a beautiful sunny day with temperatures in the mid-60s and a gentle breeze finding its way through the harbor and into the Charles. A terrific day for fishing!

While the two men topside actively fished, the third man exited the boat via an enlarged hatch forward under the hull. Outfitted with a compact conformal rebreather, he steered a heavy canister made neutrally buoyant because of some inflatable tubes fitted along its length...a special Independence Day gift for the city that would be delivered early. Though the water inside the basin still had unhealthy levels of coliform bacteria and a host of other chemicals accumulated on the bottom discharged from factories as far west as Watertown, it was now clean enough for swimming during scheduled events.

Surprised with the six to eight feet of visibility, the man stayed close to the bottom and didn't care about water quality. He kicked slowly and steadily, guided by a simple sound source activated the same morning. His mission would be carried out without any permission. After nearly an hour of fishing, the two men stowed their rods and retrieved the anchor, then headed slowly east, maybe to see how the fishing outside the harbor might be. There were reports of striped bass being caught off the southern cape and in the Cape Cod Canal. Late that evening, the boat docked in Portsmouth, NH and three men left the boat together.

Chapter 109

Double Eagle Headquarters
M Street Georgetown
Washington, DC
May 08, 2018

The small pager device on Spence's desk buzzed and the small window lit up with the numeral "1". Spence smiled. Delighted, he buzzed security and told them he would depart in five minutes. The car waited for him outside the elevator and departed via the open metal door into the black night.

Chapter 110

Andrews Air Force Base
Maryland
May 14, 2018

The scheduled departure of the Advance Team was delayed by a storm moving up the East Coast which dumped heavy rain in the Mid-Atlantic and impacted the flow of cargo into Andrews. No one thought that the delay would alter the preparations for the President's visit to Boston. The Secret Service agent addressed a group of 200 uniformed personnel and civilians assembled in one of the hangars for the pre-departure briefing. On the airport's aprons, pallets of electronics, computers, and communications gear and a full armory disappeared into the cargo bays of the two story heavy lift transport planes. The event's choreographer, a tall loadmaster with a bullhorn, directed a complex logistics event being executed with a discipline that only comes with practice and having a "zero defects" attitude. Known as the Advance Team, this group of specialists would be heading to Boston in three large C-17 Globemaster transport planes being loaded with a fleet of armored cars, the White House Communications team, a cadre of media specialists and security experts from the other countries whose Heads of State were expected to attend.

Most of the aircraft space was dedicated to cargo but each of the planes had seating for 100 people on the upper deck. All the RSVPs were not in, but the plan needed to be executed now, even if the President had to cancel at the last minute. The team would take over the town unobtrusively and were now leaving after months of planning. There would be about 3,000 people ultimately descending on Boston to ensure the President was protected against any potential contingency, that the other Heads of State would be protected in the same manner and the celebration would take place without a hitch. There would be no stone left unturned nor any contingency, regardless of how farfetched, left to chance. This team would make the President's Independence Day visit to Boston like a routine day at the office.

Chapter 111

Double Eagle Headquarters
M Street Georgetown
Washington, DC
May 15, 2018

Jack avoided Spence since their last unpleasant exchange but had no good reason to ignore his request for an office meeting. Lately, things about his boss started to bother him. He couldn't put his finger on it, but he just harbored growing doubts about the businesses that operated under the Double Eagle logo. He paused at the door to Spence's office and felt relieved with the warm welcome.

"Come in, Jack, it's been a long time since we've had a chance to catch up. Where have you been?" Spence closed the distance between them and embraced Jack warmly.

"Sit down, Jack, would you like anything to drink? Coffee or tea?"

"No, I'm fine thanks. I just got back from our Berlin office where I facilitated an employee development program. Frankly, I found it a waste of my time and something HR could surely handle. Please don't misunderstand me. I enjoy the travel and representing the company at our affiliates but just think I'm better suited for some of the line responsibilities in the company rather than the staff stuff."

"I understand. We do have career plans for you, and I'd like nothing better than to see you running one of our companies in the future, either here or internationally. We are blessed to have a group of loyal senior managers who are still working and have not signaled any intention of leaving their posts. I cannot just let one of these stalwarts go for no reason. We are a growing business that will need capable, strong leaders in the near term and that's what I'm preparing you for— to lead one of our operating companies."

Spence took in an audible breath and he stood and faced Jack. "I must say I was deeply troubled by our last meeting. I hope you understand how important loyalty is to the leadership of this company. I trust the senior leaders to run their businesses in an aggressive manner and to be successful carrying out both the annual financial plan as well as the strategic plan on which they are all measured and held accountable. That's also what their compensation and bonus package is based on. You must be patient and prove yourself to move up to that level. I've made it a practice to consult with my senior leaders before making assignments to key positions. You've met many of those men and have made a good impression, but there's more to do. Do you understand?"

"Yes, I do. I see my contemporaries moving up to the VP slots in their companies but don't see the career path ahead for me as clearly as I want to."

"I can confirm you are on the fast track for promotion. It just takes a little longer in a company like ours." Sitting down, he took a sip of coffee. "Have you heard anything of interest from the old Stormy Weather team at DHS?"

"I lunched with one of the CIA guys the day I flew to Berlin. He said that things were quiet. He thinks the program was terminated because of budget pressures. Seems like they have started the summer sweep-up of appropriated funds early this year, and the formal program reviews will be starting in the next few weeks for most of the agencies. He thought DHS would take some hits and that the President might seek some relief but reminded me that the Oval Office can only spend so much good will on a single agency. This year, he'll need some strong support to get the Overseas Contingency Operations Funding he wants. I expect there will be some serious deal-making up on the Hill."

"What about Steele? He's been an active thorn in my side since the group stood up and he seems to turn up everywhere. I have to give him credit, though. As a new player here in town, he's made his mark."

"No, nothing much from him. Last time we talked he told me I should look for employment outside the company. He didn't provide any justification for that suggestion, but I found it curious and a bit surprising. A warning almost so I think he's holding any cards close to his vest. What do you think?"

"He is stepping way out of bounds. He doesn't understand business or contractors and seems oblivious to the relationship between the government and its primes. He is not someone to listen to. If he's not careful, he could find himself in real trouble. Please keep me up to speed on him."

The two talked for another forty-five minutes. Jack was traveling again out to the West Coast for an Award Fee Presentation and would leave later in the afternoon.

"Let's have lunch when you get back in town."

"Sure, I'll look forward to it."

Chapter 112

Boston, Massachusetts
May 16, 2018

The Advance Team occupied the top five floors of a hotel where they'd reserved all 300 rooms starting in early June. Located at the former site of the Charles Street jail on Beacon Hill and now upgraded into a luxury hotel boasting a new sixteen story tower, the hotel retained some of the original architecture including the thick granite walls and the remnants of several cells adjacent to the lobby bar. The location couldn't have been better. The hotel had a commanding view of the Charles River basin and looked down on the Esplanade and Hatch Shell. Adjacent to Storrow Drive and the Longfellow Bridge, two blocks from Massachusetts General Hospital, and about 500 yards northeast of the Hatch Shell, the location offered all the things they needed: access with multiple routes, proximity to the venue, height with a commanding view of an area protected by water, first class hospital facilities and a venue that could be locked down by any number of security teams.

Chapter 113

Hatch Shell
The Esplanade
Boston, Massachusetts
May 21, 2018

The city's Project Lead, Jim Ward, walked with his boss around the Hatch Shell where the newly seeded lawn had already been cut twice and there were no visible signs of the recently completed excavation project. The Beverly Inshore site manager trailed the two men.

"I knew I picked the right person to lead this effort. You delivered early and under budget- that's a first since I've had this job. And the site looks terrific. I'm certain none of the Feds descending on this place will appreciate all the hard work that's been accomplished here on a challenging timeline. They'll treat this place like an abandoned parking lot, but you've really shown your stuff here. This is first class work!"

"Thanks. Fortunately, I had a capable sub on this job. Beverly Inshore proved in spades that they were up to the task."

"A team effort, that's what I like to hear. Good on you. Why don't you come by sometime in the next couple of weeks, and we'll talk about what you'd like to manage next. Looks to me as if you've got one bright future ahead."

Chapter 114

IRS Headquarters
Washington, DC
May 24, 2018

After months of investigation that started in Double Eagle's West Virginia mine, the IRS finally had the evidence to charge the company with circumventing import laws by changing the cargo manifest and bringing the Swiss-made drilling machine into the United States. Of course it would be difficult to prove whether this was a clerical error or a conscious act to avoid the scrutiny of the customs agents who monitor goods coming into the United States.

Unfortunately, the judge reviewed the DHS probable cause petition yet again and determined that there was insufficient linkage between the violation and the proposed search of the company's Washington Headquarters.

The ruling disappointed Dan, but he was working on multiple fronts and one of those fronts was bound to yield something in time. What he didn't know was how much time he actually had to prevent the next act of terror. He had great respect for the law and would forge ahead in compliance until he thought it necessary to make some excursions on his own.

Chapter 115

DHS–Domestic Terrorism Annex
Washington, DC
May 30, 2018

A team of interrogators worked on Martin for nearly two months and concluded he was a very skillful liar and that the organization recruiting him as an insider structured the relationship so no one ever got a peek at its inner workings. Martin claimed his contact with the company had been mostly through the mail. He used the data pager only a few times. He explained that the pace of government made the mail system a good means of keeping people advised, and he'd found his detailed reports sent by mail generally resulted in higher payments. Recent information did not generate any payments so either the information had no particular value or perhaps the other side knew that Martin was compromised.

"So, what do we do now?"

"Well, I frankly think we've gotten everything we are going to get, Admiral," the interrogation lead responded. "We can continue but I'm not convinced he's got much more to give. The truth is that his phone records and bank statements were the best sources of information. I think he is a low level paper pusher who saw a chance to make a few bucks and took it."

"I'll bring in the personnel people, and we'll try to discharge Martin from government service and see if they'll impose a lifetime ban on his working anywhere in the Federal government. I wonder how many others are working in this building right now that are reporting to some other organization?"

Chapter 116

Double Eagle Headquarters
Berlin, Germany
June 12, 2018

German investigators were aware of the intense focus on Double Eagle in the United States. They followed an internal lead for months involving a German Air Force procurement of secure communications equipment. Though a routine process, it spawned a sting operation that uncovered bribery of an acquisition official by an employee of Double Eagle Industries. The procurement official did not follow protocol and directed the contract award go to a small German company with a poor track record of delivery and previous quality issues.

Their participation in the tender required a waiver that the official personally signed over the objections of his staff. Granting a waiver proved to be a critical misstep. Reported anonymously, the procurement Director asked for the matter to be investigated and the evidence fell into place. The bribery had been going on for a long period of time, and the two men became lax. A cash transaction being made right in the government office was captured on videotape. While bribery charges were brought against the Double Eagle employee, they were not sufficient to extend to the company that protested they had no knowledge of the employee's actions and their ethics policy prohibited such payments. He would be terminated immediately.

Chapter 117

DHS–Domestic Terrorism Annex
Washington, DC
June 18, 2018

Cass walked into the office and asked, "How was the weekend...do you do anything other than work and work-out?"

"Yeah, I went back to Virginia Beach for a hail and farewell for one of my old teammates. Also met with a realtor about the house, but I just can't go through it now. Every time I'm there I'll hear a sound and look up hoping to see Jill walk into the room."

"I've seen nothing new in the weekend traffic that would give us a stronger case to get a search warrant. They always seem to be one step ahead of us."

"I think we'd both be shocked if we really knew the extent they've penetrated the government. Like my mother used to say, 'Money is the root of all evil' and from what I can see, she was right. I got a call from this DHS security guy located over in one of the Anacostia buildings, and he said he wants to talk about some other connection they've found. I expect to be back here before noon."

He called for a local cab, and it was waiting when he walked outside the building. He leaned into the open sidewalk window and asked, "Steele?"

"Yes, that's right."

The cab pulled away from the curb and headed across town. Dan looked at his phone, and the screen suddenly looked out of focus. He saw the Plexiglas partition separating him from the driver was completely sealed and that a small vent in the roof liner was spewing a cloud of vapor into the passenger compartment. He reached for the window button and it was locked. His hand moved to the door handle when he blacked out. It didn't matter because it was locked too.

When he regained consciousness, he found himself seated in a small, windowless room with poured concrete walls and a heavy reinforced metal door with a viewing port. A small surveillance camera was mounted in the corner of the room. He tried to lift his arms but they were strapped to a heavy metal chair bolted securely to the floor. Still clothed in his suit pants and a dress shirt, his jacket and shoes had been removed.

"Well, well," boomed a voice echoing from a speaker in the wall, "I apologize for the informal welcome but hope you are comfortable in our guest room. We have called for a doctor to examine you. You will tell us about Stormy Weather and other things of interest. This is a new doctor. I'm afraid our long time doctor of persuasion took another position after he failed to get much information out of your former colleague, a Ms. Andrews I believe."

Dan clenched his arms and wanted to test the strength of the wide leather straps holding each of his arms and legs but realized that this game of provocation would be much more difficult if he revealed his pent up rage about Meg's death.

"I'm not sure I know a Ms. Andrews but I doubt I have any worthwhile information to share. You've got plenty of contacts inside the government. I'm just a small fish in a large tank."

"We shall find out just how small you are and also how tough a former Seal really is. Welcome and I'll look forward to meeting you soon."

The speaker clicked off. Dan started to assess his situation. Orient, he commanded himself.

Chapter 118

DHS–Domestic Terrorism Annex
Washington, DC
June 18, 2018

Cass realized it was almost 4:00 p.m. Dan told her he'd be back early so she tried his cell phone, and it rolled to a robotic not in service message. This happened frequently when he was brought into a SCIF somewhere and had to power down a phone and deposit it into a lock box before entering. She tried to push the thought out of her mind but was getting nervous. At 5:00 p.m., she called DHS security to see if there was a record of Dan's entering the Anacostia facility. No record could be found. She called Sandy, and he reassured her that Dan probably got involved in something and would be back soon. By 6:00 p.m., both Cass and Sandy were in the War Room with Admiral Wright discussing next steps.

"This is not like Dan, Admiral. He's always has a plan and follows it. I've only known him for a few months, but I've never seen anything like this. I'm thinking he may have been picked up by someone."

"Me too," said Cass, "If he's not in a meeting, he always has his cell phone close-by."

"Let's give him one more hour. If we haven't heard anything by then, let's make the reports and start getting the word out."

Cass left the building after 11:00 p.m. fearing the worst. She knew he was tough and clear-headed but also knew he was on at least one target list and possible others. Once inside her apartment, she downed a large glass of whiskey before going to bed. Dan would still be missing when she awoke the next morning with a painful headache that would not go away.

Chapter 119

Double Eagle Headquarters
M Street Georgetown
Washington, DC
June 19, 2018

Dan awoke and felt stiff and sore all over. He remained strapped to the metal chair for the entire night. His legs were cramping, and he needed to stretch but more important, he needed the bathroom. He yelled to see if there was anyone within earshot. There was no response.

Confined in a ten by ten foot square box with concrete walls and a ceiling covered with thick rigid insulation panels to keep any sound inside the room, the quiet reminded him of a deep dive he'd once made where the only sound at 200' was his own breathing. Deathly quiet, just like this room.

Within a few minutes, a guard with a machine pistol of European origin slung across his chest came in carrying a paper sack advertising a well-known fast food restaurant. He also brought a towel and a packaged chip of soap. He left and returned with a bucket of fresh water joined by a second guard, empty-handed but armed in a similar way. The first guard spoke to Dan with an authoritative tone that could have only been developed within the military.

"I'm going to release these straps and your hands and legs are to remain in place, understood? Here's some breakfast, and there's a bucket of water for you to wash with. The floor drain in the corner is your toilet. Any sudden moves and my partner will shoot you. We have been ordered to keep you in good health unless you do something stupid. I'm certain the doctor will discover some medical conditions you were not aware of that he will need to explore with some razor-sharp instruments."

Both men laughed loudly as they left the cell. They'd obviously observed similar interrogations in the past and probably had to clean up after them. This was not the time to try an escape. He hobbled over to the drain and relieved himself and then stripped and washed as best he could with water in the bucket. It reminded him of the stories he'd read about Vietnam POWs and how they'd been treated at what they called the Hanoi Hilton.

Returning to the chair, he noticed blood stains on the frame that were never completely scrubbed off. It had been used to question others in the past. He ate the breakfast sandwich knowing he needed all the energy he could get into his body, regardless of the source. Both men returned within what he estimated was thirty minutes, and Dan was re-strapped to the chair. As the two were leaving the room, he spoke again.

"Hey, do either of you know whether I'll get frequent flyer points for this stay?"

The door closed without a response. The same routine was repeated for two long days.

Chapter 120

DHS-Domestic Terrorism Annex
Washington, DC
June 22, 2018

There were no leads in Dan's disappearance. The cab company claimed the driver responding to the call was mugged by someone he didn't even see. No one at DHS knew anything about an invitation to Anacostia or any new information. Events had taken a dangerous turn, and with no ransom note or communication whatsoever, everyone at the Annex learned of the abduction and took additional precautions for themselves and their families. A buddy system was put in place to keep employee's movements known to at least one other person, and the check-in procedure would now be overseen by an armed guard. The local police conducted door to door searches. Grainy city surveillance tapes confirmed he had entered the cab, but camera coverage between the downtown area and Anacostia was non-existent. He had disappeared without a trace.

The decision was made to smoke out some leads so Dan's picture appeared on Page Two of the Washington Post. It was a move calculated to provoke a response that could enable a deal or possibly a rescue. At a minimum, it would buy some additional time.

Jack saw the newspaper and Dan's photo being carried on the news and wondered if Spence had anything to do with this disappearance. He called Spence's Executive Secretary and made an appointment for later in the morning.

"Good morning, Jack. You look great!" Spence exclaimed, "How is everything?"

Jack held the newspaper in his hand with Dan's photo.

"Tell me you and the company are not involved in this," Jack demanded his eyes flashing.

"What is this?" asked Spence who held the paper and saw his Dan's US Navy photo. "I guess he's quite a hero. Look at all those ribbons. And he's missing? Isn't that odd. Now why would you think I would know anything about this? It looks like one of those government stunts to get someone under cover."

"And I think you know more about this than you are telling me. You said I was on the fast track with the company, and then you treat me like a mushroom. I don't get it. I know sometimes circumstances can force anyone to take action they ordinarily would not take, but tell me why you are so guarded on this. You want loyalty, and, in return, I want the truth."

"Double Eagle makes pragmatic decisions and sometimes has to take extraordinary action to gain an advantage. I know you understand that. But again, why would I waste my time on someone like Steele?"

"I guess it's just a gut feeling."

"Well, Jack that's good news. Some of the best decisions I've ever made were based on my gut or my heart and not my head."

"The whole city is looking for him in force, and this could give DHS the ammunition they need to get the search warrant they've been trying to get on us for weeks."

"There's no cause for alarm Jack," Spence said in a soothing tone. "The judge is a good friend of ours, and I am confident he'll not change his mind based on someone that's gone missing. He's probably out on a bender somewhere with his old US Navy buddies."

"Yeah, maybe you are right."

"Jack, I'm glad you remembered that we talked last time about your future with the company and your impatience to move up. And I told you about the importance of loyalty. At the end of the day, loyalty is what motivates people and keeps them working as a team with a single-minded purpose. That's an important ingredient in making Double Eagle successful and keeps our leadership team together. We test our leaders to make sure they are ready and possess the strong commitment needed to operate as we do."

"How do you test them?"

Spence picked up a slim remote controller and the wide screen monitor on the wall revealed a man with his head down strapped to a metal chair.

"What the hell is that?" Jack spat the words at the monitor while his mouth filled with a harsh acid reflux making him choke.

"This is your test, Jack. Steele was kind enough to stop by at my invitation. I have someone coming later in the day to begin questioning him. Extracting information from a strong man or woman often requires the imposition of pain. Generally, people are quick to give up what they know rather than enduring any additional procedures. Perhaps you can pass this simple test and also give him a chance to avoid the pain."

"What do you mean?"

Spence opened his desk drawer and slid a matte black pistol across the library table.

"Kill him."

He looked into Spence's eyes that had the hard, cold look of flint. He was dead serious.

"This is my test and ticket to better things here at the company?"

"Correct."

"Where is this room?"

"Right here in the building. On the garage level behind the elevators and down another floor."

"This is easy. I won't let him or anyone else stand in my way."

He had been in the gun club in college and had a collection of handguns from around the world. This particular 9 mm pistol felt very natural in his hand. He released the magazine and studied the neat little row of shiny bullets. He returned the magazine with the butt of his left hand.

"Can I keep this gun for my collection after dispatching Mr. Steele?" Jack's wolfish grin caused Spence to squirm with anticipation.

"Certainly."

Spence called Paul McGovern over and asked him to accompany Jack. The two rode the elevator to the garage, and McGovern led Jack around the corner to the steel door leading down a set of cement stairs to a landing where an armed guard relaxed comfortably in an overstuffed chair.

Jack addressed the guard with authority, "Open the door. I have some important business with our guest. He's still strapped in the chair, right?"

"Yes, he's not going anywhere."

The three men entered the poorly ventilated room that now smelled like an economy bathroom at the end of a long overseas flight from a country where personal hygiene was not a daily practice. Dan's head rose as he looked up to see his visitors.

Jack stepped in front of the chair. "Well, I never imagined you'd be here at Double Eagle having not come through the front door."

"I'm not sure what door I was brought in. So you've been part of this all along?"

"As you know, I'm part of the company and now have an opportunity to demonstrate my loyalty by actions, not just words."

"What does that mean? You kill me and they kill you? Loyalty? Sounds like a fool's test to me."

"No, you've got it wrong again. We keep the peace in this country and others, and you are trying to upset the balance we've put in place after years of work. Plus you should be thankful. I'm doing you a favor because someone is on his way here to take all the information that you have stored in your brain. I'm told he is very persuasive."

"Fire away and know now you'll rot in Hell along with many of your Double Eagle associates."

Jack stepped forward and chambered a round. Cocked and ready, he took a double-handed grip and aimed at Dan's forehead, visually making an "X" with the lines connecting the right ear and left eye and right eye and left ear. He moved his finger inside the trigger guard and remembered that his pistol instructor always taught him to put steady pressure on the trigger as he fired. Jack adjusted his aim to slightly above Dan's head and pulled the trigger. Despite the sound-proofing insulation, the shot was deafening in the small room. Nothing happened. No bullet came out of the barrel.

Jack looked around and stared at the camera in a fury, "What is this Spence, a joke? You gave me a gun with blanks?"

He reached over and took the machine pistol from one of the guards, chambering a round and standing in front of Jack.

Spence's voice came over the speaker. "Jack, you've passed the test with flying colors. I'm proud of you. I want to save Dan for the doctor. It's important we get all the information he knows about our operations."

"Sorry, Spence, you said this was my test. Steele is mine."

Eyes blazing with sick determination, Jack took his stance in front of Dan and aimed at his forehead. His finger rested on the trigger.

Jack then spun around and fired a round into the guard's chest, where a red flower bloomed immediately. He then fired two shots into Paul McGovern, one in the forehead and the other into his gaping mouth. The fourth shot killed the video feed. Jack unbuckled the straps binding Dan to the chair. He grabbed the other machine pistol and hobbled behind Jack. Three days in a chair had left his legs in very bad condition.

Another security guard was coming around the corner when Jack dropped him with a single shot. He dashed into the security station and grabbed the keys to Spence's armored limo from a row of pegs in front of the desk. He knew a silent alarm had been sounded and additional guards were being summoned to the garage from all over the building.

"How many guards are on duty?"

"Maybe six to eight. Let's get out of here." Jack took the wheel and floored the car just as a heavy stainless steel curtain with solid one inch bars emerged from the floor to block the garage door. Jack slammed on the brakes and made a wide turn to build-up speed. Modest in size, the parking garage structural supports stood at twelve foot intervals through the bay.

"Hold on!" he said, flooring the accelerator. Tires squealing, he steered the heavy car straight ahead trying to ram through the barrier. The front end slammed into the gleaming steel curtain bending a number of steel bars, pushing the front grillwork and bumper rearward into the engine block and activating the air bags but without the desired effect. With the exit blocked, the car was going nowhere.

Bullets ricocheted off the armor plating and thick bulletproof glass. Jack looked in the rear view mirror and saw four more armed guards advancing towards the car. All their weapons were silenced to avoid any sounds reaching the street but they were spitting a hail of bullets causing sharp metallic plinks as they struck the car. Dan glanced up at the solid concrete walls and saw no other exits.

Jack looked at his lame passenger. "Look, these guys are closing in. There is an escape chute over in the corner of the garage on your side under the green garbage can. I don't know where it leads, but it's our only chance. I'll try to keep them diverted while you head for the chute. I'll come around the front of the car and be right behind you."

Jack took position on the other side of the armored door firing the machine pistol on full automatic and giving Dan the cover he needed to hobble to the corner of the garage. He lifted up the green can and exposed a thick composite cover. Shots whizzed over his head as he jerked off the cover and looked back as Jack skidded over the hood of the car. Dan leaned into the wall and squeezed off two quick bursts, hitting one of the guards and forcing another to take cover behind a support column. Running like a halfback headed to the goal line, a bullet found one of Jack's legs, and the force of its impact spun him around. He crumbled to the floor just short of the chute.

Dan returned fire, wounding the shooter and started to move towards him.

Jack yelled, "Go, Go," as he held off the guards with return fire from a prone position on the garage floor.

Dan jumped in the chute feet first.

The chute turned out to be just a smooth plastic trough similar to the ones at water parks. He had no idea where he was going, but the acceleration rapidly increased. Completely dark, the chute made several quick turns on a steep slope. On a straight-away, he thought he saw some light at the end of the tunnel but then the trough banked sharply to the left. Suddenly, the tunnel curved upward into space and he tumbled out into a room padded all around with inflatable panels like the Space Walks kids use for birthday parties.

Not knowing if a team of armed shock troopers were in pursuit or now guarding the terminus of this ride, Dan oriented and looked for an exit. A solid wooden door dead-bolted to a stout jamb stood between him and freedom. He backed off and ran through the door, tumbling down a set of steps before hitting the ground in an alleyway between two buildings. With no one in sight, he headed up the alley's slope towards the sounds of traffic, thinking he landed somewhere near the C&O canal that paralleled the Potomac.

In less than a minute, he was standing back on M street in the middle of another routine week day in Washington. He crossed the street and ducked into a coffee shop full of patrons. With bare feet, a stained shirt and not having a proper shower for days, he looked and smelled like a wild man. He also had a machine pistol in his hands. A teenage girl dropped her whipped-cream topped latte when he grabbed her cell phone and dialed the Annex. Minutes later, he was picked up by a heavily armed security detail and whisked away to Headquarters. People in the lobby just cheered as they recognized him coming through the building.

He related the story to Sandy and Cass and told them to alert the surveillance team already on station to surround the place. Hours later, he was told that multiple units stormed the Double Eagle Headquarters and began searching it with a fine tooth comb. Several armed men were found dead in the garage and two others in a room on a lower floor which resembled a prison cell.

Another man on the top floor had been seated in a heavy leather armless side chair when his head and right arm were severed from his body with a single stroke of a massive two-handed sword. He didn't need to see the photos to know Jack had been killed by Spence. But by a sword? The loyal Executive Secretary had a single bullet hole in her flawless forehead and would not be able to give any information to the investigators. There was much more to Double Eagle Industries than met the eye. Spence somehow managed to escape from the building without a trace and successfully eluded the police lockdown of Georgetown.

Chapter 121

National Naval Medical Center
Bethesda, Maryland
June 22, 2018

Under heavy guard, Dan was transported to Bethesda for an examination and to begin recovering from his ordeal. At least he'd be in a safe place for a while. He was thoroughly examined and given a sedative to ease the leg pain. The doctors expected he had some clotting in his extremities. He awoke the next day feeling like a new person but still hobbling on his damaged limbs. Prepared to rejoin the fray and knowing that prompt follow-up action needed to be taken, he asked to replace his hospital Johnnie with some fresh clothes so he could leave. The answer: an emphatic no.

Chapter 122

National Naval Medical Center
Bethesda, Maryland
June 23, 2018

Later in the morning, the Admiral, Sandy and Cass came for a visit.

"Have you come to take me home?" Dan asked.

"No," the three said in unison.

The Admiral took charge. "You are going to stay in the hospital for the weekend until we have the situation in Georgetown under control. We are going through both sides of the building, and they are carting out evidence which makes my head swim. They are some encrypted file servers we've already transported to the NSA. I just don't know why you didn't have the patience to wait for the judge to make his probable cause ruling."

"I guess I'm just naturally curious, that's all. Really, Admiral, are you serious about making me stay here all weekend?"

"Yes and there will be no negotiation on that point. You are here to recover, and assuming the medical staff agrees, I'll expect you to be escorted back to the office sometime next week. Understood?"

"Yes, sir."

Chapter 123

DHS–Domestic Terrorism Annex
Washington, DC
June 25, 2018

Dan was discharged early Monday morning, walked out of Bethesda under his own power with three no-nonsense plainclothes escorts and arrived at the Annex before 10:00 a.m.

"Morning, Cass. I'm back."

"Great. How are you feeling?"

"Better than ever. I needed the rest and hadn't realized how bad my legs were affected. As you might guess, I've been thinking about last Friday all weekend and want to look at all the unknowns from a different angle. If you make a side-by-side of what we don't know versus what we do, it's clear we don't have a good picture of how the company operates, how it's managed, how decisions are made and at what level and perhaps most important, an understanding of how the visible public part of the business is related to the back part run in secret. It's similar to the compartments we use to protect the important stuff that can be accessed only by those with the proper level of clearance and the need to know. To use the iceberg analogy, the top quarter of it showing above the water is what's fronted on M street in Georgetown, but there's three quarters in the back of the building where the real power is centered. I don't think most of the employees even know about the other part of the company."

"I agree. Maybe we'll get some more insight once the NSA is able to crack those encrypted file servers, but I don't have any idea how long that will take. Are you able to step across the street for some coffee? My treat."

"Thanks, but I can't go anywhere without my friends. I don't know how it will work tonight, but only the Admiral has the authority to change their orders."

Sandy stood in the doorway and said, "Welcome home. Ready to get back to work?"

"Right after I enjoy a cup of coffee from across the street. Cass is buying and flying."

"OK, I'll have my usual. Do you need help?"

"No, I've got it."

Sandy took a chair next to Dan, wincing as he sat. His internal injuries were healing slowly and still caused pain from time to time.

"You came very close this time, my friend. I was worried."

"A lot closer than I planned, that's for sure. Someone is looking out for me."

"How safe do you feel now?"

"I think this is a real setback for the bad guys, and it will take some time for them to recover. Personally, I'm not sure. Seems like I've got a price on my head, and I just knocked down a live wasps nest. I expect they'll try to take me out again."

"My point exactly, Dan. Is it time for you to get out?"

Cass barged through the door carrying a paper tray with three coffees and a couple of fresh blueberry scones, giving Dan an opportunity to dodge Sandy's question which he'd wrestled with during his time in Bethesda. The three drank coffee and shared the scones and talked about everything except Double Eagle.

Chapter 124

Boston, Massachusetts
June 27, 2018

After a week of hoping for a major break in the case that would provide the answers to questions nagging at him for months and two return visits to Bethesda for blood work and a final exam, Dan persuaded the Admiral he needed to go to Boston. Security in Boston would be adequate to protect him, and he promised to stay within the security perimeter that included the designated hotel where he'd reserved a room. The Admiral reluctantly agreed to the restrictive rules Dan had outlined. All agreed that POTUS and the other world leaders invited to Boston made a very juicy target.

He flew to Logan and a government car took him to the Security area where his identification was checked against the computer database, and he received a photo badge to wear around his neck at all times within the perimeter. He took a long walk within the secured area and got details on the Advance Team organization, briefing times and even got a desk assigned within the designated command center. He was restricted to the security area and couldn't join others who were heading out to some of the city's best restaurants to enjoy some New England fare at taxpayer's expense. He overheard one very large communications tech bragging that he'd eaten three two pound baked stuffed lobsters at a single sitting.

Dan had a full week to get acclimated and to think about how Double Eagle could make Boston their next target. He walked every square inch of the small area of the Esplanade, knew every entry point, and had implanted an interactive topographic map in his brain which would alert him to any changes. He also ate every entree in each of the hotel's three restaurants at least once. This was like embarking on a ship sailing to an objective area and spending a week waiting for the action to begin. He felt like a caged animal.

He stayed in constant contact with the office, and the daily flow of new information never stopped. While the Double Eagle servers were giving our very best NSA hackers a challenge, other documents provided insight into the company's finances, but only on the customer-facing companies. Little had been uncovered on the backroom side.

The sword which killed Jack had been identified as a very fine replica of the sword carried by Skanderbeg, an Albanian forced into military service for the Ottoman Empire. The recent terrorists' recruiting practices in Iraq and Syria followed a similar pattern. Skanderbeg's reputation on the battlefield made him a hero in the service of the oppressive Ottoman Turks. After many years, he finally abandoned the homeland and its religion and returned to Albania with three hundred loyal soldiers.

He converted back to Christianity and defeated army after army attempting to bring his head back to the ruler. A hero in two worlds, Skanderbeg's legend invoked strong feelings from the downtrodden people of Albania and inspired others to push it to a new beginning. The large, heavy sword with cutting edges on both sides lay tagged in the evidence cage at the Georgetown police station. "What could be the connection between Spence and Skanderbeg?" Dan wondered.

For all his complaints about being restricted to a small area along the Esplanade, the week passed quickly, and Dan could not believe the thousands of details being addressed by the Advance Team. These people were professionals that knew how to make things happen.

Chapter 125

Boston, Massachusetts
July 01, 2018
08:00 a.m.

Boston was in a festive mood. Because July 4th fell on a Wednesday, many businesses closed their doors for the entire week. The narrow streets became gridlocked with thousands of additional cars, tourists, protesters, bands and crazies. Protective service teams from six countries were struggling to understand how the process would go with all the security that would effectively lock down the city for days. Were people here to celebrate Independence Day, get a glimpse of the dignitaries or did their plans include an attack? Sorting out the good guys from the bad would be next to impossible.

"OK, folks. Listen-up. We've got three more days of making this city safe for a lot of important people. They are counting on us and have their own security teams working with us. All the protective services personnel will be wearing an earpiece, and we'll have a dedicated circuit up and running. Each of the radios has a biometric keypad and numeric password. Uniformed Police, SWAT and DHS federal teams will be linked via data ports and one way broadcast. Each of the teams has the capability to transmit emergency voice reports into the command center. Again, primary is here at the hotel near the Longfellow bridge and the back-up is a few blocks east in city hall. Our mobile command center here at the Esplanade will direct the teams located inside area One. Questions?"

He continued, "I'd like to test all the security communications this morning to ensure we have connectivity. One reminder, I want to take a hard look at the Esplanade this afternoon before the Boston Pops dress rehearsal that begins at 3:00 p.m. This will likely be the last opportunity for any party crashers to make a final check of the objective area and plan any last minute adjustments. The Pops will review the timing for all the acts and practice the final choreography. Tomorrow we've got the TV stations coming into the area to set up their equipment. More on that in the morning. Any questions? Good. Next briefing at 1:00 p.m. for the security leads."

There were surveillance assets stationed at local military bases to the west of the city, south to Cape Cod, and north to Maine. Check points and perimeter defense positions ringed the city on all sides, including the water. Two US Navy destroyers took positions well outside the sea approaches to Boston, on alert for any submarine or commando-type attack. Within the harbor, the Coast Guard coordinated all traffic entering the traffic separation scheme and commanded fast reaction boats to intercept any waterborne traffic. A sixteen man Seal Platoon operated under cover in four high-powered fishing boats near the Charlestown Bridge and on the Charles River itself. Garbed in shorts and boat shoes, they blended in with the waterborne crowd. Despite the party atmosphere, there were thousands of people on duty, assigned to protect the President and his guests.

Chapter 126

Boston, Massachusetts
July 02, 2018
09:30 a.m.

Located in one of the hotel conference rooms on a lower floor, the intelligence center networked domestic and international intelligence services via a large bank of servers and a dozen workstations and data terminals, most of which paralleled the capability in Washington. The center had been manned 24/7 for weeks with a cadre of interagency analysts.

"Well, good morning, Mr. Steele. You are off to an early start this morning. All is quiet here, and there was nothing of interest overnight."

"OK, Marty. I'll read the traffic and wait for George's shift to come in. I'm getting nervous. Everything seems too quiet."

He wondered how many people in the Intelligence center or the command center having insight into the security plan might be feeding information to Double Eagle. While cloaked in secrecy, most of the security preparations were straightforward applications of common sense, not the high tech capabilities that only a few people knew about or understood.

Dan scanned the large white board dividing the threats by domestic and international and featuring a visual assessment of the likelihood of any activity by the groups on the watch list. He thumbed through the thick stack of the morning cables and found a report from Turkey on Mikhail Zubov. After just a day in prison, the Turks discovered Zubov exhibited common withdrawal symptoms. One of the country's few addiction specialists came to the underground aquifer and after five minutes of questions, concluded that Zubov had gotten hooked on prescription painkillers years before.

Like most addicts, he would willingly trade almost anything to escape reality. He admitted he'd been in Istanbul to conclude financial arrangements tied to a recent transaction involving both radioactive material and a cylinder of a deadly gas. He had no idea what organization had purchased the material or where they intended to use it. However, the package had been crated for handling by a forklift so Zubov thought it might be going overseas.

Dan carried the pile of cables to the other desk and addressed the man who had just assumed the morning shift. "George, I'd like you to query the Turks and see if there is any more detail on this Zubov disclosure. Yes, call me paranoid, but I can't help but believe that someone may be trying to add to the fireworks display coming up on Wednesday. My gut tells me we are very close to ground zero."

Dan left the room, wondering why Marty's shift didn't pick up on the report on Zubov. Was Marty on someone else's payroll in addition to DHS?

Chapter 127

Boston, Massachusetts
July 02, 2018
12:45 p.m.

Spence had always had a dramatic flair. He would have enjoyed joining a theatre company on Broadway. As a young man in Vienna, Spence would sometimes attend the opera from a small section in the back of the house where walk-ins were accommodated with tickets costing the equivalent of a single dollar. Just feet from the beautiful people in formal wear and ladies swathed in stylish gowns dripping with jewels, he longed for the days when he too would be seated with the people known throughout the Austrian society.

The man sitting at a table in a small eight table restaurant in Boston's north end enjoying an antipasto and a glass of dry Chianti Classico didn't look like Spence at all. Attired as a Texas oil man with a large white hat, there were distinct western touches on his suit which complemented the classic alligator cowboy boots. His face had been transformed with addition of multiple squinting wrinkles which made him look as if he had just come off the range the day before. His skin had the look of polished leather, and a small goatee completed the make-over. He had taken on a flat Western drawl as well.

The fresh mozzarella was particularly good. The north end had always been the home to the city's best restaurants, mostly modest establishments that did not attract the hordes of tourists because they were so difficult to get to. There was no parking, anywhere. Often, the diners' cars were taken by valets who would drive the streets for two hours in exchange for a healthy tip. There was no other way to deal with a small area of the overcrowded city.

Spence looked out the window past the adjacent building and thought about what the city might look like in just over forty-eight hours. Satisfied, he finished the wine and thanked the staff in fluent Italian. Because he demanded that no other diners be in the restaurant at the same time, he left a thick envelope on the table to offset the lost business and entered the back seat of a waiting black Town Car with dark-tinted windows. How different his life would have been if he'd followed his artistic muse.

Chapter 128

Boston, Massachusetts
July 03, 2018
08:00 a.m.

"Good morning everyone. Air Force One will land at Logan this morning at 10:00 a.m. He'll have a full plane including members of his Cabinet and Staff and their families and of course the beloved press corps with their White House correspondents. None of the international dignitaries will accompany the President. All the passengers will be screened in Washington prior to take-off, so we are confident that our risk assessment will remain unchanged. The President's motorcade will proceed through the Ted Williams tunnel and begin a windshield tour of the city's historic sites. They will travel out past the Commons and then follow the Freedom Trail through the city, ending up over in Charlestown for lunch aboard the USS Constitution which just opened after a three year overhaul."

The briefer paused to glance across the room to ensure he had everyone's attention. "After lunch, the motorcade will travel to the Statehouse for his scheduled meeting with the other Heads of State. The State Dinner will be held there. The overall Risk Assessment is low. Do any of my colleagues from the FBI, CIA, DHS or State have anything to add?"

Chapter 129

Boston, Massachusetts
July 03, 2018
10:00 a.m.

Air Force One landed right on time. Spence watched the landing from the General Aviation terminal where his plane had been backed up by the President's arrival. Air Traffic Control had rescheduled his departure timeslot to 12:30 p.m. to accommodate the commercial jets stacked up on all the ramps and staging areas, including the big package and cargo delivery aircraft. He rented an executive jet for the trip to Paris. He told the Customs and Border Patrol agents he would be meeting some Texans gathering in the City of Light to repay a bet he'd lost. After boarding, he reclined the seat and felt the buttery leather softly embrace his frame. He fell asleep, waking just before taxiing and taking off. The plane departed at 12:45 p.m. heading to Paris. The plane would stop there before continuing on to Tirana.

Spence would watch America's Independence Day unfold in a small theatre that looked similar to the Intelligence Center set up in the hotel in Boston, fitted with multiple communications terminals, where the data and voice feeds would be collected, interpreted, and rolled up to summary information to the six Level 1 leaders of Double Eagle. There would be a number of separate reports coming in from people in the Advance Team as well as other sources inside America's security apparatus.

A bank of large screen displays would carry the live broadcasts of the major US and European networks. Though there would be some slight time delays in the reporting from the field, Spence eagerly anticipated the panicked and confusing events covered by the Primetime networks on Independence Day. Fear would grip the city instantaneously and strip away any semblance of civility and order. A stampede would overrun the police barriers. Panic would provoke the opportunists to set fires, to loot the upscale shops and to turn the Boston Commons into a new place of confrontation 242 years after the Independence Day skirmish. Watched in real time from comfortable chairs with full food and beverage service to meet every taste and need, the celebration planned in Albania would mark another important though far different milestone.

Chapter 130

Boston, Massachusetts
July 03, 2018
3:00 p.m.

Dan paged through the security plan in the makeshift SCIF created in the hotel's basement. Hundreds of thick black fiber, landline and secure communications cables terminated in the basement, connected to a neural network with multi-level security and controlled access. The SCIF maintained the master security plan he had reviewed at least five previous times. It tracked resources and potential vulnerabilities defined by security experts from all the agencies. Just hours before the day's festivities began, the President and other Heads of State would start a series of meetings on proposed joint terrorism initiatives followed by the extravaganza planned for the city that night. The focal point would be the Hatch Shell. Evacuation and contingency plans filled endless binders. He shook his head with the realization that most of these plans had been crafted in isolation, that the vaunted coordination was really no more than a thin veneer hiding the organizational in-fighting which routinely marked the planning and preparation for such events.

Closing the detailed schedule book, he left the room, walking slowly towards the Esplanade and planning the attack as if he were leading a small team of motivated, well-trained, and experienced fighters. People like him. For years, his biggest fear was the active recruitment of disenfranchised military personnel with the inside knowledge and will to beat the stateside security plans. He began to vision the likely attack points in a completely different way.

The streets had been cordoned off for days, snarling the traffic even more in this city where everyone needs a car or two and insists on driving them everywhere. He stood in the center of the Hatch Shell amphitheater and took tactical stock of his surroundings, planning a mission for one of his platoons. It became his mission, his team, and his plan. What were the approach lanes, the hard points which would be difficult to penetrate, could a weapons or communications cache be put in place in advance? What was the window for the attack, its objective and the center of gravity? How would he do it? His personal cross-examination led to some simple conclusions.

Air—almost impossible. The no-fly zone extended two hundred miles from the city and would be monitored in a dozen locations. To the west of the city tethered over Wellesley, the Army's low altitude dirigible carried a suite of sensors which included long range surveillance radar as well as a short range system capable of detecting missiles, mortars, and artillery fire. A passive electronic warfare listening and direction-finding package rounded out the capabilities. To the east, two US Navy destroyers enforced the no-fly zone and the prescribed air corridors. The ship's air controllers monitored the transmissions from all aircraft in parallel with Logan's tower.

Ground—the narrow streets and barricades created an effective perimeter. A ground force would rely on speed and multiple points of attack, and this city offered little opportunity for delivering a knock-out punch. The people in the streets formed yet another moving barrier that would complicate a quick strike. It would be very difficult to mass a force of any size clandestinely. Heavy forces were out of the question. There was simply not enough room for maneuver. Pick-ups with heavy machine guns mounted in the back would be stopped by the sharpshooters lining the city's roof tops. No, any assault would have to be carried out by a platoon size force of commandos. Still it seemed improbable.

By sea—again, the field of battle was narrow and constricted. A perimeter was established well out from the shoreline, and the narrow waterway into the Charles could be closed, effectively ruling out a quick strike from the sea. According to all the intelligence teams, precision guided munitions or cruise missiles were considered next to impossible. The Charles would be patrolled by a number of fast boats from the USCG and well as the Navy, and there had been a network of acoustic sensors placed in the water along the Esplanade that would detect anything of any size moving underwater towards the shore. His mind kept working as he pulled on a single thread from this Gordian Knot.

"Good afternoon, I'm Dan Steele with the DHS team. I thought you might know if there were any construction efforts here in the last year that involved excavation?" he asked the city's on-call engineer manning a desk in a small trailer located near the Hatch Shell.

"As a matter of fact, we had a longstanding drainage problem near the shell where a large pool of standing water led to some serious structural deterioration. We installed a new support structure and drainage system earlier this year, I'd say late January early February. As a matter of fact, I was the construction supervisor for the job, and a local company, Beverly Inshore, was the prime contractor. You can't believe what this site looked like then compared to now. They finished the work over a month ago. Can you believe it?"

"I bet. How often did you work with them in the past?"

"Never in the past. Just on this job. When I first got assigned, I heard they had a shaky reputation and mostly bid on harbor work, rip rap, piling replacement and so forth, but they brought in a new management team which was terrific. They presented a construction schedule that anticipated everything and pulled all their permits the first week. To my knowledge, they didn't lose a single day because of an inspector shutdown, and I can tell you this city has a lot of inspectors. First time I've ever heard of such a thing in Boston. They were the low bidder but brought this job in ahead of schedule and on cost. They made my job easy."

"What was the scope of the work?"

"I'll show you," replied the engineer as the two walked over to the front of the shell.

"Like I said, we had two problems: the support structure and the drainage. They drove piles down to the bedrock along here and then poured a reinforced concrete support apron here along this part of the shell and then channeled a perimeter drain field into a concrete chamber right about here and then connected it to a large storm drain that ran right out into the Charles. The discharge is about eight feet underwater and surrounded with crushed stone. We haven't had a problem since. There's been no settling, and the ground drains like a golf green without any standing water. I know it may sound simple but it's more complicated than you realize."

"Could you get me the site plans?"

"Sure. When do you want them?"

"Yesterday, but anytime in the next hour will be fine."

"Are you kidding me? It will take me over an hour to get back to our office. With the way Boston's finest have routed the traffic, you damned near have to travel to Southie to get back into the downtown area."

"Can you ask someone to bring the drawings here?"

"Can't this wait until tomorrow?"

"No."

"OK, OK. Let me call the office."

"I'll be in the Command Center most of the evening. My cell phone number is on the board."

Instead of attending the State Dinner with all the dignitaries, Dan focused all his energy on devising an attack plan where the probability of success outweighed the negative outcomes on the other side of the balance scale. He had to recalibrate his normal approach because unlike a mission assigned to a Seal Platoon, the other side often took a different view of the value of life. In the US military, people were not expendable. How would a plan change if they were?

Chapter 131

Boston, Massachusetts
July 03, 2018
6:30 p.m.

Furious with the two hour trip he had to make to retrieve the drawings, Jim Ward entered the command center ready for a fight. Dan looked up and saw him charging into the room. He needed to defuse the situation.

"Hi Jim. This is really important, and I appreciate all your effort to get these back tonight. Maybe we could sit down and look at these together and wrap this up now. What do you say? I just brewed a pot of coffee if you need caffeine or I can snag you a bottle of spring water. Preference?"

"Sure, I'll have some coffee, my shift doesn't end until mid-night anyway. Thanks."

"Let's go over here to the conference table so we can spread out."

The new concrete apron poured to support the settling side of the Hatch Shell seemed straightforward, but the detailed drawings of the drainage system that emptied into the Charles got Dan's attention. He traced the drainage flow along the building's perimeter to a concrete collection box. The engineer responded to Dan tapping the box without being prompted.

"Think of it as a large concrete vault for a closed septic system. I would say it's probably six feet square and it's got a manhole cover for service right here, which is eighteen inches under the grade, pointing to the drawing."

"Did any of the Advance Team take a look inside the vault in the last month?"

"Not that I know of. I showed them the close-out photos and the soil has not been disturbed since then, so they didn't think it was necessary to inspect. Like one of the guys said, why would anyone want to fill an underground concrete bunker with explosives? It's self-defeating."

"But the vault then empties into this eighteen inch CPVC pipe which terminates under water here."

"Correct. The end of the pipe is protected with a steel thimble to prevent crushing. The FBI had a team of divers inspect the pipe's termination grate that's been welded on. Beverly gave me a virtual tour of the system including the grate using a remote-controlled flexible, neutrally buoyant cable fitted with a camera. They videotaped the line from the end of that pipe all the way back to the box. They told me the guy invented the flexible cable for colonoscopies and adapted the technology."

"Well it looks like you supervised a very thorough job. If we had all this much previous attention on the construction, I'm satisfied. Thanks and I apologize for putting you through the wringer. Will you be here tomorrow night for the show?"

"No, Smith has the watch tomorrow."

"Can I hang on to the drawings for another day?"

"Sure, I tell Smith to come and collect them before his shift ends tomorrow at midnight."

"That'll work. Thanks again."

Chapter 132

Boston, Massachusetts
July 03, 2018
9:30 p.m.

After tapping out a priority query on Beverly Inshore, Dan changed into a pair of khaki shorts and a green t-shirt and returned to the Hatch Shell. He had triangulated the drainage vault cover in his mind and went in search of a spade. He had some digging to do. Though incredulous that Dan wanted to pursue something so ridiculous, Jim Ward found a spade located in the watch station used by the first shift to collect any dog droppings left overnight and a well-worn blue plastic tarp. Dan also managed to borrow a flashlight that he promised to return before the end of the shift.

"Jim, I know it sounds crazy, but I need to take a peek inside the drainage vault. And I promise to do it carefully enough so even the groundskeeper will never know. See you later."

"OK, if you want to wait ten minutes, I'll send one of the guys out to help you when he gets back from his coffee run."

"Fine. I'll just get started and probably be finished about the same time."

"Suit yourself. But I'm telling you my boss will not be happy if that ground is disturbed, got it?"

Though the area forward of the shell resembled mid-day with lighting rigged to avoid any shadows, the back of the Shell remained in the shadows. Working by flashlight, the spade bit into the screened topsoil easily and the top three inches of sod was moved aside on the tarp in one neat round piece. Digging carefully, Dan enlarged the hole. A hard metallic scrape revealed the top of the vault. After a few minutes of digging by hand, he exposed the top of the cast iron manhole. He grasped the metal handles recessed into its face and lifted the heavy cover through the hole and placed it on the tarp.

The flashlight's bright beam panned the sides and bottom of the vault. Clean except for some mud at the bottom. Just what he expected. The light revealed the individual pipes feeding the collection vault and the mouth of the CPVC drainage pipe channeled any collected water into the river. Just as he expected. To make sure, he lowered himself into the vault head-first into a handstand and gently dropped to the floor. At the Hatch Shell end of the vault, all the perimeter drains were clear. He went to the larger corrugated pipe on the discharge side and decided that he could easily check the welds at the termination, judging that the pipe was perhaps twenty to twenty-five feet in length with probably the last eight feet underwater. With an outside diameter of only eighteen inches, it would be a tight fit but he could go feet first and get his shoulders inside the pipe with his arms extended. He placed the plastic flashlight against the vault wall and pulled himself feet first into the darkness.

The pipe's corrugations were filled with cold slimy water that made it uncomfortable but easier to move down the pipe. His feet touched the water in less than thirty seconds. He took a long slow breath, exhaled and then inhaled again and pushed himself down into the water. Nothing strange here. His sneakers touched the heavy steel grate and he pushed hard against it. Solid as a rock. Using the upper part of the pipe, he pulled himself along the inclined corrugations and broke the surface of the water. Finally satisfied, he grabbed the flashlight and crouched forward to the opening to crawl back out through the hole he'd just dug. As he stood upright, out of the corner of his eye, he saw the downward motion of an arm connected to a sharp blow to his head.

Chapter 133

Boston, Massachusetts
July 04, 2018
02:00 a.m.

In total darkness, Dan reached for the painful lump on his right temple and traced a crease crusted over with dried blood. He found the flashlight and got his bearings after seeing the rounded platter-sized pool of coagulated blood that spread onto the floor. He didn't know whether he'd been out for sixty minutes or six hours. Looking up, he saw that the manhole cover had been put back in place.

"Orient" he disciplined himself. I'm in an underground pre-cast concrete vault that collects a set of perimeter drains with eight inch pipe which is too small for me to crawl through and an eighteen inch diameter corrugated CVPC with a welded termination under the Charles River that I can't budge. The vault is four feet square with a manhole access that's been put in place and is likely supporting a circle of earth eighteen inches in diameter and eighteen inches deep. And, since this place doesn't have any air flow to speak of, either I find a way out or die from asphyxiation. Had he tried hard enough to move the welded grate in the river? He again lowered himself down the gentle incline and, holding his breath pushed hard against the heavy grate. Solid. He concentrated on the edges. No movement. He pulled himself back through the pipe to re-group. The coffin-like vault felt confining, and the stale air lacked oxygen.

Plan B. He spread his feet shoulder width apart and raised up until the back of his head and two palms were evenly distributed against the manhole and used the strength of his legs to push for nearly thirty seconds. Nothing moved. Now gulping the stale air, he knew the oxygen was being rapidly depleted. He had a brief flashback to his Navy days when sailors would enter unventilated sealed compartments without being tested and were later found dead. He needed to get out. Again he tried the same three point push on the underside of the manhole. This time he felt a few grains of soil fall on his face. Catching his breath, he pushed again against the same side and felt a slight movement of the cover and another stream of soil. And again. The manhole cover had moved up past the edge of the metal support ring cast in the surface of the concrete. More soil streamed onto the vault floor.

His arms, back and legs ached from the resistance, and his muscles were fatigued from the lack of oxygen. He wedged his T-Shirt into the opening so his fingertips could reach the narrow slit to excavate. Now gasping for air while using the index fingers of both hands to remove the dirt, he estimated that he'd die of asphyxiation at this rate of progress.

He pushed hard again and the manhole opened another quarter inch. With both hands on the cover's rim, he pushed with all the strength he had. Dirt poured down on him and he frantically pulled at the soil. Breathing heavily with his temples pounding and his legs numbed, he knew he could pass out any second. He jabbed a fist through the opening and thrust forward. This time he saw a different kind of darkness and sucked in a lungful of fresh air. Maybe twenty more minutes of digging and he finally pushed the cover out of the hole and pulled himself out of the vault. He lay on the damp grass exhausted. The spade and tarp were nowhere to be found. He didn't know how or where but now felt certain Boston was the target.

Chapter 134

Boston, Massachusetts
July 04, 2018
02:30 a.m.

He walked into the command center.

"Well. Look what the cat dragged in. Where the hell have you been?" asked the watch officer.

"I saw a large night-crawler wearing a Rangers jersey and followed him back into his hole."

"Looks like you bumped your head on the way in. It looks bad. You should swing by medical and see if you lost any gray matter in the process. By the way, the DHS liaison officer has been looking for you for the past couple of hours."

Dan looked at the clock. Five hours had elapsed. I must have been unconscious for almost four hours....the tunneling job that almost killed him couldn't have taken more than an hour. It felt as if he'd been gone the better part of the night.

The DHS liaison officer approached a bedraggled Dan standing in the command post.

"What happened?"

"It's a long story, and I've got to get over to medical. Anything new?"

"We just got a response on the Beverly Inshore query you sent out last evening. The company was purchased last winter by a wholly owned subsidiary of Double Eagle Industries. We tracked down the previous owner living in Florida and should have something back later this morning."

"Good work!"

"Do you need a hand?"

"No, but see if you can find the video tapes from the area between the Hatch Shell and the Charles River. I'd like to identify the person who coldcocked me and left me to die in a drainage vault. Start at 9:30 p.m. tonight... I mean last night."

"Got it."

The nurse at the Medical Station scrubbed his wound with what felt like a wire brush, rinsed off all the dirt and blood and stood back to examine her handiwork.

"I'm betting ten stitches will do it but if you think you have a future as a leading man in Hollywood, ask for fifteen. The doctor is on his way."

"Well, that's quite a gash you've got there Mr. Steele. Did you try to re-enact the Boston massacre?"

"No. I was on the receiving end of a small club or sap from someone who doesn't like me."

The doctor felt the area around the laceration and expressed his findings in a clinical monotone, "Your head is very hard and from the look of your scalp, you've had a few stitches in the past. So, I'll close the wound and give you a tetanus shot and a course of antibiotics just to be on the safe side. You'll need to take it easy for the next few days. Nothing too strenuous, lots of fluids and wear a bathing cap when you shower. You should be fine. I'll ask the neurologist if he sees any signs of a concussion or if he thinks we need more X-Rays."

"Thanks, Doc. I feel better already."

He returned to the hotel and got a number of strange looks on his way to the men's locker room, showered, wrapped himself in a thick hotel bathrobe and returned to his room for a change of clothes. He'd concluded that Independence Day was D-Day for the attack on the President of the United States, several world leaders who were his guests and thousands in the city of Boston. The clock was ticking. How, where, and when kept his eyes open and his mind working for the rest of the short night. Adrenaline kept him pumped up.

Chapter 135

Boston, Massachusetts
July 04, 2018
06:30 a.m.

Dan badged into the Command Center and spied the red-rimmed eyes of the DHS liaison officer almost immediately. He walked over and quietly took a seat in front of his work table until the young man looked up.

"My God, what happened to your head?" seeing the large bandage which covered the stiches and puffy bruise that offered several shades of purple and yellow around its periphery.

"I tried some new mousse in my hair and had a bad reaction to it."

He walked over to the Engineer's trailer and introduced himself.

"Is there a contracts person who reviewed the Beverly Inshore bid for the construction work here at the Hatch Shell?"

"Sure, but I don't expect you'll get anything from contracts today. Everybody's off."

"Do you have Jim Ward's home number?"

"Yes, but don't tell him where you got it."

Dan walked back to the Command Center and used the desk set to make the call. He expected a bad reaction.

"Morning Jim and Happy Independence Day! It's Dan Steele from DHS. Look, I know it's early but just wondered if you could spare a minute to tell me more about the Beverly Inshore contract."

"Give me a minute to get downstairs." In the background, it sounded like someone had been awakened from a deep sleep and wasn't happy.

"You've really got some nerve, Steele. You told me you'd be back before the end of my watch last night to return the flashlight, tarp and shovel and you bail out. My guy ended up filling in the hole you left. I just don't get it. And then you get me out of bed on a National Holiday. What's up with you?"

"I guess you could say I was a troubled child."

"Sure. Have you tried stand-up? Forget it, what do you want to know now?"

"They were the low bidder, right."

"Who?"

"Beverly Inshore."

"Yeah, my eyes are still closed, and I haven't had my coffee yet. Yeah, they were 40% lower than the guy who usually bids and wins most of the work of that sort in the city."

"How closely did you monitor the excavation?"

"I was there every day except for a couple days when I went up north skiing with my son. That's when the trenching was completed and the CPVC went in. I came on site and inspected the job before they backfilled the trenches."

"So you weren't there when they did the trenching?"

"No, they had the area staked out, and I checked the layout against the plan. They followed the plans with no deviations or exceptions but I wasn't there during the digging."

"Beverly Inshore was purchased earlier in the year by a company that's been under surveillance for several months now because of some links to a terrorist organization. I explored the inside of the drainage vault last night and got bumped on the head on my way out. Someone tried to bury me alive. Did anyone else know that I wanted to look inside the vault last night?"

"No one except the groundskeeper who I sent out there after he returned with coffee. What a character. Twenty minutes for a coffee run here within the security boundary. Not too swift. We brought him on to take care of the trash."

"What's his name?"

"Jimmie. He works for DCR."

"DCR?"

"Yes, the Department of Conservancy and Recreation here in Boston."

The WBZ weather guesser ecstatically announced that the area of high pressure would continue to dominate New England's weather and predicted a picture perfect Independence Day. She was unaware that other people were planning to change the course of nature that day and were predicting something far different, high pressure or not.

Chapter 136

Boston, Massachusetts
July 04, 2018
07:30 a.m.

Dan kept trying to see the landscape from inside the minds of the enemy as he had been doing during the previous trips the President had made in the last month. He had been acting as a security advisor to the Advance Party. The multiple recent attempts on Dan's life made him ineligible for the traveling crew. With no clear role and no direct responsibility, he would merely review the security plan and offer his comments. Being on the ground in Boston brought a different perspective. His gut told him the city would be the target. Something horrific would be carried out which the security team did not expect.

He'd been up for several hours when the summer sun peeked its way down the narrow streets. A fresh breeze came out of the northeast carrying the scent of low tide. Dan pushed the chair back from a table in the war-room established in a building adjacent to the Esplanade the FBI called home. He joined about twenty others for the morning brief. Dan glanced around and saw representatives from the Secret Service, Homeland Security, FBI, USCG, the White House Communications Team, State Police, Boston Police, and the mayor's security team. Dan knew how the larger team operated. He laughed and thought the only group not represented was the Boston Pops.

"Good morning! Today's the big day. Ryan will cover the President's detailed schedule later in the brief. Overnight reporting has not changed the threat profile, and the net assessment from the FBI is in synch with ours. Homeland Security agrees with the exception of our colleague Dan Steele who believes that today is the day when his terrorist group from Albania will strike." Special Agent Gibson smiled at Dan, pausing for the laughter to die down. "We will stick to our current deployment plan. Next briefing at 2:00 p.m. this afternoon. Stay sharp."

Dan looked at Gibson as he sat at the conference table. The minute by minute details of the President's schedule were reviewed, and the emergency fire and rescue plans spelled out. The details hummed in the back of his mind. He regarded Gibson as a real pro with lots of field experience and an unblemished record of success. He didn't mind the constant ribbing, even from his own organization. Something deep in his core made him confident that there would be no laughter at the end of this day. But decisions were made on facts, and there had been nothing new to suggest this visit would be anything other than routine.

After the formal briefing, Dan approached Gibson.

"I heard you had a close call last night. How are you feeling?"

"I'm OK but just wanted to let you know that we connected the dots between the company that worked on the Hatch Shell and Double Eagle, the outfit that we think is our domestic terror cell."

"Good. You think they'd really try to go after the President here?"

"It looks that way to me. I haven't figured how they could pull it off but, yeah, I think something will happen here today."

Gibson looked at him with tired eyes. "Look, Dan, I respect your judgment and know you are committed to the success of this visit. But we are way past the point of being able to pull the plug. The Chief of Staff made the "go" decision a week ago. He expects us to deal with pop-ups like this by applying more resources to make sure nothing does happen. That's the reality."

"That's what I figured."

"Heh, if we don't see each other again, I've enjoyed having you on the team and would love to have you join us if things get slow over at DHS."

The two shook hands and Dan left the building. He had just gotten a first-hand lesson on bureaucratic momentum. Pop-ups at the 11th hour were not welcome.

Though the Secret Service did not like the Esplanade venue, they could not change it. The thick foliage was problematic for the snipers positioned on nearby towers and roofs, but the city refused all the radical tree trimming they had suggested. All the other accesses had been sewn up tight. Traffic control would be in place by mid-day and the perimeter of the park was outlined by metal detector portals manned by teams of TSA and other agents. Manholes were welded shut and would be checked again mid-afternoon. The city changed Storrow Drive into a pedestrian walkway.

The USCG patrolled the Charles River and established a perimeter marked by bright red buoys to prevent access to the shore. Lights strung on poles along the banks permitted constant surveillance. Daily satellite and Infra-Red images had been compared for a month to detect any unexpected changes in the venue. Plain clothes detectives watched the streets and passersby for anything unusual. Two independent teams checked flight manifests into Logan looking for anything suspicious. A number of people arriving from overseas were invited to describe their travel plans in greater detail to agents at the airport. Aggressive profiling was the order of the day. Boston's size presented the biggest challenge. The small city just simply couldn't handle the number of people and the traffic. Gridlock cut both ways, slowing the movement of forces to concentrate on a specific area and giving the bad guys lots of escape routes.

Chapter 137

Kruje, Albania
July 04, 2018
Noontime

With bright sunlight and a cloudless, clear blue sky canopied above them, Spence and several other Sons enjoyed a relaxed lunch on an outside terrace adjacent to the castle. They eagerly looked forward to the evening when they would witness Boston explode with a fury that hadn't been felt since 'the shot heard round the world' was fired by some unknown soul in neighboring Concord in April of 1775.

In a jocular, confident mood, Spence talked and laughed and ate with gusto. The 2018 Boston Massacre he planned would not be a street fight but a decisive military operation that would herald a new era and serve to fully consolidate his power. As the country's warrior-king, he would fulfill a long held dream of creating a new monarchy in Albania. The country's first modern-day renaissance would begin under his reign with the populace shrugging off the past and inspired to great future accomplishments. They would never be oppressed or subjugated again by the more developed countries. A vibrant prosperity lay just ahead, and no one would dare treat the country in any way other than an equal on the European stage or in the grander world order.

Chapter 138

Boston, MA
July 04, 2018
08:30 a.m.

A series of briefings including an overview of Stormy Weather updated for recent events were listed on the day's agenda. Dan intercepted the President's National Security Advisor after breakfast and gave him an update on the attempt to bury him alive the previous night.

"Look, Peter," staring through the rimless glasses worn by the rail thin man with an oversized brain housed inside a very large head, "I know we've got this town covered like a blanket, but I have a strong suspicion that Boston is the target."

"I understand. I'm assured we've got a handle on this from your boss and the FBI. Let's not get into any unnecessary fear-mongering on our Independence Day, all right?" The waxy smile looked like it had been painted on by a doll-maker. Venom spewed from his pretty mouth, "Just give your briefing and try to not whip up the attendees because of some shadow boxing that you are still trying to do. Let's not embarrass the Commander in Chief. Understood?"

"Got it."

"And try to look a little more presentable this afternoon."

Chapter 139

Boston, MA
July 04, 2018
09:15 a.m.

He returned to the Command Center where he reviewed overnight cables and called Cass back at the office.

"I am convinced an attack is planned for today here in Boston. The connection between Beverly Onshore and Double Eagle is the last piece in the puzzle. The President and other world leaders are at risk."

"Did you tell anyone?"

"I got to his National Security Advisor who believes I am speculating, and he's been assured by the Law enforcement agencies, the FBI, the Secret Service and of course our own DHS director that we are good to go today."

"So have you figured out how they'll do it?"

"No, but I'm working on it."

"Good luck."

"Thanks, I'll need it."

Chapter 140

Boston, MA
July 04, 2018
10:00 a.m.

The daily briefing confirmed the adequacy of the security plans being executed. No additional measures were expected.

Dan suggested an attack would be carried out later in the day though he couldn't point to any specific actionable intelligence. People listened politely while he explained the attack on him and the confirmation that the company that finished work on the Hatch Shell a month earlier was linked to Double Eagle, with a few muffled snickers in the room. They were also in denial about how tightly they'd locked down the small city. Most of the people thought their jobs were done, and that this was a night when they could be part of the magic of an Independence Day in a town where the United States had been violently birthed. The fat lady began singing, but there were still fourteen hours left in the day.

Chapter 141

The Commonwealth State House
Boston, Massachusetts
July 04, 2018
Noon

Though he'd tried to duck the assignment, Dan attended the luncheon prior to the National Security briefing on terrorism at 1:30 p.m. He sat at a table for eight with a Foreign Chief of Defense, two State Department Under-Secretaries, the liaison officer from DHS, a Protocol Officer from Australia, the Special Economic advisor to the German Chancellor, and a Presidential biographer. Dan tried to be friendly, but his mind was miles away from the lunchtime chatter. He pushed the food around on his plate but ate nothing.

After adjoining to a small conference room, the President made some brief opening remarks and then introduced him to the entire group.

"Dan has been the point man for an effort begun earlier this year to determine if the attacks we've all seen around the world and attributed to Al-Qaeda, ISIS or one of their many offshoots were instead perpetrated by a group operating within this country and camouflaging their efforts to look like they originated elsewhere. The findings are sobering, and I thought you should hear them first hand."

He walked to the podium without the polite applause that usually accompanied a speaker for such an event. "Good afternoon, Ladies and Gentlemen, I'm here to give you an overview of a program initially called Stormy Weather. You may well have been briefed on the program as we've engaged many of your country's security teams to identify a threat we all face. Our intelligence suggests there is at least one if not more very well-funded groups operating within the United States today. We cannot confirm any association with Al-Qaeda, but I can say with strong confidence that this group or groups has modeled Al-Qaeda's tactics and done what they could to point to them as the responsible party. I wish I could be more definitive, but they are also very good at covering their tracks and evading the domestic and international police dragnet we've put into place. While I do not know exactly what their motivation is, I do believe they have penetrated key security agencies within the United States and perhaps in your countries as well. We also have confirmed there are insiders working in some of our international security organizations such as INTERPOL."

Dan glanced at the National Security Advisor whose contorted face signaled his annoyance that these comments were "off-roading" and he didn't appreciate it. There would be Hell to pay Dan thought absently.

A hand waved from one of the tables. "Excuse me, Mr. Steele, are you suggesting this nameless, faceless group could be preparing to attack Boston?"

"I can't predict where or when they will strike next. I can assure you every possible precaution has been taken to protect all of you and the city of Boston during this celebration of our Independence Day. We are getting closer to connecting the dots so this group can be tracked down and stopped. The truth is we are not there yet." Dan paused and looked around the room and then told the audience what he believed. "My gut tells me something will happen here in Boston tonight."

The room erupted. The decorum was rudely abandoned as several Heads of State looked around anxiously for their Security leads. A number of people recycled the delicious lunch on the carpet. Gone were the confident faces gathered here in Boston for a first class party, where the price of admission consisted of listening to some politically correct speeches and trying to muster the excitement to be truly concerned about terrorism. The premise was blown out of the water and left the crowd aghast. Panic filled the room after Dan's comments. The Protective Services teams went on full alert as the venue spun out of control.

President Bowles jumped to the podium alongside Dan and faced his counterparts from around the globe trying to restore some semblance of order, beckoning the crowd to remain calm with his outstretched hands. He would have been more effective had he fallen to his knees and held his clenched hands to the heavens.

"Ladies and Gentlemen, please. Please take your seats," the President pleaded, raising his voice to the level of being rude and directive. "This briefing was not intended to frighten you, but we can no longer sugar-coat the situation. I found this news as disconcerting as all of you have. However, Mr. Steele, your last statement represents a personal opinion not shared by any of the agencies involved in assessing the likelihood of an attack. I am personally embarrassed by your outburst."

The President had the audience's attention now and continued, addressing a quieter, shell-shocked audience, "These are troubling developments. I never thought we'd be fighting terrorists on this scale within our own country but we are. I know all of you have similar fears. We've had great cooperation from many nations, and I appreciate all your personal help. Now we must re-double our efforts including data sharing and intelligence cooperation and focus our resources on these terror groups that are growing like a cancer on our free societies. We'll get into more details on a number of anti-terrorist initiatives and want to learn of similar things you are doing. That's the main reason why I asked you to participate in this summit."

The President flashed a weak smile in Dan's direction that said you've ruined our Independence Day gala here in Boston and I don't understand why.

The tortured faces in the group confirmed Dan's bombshell would cause some invitees to re-think their plans for the evening. The remaining agenda fell apart while questions and details were sought and risk assessments were made in real time. Dan retreated from the podium and found the nearest exit, avoiding the daggers being thrown his way by the Presidents' men. He jogged passed the thickening crowds oblivious to the very real threat facing their city, weaving his way back to the Esplanade. Anyone on these streets would dismiss his prediction outright and think that he himself presented the only threat to their fair city on this grand day. It would have been easy to shrug off the truth, stand tall and tell the story that all the politically correct people wanted to hear. He just couldn't bring himself to take the easy way out.

Chapter 142

Boston, Massachusetts
July 04, 2018
2:15 p.m.

He ducked into the command center to catch up on any last minute intelligence or reports from the Double Eagle surveillance. The DHS liaison looked up and waved him over.

"So what's new?"

"The surveillance tapes from last night show the two men who tried to entomb you. Because of the lighting, it's impossible to get a positive facial ID but one of the individuals was wearing a Department of Conservation and Recreation ball cap with 'TEX' embroidered on the back. The police are following-up."

"Anything from HQ on the surveillance effort in DC? Cass or Sandy?"

"Nothing. I think everyone is enjoying some burgers and dogs on the grill washed down with some ice cold beer."

"Yeah, I forgot, it is our national holiday."

Chapter 143

Boston, Massachusetts
July 04, 2018
3:30 p.m.

Choreographed down to the second as it would be carried
nationwide by all the prime time channels, the Independence Day
celebration became theatre. Security had been very tight in recent
years, and this year reached an even higher level. The Hatch Shell had
been ringed with portable barricades and controlled entry points with
metal detection portals. The gates opened at 09:00 a.m. with the
seemingly endless list of prohibited items posted all along the
perimeter: no coolers, no blankets exceeding ten feet by ten feet,
personal articles in a clear plastic bag, no cans or bottles, and nothing
that looked like or could be used as a weapon.

Those disappointed with the expanded rules elected to watch the
festivities from the Longfellow or Harvard Bridges or even from the
Cambridge Parkway on the northern side of the Charles River.
Hundreds of others joined a growing flotilla that had gotten into the
Charles River Basin before the narrow passage located south of the
Museum of Science closed to boat traffic. Boat ramps to the west of
the basin all the way to Waltham had similar restrictions imposed to
prevent additional boats from being launched up river.

The small, densely packed city was traditionally overrun during
the Fourth. With the President returning to his home town this year,
officials estimated nearly a million people would attend the
celebration. Bostonians asserted their rights and freedoms vehemently,
especially when it came to their beloved sports teams and patriotic
holidays such as Veterans Day, the Fourth of July and Presidents' Day.
They quickly became indignant about their celebrations, and anyone
trying to impose rules they did not agree with would be subject to loud
verbal abuse. Escalation seemed evitable. If the consequence meant a
night in jail, so be it. The attitude seemed unanimous: just don't mess
with my holidays or my way of celebrating them. Most times, alcohol

fueled the city's celebrations and led to all the bad things that go with it.

Chapter 144

Boston, Massachusetts
July 04, 2018
4:00 p.m.

Dan returned to the scene of last night's close call and looked around at the ground that had been carefully restored after his escape. Something about this excavation still gnawed at him. During his short sleepless night, he'd again ruled out any air attack and concluded a ground assault would be impossible with all the checkpoints and barricades around the city. Even a team of suicide bombers with explosive vests would not get close to the VIPs. The Charles River basin had been secured from the Charlestown Dam all the way to Watertown and every boat coming within 200 yards of the Hatch Shell would be intercepted. Boat registrations were verified and the operators questioned.

With the shallow depth of the river and the listening devices placed along the basin's banks, the likelihood of any attack coming from on or under the water was remote. Even the few deep fishing holes in the basin had been inspected again. So, he reasoned there had to be something already pre-positioned and hidden somewhere that could be activated remotely. He walked over the ground covering the discharge pipe that he'd slithered down hours before and looked down at the water where the discharge grate had been tested with as much strength as he could muster. The gnawing just wouldn't stop.

Chapter 145

Boston, Massachusetts
July 04, 2018
5:30 p.m.

He tracked down the FBI dive team that remained on site for any contingencies. They had inspected all the drainage outflows, and Dan asked about the discharge from the Hatch Shell. One of divers had started the celebration early and remained on standby with no chance of getting called into action.

"So what did you see down there."

"Look, man, we inspected almost four weeks ago so I'm a little fuzzy on exactly where you are talking about." He smelled strongly of beer and constantly eyed the nearby cooler.

"You would remember the discharge pipe. It was constructed of black eighteen inch CPVC and had a shiny steel thimble at the termination with a heavy grate welded in place."

"Yeah, I do remember that one. The pipe fitter didn't have to get suited up to do any welding down there. Looked like a recent job. A gold-plated job if you ask me."

"That's it. Anything else you can remember about it."

"No, all I did was check the bottom and the grate."

"What was under the pipe?"

"What I remember looked like fist-sized backfill stone," holding up his balled fist.

"OK, thanks. Happy 4th!"

Chapter 146

Boston, Massachusetts
July 04, 2018
7:55 p.m.

Now jammed with people on the Hatch Shell front lawn and on all sides, the Esplanade crowd anxiously awaited the Presidential party. The motorcade arrived right on cue, and some of the prime time commentators had already dubbed the event historic. The President and his guests took their seats, ringed with security forces from multiple countries. Special care had been taken to surround the President with US security teams. The seating plan had to be adjusted on the fly as several chairs suddenly became available after the early afternoon briefing. Dan expected to be permanently labeled persona non grata at the White House.

A popular country music singer who'd been in the forefront of the Wounded Warriors Project hosted the show. He lifted his trademark straw cowboy hat and welcomed the local crowd and the millions of viewers tuning in from around the globe with a stylized twang before launching into a Boston favorite: "Proud to be an American." The long time conductor of the Boston Pops had strung together a rousing playlist that kept people in motion, dancing and singing along. Boston would show the entire country how to put on an Independence Day party.

Chapter 147

Boston, Massachusetts
July 04, 2018
9:30 p.m.

The sun set at 08:17 p.m. and the natural light in Boston got sucked up quickly into the night. The planned fireworks would start promptly at 10:00 p.m. as the smoke from the cannons cleared from the last strains of Tchaikovsky's 1812 Overture. Ironically, the music celebrated the valiant Russian stand against Napoleon's army at Borodino. Made popular when Arthur Fiedler conducted the Boston Pops, the stirring piece traced the key historical elements of the battle's evolution and became the traditional finale of the evening. The Esplanade honored the conductor permanently with a massive sculpture of Fiedler's head carved from aluminum plates. Clear skies and moderate temperatures combined for a near perfect night for the outdoor celebration the city would long remember.

Dan couldn't stand it any longer. After analyzing all the possible scenarios in his head for the umpteenth time, he still had doubts and could not silence the little voice in his head telling him to overturn the last stone: he needed to look under the discharge pipe to ensure there was nothing else hidden in the rocks along the bank. He stepped down to the water's edge and got the attention of a crewman on a US Coast Guard forty-two foot fast response boat that idled with the throaty rumble of its engines fifty feet away. Powered by two 565 HP diesels driving waterjets for propulsion, the boat could reach speeds in excess of forty-five knots while only drawing thirty inches of water. Dan waved the boat in and the boat backed confidently until its stern lay just six feet off the river bank.

"You have a rescue swimmer aboard? I need to borrow a mask."

A Senior Chief Boatswain's Mate wearing a ball cap emblazoned with the boat's name and hull number stood on the aft deck and studied Dan over the stern. He asked, "Are you going to use the mask instead of beer goggles or are you planning to dive in the water with your polished Washington pumps and fancy suit? And what's the bandage on your head? Are you sure you're feeling right, son?" The chief was nobody's fool. He had operated boats his entire career and understood how to operate, repair, and keep them ship shape. He could also recognize a question that didn't pass the common sense test.

Dan shook his head and replied directly making sure that no one thought he was joking and expected an answer. "No, Senior Chief. I'm going to remove my suit and shoes before I strip down to my boxers and then conduct a little last minute underwater research. Now, I can borrow a mask?"

The swimmer tossed a mask to him and the four man crew watched as Dan undressed, spit in the mask to reduce any fogging and waded into the water. People near-by got the attention of a policeman and reported a man was swimming near the Hatch Shell. Several women admired his physique and wondered if this was a prelude to a naked run across the Hatch Shell lawn to flash the dignitaries. Cell phone cameras captured the scene unfolding. The images would be passed around the world in seconds via all the social media feeds.

Standing in waist-deep water, Dan took a series of deep, slow breaths before submerging. He found the discharge pipe's termination and tested the grate. It was solid. He stuck his fingers in the grate to remain submerged and began clearing the stones under the termination. He finally surfaced. A number of security personnel stood on the bank demanding his identification and an explanation. This event had not been planned.

"Dan Steele, DHS. My badge is right there on top of my suit."

"I see that but what in the hell are you doing?"

"Protecting the President," Dan replied as he again submerged. He continued to excavate under the pipe for another minute before he felt something unusual. A thin, curved surface that felt clean and metallic to his bare hands.

When he surfaced, an angry Boston policeman stood on the muddy bank with the Charles River lapping over his dress black shoes, ordering him to come out of the water.

"Lieutenant, you'll have to come in after me because I need one more pass before I'll come out, OK?"

Dan submerged as the Lieutenant barked into his brick radio. He found the curved surface again and further excavation revealed the mouth of another pipe. It could be part of an old drainage system just left in place or could be something new. Just the smooth feel of it told him it was new. With a faint glow in the western sky following sunset and the dim lamps along the Esplanade there for ambiance rather than illumination, he was searching blindly, with his hands alone. The curve of the metal seemed slightly larger than the new drain pipe run by Beverly Inshore but still too narrow for anyone to get through with scuba gear.

Dan rose to the surface again and was greeted with a bank of flashlights shining on him. The police Lieutenant's apoplectic look felt intimidating, even from twelve feet away. He looked as if he were ready to draw his sidearm.

"Now, listen up mister. If you don't come out of the water now, we will come in and get you out. Do you understand?" The Boston accent left no doubt in Dan's mind that the Lieutenant would carry out his plan just as he described.

"Lieutenant, I've got a pair of boxer shorts and a mask on, but there's something down there I must check, so I need to dive one more time to see if it's anything to worry about."

He submerged before the Lieutenant could sputter anything further.

He removed the remaining rocks blocking the pipe's mouth and ordinarily would have surfaced to get a deep breath of fresh air but realized he might not get that opportunity. Dan pulled himself into a black void. After fifteen feet of pulling himself through the pipe that seemed to have a slight upslope, his head broke the surface of the water. He immediately heard the orchestra above. He continued to crawl through the narrow pipe ending in a dark void somewhere under the stage. He pulled off the mask and took a deep breath of the dank air. Tiny shafts of dim light leaking from stage fixtures diffused into the darkness. He estimated he was at one end of a narrow void eight feet long and four feet wide. The light was too dim to reach the concrete surface that he crawled along on his knees, searching with his arms extended in front of his body.

Feeling the cold end of a smooth rounded cylinder, he was reminded of the old fable about the blind men trying to guess the elephant from its individual parts. After following its length with his hands, Dan surmised he'd found a long canister about the size of a ninety cubic foot scuba tank supported on a simple metal cradle made of angle iron. Whatever it was, it clearly didn't belong there. As he carefully maneuvered around the canister, the irony struck him: a national celebration was in full swing a few feet above him and here he was, crawling under the Hatch Shell on his hands and knees about to die in a terrible catastrophe likely already set in motion and programmed to begin automatically.

Chapter 148

Kruje, Albania
July 5, 2018
03:42 a.m.

A large screen television displayed a very clear image of the Boston Pops as they wrapped up a medley of well-known patriotic songs. The conductor then walked to the front of the stage and began reciting the history of Boston's favorite Independence Day piece. As he turned to signal the musicians, Spence depressed a small button on his pager and thought, how apt that the 'shot heard round the world' would be heard a second time.

The conductor took the podium and brought the orchestra to the ready. They enthusiastically began the 1812 Overture, an arrangement taking a full fifteen minutes of orchestra time with ear-ringing accompaniment from some full-sized saluting cannons manned by the US Army. The stirring piece included every instrument on stage including the bassoon for a captivating solo, bells, and a driving tympani. The enormity of the music's reach led anyone to understand how it motivated the Russian peasants from Borodino to rise up against the juggernaut of Napoleon's Army. The music told a colorful tale and inspired all the way to the finale.

Spence licked his dry lips in anticipation of the holocaust that would soon be unleashed. The city would react like a frightened school boy wetting his pants. It would take days to tally up the human toll from this night. He sat down but knew he'd be on his feet seconds later. Despite the months of complicated logistics and detailed planning, an intense emotional jolt coursed through his body like an involuntary petit mal.

Over the social media feeds came a bizarre scene of a man in the Charles River near the Hatch Shell. While most people believed that the man was a drunken reveler who would be apprehended by the policeman standing on the bank, Spence stared at the screen in shock. Though the picture the picture was not clear, one video clip came onto the screen that zoomed onto the man's face. It was Dan Steele. Spence looked at his watch and his anxiety subsided. There was no way that Steele could disrupt the plans he'd just set in motion.

Chapter 149

Boston, Massachusetts
July 04, 2018
9:46 p.m.

Dan judged the sealed canister to be about eight inches in diameter and perhaps three feet long. His hands found no wires or connections to the cold metal object, and his search revealed no access panels, fittings or fasteners. Carefully crawling around the object, he found a small lighted LED window on one end showing 00:13:50....then 00:13:49, followed by 00:13:48. A countdown clock clicked down the time, second by second. Something catastrophic would occur in less than a quarter of an hour. With his mind in overdrive, he glanced at the small window. He now had just over twelve minutes to disable, disarm or get rid of this device before the timer hit 00:00:00 at some point during the tumultuous finale of the 1812 Overture. He didn't even know what it was. Explosives? Dirty Bomb? Gas?

The LED read 00:11:30 as Dan lifted and maneuvered the heavy canister to the pipe and followed it down the slope to the water. He cradled it out of the pipe and into the river, scraping the bottom. Without the support of the pipe, it was much heavier than he realized, and he lost his grip and dropped it before heading to the surface. He frantically yelled to the FRB crew before submerging.

"I've got a device. Need to get it to deep water ASAP."

Dan dove to the bottom and frantically searched with his hands for the canister. He found something on the bottom but it felt much lighter. It turned out to be a piece of PVC drain pipe packed with mud. He again took a quick breath on the surface and submerged again, searching desperately. His bare hands finally grasped the canister. With no fins, trying to bring it to the surface and get it onto the boat would be next to impossible. The police Lieutenant on the river bank stood dumbfounded and speechless. He thought the crazy man was dead after spending nearly three minutes under water.

With the help of a strong rescue swimmer, the two wrestled the unwieldy canister to the back of the boat where the other two crewmen pulled it aboard. They were barely over the transom when the Chief threw the throttles full ahead. The boat squatted with the power of the inboard engines driving a mind-boggling volume of water through the steerable waterjets. In thirty seconds, the boat was flying at forty-five knots, a nautical speed of advance of 1,500 yards per minute. Dan stooped and rolled the canister to see the LED now read 00:09:20. He cursed that his fumbling cost so much time. He walked forward and stood in back of the two seat cockpit that looked like it belonged in an airplane.

"Chief, I don't know what's in the package, but I guessing it's a bomb of some sort. It's got a countdown timer that says whatever is in there will be done in about nine minutes. I'm a little nervous about what's cooking."

"Yeah, so I figured." Calm and collected, the Chief seemed comfortable with the situation and completely focused on the task of getting out of the basin and dumping the device. He worked the time and distance calculations with the aid of a state-of-the-art electronic charting system which displayed a route planner among other things. "I radioed the Charlestown lock operator and ordered him to open one of the locks on both ends. He told me he couldn't do it but changed his mind when I told him we were carrying a bomb and that the locks better be open when we arrived in two-three minutes." The boat flew under the Longfellow Bridge twenty seconds later. The Chief had started a countdown clock on the boat's dashboard to monitor the time by the second.

The boat had to maintain speed in order to reach open, deep water and get as far from the waterfront as possible. But tonight, boats of every size clogged the Charles, each representing the equivalent of dangerous and sometimes moving shoal water affecting both speed and safety. The evening sky was clear but dark, and the background lights from the buildings and other boats made the transit even more difficult. Moving at any speed was dangerous and the risk of collateral damage very high. A collision here in the basin would end any hope of getting away from the crowds and minimizing the effect of the blast. The radar showed hundreds of blips, forcing the Chief to reduce his speed to avoid ramming the boats that drifted on the water. Only the larger boats anchored, and few boats displayed the navigation lights needed to avoid each other on the water. After all, this July 4th celebration meant a memorable night without a care!

The FRB had a loudspeaker system and a set of flashing lights, but no one had ever tried to slalom the basin at night with so much traffic and at full throttle. Both the security frequency and channel sixteen were used to alert boaters that a USCG boat was transiting the basin for an emergency and to clear the way. Kayakers out for the evening were swamped as the twin waterjets pushed up a rooster tail and a rolling wake. How many others would end up in the drink? Dan asked the Chief if his crew wanted to leave the boat for their own safety.

"Hell no, we're all in on this and ready to execute." He turned and yelled at the afterdeck, "Anyone want to go ashore now or all go to Hell together?"

With all their thumbs up, the crew would stick with it.

"With that question behind us and while we've got a few seconds of dead time during this transit, perhaps you can share your plan with me?" The Chief stuck out his hand, "By the way, I'm Senior Chief Boatswain's Mate Kevin Ramsey." On any other occasion, Dan would have roared with laughter at the dead-panned question. Tonight there was no time.

"Nice to meet you Senior Chief. Dan Steele. Former Navy Seal Lieutenant now with DHS. Glad to be aboard. Here's the plan: Head for the deepest point outside the harbor you can get to in..." Dan stopped and moved aft and looked at the LED countdown clock and finished the plan "in seven minutes. I'd like a place with a muddy bottom to reduce the blast effect. I'm assuming what we have here is a conventional explosive."

Dan watched the Chief's hands deftly fly over the console, keeping up a running warning on the radio's handheld microphone and topside speakers, refining the course on the electronic chart system, pushing the diesels to their maximum RPMs, slaving the track to way points and synchronizing the console's countdown clock with the LED.

"How do you drop the anchor?"

"I can release it from here or from the foredeck."

"So my working plan is to get into the deepest water you can find, wrestle the canister into the water and then ride the anchor down to the bottom. I'd like to use the weight of the anchor to crush the canister between it and whatever it hits on the bottom.

"Just so you're not surprised, Lieutenant, our anchor weighs in at a massive forty-four pounds and is attached to six feet of chain so it's not going to speed your trip to the bottom."

With 00:08:05 on the countdown clock, the boat roared past the pedestrian walkway near the Museum of Science curling a deep wake which pounded the seawall, soaking everyone on either side. After nearly careening off the old pilings on the seaward side of the fifty foot wide channel, the Chief didn't flinch, keeping the engines at full throttle, passing under I-93 and boring down on the locks' narrow trough.

The operator radioed the southernmost lock was opening and reported an unusually strong current flowing into the Charles. The boat roared through the open locks at top speed while the sounds of the 1812 Overture echoed off the nearby buildings. Time to go: 00:07:30. Dan's mind raced as the boat shot under the Charlestown Bridge, its 25,000 pounds becoming airborne with the water boiling into the opened lock.

"What else is aboard to get me down to the bottom fast?"

Standing next to Dan, the rescue swimmer answered, "Jacob always brings his dumbbell aboard when the ship is operating to keep his biceps in shape."

"See if you can get it up here on deck pronto," said the Chief, keeping a constant watch on the gauge board and the pop-up window now counting in unison with the canister's LED. Dan went aft to the small working deck to see the dumbbell and revise his free diving plan.

Jacob arrived from a below decks hatch with a gleaming stainless steel dumbbell he carried like a newspaper.

"How much does it weigh?"

"Eighty-five pounds," he replied nonchalantly.

Dan issued some quick orders and returned to the cockpit. The boat flew around Boston's north end and took a southerly course to open water. Fortunately, boat traffic was light, and the normal chop in the inner harbor had no effect on the FRB as it continued at top speed. The boat diverted from its track once to avoid an anchored ship backing and twisting to its outbound course. The Chief called out 'mark' when the boat passed the next way point at the Sumner and Callahan tunnels that link the city with East Boston and the man-made island constructed to keep Logan Airport a safe distance away. The countdown clock read 00:06:10.

Tunnel? Dan shuddered involuntarily when the Chief mentioned the word. He felt a hot flash surge through his head and extend down his body ending in a convulsive twitch. He'd had visceral reactions before but none like this. He tried to focus and ignore the fear that choked him with a shot of acid reflux from his empty stomach.

Chapter 150

Kruje, Albania
July 05, 2018
03:55 a.m.

On his feet and pacing like a nervous cat, Spence couldn't calm his rapid heartbeat and the excitement of the moment. His brain felt hot, and his nervous system pumped adrenalin into his body like never before. His lifelong dreams were about to become reality on the world's stage, and he would be the faceless star of the show. He showed a wide smile to his leadership team and hoisted a glass of wine to his lips, glancing at his watch for the hundredth time in the last minute. He licked his dry lips and mopped the sweat from his forehead.

Chapter 151

Boston Harbor
July 04, 2018
9:56 p.m.

The Chief displayed a destination symbol on the electronic chart system defining a new navigation point between the easternmost tip of Logan Airport and the Head Island Lighthouse. "This is where we're headed. I estimate you'll have thirty seconds to get to the bottom after we stop. Is that enough time?"

"Sorry Chief, I'm too brain dead to do the calculation in my head. Let's assume that it's enough. If you can give me another second or two, great." Dan looked east towards Logan where the air controllers were unaware of what was being carried at high speed to a point just south of the airport. Had they known, a ground hold would have been imposed and in-bound aircraft diverted or re-routed to land from the north.

"We've got 00:04:35 minutes left on the clock. Are you on track?"

"Yep. We'll be over the Ted Williams tunnel in another ninety seconds. Just under three minutes to go. You'll have thirty seconds to get in the water and get down to the bottom."

"Listen, Chief," Dan said in a quiet voice, "We wouldn't have made it this far without you and your crew. As soon as I start to descend, I want you to get the hell out of here and don't look back. Understood?"

"No, Lieutenant, your message is coming in garbled, and I can't understand a word you're saying. Understood?" The Chief gave him a knowing grin and shifted his attention to the chart display and the countdown clock. He changed the scale on the chart so the last thousand yards filled the entire screen. Using the general announcing microphone, he gave a last order to the crew over the blaring topside speakers, "Men, we're almost there. Stand-by for a quick stop."

"OK, my GPS says we are there. Eighty feet deep with a soft bottom. Good luck!"

Still wearing his boxer shorts, Dan headed aft.

"All stop," came the voice from the announcing system.

The countdown clock passed 00:00:32 when the boat's forward movement stopped. A bright spotlight illuminated the after deck and the black water.

The canister had been lashed to Jacob's dumbbell with its midpoint secured against the short handle connecting the heavy metal plates on either end. Dan cinched the rescue diver's twenty pound shot-filled weight belt around his waist. Jacob lifted the canister and placed it on the boat rail. Dan donned a mask and jumped over the side, treading water alongside the gently bobbing hull. The seawater felt much colder than the shallow water in the basin. Countdown clock: 00:00:27.

"OK, Jacob. Hand me the package." Taking a final deep breath, Dan placed his hands on either end of the black canister and nodded to Jacob to release the package. With the canister weighing an estimated one-hundred pounds, the weight belt another twenty and Jacob's eighty-five pound dumbbell on the bottom, Dan began a high speed descent down into the inky depths of Boston harbor. The air in his lungs compressed with the depth, and the rapid pressure changes caused his ears to equalize like popcorn on a hot stove.

He locked his elbows for the descent and held the canister with both hands in front of his outstretched arms. His lungs carried more than enough air for this trip. It seemed like an eternity, but it was only eighty feet. Besides, it would likely be a one way trip. He hadn't bothered to calculate the duration of the drop or even count the seconds. If he didn't die from the direct blast effect of the underwater explosion, the shock wave would find the air-filled organs and cavities in his body and the internal damage would be fatal. At least it would be quick and painless.

He felt the water change as he slammed into a thick black ooze that covered the harbor floor and suddenly stopped when the dumbbell clanged against something solid. He felt the canister give way on both ends as the force of the impact sheared it into two pieces. His chest hit the makeshift anvil that felt like a thick steel plate trying to punch through his sternum.

The sharp blow to his chest caused him to swallow a mouthful of thick suspension that was likely rich with PCBs and other deadly contaminants that had collected on the bottom over the centuries that Boston had served as a trading port. At the same time, he felt a sharp pain as if a handful of sharp blades were being pushed into his right shoulder. The pain intensified as he continued deeper holding half of the canister with his left hand, waiting for the explosion. He remained conscious and wondered if the countdown clock had expired. Nothing had happened, yet. His leg rubbed against a very solid piece of steel as he continued to descend with time seeming to shift into slow motion. How could his timing be that far off?

The explosion boiled the water with a sound like some banshee from hell. He felt the shock wave bend his body in half. A piece of hot metal shrapnel struck his exposed right arm and right leg simultaneously but the unbearable sound of the explosion and the shock wave bending his body around made him incapable of logical thought. He was caught in a maelstrom of the kinetic effects of the explosion and the sensory overload that accompanied it.

Topside, Senior Chief Ramsey and the FRB crew watched as the dark water blossomed with muddy clouds of sediment around the boat and boiled with the gas created by the explosion. They could also hear the sharp pings of something hitting the boat's 5/16" thick, high strength alloy hull. At the same time, small projectiles broke the water's surface at high velocity, causing everyone to hit the deck and take cover without an order. One round serrated ball of death landed on the afterdeck and rolled to one side when Jacob snagged it. He opened a bloody hand where the serrations had sliced open up his calloused palm. All of them came to the same conclusion about the passenger who took the canister to the bottom. There was no way he could survive the force of the hellish explosion at eighty feet they saw on the surface. After the surface torment subsided, the crew looked around expectantly, anticipating bits and pieces of Dan Steele to surface in the midst of the muck stirred up from the bottom of the harbor.

Shocked, Dan suddenly realized he'd survived the blast and started to stroke towards what he thought had to be the surface. He somehow survived the shock wave that should have burst his eardrums and compressed then ripped apart his internal organs. Maybe his internal equilibrium was so disrupted that he was swimming along the bottom without knowing it?

Chapter 152

Kruje, Albania
July 05, 2018
04:00 a.m.

Dumbfounded, Spence watched the Boston crowd erupt with excitement as the smoke from the cannons cleared and the fireworks thumped skyward like a volley of mortars from the barges moored in the Charles. The other "Sons" looked at him expectantly. Spence tried to swallow, but his throat seems paralyzed, and his overworked nervous system started to shut down. He watched the screens as nothing interrupted the festivities. The fireworks filled the skies over the Charles punctuated with sharp reports as the multi-colored plumes winked out a few hundred feet in the air. What had gone wrong? He planned the event himself. He slumped heavily into his chair and buried his head in his hands. Several minutes later, he regained his composure as he pounded the table with his fist as he stood.

He addressed the "Sons" leadership with a steady and determined voice. "My brothers, I promise you I will find out why our plan failed tonight. But now is not the time to dwell on this set-back to our larger plans. We must rebuild Double Eagle and take a new course to achieve our goals. Try to get some rest before the sun rises in another hour. Join me for lunch at 1:00 p.m. We will set up the conference room to begin a damage assessment of our network and where we might be vulnerable. I want us all to agree on the next steps together here in our homeland. We will define the future in broad strokes and rise again."

All glasses were recharged by the waiter. Spence raised his glass of wine and toasted the "Sons" in his native tongue. All of them drank, and Spence threw his empty glass through the largest of the television screens as he left the room.

Chapter 153

Boston, Harbor
July 04, 2018
10:02 p.m.

Racked with pain, he dropped the weight belt and continued to move his usable limbs. On the way to the surface, he took a quick inventory: unusable, his right arm just would not operate with his left. He couldn't feel his right leg. On fire, his right shoulder winced with every stroke. He wondered if the poisons on the bottom of the harbor would kill him before he got to the surface. Disoriented and drowning, he wondered how much further his broken body could take him without oxygen.

What a sight when he finally did surface and saw the FRB bobbing nearby. The rescue swimmer reached him in seconds. He was on his back, with no feeling in his extremities, being towed to the boat when the post 1812 overture fireworks illuminated the skies over the Charles with joyous celebration. He'd never seen such a beautiful sight! His mind flashed back to a time not quite eight months ago when he swam towards another USCG boat after surviving the explosion that breached the Chesapeake Bay Bridge and Tunnel walls and killed his family. He'd cheated death twice but didn't know whether what was left of his broken body was worth saving.

While the three crewmembers tried to render first aid, Senior Chief Ramsey manned the radio. "This is US Coast Guard Fast Response Boat in Boston harbor with an emergency. I've got an adult male with multiple external injuries from an underwater explosion. Extent of any internal injuries unknown. Victim is stabilized and conscious but has lost a lot of blood. Need an ambulance to transport to the closest trauma center from the cruise port along the South Boston waterfront."

Moving at flank speed, Dan heard the radio crackle with rapid fire responses to the Chief's request and drifted in and out of consciousness. His mind seemed disconnected from his body because he couldn't assess the extent of his injuries. He knew there were several active sites on different parts of his body but could not pinpoint any of the injuries: intense pain in his right shoulder had been immobilized by direct pressure. The crew had been trained in first aid but certainly not addressing mass casualties in a single person. The fireworks seemed to be a distant glow in the western sky as the FRB docked alongside a jetty, and the crew lifted Dan onto a gurney. Two EMTs shoved him into an ambulance which sped off into the night with all its lights flashing.

He awoke in a hospital bed unable to move. An inflatable cast securely fixed his throbbing shoulder, and he raised his head slightly to see a full white plaster cast on his right arm. Returning to the inventory that he'd conducted before surfacing, he concentrated on his right leg to see if he could detect or feel anything. He could not. Turning his head to the left, he spotted Senior Chief Ramsey sitting in a chair snoring.

"Heh, Chief, am I still alive or what?"

The question did not disrupt the pattern of deep snoring. A nurse arrived at his bedside moments later.

"Where am I? What are my injuries? Did I lose anything? When can I talk with the doctor? Has the Senior Chief been here all night?

The nurse expected to be peppered with questions and sternly held up her hand. "You are at Tufts Medical Center in Boston, Massachusetts. The doctor is making rounds and should be here within the next twenty minutes, OK?" Though she ended the question with OK, it did not represent a question that needed an answer. Dan would have to be patient. The conversation did however wake the Chief from his slumber.

"Welcome back Lieutenant. How are you feeling?"

"I'm not quite sure. The nurse wouldn't give me any details. I don't remember much after surfacing. What happened?"

"Truth is I really don't know. You were in pretty bad shape when we hauled you aboard and kind of drifting between this world and the next one. We got you over to a landing where you were picked up. I've heard of Nantucket sleigh rides before, but that's the strangest one I've ever witnessed. Jacob wants to know if he'll get his dumbbell back."

Dan touched his thick forearm with his left hand. "Well, it wasn't pretty but it worked. Thanks, Chief. I hope I'll be able to come back aboard to thank the rest of your crew. They saved me last night."

"I'll pass it on. We'd be honored to have you back aboard. I'll try to stop back later in the day to see how you're making out."

"Thanks, I'll look forward to it."

Chapter 154

Boston, Massachusetts
July 05, 2018

A large area in the outer harbor had been restricted to shipping early that morning, forcing all marine traffic to take the northern channel to get out to sea. Exposed areas around the city's wharfs were cleared of people and a buffer zone established by the police. Logan operated at a reduced capacity using only the northern approaches and East-West runways. Visitors and locals alike who thought the Independence Day celebration and yesterday's POTUS visit had imposed unnecessary constraints were beside themselves.

Sandy concocted another cover story which involved a US Navy submarine-hunting P-3 aircraft operating from the old naval air station in Brunswick, Maine that had inadvertently dropped a live torpedo in the outer harbor while on a training mission. It sounded farfetched, but Sandy wrote it so believably no one would question its veracity. Of course, the Admiral got a one way call from a very irate Chief of Naval Operations who had to appear at a press conference and explain the mishap. He added that an EOD team had already been dispatched to the scene and expected the weapon would be recovered in short order. He sheepishly announced an investigation was underway.

The President would remain in Boston for the day and depart on Air Force One late that night. The morning's press conference deferred any details regarding the lost torpedo to the Department of the Navy. The Press Secretary conveyed the President's thanks for a wonderful celebration in Boston and specifically mentioned how proud he was of his hometown.

Embarked in a US Navy destroyer with the coordinates from the USCG FRB and armed with an underwater robot equipped with high resolution side-scanning sonar, the EOD team quickly found what remained of the canister and its contents by 10:00 a.m. The divers found two-thirds of the composite canister intact and fragments from the other third which contained the bulk of the explosive material. The team referred to it as a Double Ender. One part of the canister contained a shaped charge of C4 explosive and the other a large glass cylinder filled with an amber liquid thought to be poison gas. Miraculously, the glass was found unbroken in the mud at the base of an old I-Beam with a two foot web that separated its top and bottom flanges. What was left of the canister and its contents was deposited in an armored drum pressurized with inert nitrogen and fitted with chemical sniffers.

With the cargo secured, the destroyer headed due east and further out to sea. One of the EOD team referred to the configuration as the terrorist's version of the famous hors d'oeuvres, pigs in a blanket. By noon, the city began to return to normal. Most of the drunks were still sleeping off the celebration or nursing their hangovers and didn't care anyway.

From the scene, the EOD team's preliminary reconstruction assessment suggested the weapon had been remotely activated, and the triggering circuit had closed shortly after the canister sheared in two pieces by the impact of the dumbbell hitting a large I-beam that had somehow found its way to the harbor floor. Covered with years of accumulated marine growth, it stood proud of the bottom by a good eight feet, a single piece of steel buried and sticking upright just at the place the canister was being guided to the bottom. It was just dumb luck that the canister hit the I-beam as it did. The divers found one side of the I-beam's two foot wide web looked like it had been sandblasted down to bare metal as the serrated ball bearings were expelled by the explosive force which was largely contained within the three sides of the I-beam. The divers found a small pile of shiny serrated ball bearings at its base. They surmised that the only way Dan Steele survived was continuing his descent protected from the overpressure and shock wave by the width of the I-beam's web.

When a Navy weapons lab analyzed the contents of the flask a few days later, they did find a very concentrated agent that had not been seen before. It had been sealed with a dollop of molten glass. Once broken and vaporized by the explosion, the wind would have randomly carried the gas to find its victims. Death would occur within minutes as the lungs' soft porous lining turned into a gelatinous mass that could no longer oxygenate the blood.

Epilog

A full week had passed since the Independence Day celebration in Boston. The people of the city proudly pointed to the day as the finest anniversary of our nation's quest for freedom ever put on. The President and other leaders attending were welcomed in a very special way, and the international visitors were made honorary citizens of the United States. The halo effect would be short-lived.

Few people knew about the frantic activity alongside the Hatch Shell that began a race against time. The after action account about how close a major terrorist attack had come to being successful would never become public knowledge. The dangerous, high speed movements of the Coast Guard boat were explained away by creating an imaginary waterfront disturbance in the North End. The local Coast Guard commander told the story to the press and provided contact information for any citizens interested in filing claims for personal injury or property damage.

Dan left the hospital in a wheel chair after four long days. His final meeting with the doctor buoyed him up with hope.

"Your discharge instructions are not complicated but must be followed. As I said before, my choice would be to keep you here for another week or ten days. Your right shoulder is healing very well and should be ready for some limited physical therapy next week. The permanent damage to the shoulder muscle can be minimized over time with physical therapy. However, the fractured ulna in your right arm will complicate that healing process as your arm will remain in the cast for another four weeks. The large scoop of flesh taken out of your upper right thigh is healing well. The drains should be removed in another week or so, and I anticipate your leg strength can be re-established with a good physical therapy regimen. The scalp wound you re-opened has been closed with both stitches and staples, and it's important that you take all precautions to not open it again. You will remain on antibiotics for another ten days based on the material that we removed when your stomach was pumped. Now, do you have any questions?"

"Doc, thanks for taking care of me. I couldn't have been in better hands.

Admiral Wright, Sandy Matthews, and Dan Steele sat in Wright's office drinking cup after cup of coffee to recover from getting hammered the night before. The three began the day in the Oval office where the President awarded Dan the Presidential Freedom Award for his actions that had saved countless lives and protected like-minded world leaders as well as himself.

"Dan, our nation and the free world owe you a debt of gratitude. Your selfless actions set a new standard for service and dedication. I am proud to make this presentation and know I speak for the entire nation in recognizing your courage. It's unfortunate only a few of us will ever know the details of what happened in Boston."

"Thank you Mr. President."

The President awarded the Admiral and Sandy similar commendations. Sandy helped Dan out of his wheel chair for a brief photo with the President before the three returned to the office. The White House Staff, particularly the Chief of Staff, found the trio disrespectful because they looked as if they'd stumbled in from a nearby bar directly to the White House. The strong smell of alcohol surrounded them.

"Dan, I'm glad we had a chance to wind down last night. Maybe we overdid it a little, but that's what sailors sometimes do. I'm way too old for this type of behavior!" The Admiral took another gulp of coffee and looked serious, "I also got your letter yesterday afternoon, and it caught me a little off-guard. Are you sure you are thinking clearly?"

"Yes, Admiral. When I look back over the last eight months, it's a blur. And it's exactly the pace and the challenge I needed to start putting my life back in order. I appreciate everything you and Sandy did for me. I learned a lot about myself and other people and the reality of the Beltway that I never had to understand leading a Seal Platoon. While the adventure that came along with this assignment has been stimulating, I've also done a lot of soul searching. I don't have a clue what's next but am convinced this is not the life I want to continue right now. I should be able to get around without this wheelchair in another week or so when the drains are removed from my upper thigh. My arm will remain casted for another month and my shoulder seems to be getting better every day. I'll never complain about a splinter from a pine board again. That graphite reinforced plastic is nasty stuff and when it's broken, the ragged edge is like a series of daggers sharpened like a razor. Not to mention the deep scalp wound that's been re-opened and exposed to the bottom of Boston Harbor. The thought of dying of natural causes doesn't seem quite so boring today. So yes, I'm thinking clearly. But if I slur some words this morning, please forgive me."

The three men roared with laughter reminiscent of the night at Sandy's house when they were pinned down by a Double Eagle SWAT team. Tears streamed down the Admiral's face.

"What are your immediate plans?"

"Well, I need to visit Jill's parents and see what I can do for them. I'll tell them some of what I've been doing since we buried Jill and the boys. I haven't finished the job I promised both of them I'd do. Spence is still alive. I also need to spend some time with my family and some people who I've ignored and try to mend fences with some of our old friends. I've been focused on one thing for a long time and need a break from the action. I hope to find out what the rest of my life might be about. I don't think it has much meaning now."

"What about you, Sandy?"

"Well, I'd like to get ready to rejoin the Appalachian Trail where I left it to come down here, but I will start planning that for later in the fall when I'm physically stronger."

"Admiral?"

"Well, I've been asked to coordinate the top-to-bottom review the President has directed. I expect there will be a number of open positions throughout our government after we vet the Presidents' Staff and move down through the agencies. No one gets a waiver. The Double Eagle infrastructure and organization are still out there, and no one knows how this strategic pause will affect their efforts. We don't know today what the endgame will be. I'm told the big DHS contract for homeland defense has been put on hold indefinitely so that will block any attempt by the Double Eagle we know from penetrating further. But there's a big task ahead to ensure people in leadership positions are working for this country's interests and not someone else's."

After staring at the floor for a moment, he said, "Much as I love this country and would do anything in my power to protect it, I just don't want to go through the process of second-guessing whether I'm being supported or stabbed in the back. I'm ready to move to Rhode Island and do some clamming with Carole and work on us. I submitted my letter of resignation when you two were over in Albania, and I'll retire next month. The Director doesn't know whether to keep this office up and running or close it. Of course, I voted to maintain the momentum and bring in some fresh blood to run it. Dan, I sense you'll be back in the action before you know it, and I hope you'll visit Carole and me when you're up north. You too, Sandy. Best of luck! Both of you are great shipmates and friends."

Dan thought back to when he left the Seal Team and everything that had transpired since as he wheeled himself down the hall. Cass had moved into Dan's office and was unpacking a Bankers Box when he knocked and stopped in the doorway.

"Thanks for everything, Cass. I couldn't have done this without your help. Let's keep in touch. I hope our paths cross again."

"I'm counting on it."

The elevator door opened into the lobby where a large group of Annex employees gathered to send him off. He smiled and waved his thanks to the people who'd made our nation's security their sole purpose in life. The steady sound of clapping hands followed him out through the main entrance doors held open by a plainclothes policeman.

He stopped the wheelchair feeling the hot sun warm his face, closing a restless chapter in his life still filled with many lingering questions and the "eye for an eye" covenant not yet imposed.

Ramping down to the sidewalk, he pushed himself along deliberately, his mind flashing with images of Jill and the boys, of Meg, of Jack and Spence. His work was not finished but just beginning.

Made in the USA
Monee, IL
14 September 2020